GLORIOUS
APPEARING

Also by Tim LaHaye
and Jerry B. Jenkins
in Large Print:

Left Behind®
Tribulation Force
Nicolae
Soul Harvest
Apollyon
Assassins
The Indwelling
The Mark
Desecration
The Remnant
Armageddon

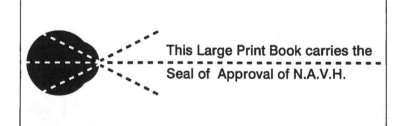

This Large Print Book carries the
Seal of Approval of N.A.V.H.

GLORIOUS APPEARING

THE END OF DAYS

Tim LaHaye

Jerry B. Jenkins

Thorndike Press • Waterville, Maine

Published in 2004 by arrangement with Tyndale House Publishers, Inc.

Thorndike Press® Large Print Basic.

The tree indicium is a trademark of Thorndike Press.

The text of this Large Print edition is unabridged.
Other aspects of the book may vary from the original edition.

Set in 16 pt. Plantin by Elena Picard.

Printed in the United States on permanent paper.

Library of Congress Cataloging-in-Publication Data

LaHaye, Tim F.
    Glorious appearing : the end of days / Tim LaHaye,
Jerry B. Jenkins.
        p. cm. — (The left behind series)
    ISBN 0-7862-6651-1 (lg. print : hc : alk. paper)
    1. Steele, Rayford (Fictitious character) — Fiction.
2. Tribulation (Christian eschatology) — Fiction. 3. Rapture
(Christian eschatology) — Fiction. 4. End of the world — Fiction.
5. Second coming — Fiction. 6. Large type books. I. Jenkins,
Jerry B. II. Title.
PS3562.A315G58 2004
    813'.54—dc22   2004048064

To the memories of
Frank LaHaye
and Harry Jenkins,
whom we shall again see

Special thanks
to David Allen
for expert technical consultation,
and to John Perrodin
for additional biblical research

As the Founder/CEO of NAVH, the only national health agency solely devoted to those who, although not totally blind, have an eye disease which could lead to serious visual impairment, I am pleased to recognize Thorndike Press* as one of the leading publishers in the large print field.

Founded in 1954 in San Francisco to prepare large print textbooks for partially seeing children, NAVH became the pioneer and standard setting agency in the preparation of large type.

Today, those publishers who meet our standards carry the prestigious "Seal of Approval" indicating high quality large print. We are delighted that Thorndike Press is one of the publishers whose titles meet these standards. We are also pleased to recognize the significant contribution Thorndike Press is making in this important and growing field.

Lorraine H. Marchi, L.H.D.
Founder/CEO
NAVH

* Thorndike Press encompasses the following imprints: Thorndike, Wheeler, Walker and Large Pr int Press.

Seven Years into the Tribulation; Three and One-half Years into the Great Tribulation

The Believers

Enoch Dumas, early thirties; Spanish-American; shepherd of thirty members of The Place ministry in Chicago; relocated underground in Palos Hills, Illinois

Montgomery Cleburn ("Mac") McCullum, early sixties; former pilot for Global Community Supreme Potentate Nicolae Carpathia; faked death in plane crash; chief Tribulation Force pilot on assignment at Petra

Hannah Palemoon, mid-thirties; former GC nurse; faked death in plane crash; on Trib Force assignment at Petra; on staff of the International Commodity Co-op, an underground network of believers

Razor, early twenties; Mexican; military aide to George Sebastian; Petra

Leah Rose, early forties; former head nurse, Arthur Young Memorial Hospital, Palatine, Illinois; on Trib Force assignment at Petra; on staff of the Co-op

Dr. Chaim Rosenzweig (aka "Micah"), mid-seventies; Nobel Prize–winning Israeli botanist and statesman; former *Global Weekly* Newsmaker of the Year; murderer of Carpathia; leader of the million-plus Jewish remnant at Petra

George Sebastian, late twenties; former San Diego–based U.S. Air Force combat helicopter pilot; underground with Trib Force and Co-op; defending Petra

Priscilla Sebastian, thirty, wife of George Sebastian; mother of Beth Ann; Petra

Abdullah Smith, mid-thirties; former Jordanian fighter pilot; former first officer, Phoenix 216; faked death in plane crash; a principal Trib Force pilot on assignment at Petra

Rayford Steele, late forties; former 747 captain for Pan-Continental; lost wife and son in the Rapture; lost second wife to plane crash; former pilot for Global Community Potentate Nicolae Carpathia; original member of the Trib Force; international fugitive last seen on the Petra perimeter

Eleazar Tiberius, early fifties; an elder at Petra; father of Naomi

Naomi Tiberius, twenty; daughter of Eleazar; computer whiz; in love with Chang Wong; Petra

Otto Weser, fifty; head of small band of German believers who fled New Babylon; Petra

Lionel Whalum, late forties; former businessman; former Co-op pilot; on Trib Force assignment at Petra as new director of the Co-op

Cameron ("Buck") Williams, mid-thirties; former senior writer for *Global Weekly*; former publisher of *Global Community Weekly* for Carpathia; original member of the Trib Force; editor of cybermagazine *The Truth*; lost wife, Chloe, to Global Community guillotine; last seen defending the Old City in Jerusalem

Chang Wong, twenty; former Trib Force mole at Global Community Headquarters, New Babylon; on Trib Force assignment at Petra as head of computer facility

Ming Toy Woo, mid-twenties; Chang Wong's sister; former widow, remarried to Ree Woo; former guard at the Belgium Facility for Female Rehabilitation (Buffer); AWOL, on Trib Force assignment at Petra, assisting with Co-op

Ree Woo, mid-twenties; husband to Ming Toy Woo; a principal pilot on Trib Force assignment at Petra

Gustav Zukermandel Jr. (aka "Zeke", or "Z"), late twenties; document and appearance forger; lost father to guillotine; on Trib Force assignment at Petra

The Recently Martyred

Al B. (aka "Albie"), early fifties; native of Al Basrah, north of Kuwait; pilot; former international black marketer; member of Trib Force; murdered in Al Basrah

Tsion Ben-Judah, early fifties; former rabbinical scholar and Israeli statesman; revealed belief in Jesus as the Messiah on international TV — wife and two teenagers subsequently murdered; escaped to U.S.; former spiritual leader and teacher of Trib Force; had cyberaudience of more than a billion daily; taught the Jewish remnant at Petra; slain defending the Old City in Jerusalem

Chloe Steele Williams, mid-twenties; former student, Stanford University; lost mother and brother in the Rapture; daughter of Rayford; wife of Buck; mother of four-and-a-half-year-old Kenny Bruce; original Trib Force member; former CEO of the Co-op; guillotined by the GC at the former Stateville Correctional Center in Joliet, Illinois

The Enemies

Suhail Akbar, mid-forties; Carpathia's chief of Security and Intelligence; One World Unity Army command post, Megiddo

Nicolae Jetty Carpathia, late thirties; former president of Romania; former secretary-general, United Nations; self-appointed Global Community potentate; assassinated in Jerusalem; resurrected at GC Palace complex,

11

New Babylon; leading massive Unity Army forces in the Valley of Megiddo; last seen outside Herod's Gate on the Suleiman Road in Jerusalem

Leon Fortunato, late fifties; former supreme commander and Carpathia's right hand; now Most High Reverend Father of Carpathianism, proclaiming the potentate as the risen god; Unity Army command post, Megiddo

Viv Ivins, early seventies, lifelong friend of Carpathia; GC operative; Unity Army command post, Meggido

Mediterranean Sea

Sea of
Galilee

Haifa

Mt. Carmel

Jezreel Valley

Jordan River

Megiddo

Jezreel

Valley of Jehoshaphat

Mount of Olives ▲

Jerusalem

• City
○ City (modern name)
▲ Mountain peak

Dead
Sea

Direction
of view

Bozrah

EDOM

Petra

KEY LOCATIONS FOR ARMAGEDDON
AND THE GLORIOUS APPEARING

13

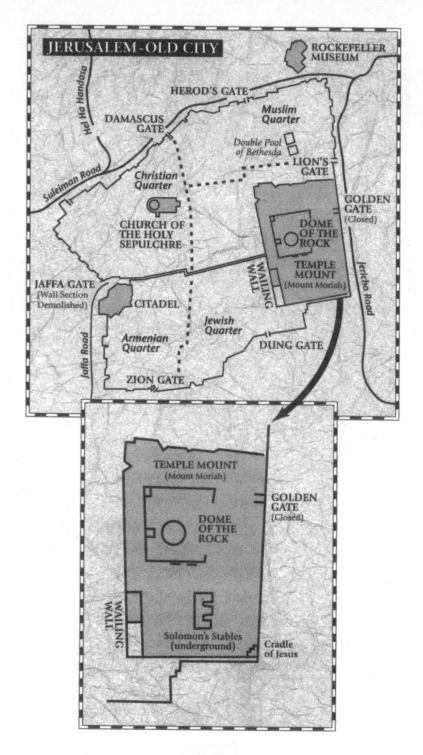

JERUSALEM-OLD CITY

ROCKEFELLER MUSEUM

Hel Ha Handaa

HEROD'S GATE

DAMASCUS GATE

Muslim Quarter

Double Pool of Bethesda

LION'S GATE

Suleiman Road

Christian Quarter

GOLDEN GATE (Closed)

CHURCH OF THE HOLY SEPULCHRE

DOME OF THE ROCK

TEMPLE MOUNT (Mount Moriah)

WAILING WALL

Jericho Road

JAFFA GATE (Wall Section Demolished)

CITADEL

Jewish Quarter

Jaffa Road

Armenian Quarter

DUNG GATE

ZION GATE

TEMPLE MOUNT (Mount Moriah)

GOLDEN GATE (Closed)

DOME OF THE ROCK

WAILING WALL

Solomon's Stables (underground)

Cradle of Jesus

14

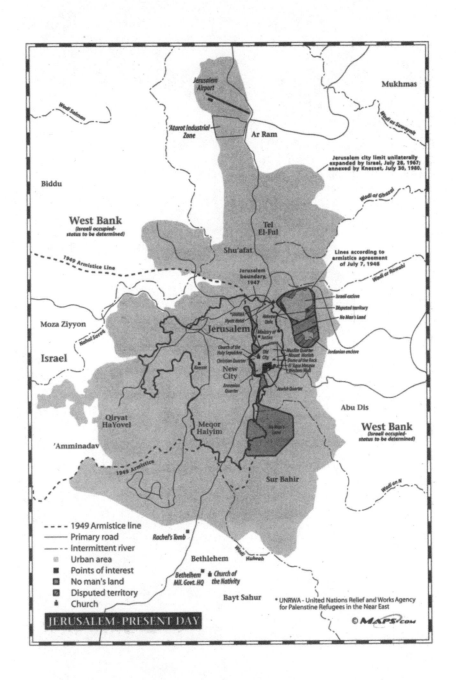

JERUSALEM - PRESENT DAY

Mukhmas

Wadi Soliman

Jerusalem
Airport

'Atarot Industrial
Zone

Ar Ram

Wadi as Suwaynit

Biddu

Jerusalem city limit unilaterally
expanded by Israel, July 28, 1967;
annexed by Knesset, July 30, 1980.

Wadi al Ghazal

West Bank
(Israeli occupied-
status to be determined)

Tel
El-Ful

Shu'afat

1949 Armistice Line

Jerusalem
boundary,
1947

Lines according to
armistice agreement
of July 7, 1948

Wadi ar Rawabi

Moza Ziyyon

Nahal Sorek

Israel enclave

Disputed territory

No Man's Land

Jerusalem

Ministry of
Justice

Jordanian enclave

Israel

Church of the
Holy Sepulchre

Christian Quarter

Muslim Quarter
Mount Moriah
Dome of the Rock
El'Aqsa Mosque
Western Wall

Old
City

Knesset

**New
City**

Armenian
Quarter

Jewish Quarter

Abu Dis

Qiryat
HaYovel

Meqor
Halyim

No Man's
Land

West Bank
(Israeli occupied-
status to be determined)

'Amminadav

1949 Armistice

Sur Bahir

Wadi an N

- - - - 1949 Armistice line
——— Primary road
——- Intermittent river
▦ Urban area
■ Points of interest
▣ No man's land
▨ Disputed territory
⛪ Church

Rachel's Tomb

Bethlehem

Wadi Hulwah

Bethlehem
Mil. Govt. HQ

Church of
the Nativity

Bayt Sahur

* UNRWA - United Nations Relief and Works Agency
for Palestine Refugees in the Near East

JERUSALEM - PRESENT DAY

© MAPS.com

Prologue

From **Armageddon**

Rayford started down the backside of Petra, finding it even more harrowing than coming up. He had stayed with Chang and Naomi a little longer than he had planned, so he assumed Mac would be looking for him and that George thought he had already arrived.

From his vantage point he had a good view of the army a mile off. He was reaching for his phone to reassure Mac when it became clear something had happened. The front lines were recoiling again, so George must have initiated another burst of the directed energy weapons.

This time, however, despite the ensuing chaos, the Unity Army didn't take it sitting down. Rayford heard the booms of retaliatory fire, like thunder from a storm head a hundred miles wide. He knew enough about munitions to know that Carpathia's forces were a little far away to be using the mortar cannons and shooting at high angles. He guessed the shells would drop short of the Petra perimeter.

He was wrong. Maybe their cannons were bigger than the typical unrifled short barrels. The shells flew past the perimeter and began dropping all around him. When one exploded right in front of him, Rayford was nearly pitched off the ATV. Grabbing for the handlebar with his free hand, he saw his phone go flying, bouncing a hundred yards down the rocky steep.

And now his vehicle was out of control. He bounced high off the seat and realized he was soaring through the air with only his hands attached to the ATV. He came down hard, and the contraption bounced and rolled sideways. To hang on or not was the only thing on his mind, and quickly that option was gone too. The four-wheeler hit yet again, ripping his grip away. As he bounced and rolled he kept picking up the sight of the vehicle disintegrating as it smashed into rocks all the way into a valley.

Rayford reminded himself not to try to break his own fall. He tucked hands and arms in and tried to relax, fighting his natural instinct for all he was worth. The grade was too steep and his speed too fast to control himself. The best he could wish for was a soft landing place.

A shell deafened him from about ten feet to his right, knocking him into a sideways roll. Rayford felt his temple smash into a sharp rock and was aware of what sounded like rushing water as he rolled toward thorny overgrowth. Scary as the thorns looked, they had to be softer than what he had been hitting.

Rayford was able to shift his body weight as he slowed and backed into the thorns. It was then he realized what the liquid sound was. With each beat of his heart, galloping now, his life's blood spurted six feet from the wound in his temple.

He pressed his palm hard against his head and felt the gush against his hand. He pressed with all his might and felt he might be containing it somewhat. But Rayford was in danger now — mortal danger. No one knew exactly where he was. He was without communications or transportation. He didn't even want to inventory his injuries, because regardless, they were minor compared to the hole in his head. He had to get help — and fast — or he would be dead in minutes.

Rayford's arms were gashed, and he felt sharp pains in both knees and one ankle. He reached with his free hand to pull up his pant leg and wished he hadn't. Not only had something sliced the flesh from his ankle, but something had taken part of the bone too.

Could he walk? Dare he try? He was too far from anywhere to crawl. He waited for his pulse to abate and for his equilibrium to return. He had to be a mile from Mac and his people, and he could not see them. There was no going back up. He rolled up onto his feet, squatting, one hand desperately trying to keep himself from bleeding to death.

Rayford tried to stand. Only one leg worked, and it was the one with the nearly totaled ankle. He may have broken a shinbone in the other. He tried to hop, but the incline was so great, he found himself pitching forward again. And now he was out of control one more time, trying to hop to keep from falling but picking up speed with every bounce. Whatever he did, he could not take his hand from his temple, and he dare not land on one more hard thing. "Lord, now would be a most appropriate time for you to come."

Chang sensed something was about to

give. He had succeeded in intercepting signals from geosynchronistic satellites that supported communications among the millions of troops. They were about to move, and his key people needed to know.

He called George. "Expect an advance within sixty seconds," he said.

"We've already been shelled," George yelled. "You mean more than that?"

"Yes, they will be coming."

"Rayford see you?"

"Left a little while ago. On his way to see Mac."

"Thanks. Call Mac, would you? I'll inform the others."

Chang called and told Mac the same.

"Hey," Mac said, "I can't raise Sebastian, and Ray is overdue."

"On his way," Chang said.

He called Buck. "Expect ad—"

But he was cut off. He redialed. Nothing.

"They're coming! They're coming!"

Buck heard a young rebel shrieking just as his phone chirped, and he saw an incendiary device hurled over the Rockefeller Museum, right at his position. He saw Unity Army troop movement from every side, and he grabbed his phone and held it up to his ear just as the bomb hit the wall right in front of him and clattered to the ground outside.

He recognized Chang's voice just before the bomb blew a hole in the wall. Rock and shrapnel slammed his whole right side, killed his phone, and made him drop one Uzi. He felt something give way in his hip and his neck as his perch disintegrated.

One of the young boys near him had been blown into the air and cartwheeled to the pavement. Buck was determined to ride the wall as it fell. He reached for his neck and felt a torrent of blood. He was no medical student, but he could tell something had sliced his carotid artery — no small problem.

As the wall crumbled, he danced and high-stepped to stay upright, but he had to keep a hand on his neck. The remaining Uzi slid down into his left hand, but when he stabbed it into something to keep his balance, it fell away. He was unarmed, falling, and mortally wounded.

And the enemy was coming.

Rayford could break his fall only with his free hand, not daring to take pressure off his temple. His chin took as much of the brunt as the heel of his hand as he slid at what he guessed was a forty-five-degree angle. There would be no walking. All he could do was crawl now and try to stay alive.

Buck's feet caught in a crevasse of shifting rock, and his upper body flopped forward. He was hanging upside down from the crumbling wall over the Old City. His hip was torn and bleeding too, and blood rushed to his head.

Even inside the tech center of a city made of rock, Chang felt the vibration of the millions of soldiers advancing on Petra. He was clicking here and there, flipping switches, and trying to make calls. How far would God let this go before sending the conquering king?

Fighting unconsciousness, he tried gingerly edging along, one hand ahead of him, the other occupied. Each inch made the angle seem steeper, the way more unstable. With every beat of his heart, every rush of blood, every stab of pain, he wondered what was the use. How important was it to stay alive? For what? For whom? "Come, Lord Jesus."

Dizziness overwhelmed, pain stabbed. A lung had to be punctured. His breath came in wheezes, agonizing, piercing. The first hint of the end was the crazy rhythm of his heart. Racing, then skipping, then fluttering. Too much blood loss. Not enough to the brain. Not enough oxygen. Drowsiness overtook panic. Unconsciousness would be such a relief.

And so he allowed it. The lung was ready to burst. The heart fluttered and stopped. The pulsing blood became a pool.

He saw nothing through wide-open eyes. "Lord, please." He heard the approach of the enemy. He felt it. But soon he felt nothing. With no blood pumping, no air moving, he fell limp and died.

Immediately after the tribulation of those days the sun will be darkened, and the moon will not give its light; the stars will fall from heaven, and the powers of the heavens will be shaken.

Then the sign of the Son of Man will appear in heaven, and then all the tribes of the earth will mourn, and they will see the Son of Man coming on the clouds of heaven with power and great glory.

Matthew 24:29–30

One

Mac McCullum scanned the Petra perimeter with high-powered field glasses. Rayford should have reached him by now.

Mac's watch showed 1300 hours — one in the afternoon, Carpathia Time. It had to be more than a hundred degrees Fahrenheit. Sweat ran down his neck from the grayish red hair peeking out from under his cap, soaking his shirt. Mac detected not even a wisp of wind and wondered what his freckled, leathery face would look like in a few days.

Without taking his eyes from the lenses, Mac unholstered his phone and punched in the connection to Chang Wong in the computer center. "Where's Ray?"

"I was about to ask you," Chang said. "He left here forty-five minutes ago, and no one else has seen him either."

"What do we hear from Buck?"

Mac noticed the hesitation. "Nothing new."

"Since when?"

"Uh, Rayford heard from him late this morning."

"And?"

Another beat. "Nothing to speak of."

"What're you sayin', Chang?"

"Nothing."

"I gathered. What's wrong?"

"Nothing that won't be cured in a little —"

"I don't need double-talk, buddy." Mac continued surveying the rocky slopes, feeling his pulse quicken despite his years and experience. "If you won't tell me, I'll call him myself."

"Buck?"

"Well, who else?"

"I've tried. My sensor shows his phone inoperable."

"Turned off?"

"Unlikely, Mr. McCullum."

"Well, I should guess so. Malfunctioning? Damaged?"

"I'm hoping the former, sir."

"Global Positioning System active, at least?"

"No, sir."

Chaim Rosenzweig had not slept, and after only two light meals of manna, he expected to feel the fatigue. But no. The best he could calculate, this was the day. He felt the swelling anticipation in both his head and his chest. It was as if his mind raced as his heart ached for the greatest event in the history of the cosmos.

The old man's senior advisers, a half-dozen elders, sat with him deep in the stone compound of Petra. Eleazar Tiberius, a broad globe of a man, offered that the million-plus pilgrims under their charge "are clearly as restless as we. Is there nothing we can tell them?"

"I have an activity in mind," Chaim said. "But what would you have me say?"

"I am newer to this than you, Rabbi, but —"

"Please," Chaim said, raising a hand. "Reserve such a title for Dr. Ben-Judah. I am merely a student, thrust into this —"

"Nonetheless," Eleazar continued, "I sense the populace is as eager as I to know the exact moment of Messiah's return. I mean, if it is, as you and Dr. Ben-Judah have for so long taught, seven years from the signing of the covenant between Antichrist and Israel, does that mean it will be to the minute? I recall the signing being at around four in the afternoon, Israel time, seven years ago today."

Chaim smiled. "I have no idea. I do know this: God has His own economy of time. Do I believe Messiah will return today? Yes. Will it trouble me if He does not appear until tomorrow? No. My faith will not be shaken. But I expect Him soon."

"And this activity you mentioned?"

"Yes, something to occupy the minds of the people while we wait. I came across a videodisc of a dramatic sermon from before the turn of the century by an African-American preacher, long since in heaven, of course. I propose calling the people together and showing it."

"The Lord may come while it is playing," an elder said.

"So much the better."

"There remain unbelievers among us," Eleazar said.

Chaim shook his head. "I confess that puzzles and disturbs me, but it also fulfills prophecy. There are those who enjoy the safety of Petra, even many who believe Jesus was the most influential person who ever lived, who have not yet put their faith in Him. They do not recognize Him as the long-awaited Messiah, and they have not acknowledged Him as their Savior. This sermon is also evangelistic. Perhaps many of the undecided will take their stand before Messiah appears."

"Better than waiting until the event itself," someone said.

"Gather the people for a two-o'clock showing," Chaim said, rising. "And let's close in prayer."

"Begging your pardon," Eleazar said, "but do you feel the absence of Dr. Ben-Judah as keenly as I do?"

"More than you know, Eleazar. Let's pray for him right now, and I will call him in a few minutes. I would love to share his greeting with the people and hear what has been happening in Jerusalem."

Mac's magnified vision fell upon colorful, metallic pieces glinting in the sun, perhaps a mile from his position. *Oh no.*

A red fuel tank and a tire looked very much like parts from Rayford's all-terrain vehicle. Mac tried to steady his hands as he panned in a wide arc, looking for signs of his friend. It appeared the ATV could have been hit by a heat-seeking missile or smashed to bits by tumbling. Perhaps, he thought, no sign of Rayford nearby was good news.

Mac raised Chang again. "Sorry to be a nuisance," he said, "but what does your sensor say about Ray's phone?"

"I was afraid you'd ask. It's inoperable too, but its GPS is still pulsing. My screen shows it deep in a narrow crevasse a little over forty-five hundred feet below you."

"I'm heading down there."

"Wait, Mr. McCullum."

"What?"

"I've got a lens pointed that way, and there's no room in the opening for a person."

"You can see the phone?"

"No, but I know it's there. It can be the only thing there. The opening is too narrow for anything else."

"So have you seen his ATV too?"

"I'm looking."

"Well, I have. If that phone is due south of me, look about twenty degrees east."

"Hang on . . . I see it."

"But no sign of Ray, Chang. I'm going to look."

"Sir? Could you send someone else?"

"Why? I'm twiddling my thumbs here. Big Dog One has the troops under control."

"Frankly, I'd rather you go to Jerusalem."

"You gonna tell me what's goin' on?"

"Come see me, Mr. McCullum. I was

honoring the confidence of Captain Steele, but I think you — and Dr. Rosenzweig — should know."

Mac arrived at the tech center, deep in the bowels of Petra, a few minutes after one-thirty in the afternoon. Chaim rose to meet him while Chang acknowledged him with a look but kept turning back to his numerous screens. Finally Chang pulled away and the three sat, far from the ears of others. Mac noticed, however, that many techies and others frequently stole glances in their direction.

"There's no delicate way to say this," Chang began. "Captain Steele told Naomi and me this morning that Mr. Williams had told him that Dr. Ben-Judah was killed in the fighting at Jerusalem."

Mac stiffened.

Chaim buried his face in his hands. "I hope he did not suffer terribly," the old man said.

"With Captain Steele missing now and —"

"What? Him too?" Chaim said. "And I am unable to raise Cameron on the phone . . ."

"I felt you both should know. I mean, I know this may all be moot by this time tomorrow."

"Perhaps even by four this afternoon,"

Chaim said. "The question now is what to say, what to do."

"Nothin' we *can* do," Mac said. "I've got Abdullah Smith looking for Ray. Chang here thinks I ought to go to Jerusalem."

Chaim looked up in apparent surprise.

"I do," Chang said. "From the looks of what's left of his vehicle and his phone, odds are all Mr. Smith is going to find are Captain Steele's remains. I'm sorry to be so blunt."

"But a flight to Jerusalem now?" Chaim said. "Just to see whether Cameron —"

"It's what I would want if it was me," Mac said. "I know he may be dead, and either way, Jesus is comin', but with Tsion gone, I'd just as soon get Buck outta there and back here with us."

"Even for as little as an hour," Chaim said, more a statement than a question.

"Like I say, that's what I'd want."

"And what do we tell the people?" Chaim said.

Minutes later, Mac was in Gus Zuckermandel's quarters. He filled in the young man on his plans. "And here's the hard part, Z. I want to leave in ten minutes."

"Can you give me twenty?"

"Fifteen."

"Deal."

"What've you got, Z?" Mac said, as the forger yanked open a file drawer, riffled through several folders, and slapped one open on his desk.

"Your new identity," Zeke said, moving to a closet, which he opened with a flourish. There were two dozen black-on-black Global Community Unity Army uniforms, from tinted eye-shield helmets to calf-length boots. "Find one that fits while I'm working on your documents. Don't forget the gloves. Nobody's checking for marks of loyalty anymore anyway, but just to be safe."

"How do you do this, Z?" Mac said, approaching garments that looked his size.

"With lots of help. Sebastian's boys have killed a few of 'em, and I got me a little crew that runs out and gathers up their stuff — papers, clothes, and all."

"Weapons?"

" 'Course."

When Mac emerged with the uniform a perfect fit, he found Zeke mixing some sort of a brew.

"You look good, Mac," he said. "Problem is, you got to be black."

"And you can manage that in a few minutes?"

"If you're game."

"Whatever it takes."

Mac whipped off his helmet, jacket, shirt, and gloves. Zeke used the mix to paint him dark brown from the shoulders to the hairline. "Keep the helmet on, 'cause I haven't got time to make the hair authentic."

"Check."

"And let's do your hands, just in case." Zeke dyed Mac's skin from midforearm to fingertips. "This should dry in two and a half minutes. Then an instant photo, and you're on your way. Give my best to Buck and Tsion."

Mac hesitated. "You betcha. Zeke, you're a genius."

The younger man snorted. "Just here to serve."

Mac was sprinting to a chopper when he reached Abdullah Smith by phone.

"Nothing yet, Mac. I will let you know as soon as I discover anything."

As Mac lifted off, he saw multitudes streaming from all corners of Petra and gathering at the central meeting place.

Chaim was alarmed at the mood of the throng. It was the biggest crowd he had ever drawn at Petra, and it was noisy, clearly preoccupied, antsy. He heard nervous laughter, saw lots of embracing. When one or two would look to the skies, hundreds — sometimes thousands — did likewise.

"My beloved brothers and sisters in Messiah," he began, "as well as the seekers and undecided among us, please try to quiet yourselves and settle for a moment. Please! I know we all expect the imminent return of our Lord and Savior, and I can think of no greater privilege than to have Him appear as we speak. But —"

He was interrupted by thunderous applause and cheering.

Chaim gestured that they should be seated. "I share your enthusiasm! And while I know that there will be nothing else on your minds until He comes, I thought there might be value in focusing specifically on Him this afternoon. I know there remain among us many who are withholding their decisions about Him until He appears. Consider this my last effort to persuade you not to wait. We do not know what may befall us at that moment, whether God will allow scoffers and mockers and rejecters to change their minds. Pray He will not harden your heart due to your rebellion or unbelief. Surely there has been more than enough evidence than anyone could need to reveal the truth of God's plan.

"While we watch and wait, consider the thoughts of a great preacher from decades past. His name was Dr. Shadrach Meshach Lockridge, and his message is entitled 'My King Is . . .' "

Chaim signaled for the disc to play, and it was projected off two white walls of smooth stone, each several stories high, where all could see it. The sound system carried it to the ends of the seated masses.

Lockridge proved to be animated and thunderous, interrupting his own cadence of shouts and growls with whispers and huge smiles. The disc caught him near the end of his sermon, and he was picking up steam.

"The Bible says my king is a seven-way king. He's the king of the Jews; that's a racial king. He's the king of Israel; that's a national king. He's the king of righteousness. He's the king of the ages. He's the king of heaven. He's the king of glory. He's the king of kings. Besides being a seven-way king, He's the Lord of lords. That's my king. Well, I wonder, do you know Him?"

Hundreds of thousands applauded, and many stood, only to sit again as Lockridge continued.

"David said, 'The heavens declare the glory of God, and the firmament showeth His handiwork.' My king is a sovereign king. No means of measure can define His limitless love. No far-seeing telescope can bring into visibility the coastline of His shoreless supply. No barrier can hinder Him from pouring out His blessings.

"He's enduringly strong. He's entirely sincere. He's eternally steadfast. He's immortally graceful. He's infinitely powerful. He's impartially merciful. Do you know Him?"

Many shouted their agreement.

"He's the greatest phenomenon that has ever crossed the horizon of this world. He's God's Son. He's the sinner's Savior. He's the centerpiece of civilization. He stands in the solitude of Himself. He's honest and He's unique. He's unparalleled. He's unprecedented.

"He is the loftiest idea in literature. He's the highest personality in philosophy. He is the supreme problem in higher criticism. He's the fundamental doctrine of true theology. He's the core, the necessity for spiritual religion. He's the miracle of the ages. Yes, He is. He's the superlative of everything good that you choose to call Him. He's the only one qualified to be our all-sufficiency. I wonder if you know Him today."

As the preacher continued, more and more listeners stood, some raising their hands, others shouting agreement, others nodding.

"He supplies strength for the weak. He's available for the tempted and tried. He sympathizes and He saves. He strengthens and sustains. He guards and He guides. He heals the sick. He cleanses the leper. He forgives the sinner. He discharges debtors. He delivers the captive. He defends the feeble. He blesses the young. He serves the unfortunate. He regards the aged. He rewards the diligent. And He beautifies the meek. I wonder if you know Him.

"Well, this is my king. He's the key to knowledge. He's the wellspring of wisdom. He's the doorway of deliverance. He's the pathway of peace. He's the roadway of righteousness. He's the highway of holiness. He's the gateway of glory. Do you know Him?

"Well, His office is manifold. His promise is sure. His life is matchless. His goodness is limitless. His mercy is everlasting. His love never changes. His word is enough. His grace is sufficient. His reign is righteous. His yoke is easy and His burden is light. I wish I could describe Him to you."

That elicited an ocean of laughter and more applause. The same had happened with his original audience, and Lockridge had paused, allowing it to fade before he continued.

40

"He's indescribable. He's incomprehensible. He's invincible. He's irresistible. Well, you can't get Him out of your mind. You can't get Him off of your hand. You can't outlive Him and you can't live without Him. The Pharisees couldn't stand Him, but they found they couldn't stop Him. Pilate couldn't find any fault in Him. Herod couldn't kill Him. Death couldn't handle Him, and the grave couldn't hold Him. That's my king!"

Everyone was standing now, hands raised, many applauding, shouting, some dancing.

"And Thine is the kingdom and the power and the glory forever and ever and ever and ever! How long is that? And ever and ever! And when you get through with all the forevers, then amen! Good God Almighty! Amen!"

By the time Mac found himself within sight of the rocky Judean hills where Jerusalem lay smoking in the early afternoon sun, he had begun to despair of finding Buck. If he was all right, would he not have borrowed a phone to check in? The latest intelligence from Chang was that Buck had reported Tsion's death to Rayford from inside the Old City.

Though the colossal armies of the

world — now amalgamated into Carpathia's Global Community Unity Army — stretched by the multimillions from north of Jerusalem to Edom, it was clear from the air that the current major offensive focused on the Old City.

Mac looked for a place to land. He had to look like a GC officer on assignment and head on foot to the Old City as if he knew what he was doing. In fact, he didn't have a clue. The Old City was only a third of a mile square. And if he found Buck alive, what was he to do? Arrest him and muscle him to the chopper? Finding Buck dead or alive, Mac decided, would be like discovering a patch of dry ground in the Louisiana bayou.

Mac's phone chirped, and he saw it was Chang. "Give me some good news."

"Such as?"

"Such as Buck's dead phone all of a sudden started showin' his position."

"No such luck. But I do have something. Carpathia's on the rampage about the destruction of New Babylon, and he's taking heat from all over the world."

"Heat?"

"Everybody who depended on New Babylon is crying over the loss. I'm picking up televised reports from everywhere of leaders, diplomats, businessmen — you name it —

literally weeping, decrying what's become of New Babylon and their own interests. Some are committing suicide right on camera."

"No way the GC is puttin' that stuff on the air."

"No, *they* aren't, but yours truly still has his ways."

"Attaboy, Chang, but how does that help me find Buck?"

"You're not going to find Buck, Mr. McCullum."

"What? You know that for sure?"

"I'm just stating the obvious."

"Ye of little faith."

"Sorry. But I figured as long as you're there and undercover, you might want to know where Carpathia is."

"I don't care where he is. I'm here to find Buck."

"All right then."

"But just for smiles, where is he? Last I heard he was on a bullhorn outside Herod's Gate. Moved there from his bunker near the Sea of Galilee. Unless they were just broadcasting his voice."

"No, it was him all right. He's moved his entire command post inside the Old City."

"Impossible. I'm lookin' down on it right now, and the place is crawling with —"

"I thought so too until I heard where. Underground."

"You don't mean —"

"Solomon's Stables."

"How do I get in there?"

"Follow somebody. Carpathia's got an entire regiment there, and I got your new name on the list."

"That might not have been prudent, Chang."

"Why?"

"What if I choose not to go, am discovered missing, and someone sees me elsewhere?"

"Well, there *is* that possibility, yes. Tell them you're on your way."

"What if I'm not? I mean, I'd love to be your eyes and ears here, Chang, but my priority is Buck. And nothin' we know about Carpathia now is going to amount to a hill of beans anyway. What's gonna happen is gonna happen. Can you get me off that list?"

"Not without looking suspicious. Sorry, Mr. McCullum. I thought I was doing the right —"

"Don't worry about it. None of it will matter tomorrow, will it?"

Mac saw GC activity and other choppers putting down at the Tombs of the Prophets, south of the Mount of Olives, east of the Old

City. Caravans of jeeps quickly loaded the disgorged personnel and raced them toward the conflict. As soon as Mac stepped out of his copter at 2:45 p.m., an officer directing traffic pointed him to an armored personnel carrier. Mac saluted and jogged that way. He joined a dozen other like-uniformed soldiers, who merely nodded at each other, tight-lipped, and rode in stony silence.

The cavalcade headed north on Jericho Road and turned west in front of the Rockefeller Museum onto Suleiman Street.

"We headed to Herod's Gate?" someone said.

"Is it open?" someone else said.

"Damascus Gate," the driver announced.

As they passed Herod's Gate, Mac joined the others in pressing against the windows on the south side of the vehicle. Somehow the resistance continued to hold the gate.

"If you're assigned to the potentate," the driver said, "follow me to the entrance to the stables. Everybody else head for the staging area at the Church of the Flagellation. When we have enough personnel, we'll attack the insurgents from behind and blow 'em out Herod's Gate."

Mac felt himself swelling with pride over what Tsion and Buck had apparently accomplished before the rabbi was killed. If they had been at Herod's Gate, they were responsible for helping hold that position against overwhelming odds. *And neither of them battle trained.*

Mac assumed Buck would agree that Tsion would not want his body removed from the Old City. He only hoped Buck had found an appropriate spot for the rabbi. Bodies fallen in an active battle had a way of getting trampled beyond recognition. That wouldn't matter tomorrow either, but Mac knew he and Buck would be on the same page.

Mac found himself fighting anguish. No way Buck would let them worry and wonder for this long. Surely he could have found a way to check in if he was alive.

When the vehicle stopped and the driver gave the order, Mac and the soldiers got out and moved as directed. Mac dropped several paces behind his group and phoned Chang, speaking quietly. "Anything?"

"Nothing."

"I'm not going to succeed, am I?"

"What do you want to hear, sir?"

"You know."

"I'm past pretending, Mr. McCullum."

"I appreciate that. Maybe I should just proceed to my assignment."

"To the compound?"

46

"Yeah. I know I should have my head examined, but I'd love to be with ol' Nick when Jesus gets here."

Chang felt Naomi's strong fingers on either side of his neck.

"You're tense," she said.

"Aren't you?" he said.

"Relax, love. Messiah is coming."

Chang couldn't turn from the screens. "I'd like to lose no one else before that. No matter how much I tell myself they'll be dead only a short while, it all seems so pointless now. I don't want anyone hurt, let alone suffering, then dying. Mr. McCullum's going was my idea."

"But he sure jumped on it, didn't he?"

"I knew he would. I wish I could have gone."

"You know this place can't function without your —"

"Don't start, Naomi."

"You know it's true."

"Regardless, I sent him for my own vicarious thrill. No way he's going to find Buck, and if he does, Buck will be dead. Then what's Mac supposed to do? If he gets found out, he's history. And for what? He could be here watching for the return with everyone else."

47

Naomi pulled a chair next to Chang and sat. "What do you hear from Mr. Smith?"

Chang sighed. "That's turned out to be a waste of time and manpower too. So far he hasn't found a thing. Either Captain Steele was obliterated by a missile or he was buried in the sand."

"Could he have crawled to safety?"

"There's no safety in that sun, Naomi."

"That's what I mean. Maybe he found shelter or built himself some shield against the heat."

Chang shrugged. "Best-case scenario, I guess. But wouldn't he think to leave some sign for us?"

"Maybe he was hurt too badly or simply had no resources."

"He could arrange sticks or rocks, even a piece of clothing."

"If he was able," Naomi said.

Chang's phone chirping made them both jump. "Yes, Mr. Smith?"

"I'm on his trail. He was on the move for a while, at least."

"What did you find?"

"Blood, I'm afraid."

Two

Mac had never seen the ancient walls of Jerusalem in such a state. While Herod's Gate (some still called it the Flower Gate) was somehow still held by the resistance, places on either side of the walls had been blasted from their normal forty-foot height to half that. It would be only a matter of time before the Unity Army pushed through.

But for now the invading force seemed to be concentrating elsewhere. Mac would make sure he was last in line when the unit he was with jogged through the Damascus Gate. That way he could peel off at any time. He could find the entrance to the underground stables somehow, but not until he had at least tried to locate Buck.

Past sixty now, Mac remained fit with a daily run. But while the borrowed uniform looked as if it were made for him, the boots were going to leave blisters. As he hurried along, invisible in a sea of similarly attired plunderers, he recognized the irony that he could easily take a bullet from snipers who didn't realize he was on their side of the conflict.

Mac had seen enough carnage in seven years to last an eternity, but nothing could have steeled him against the images that came into view as his little unit mince-stepped into the Old City. The narrow cobblestone streets that snaked through the markets and crowded houses were so full of broken and dead bodies that he had to keep his focus to keep from tripping over them. His eyes darted everywhere, looking for Buck, praying he was not already on the ground.

Mac's nostrils were assaulted by smoke, sweat, gunpowder, burning flesh, manure, and the sickly sweet stench of overturned fruit and vegetable carts. He recoiled at two quick gunshots until he saw it was a Unity Army commander putting a horse and a mule out of their misery.

A bullhorn announced that Unity forces had occupied the Armenian Quarter to the south, the Christian Quarter to the west, and much of the Jewish Quarter outside the

Temple Mount. The insurgents still held the Temple Mount to the southeast and the Muslim Quarter to the northeast, from Herod's Gate to just east of the Church of the Flagellation. Mac wondered how Carpathia and his staff had access to Solomon's Stables beneath the Temple Mount.

He prayed that Buck was somewhere in the Muslim Quarter or the Temple Mount, knowing that if he found him anywhere else, Buck was likely dead. If only Mac could "capture" Buck and convincingly drag him out of the Old City . . .

Unity Army foot soldiers were filling the west side of the Church of the Flagellation, avoiding the other side, which was taking fire from the rebels. A GC commander shouted that the assembled were to be ready to storm the Pools of Bethesda after the next artillery volley.

"The rebels have apparently constructed a makeshift shrine to a dead rabbi there. They'll be easy to spot. The body is hidden, but they have surrounded it with personnel and cardboard signs pleading that no one defile his resting place. We're less than five minutes from a mortar launch that will obliterate that whole site. We will shell the enclave in such a way that there will be no escape through the Lion's Gate to the east. Survivors will be pushed north toward Herod's Gate, and we'll be right behind them. The gate they have so ferociously held since yesterday they will now open themselves."

The commander assigned various troops and platoons, some to follow the shelling of the pools and others to attack the fleeing rebels as they headed toward Herod's Gate.

Mac racked his brain. There was no escaping now. He was deep inside this. While he would not, of course, fire upon the Unity Army's enemies, neither could he risk being seen shooting GC forces. Surely it was Tsion's remains the rebels were foolishly trying to protect, and he couldn't imagine Buck having a part in that. Buck would have tried to entomb the body, but he would know the futility and meaninglessness of staying to guard it.

Was there a prayer that in the midst of the chaos Mac could raise his visor and be identified as a believer by even one of the rebels? Not all were believers themselves, of course. He could be seen by one and shot by another. What was he doing here? His odds were infinitely smaller than he dreamed, and getting worse every second.

"Come, Lord Jesus."

Chang had broadcast the S. M. Lockridge presentation all over the world, having hacked into the Global Community's broadcast center. The GC had been getting better at countering such invasions, but the sermon was short enough that it was over by the time they reacted. Chang also monitored the reaction to the message by those assembled at Petra.

Naomi said, "It's time to step out into the sun to see for yourself."

"I'm kind of locked in here," he said.

"There's nothing more you can do now," she said. "And you don't want to be inside when Jesus comes, do you?"

He looked at his watch. "If the elders are right, we've still got some time. Believe me, I'll be out there before four. I'll tell you what's most bizarre about all this: the reports from all over the globe that Carpathia won't allow to be broadcast."

"Everybody crying over the destruction of Babylon?"

"Exactly. They have no clue what's coming, so they can't think of anything worse than that."

"But look," she said, pointing to the screen monitoring the Petra crowd. "Hundreds, maybe thousands, are kneeling. Let's go see if they need people to counsel or —"

"In a minute. Let me show you some of these . . . look."

But in the reflection of the screen, Chang saw her leaving. Her priorities were right, he knew, and he stood to follow. He quickly realized how long he had been sitting in one spot. He ached head to toe and stretched as he continued to watch his screens. "I should check with Mr. Smith!" he called out.

"He knows your number," Naomi shot back.

"I'll be right with you," he said.

"I'm not waiting."

"I'll find you."

"I hope so."

From New York, Brussels, London, Buenos Aires, the Persian Gulf, Tokyo, Beijing, Toronto, Moscow, Johannesburg, New Delhi, Sydney, Paris, and other major cities came the laments of those in power. As they began their prepared remarks about the difficulty of suddenly being ripped away from New Babylon, of losing computer contact with the source of commerce and leadership, to a man or woman each began to weep. Their shoulders heaved, their lips quivered, their voices caught. From everywhere came vivid pictures of giants of commerce disintegrating into sobs.

54

"All is lost!" the woman in charge of the Tokyo Exchange wailed. "Had we been able to restore our connections within twenty-four hours, this might have been salvageable, but our entire economy is tied to New Babylon, and to see the pictures of her lying in utter ruin, smoke rising into space, well, it's just, just . . . hopeless!" And she fell apart. Moments later came the report that she had committed suicide, as had many in the sub-potentate's cabinet there.

A captain of industry from Europe announced that he had thousands of ships at sea that would virtually be dead in the water before the next sunrise.

Unity Army officials in the United North American States submitted their resignations en masse, "knowing that we face court-martial and execution," because they had lost all their resources and would not be able to send reinforcements to Armageddon. "And wait until the millions of troops already marshaled there realize that no more food is coming, let alone any pay."

As countless such reports flooded GC broadcast headquarters, some opportunistic official there kept forwarding them to Carpathia and asking what should be done.

Chang intercepted all such interactions and was amused at Carpathia's obvious rage. "Do not make me say it again," Carpathia shot back. "No such reports are to be made public. I am not to be quoted except to say that this seemingly devastating loss will be remedied by our victory in the Jezreel Valley, in Edom, and especially in Jerusalem, where I shall establish my eternal kingdom as the one and only true god. The temporary losses of finances and commerce will be forgotten once I have ushered in the ultimate New World Order. There will no longer be a shred of opposition from man or spirit, and this planet will become a paradise of bounty for all."

Chang hurried out and joined Naomi. "Sometimes I think I'm looking forward to the end of all this just so I can get some rest."

Naomi laughed and mimicked him. "Good to see You, Lord. Can I get back to You after a nap?"

"Go now, now, now!" the Unity Army commander hollered, rousting Mac and the other troops and their platoons out of the Church of the Flagellation. "You will be exposed only briefly! The mortars will be launched from behind you, and by the time the rebels take aim, they will be struck. Go! Go! Go!"

The troops, most half Mac's age or younger, looked wide-eyed and panicky, but they seemed to gather strength and courage from one another. Again Mac maneuvered so he was at the back as they sprinted toward the Pools of Bethesda. "Ten seconds!" came the bullhorned announcement from behind them, but it came too late. Those in the front, clearly terrified that they had come within firing range of the resistance, slowed and many stopped, crouching and aiming.

That caused those behind to run into them, and many were trampled. Mac heard swearing and screaming just before the rebels opened fire. Unity forces quickly retaliated, but every second without supporting mortar fire made them more vulnerable. To Mac it seemed as if the crowd was about to turn back in a rage, firing upon their own superiors.

And the mortars were launched. Because so many in front of Mac had dropped, he had a clear view of the scruffy rebels, their faces mirroring the terror of seeing mortar shells arcing directly at their positions. They were shoulder to shoulder, not uniformed, pale and wasted from surviving more than most of their comrades had been able to endure. They had proudly stood their ground and defied the GC to overrun them and their shrine, but in an instant it would all be over.

They could see it coming, see it happening, and Mac read it in their eyes. None turned away. There would be no escaping. Many apparently decided to go down fighting. They death-gripped their Uzis, rattling off loud bursts even as the first mortar shell hit and sent dozens of them flying in pieces.

The next hit a split second later and the place became a crater, with a hundred dead or dying and three times that many scurrying for the closest gate. As had been the plan, those who opted for the Lion's Gate to the east were quickly killed or sent scampering back by yet another mortar round. Now, as scripted, those resistance forces remaining were running for their lives toward Herod's Gate. The last vestiges of those guarding the gate had heard the blasts and seen the bloodbath, clearly realizing their compatriots had nowhere to go but toward their own positions. With the invaders on their heels, the gate had to be opened or they would all be pinned to the wall and slaughtered.

From Mac's vantage point he could plainly see what awaited the fleeing rebels outside the gate. While he and the others had entered the Damascus Gate, surreptitious Unity personnel had slipped into place with what appeared to be colossal Gatling guns on massive caissons. From the looks of the barrels, Mac guessed the guns could accommodate fifty-caliber shells.

Those in the front of the advancing Unity forces were now shooting the rebels in the back, and the more who fell, the more were fired upon. Mac stole a glance behind him. He was bringing up the rear. "Lord, forgive me," he breathed, spraying his Uzi and dropping at least a dozen GC from behind. He felt no remorse. *All's fair . . .* It was only fitting, he decided, that the devil's crew were dressed in all black. *Live by the sword, die by the sword.*

Unity personnel in front of him parted like the Red Sea as their counterparts outside the walls opened fire with the big guns. Mac, too, dived for cover, watching in horror as dozens of rebels were ripped to pieces.

It seemed to be over as quickly as it had begun. Rogue GC stepped among the bodies shooting this one and that who seemed to still be moving. Others fanned out and began helping themselves to weapons and what-ever keepsakes they could find on the shattered bodies. This was Mac's chance.

He quickly pretended to do what the GC were doing, but he was pickier. He used his weapon or his boot to roll over only those dead or dying who were the right size to possibly be Buck. Mac picked up a weapon occasionally and rifled a pocket or two, just in case anyone was watching. He didn't really want to find Buck now, not unless he remained alive in the Temple Mount. No rebels had survived in the Muslim Quarter, as far as he could see.

It was the strangest battle George Sebastian had ever been part of. One could hardly call it a battle at all. It was just he and his ragtag bunch of earnest, impassioned believers, ringing part of the Petra perimeter with a handful of fairly sophisticated armaments — some directed energy weapons that burned the skin of soldiers and horses from long distances, and too few long-range fifty-caliber rifles — against the largest fighting force in the history of mankind.

The Global Community Unity Army, spearheaded by Antichrist himself, filled the horizon, even when George backed up onto the slopes and looked through solar-powered uberbinoculars. Hundreds of thousands of black-clad troops on horseback seemed to undulate under the shimmering desert vapors, steeds champing at the bit and high-stepping in place, appearing eager to carry their charges in an attack on the hopelessly outnumbered defenders.

Yet Sebastian felt little fear. He couldn't deny a certain trepidation, scanning the tanks and armored personnel carriers, the foot soldiers, the fighters and bombers and choppers that backed up the cavalry as far as the eye could see. It was no exaggeration to call his enemy a sea of humanity, and he could not imagine a throng so massive ever having gathered in one place before. More than once he had seen most of the million-plus gathered at Petra, and impressive as that was, it was nothing compared to this.

Sebastian's occasional volleys of DEWs and Fifties had proved a nuisance for the Unity forces. He had even caused several dozen casualties, which sent Gustaf Zuckermandel's crazy underlings scampering into the field to harvest weapons, IDs, and full uniforms. And the supernatural protection of Petra seemed to hold, even out here. Sebastian had lost nary a troop.

Yet he knew well that if that great army merely advanced upon his position without

61

firing a shot, his entire cache of ammunition would make not one serious dent in the overall force aligned against him. The enemy had begun advancing at a snail's pace, and while they were neither firing nor launching artillery of any sort, the mere size of that force directing its momentum his way caused the earth to tremble and the footing to become unsure.

And of course he was worried about Rayford. He had seen the man protected like the rest of them, heat-seeking missiles appearing to fly directly through aircraft without harming a hair on anyone's head. What could have caused injury to him now, and why? Some had speculated that the pieces of his vehicle found in the hills might have evidenced damage from an incendiary. But the latest report from Abdullah Smith was that the damage appeared to be the result of a loss of control, that the ATV had rolled and tumbled, smashing to bits.

What, then, about the blood trail that could have been only Rayford's? It was way beyond Sebastian to question God, but he had to wonder. Could a missile God caused to miss Rayford have still caused an accident that mortally wounded him? And who was to blame for that? Ray himself? The enemy?

The bigger question now, of course, was what would come of this advance by the invaders. Sebastian believed with his whole heart that Petra was impregnable. What was he doing out here with his band of resisters then? Presumably giving latecomers a chance to benefit from the safety of the place. Before they came within the saving influence of the stone city, Sebastian would try everything in his power to pave the way for them. Yet none had come, and he saw none on the way.

Surely in a matter of hours — some said minutes — this would all be meaningless. Christ would appear, He would win the battle, and Rayford and Buck and even Tsion — dead, alive, or somewhere in between — would be reunited. Still, Sebastian couldn't get Rayford off his mind. He had been trained to never leave a comrade on the battlefield, regardless. It made no sense that Smitty could find the blood trail of a man severely wounded and thus moving slowly and yet not be able to find the man himself.

The best Sebastian could determine, there were no enemy personnel behind Rayford. He could not have been captured. Worst-case but most likely scenario: Ray had dug himself a shelter against the sun and died there. Did it make a difference, given that he would be with Christ — just like the rest of them — when it was all over? Of course it did. Because you don't leave a man.

How long had it been since he had checked in with Smitty? He looked at his watch. Too recently. And Abdullah said he would let him know at first opportunity. But Sebastian had to do something, short of heading to the hills himself — clearly an impossibility. He called Chang.

"No, I haven't heard a thing yet," the young man reported. "I sure wish you could be here, though. Thousands are turning to Christ, right here in Petra."

That was wonderful, but Sebastian couldn't bring himself to say so. Frankly, he carried a bit of resentment, even disgust, for those who had waited this long. Where had they been when all the judgments had come down? All the miracles? No sane person could deny that for the past seven years, God and Satan had waged war. Had these people really been undecided about which side they wanted to join? Any doubt about the reality of God and both His mercy and His judgment had long since been erased.

"I've got a call coming in," Chang said.

"So do I," Sebastian said. "Later."

"Big Dog One, this is Camel Jockey."

"Go ahead, Smitty," Sebastian said.

"And, Techie, are you there?"

"Roger," Chang said.

"I've spotted Captain Steele."

Enoch Dumas awoke just after seven-thirty in the morning. His musty mattress in the basement of an abandoned house in Palos Hills, Illinois, was warm where he had slept and cold where he hadn't. And he hadn't slept much. All night he had told himself that today was the day. He couldn't imagine sleeping past 4 A.M., but the truth was, that was about the time he finally dozed. Eight in the morning, Central Time, would mark seven years to the minute since the signing of the covenant between Antichrist and Israel, a covenant that had been broken years earlier, but which marked the years before the Glorious Appearing of Christ.

The Place, his little church of thirty or so down-and-outers from the inner city of Chicago, had incongruously burgeoned since they had been scattered to the suburbs with the compromising of the Tribulation Force safe house. They no longer had a central meeting place. While knowing that they should trust no newcomers, every time they got together, more were added to their number. And because they recognized the seal of the believer on the foreheads of the newcomers, Enoch knew they had not been infiltrated. They now numbered nearly a hundred. While some had been martyred, a surprising majority had eluded detection and capture, though they busied themselves every day trying to gather more converts — "getting more drowning people onto the life raft," Enoch called it.

Sometimes he even found himself urging caution to passionate new believers and warning them that the enemy was constantly on the lookout, eager to devour them, to make them statistics. And yet he was often reminded, usually by one of his own flock, that there was no other choice now than to be overt in their witness.

His favorite times were when the floor was opened and people who risked their very lives by assembling in secret would exude the joy of heaven when they spoke. He could not, nor did he want to, erase from his mind's eye the testimony of Carmela, a fiftyish, heavyset Latina. In an abandoned laser-tag park about ten miles west of Enoch's quarters, she had stood telling her story with tears running down her generous cheeks.

"I once was blind but now I see is the only way I can say it," she said. "I was blind to God, blind to Jesus, selling my body to buy drugs and food. I had left everything and everybody important to me. Before I knew it, I only cared about me and my next high. It was all about survival, kill or be killed, do what you gotta do.

"But then one day one of you came to me. And it was her, right there." Carmela had pointed to an older woman, an African-American named Shaniqua. "She handed me one of the brochures, about the meetings and all, and she said, 'Somebody loves you.'

"I thought, *Somebody loves me? Tell me somethin' I* don't *know! Men tryin' to love me all day.* But I knew better. Nobody loved me. Fact, they hated me. Used me. I meant nothin' more to them than their next meal or their next high. Just what they meant to me. Nobody loved me since my mama, and she died when I was little.

"I knew the brochure had to be somethin' religious, but her saying that about somebody loving me, and her havin' the courage to give me the brochure when she knew it was against the law . . . that was the only thing made me not throw it away or cuss her to her face.

"I read it that night, and I'm glad the Bible verses were in it, 'cause I ain't seen no Bible for years. What got me was that it wasn't fancy, wasn't hard to understand, didn't get all complicated. It just told me God loved me, Jesus died for me, and Jesus is comin' again. All them Scriptures sounded true to me, 'bout being a sinner, being separated from God, and Jesus being the way back to Him.

"Before I knew it, that was the only thing I wanted. I didn't know how I'd live, what I'd eat, nothing. But I knew I wanted Jesus. Next time I saw Shaniqua, I just about attacked her, didn't I, honey? I told her she had to tell me how to get Jesus in my life. She told me it was simple. All I had to do was pray and mean it. Tell God I was sorry for the mess I'd made of my life and take Jesus as my Savior. It ain't been easy, but know what? I'm ready for when Jesus comes."

The believers wanted to be together by eight this morning, and they had settled on a parking lot of a former shopping center. Enoch had warned that a daylight assembly of that size would surely bring out the GC, and they would be looking for marks of loyalty.

"Let 'em be checking us when Jesus appears," someone said, and the rest applauded.

As Enoch quickly showered and dressed, he found himself less worried about interference. The destruction of New Babylon in the space of one hour had so thrown into chaos the international economy that it seemed nothing else mattered to nonbelievers. Suicides were at an all-time high, and he sensed an anti-Carpathian spirit among the formerly loyal.

Social and community services already devastated by the population loss of the last few years were now virtually nonexistent. And rumor had it that even local GC enforcement personnel would be hamstrung without fuel or money for more. Salaries had been frozen for two years as it was, and now it seemed clear to the populace that there would be zero pay for government employees until further notice.

The private sector — what was left of it — was in disarray as well. Carpathia's tentacles had reached so far into every avenue of life and commerce that the virtual bankruptcy of the international government was certain to cripple everyone within days. Enoch had read of great depressions and bank failures throughout history, but no one had seen anything as far-reaching as this. Muggings, robberies, break-ins — all the unsavory acts that had been the purview of the under-world — now had become part and parcel of everyday life for all.

It was every man for himself now, and any vestige of politeness or manners or even lawfulness would soon be history. Enoch prayed Jesus would return right on schedule.

It was nearing 1600 hours, four o'clock in the afternoon, in Jerusalem. Mac felt slimy in his GC Unity Army uniform and had to fight the temptation to shout his true identity and open fire without worrying about who was watching. He could take out a few dozen more Carpathian troops, but what was the use? They'd be gone soon enough as it was.

The resistance, except behind the walls in the Temple Mount, had been virtually obliterated. Unity forces congratulated each other as they combed through rebel casualties, gathering the spoils. Mac pretended to do the same in a desperate last-ditch effort to find Buck, though he ignored the eyes of people who thought they were his compatriots. Nothing would give him greater satisfaction than seeing Buck standing tall on the Temple Mount when the end came.

Mac was near the half-crumbled wall just west of Herod's Gate when a phone hit the ground next to him and he heard someone curse above him. The phone looked familiar, but as he reached for it he heard, "Don't waste your time! Nothing left of it!"

Mac looked up to a young Unity soldier bending over a fallen rebel. "Nice boots, though, and my size. He left one of them in the wall here." The soldier untied the other boot and was wrenching it off the body when it pulled free and slipped from his hands, dropping toward Mac. He snatched it from the air and recognized it as Buck's.

"Hey, toss that up here, will ya?" the soldier said, digging the other boot from a crevasse where Buck had apparently left it as he struggled free.

Trembling, Mac tightened his fists around the boot. "A little help, huh, pal?" the soldier said, briefly turning back to the stuck boot.

Mac took a step to get a good angle. Just as the young man freed the boot from the crack and turned toward him, Mac harkened back to his sporting days as a youth. He fired the matching boot so hard that the raider had no chance to react. The sole caught the bridge of his nose and sent him catapulting back over the wall.

To be sure he wouldn't have to face him again, Mac hurried through the gate. He found the young man splayed on the ground, clearly dead. He ran back in and found enough holes and protrusions to hoist himself up to where Buck lay. He wanted to do something — anything — but he could think of nothing. Whatever he did besides appearing to ransack the body would only give him away, and what would be served?

Mac sucked in deep breaths as he surveyed Buck's injuries, gaping wounds that left Buck in a deep pool of black blood so sticky that it had barely begun to run down the wall when it coagulated. His whole right side had been torn open, and wounds also disfigured his hip and neck.

A bullhorn called for assignees to the potentate, and Mac knew he might be identified as an imposter if he didn't report. As he reluctantly pulled away from Buck he prayed that the same fate had not befallen Rayford. It just wouldn't be right if no one from the original Trib Force had survived to see the Glorious Appearing.

It was four o'clock.

Three

Despite his substantial injuries, Rayford had managed to crawl several hundred yards to an outcropping of rock. With his free hand — though its heel had been scraped raw — he somehow had scooped away enough topsoil from behind the rocks to allow himself to stretch out away from the relentless sun and beyond anyone's view.

He had exhausted every reserve of strength and had to trade the hope of being seen by his own people for fighting off dehydration and blood loss long enough to survive until the Glorious Appearing. He gingerly positioned his body in the shallow grave in such a way that if he lost consciousness, his gashed temple would remain pressed against his hand. Every time he thought he had stanched the blood flow long enough for it to stop pulsing, he was proven wrong when he released his palm for even an instant.

It was a relief to be out of the sun, but the benefit of the slightly lower temperature with the topsoil gone did not last. Within half an hour Rayford's mouth and tongue were dry, and he felt his lips swelling. He fought drowsiness, knowing that unconsciousness was his enemy. His wounds stabbed, and he worried about going into shock.

Delirium soon followed, and Rayford daydreamed about people spotting the ATV and following the trail of blood, only to find his lifeless body being pecked at by vultures. At times he discovered he had roused himself to consciousness by singing, praying, or just babbling.

As he stiffened and his temperature rose, he began to feel the deep pang of each injury, and he prayed God would just take him. *I wanted to see it from this side of heaven, but what's the difference? Relief, please. Relief.*

He wasn't sure, but he didn't think he could bleed to death from any wound other than the one to his temple. When it seemed everything had ebbed from him but his last breath, Rayford considered releasing his hand and letting his life's blood slip away too. But he could not.

He quickly lost all sense of time and had to remind himself that his watch seemed to be functioning properly, despite his fast-fading ability to focus. Rayford was stunned to see how little time had passed since he went careening. The sun was still high in the sky, but he would have bet hours had passed. It had been a mere fifty minutes.

When he awoke groaning, he realized he had actually dozed with enough presence of mind to keep the pulsing temple dammed. His neck was stiff, and he had the feeling he would be unable to stand or even roll into a crawling position if his life depended on it. If someone didn't find him soon, his life *would* depend on moving yet again. But that simply wasn't in the cards.

It seemed hours later, and Rayford was bereft of hope. He heard the advancing Unity Army and was surprised to see the sun still nearly directly overhead. It would remain that way until late afternoon, he knew, but he wouldn't have been surprised to open his eyes to dusk. No such luck.

Far in the distance he heard the high-pitched whine of a powerful dirt bike, the type Abdullah Smith rode. The Jordanian would buzz about Petra, careful in the crowds, then find his way out to the desolate slopes, where he would really open it up. Rayford could only pray that what he heard was Smitty searching for him. He tried to sit up but could not. If he had to guess, he'd have said Smitty was in the area where the ATV had finally landed. That was a long, long way from Rayford's meager shelter. He tried to stay conscious so he could call out if the dirt-bike sound grew nearer, but he knew it would also have to be shut off if the rider was to hear him.

Rayford realized his pain had spread past the spots that had taken the most direct abuse. His head throbbed all over. His eyes had become supersensitive to light, and he could barely open them to peek at his watch. His neck hurt, his shoulders were tight and achy, his back felt as if hot pokers were piercing his ribs. He was hungry, nauseated, and alternated between overheating and shivering. His leg muscles and even his toes cramped.

In and out of consciousness now, when he finally heard the dirt bike slowly approaching, Rayford was certain he was imagining it. When the engine died, Rayford tried to move, to grunt, to do anything to let Smitty, or whomever, know he was there.

"Big Dog One, this is Camel Jockey. . . .

76

And, Techie, are you there? . . . I've spotted Captain Steele. Or at least I think I have. The trail stops here, and I do not expect to like what I see. Hold on."

Rayford's breathing was so shallow he was certain Abdullah would not be able to tell he was alive. He couldn't move a muscle, let alone turn his head, wave, or wiggle a foot. When he heard Smitty's steps in the sand he fought to open an eye. Nothing was working. Was Smitty really there, or was this some sort of a near-death experience?

"Agh, I think he is gone," Abdullah said. "I mean, no, he is here, but I do not think he made it."

Rayford felt the index finger on his free hand bouncing, but clearly Smitty wasn't looking at it. "Oh, Captain Steele," the Jordanian said as he gently rolled Rayford onto his back. He sounded so grief-stricken that Rayford was moved.

Rayford kept his palm locked against his temple, but rather than persuading Abdullah he was alive, it must have made him think rigor mortis was already setting in. And so Rayford did the only thing he could manage. He pulled his hand away an inch. By now the blood had clotted enough that it did not immediately squirt from the wound.

And Abdullah apparently had not noticed the movement.

Rayford felt the pressure building in his temple, and as Smitty straightened Rayford's legs, the wound broke loose.

"Well, hello!" Abdullah said. "Dead men do not bleed. You are there, are you not?"

Rayford clamped his hand over the wound again and managed a "Yeah. Good to see ya."

"Do not talk, Captain. I do not want to lose you before the big event."

"Thought this *was* the big event."

But Abdullah was back on the phone. "Chang, he is alive. I need help here as quickly as you can send it. . . . Yes, Leah would be perfect. Ask her to bring everything she can carry. I will launch a flare in ten minutes."

Mac fell in with Unity Army troops in the Muslim Quarter of Jerusalem's Old City and followed them to an obscure but lavishly guarded entrance underground. No one even got close without proper credentials, and Mac fought to maintain his composure as two sentinels held his photo ID next to his cheek and studied it. He could only hope none of Zeke's dye had worn off in the skirmishes.

He and those with him were directed to a pressed-dirt path at least thirty feet wide and lined on either side with narrow wood steps that led deep under the northern wall and past the Temple Mount. They continued directly beneath the only ground in Jerusalem still held by the resistance, and it was, of course, surrounded by the Unity Army. Were the rebels holding their own, or were they virtually imprisoned?

Mac worried about Rayford and wished he'd had an opportunity to call Chang or Sebastian or Abdullah. Ree Woo was leading a platoon on the opposite side of Petra's perimeter. Maybe he'd seen Rayford. But now Mac had to turn off his phone.

The passageway to Solomon's Stables was so dimly lit that he and the others were immediately forced to raise their tinted visors. Still the effect was like coming into a dark theater from the bright sun, and the soldiers slowed and felt their way along so as not to fall down the stairs. Mac was grateful the edge of his helmet rode low over his eyebrows, not exposing that he bore no mark of loyalty.

Being a few steps out of the afternoon sun cooled his face and neck, and he was tempted to remove his gloves. He was nearly overcome by the reek of horse manure and urine, which grew worse as they neared the stables.

As they reached the southeast corner of the Temple Mount, some forty feet underground, they came within sight of Solomon's Stables, a series of pillars and arches that had once supported the southeastern platform of the courtyard above. The halls, made up of a dozen avenues of pillars, were a little over thirty yards wide, sixty yards long, and nearly thirty feet high. At least a hundred men, not in uniform, seemed to be tending more than a thousand horses.

The odor alone took Mac back to his childhood, and he wondered how he had ever grown used to it.

"Attention!" someone shouted. "Silence for your potentate!"

Everything and everyone stopped, and Mac wondered where Nicolae could be. Mac and several other uniforms had their backs pressed up against a wall, standing at attention. He recognized Carpathia's voice coming from inside a pillared room. "Gentlemen and ladies, you will be pleased to know that several months of renovations here were accomplished in the space of fewer than three weeks. The sanitation facilities are second to none, at least for humans, and best of all — per my instructions — they empty into the legendary Cradle of Jesus."

Leave it to Carpathia to sicken Mac with his first words. Mac had never heard of the Cradle of Jesus, at least in the context of the Temple Mount. Many others apparently hadn't either, for Leon Fortunato was called upon to explain.

"Thank you, Excellency. The Cradle of Jesus can be accessed down a winding staircase in the southeast corner. This leads to a chamber approximately fifty by seventy feet where in the past there have been both a basilica named for Saint Mary and a mosque. There is also, on the west wall, some ancient Byzantine art. Should you care to view the chamber, be forewarned of its current use, which we feel is more appropriate to something bearing its name. You will want to hold your nose. You'll be glad to get back to the odor of mere horses."

Suhail Akbar was next, Carpathia's chief of Security and Intelligence. "Having just arrived from Mount Megiddo," he began, "I am pleased to report that everything and everyone is in place for our soon unequivocal victory. Despite reports of discord due to the destruction of New Babyl—"

Suddenly a shout, more of a scream, but Mac clearly recognized Carpathia's voice. He cursed and cursed again. "Tell me,

Suhail!" he raged. "Tell me you are not going to violate my specific order to never again mention the name of —"

"But, sir, I merely meant to —"

"You dare interrupt me? Do you see yourself above corporal punishment?"

"No, sir, I —"

Something slammed the table. "I should have you executed this instant! I should do it myself!"

"Excellency, please! I was saying that *despite* what we have heard, the truth is —"

"The truth is that *I* will rebuild New Babylon right here in Jerusalem. She shall be restored to a thousand times her former beauty and majesty. I have decreed there shall be no more mention of what has become of her."

"My humble apologies, Potentate. I —"

"Silence! I have spoken. Back to your quarters, Chief Akbar. Your services will not be required again until further notice."

The commander in charge of Mac's unit quickly stepped forward and conferred with a colleague at the entrance to the meeting room. He backed away as a half-dozen guards led out an ashen Suhail Akbar. The commander then silently pointed to six uniformed men at attention, including Mac, and directed them inside to replace those who had left.

Rayford's lucidity had returned somewhat after Abdullah slowly worked a liter of water into him. Leah arrived on a small ATV with two coolers full of supplies and tossed a clipboard to Abdullah. "Would you do the honors, sir?"

"The honors?"

"Take notes."

"Of course."

Rayford kept interrupting her. "What's the buzz at Petra? They think Jesus is late?"

"Hush."

"C'mon, Leah. I gotta know if we've all been off by a day."

"Nobody's off," she said distractedly, coolly inventorying his injuries. "Chaim has everyone calmed down."

"How? What's he saying?"

"God's ways are not our ways. He's on His own clock. That kind of thing."

"Leah, you love this, don't you?"

"Sorry?"

"Having me at your mercy."

"I don't know what you're talking about."

"Yes, you do. We —"

"Mr. Smith," she said, "I'll be suturing the head wound. The chin, the arms, the

83

right hand, and the knees can wait. The left shinbone may be broken, but I won't attempt to set it until we can be sure. I'm going to need to study the right ankle and probably suture that too. And we're going to need some kind of conveyance to get him back up to the compound, probably within half an hour."

"You *love* this, Leah! I can tell."

"You're delirious."

"What kind of conveyance, Miss Rose?" Abdullah said.

"I need him prone."

Abdullah got back on the phone.

"You could be just a little rougher with me than you might be with another patient, just to get back at me."

Rayford was teasing and trying to smile, but Leah clearly wasn't biting. "Back at you for what?"

"For how I used to talk to you."

"Well, maybe you owe me too," she said.

"Maybe I do, but I'm in no position to exact revenge."

"And I have your flesh wounds in my hands. Now keep quiet and let me work."

It was all Mac could do not to burst out laughing when he saw Carpathia. Had the man been wearing a black hat, he would have looked like Zorro. A shirt with a frilly collar represented the only white in his ensemble. Everything else, from his knee-length boots to his leather pants, vest, and thigh-length, capelike coat, was black.

Leon was in his most resplendent, gaudiest, Day-Glo getup, including a purple felt fez with multiple hangy-downs and a cranberry vestment with gold collar, appliquéd with every religious symbol known to man, save the cross of Christ and the Star of David. A turquoise ring on his right middle finger was so large it covered the adjoining knuckles.

If only God had scheduled the Glorious Appearing on Halloween . . .

Carpathia stood at the head of an enormous, polished wood table, around which sat — if Mac could guess from their native garb — the sub-potentates from each of the ten international regions, their entourages, and Carpathia's brain trust, sans Chief Akbar, of course. There had to be more than fifty gathered.

Viv Ivins sat demurely in her customary sky blue suit (with hair to match) six chairs from Nicolae on his far left side. She seemed even paler than Mac had remembered, and he thought he detected a trembling in her fingers as she busied herself taking notes.

The others, despite their positions of high authority on Carpathia's cabinet and around the world, also seemed tentative in his presence. The outburst against Suhail Akbar had clearly shaken them all.

Mac was near the entrance, one of the last few to have entered, and he realized that the six sentries he and his platoonmates had replaced had filled out a contingent of another fifty or so who lined the walls of the long room. Knowing what it had taken even to be allowed underground, he had to wonder against whom they were protecting Carpathia. Was he afraid of his own people?

Chang had walked Naomi back into the tech center. "What am I going to do?" he said. "I'll never sleep tonight, and I'm wasted."

"Surely you don't think we'll have to wait another day."

"I don't know what to think."

"Today is the day, love. There's no question."

"I hope you're right. I'm wired, but at some point I'm going to crash. Dr. Rosenzweig wants me to get him on international TV just before dark. You may have to prop me up."

"You'll rise to it. You always do."

★ ★ ★

The wall at his back, made of large blocks of stone, cooled Mac through his uniform jacket. He desperately wanted to peek at his watch. He knew it was well after 1600 hours now, and he believed Jesus could come any second. This was the last place he wanted to be when that happened, but being here was part of the price he paid to find Buck. And there was the prospect of seeing the look on Carpathia's face.

Mac tried to appear focused on his menial task — providing showy security where none was needed — but when he ran through his mind what he really wanted to be doing, he found it difficult to concentrate. Besides being in broad daylight in the Holy City when the Lord Christ appeared, Mac's second choice was opening fire on Carpathia from his perfect vantage point. There would be none of that, he knew. It fit no prophetic scenario, but how fulfilling it would be!

Nothing would come of such foolhardiness, of course. The man had been murdered once, and was he now even a man? Drs. Ben-Judah and Rosenzweig had said he was now indwelt by Satan himself, a spirit-being using a human body — albeit a dead one.

In addition, Mac simply wanted to take a

load off. The idea of sliding to his seat on the floor, of stretching out with his hands behind his head . . . well, that was something that would come once Jesus had taken His rightful place. Mac's friends and comrades often talked about what kind of a world they would live in soon, but he kept to himself the idea that what he most longed for was simply rest.

He was certain he was not alone in this. Others had hinted at it. They had all been so busy, so stressed, so sleep deprived, and all that had only worsened as the days grew nearer to the Glorious Appearing. The idea of living in a world of peace and safety so appealed to Mac that he could barely imagine it. To be able to sleep without half an eye or ear figuratively open to danger . . . well, talk about heaven on earth.

And to be reunited with friends and loved ones. It was nearly too much to get his mind around. Best of all, of course, would be to see Jesus personally. Would he get to touch Him, to speak with Him? Mac felt so new as a believer, so limited in his knowledge of the things of God. He felt as if he had been attending seminary under the Tribulation Force's spiritual leaders ever since Rayford had led him to faith. But there was so much he didn't know.

All he knew was that Jesus loved him, had died for his sins, and was the reason he did not have to fear death and hell.

Chang had been called before Dr. Rosenzweig and the elders.

"Of course I can do it," he said, "but the GC has been improving on wresting back control of the airwaves. The shorter the broadcast, the more likely I can keep it on without interruption."

"I plan to be brief," Chaim said.

"And if, ah, if —"

"You're wondering what happens, hoping as I am, if Messiah returns first?"

"Or in the middle of it," Chang said.

"Well, I should think that event would take precedence, wouldn't you?"

Chang smiled as the elders laughed.

"Rabbi Rosenzweig is attempting," Eleazar Tiberius said, "to persuade the rest of the Jewish population — those who have refused the mark of the beast and yet who have not acknowledged Jesus as Messiah — to do just that. He, and we agree, estimates that this may constitute a third of the remaining Jewish population. You understand that these are God's chosen people, His children from the beginning of time. All of Scripture is His love letter to them, His plan for them."

"Understand it?" Chang said. "I can't say that I do. But I believe it."

Chaim stood. "We must not delay. As I have said so many times, we know the day — today — but we do not know the hour. If we thought we did, we were wrong, were we not, Eleazar?"

The big man smiled. "I acknowledge it. But is it not also true that we know the sequence of events, so we have some idea what follows by what comes next?"

"That is what I will be talking about on the broadcast, my friends."

Before the anesthetic took effect in his temple, Rayford fought to keep from recoiling from the thrust of the needle. He was amazed that a new twinge of pain could supersede all the others, and he was also struck by Leah's gentleness as she cradled his head and assured him the sting would soon fade.

"You're being much better to me than I deserve," he said, knowing he sounded groggy and hoping she understood.

"Will you stop with that now, Captain? I have work to do, and while I know you're trying to keep things light, I don't need to be worrying if you're serious."

He reached for her hand. "Take a minute,

Leah. I am serious. When you first came to us you know that we sniped at each other. I wasn't used to your types of questions and probably was threatened by them. I never made that right, but as far as I could tell, you never made me pay."

She pressed her lips together. "And I'm not about to now. Listen, Ray, you're hurt more badly than you know. My job is to stabilize you, keep you from going into shock. The fact that you haven't already is a miracle. But you apparently need to hear this, so let me tell you. My failure was that I never cleared the air between us either. Fact is, you eventually won me over. Everybody could see how much you cared for all of us, how tireless you were, how you put everybody else ahead of your own needs."

Rayford was embarrassed. He hadn't meant to elicit this, nice as it was. He squeezed her hand. "Okay, okay," he said. "We're friends again."

"Think of the people who will be in heaven because of you," she said.

"All right, enough," he said. "I was just trying to thank you for not rubbing it in."

"Now will you hush?"

"I will, ma'am."

Mac noticed Viv Ivins look up with a start

but then recover quickly. Carpathia had asked, "Photographers in place and ready, Ms. Ivins?"

"Yes, Excellency."

"I shall be on horseback," he said. "All Global Community Unity Army personnel in this room, plus their superiors, shall also ride. Your mounts are being saddled as we speak."

Mac panicked. How long had it been since he had ridden? Was it like riding a bicycle? Would it all come back to him? He had never been atop a steed the size of the Thoroughbreds in the stables. Any horse responded to a sure, confident hand. The beast had to know the rider was in charge. He might have to fake that bravado.

"Are you looking directly at me, soldier?" Carpathia demanded.

"No, sir," the young Brit next to Mac said, eyes darting everywhere but at Nicolae.

"You most certainly were! You would have done better to admit it and beg forgiveness."

"Affirmative, sir. I was and I regret it and offer my sincerest abject apologies."

"That is the second time you have referred to me as sir! Have you not been instructed neither to look directly at me nor to refer to me in any manner except as —"

"Yes, Excellency! My apologies, Supreme Pot—"

"And now you deign to interrupt me?"

The Brit's voice was quavery and Mac believed his legs were about to fail him.

"Sorry," the young man whispered.

"I cannot hear you, soldier!"

"I'm sorry, Excellency. Forgive me."

"Who is your superior officer?"

"Commander Tenzin, sir — Excellency!"

Carpathia cursed the man. "Commander Tenzin!"

The Indian commander rushed in, bowing. "At your service, Excellency!"

"Commander, have you taught your men who I am?"

"I have, lord potentate."

"All of them?"

"Yes, my king."

"And the privilege of serving god on earth?"

"Absolutely, divine one."

"Even this man? Your name, son?"

"Ipswich, Excellency," he said, tears flowing now.

Mac wanted to shoot Carpathia dead and feared he just might if the potentate approached.

"Commander Tenzin, what is that in your hand?"

"A rattan rod, Excellency. I so look forward to the privilege of riding with you today."

The rod was an inch thick and appeared to Mac about four feet long.

"If I told you that Mr. Ipswich has flouted your training, could you think of an appropriate use for your rattan rod, Commander Tenzin?"

"I could, Your Grace."

Ipswich was whimpering.

"And would you do me the honor of employing it in my presence, for my entertainment and for the education of all?"

Without another word, Tenzin stepped forward and drew back the rod. Before Ipswich could even recoil, his commander lashed his face with such speed and force that the stick caught him just to the left of his nose, splitting both lips, cracking some teeth, and slicing his left eyelid.

Ipswich screamed and grabbed his face with both hands, bending at the waist. Tenzin brought the rod down on the back of his neck, just above the hairline, opening a gash that spattered blood on Mac's face and chest. It was all he could do to keep from attacking the Indian.

As Ipswich pitched forward, Tenzin cracked him twice across the backside in quick succession, the second blow tearing his uniform pants. That drove him to the floor, and as he tried to scramble away, his commander followed, raining blows on his back.

Carpathia howled in delight. "When he can crawl no more, Commander Tenzin, spare the rod and put him out of his misery!"

Another soldier was quickly enlisted to replace Ipswich in line. He entered pale and shaky and quickly came to rigid attention.

"Ooh," Carpathia moaned, clasping his hands and gazing upward. "What a way to start the day! Leon . . ."

"Yes, holy one?"

"Ask Commander Tenzin to pay a visit to Chief Akbar."

"Certainly, lord."

"But instruct him to punish him only to the point of *near* death."

Four

Enoch Dumas led more than a hundred of The Place followers around the back of the abandoned Illinois shopping center. Just before eight in the morning he had begun to teach, trying to inform his people and a few interested others what should precede the Glorious Appearing. None of the heavenly preliminaries had begun, and he sensed the disappointment, doubt, and fear on the part of his little band of believers. But mostly he found himself looking over his shoulder at the main road.

Though there were few vehicles of any type about, given the fuel shortage and the crippled economy, he knew the local GC had not shut down completely. They would have to investigate a meeting of this size. And the discovery of that many people, not one bearing the mark of loyalty to Carpathia, would result in a bloodbath.

There was no longer any earthly excuse not to bear the mark, and punishment was execution on the spot by any means. Even a civilian had the right to put to death an insurgent. All that was required for exoneration from the crime of homicide was either to drag the victim to a local GC headquarters and prove he or she bore no visible mark, or to flag down a patrolling Morale Monitor or GC Peacekeeper and get him to confirm the same.

In fact, there was a healthy bounty on such offenders, and citizens loyal to the potentate competed for cash prizes. Many made their living as vigilantes, and some were famous for their impressive number of kills.

Perhaps that was why Enoch found his usually bold congregation willing to follow him from the public light of day to the relative seclusion of the other side of the empty mall. "If we knew Jesus would get here before the GC, we could stay where we are. But I, for one, do not want to have survived seven years, only to die just before He comes back."

The group crowded into an inner court, where it was obvious they all felt safer.

But they had questions.

"When's it gonna happen?"

"What'd we miss in the prophecies?"

"Did you only *think* the 'weeks' meant 'years,' or what?"

"Could we be off by a long ways?"

"I don't think so," Enoch said. "But I don't know. I was never a scholar or a theologian. I'm sort of a blue-collar student of all this, just like you all are. But I have been reading and studying for years. While there is a lot of disagreement and debate, so far everything, every element of the prophecies, has been fulfilled literally, the way it was spelled out. I have to believe today is the day."

"Ho'd on!" a woman shouted from the back. She was peering into a tiny TV. "Look like somebody done took over the GC's airwaves again."

People crowded around.

"That Micah guy," she said, "runnin' things at Petra, is gonna speak about what comes next."

Others pulled mini-TVs from their pockets and bags. "Should we listen, Brother Enoch? Will you be offended?"

"Hardly," Enoch said, digging out his own TV. "What could be better than this? Dr. Rosenzweig is a scholar's scholar. Let's have church."

The assembled put their tiny screens together on a concrete bench and turned them up so the combined volume reached everyone.

Mac saw the narrowing of Carpathia's eyes and feared someone else was about to catch his rage. His attention had been drawn to the entrance of the room.

"Yes, what is it?" Carpathia said.

An underling said, "Begging the potentate's pardon, but, Excellency, you asked to be informed."

"What? What!"

"The zealots at Petra, the Judah-ites —"

"I know who is at Petra! What now?"

"They have pirated their way onto GC television again."

Carpathia flushed and leaned over the table, resting on his palms. His jaw muscles tightened. "Turn it on," he said through clenched teeth.

Leon nearly toppled trying to pull out a chair. He sat heavily and made a show of reaching far up under his robe and producing a remote-control laser, which he aimed at the wall behind Nicolae. A screen descended and the picture appeared: Chaim Rosenzweig seated on a simple set, deep in the confines of Petra. His open Bible was before him, and he bore a pastoral smile. A timer showed that he would begin in less than a minute.

Carpathia looked over his shoulder at the screen, then turned back and slammed both fists on the table. "First," he shouted, "confirm that Ipswich is dead! Then tell Tenzin I have changed my mind about Akbar! I want him dead too! Finally, get hold of Security at Al Hillah. Inform them of the demise of their chief and tell them the following order comes directly from me.

"Whatever it takes, I want Security to take over our broadcast center. I want the management personnel shot to death through both eyes, one administrator at a time, from the top down through the chain of command, one every sixty seconds until someone has wrested back control of the airwaves. Understood?"

No one moved or spoke.

"Understood?!"

"Yes, Excellency!" Leon said, reaching for his phone.

"I'm on it," Viv Ivins said, phone already to her ear.

Carpathia whirled and faced the screen. "Does no one understand?" he railed. "Does no one recognize this man? This is the one who assassinated me! And while

I raised myself from the dead and reign as your living lord, he remains a thorn in my side. Well, no longer! Not after today! A third of our entire army will overrun Petra tonight, and he shall be my personal target!"

With hydration and an IV started by Leah, Rayford at last began to feel he might make it. He still felt as if he had been run over by a tank, and there would be no walking or helping himself get off this god-forsaken slope. But his mental faculties were returning, and he came to believe that Leah and Abdullah could somehow get him back to the compound.

"Two things, Miss Rose," Abdullah said.

"Shoot."

"According to Miss Palemoon, we have a problem with the conveyance."

"What problem? There's a stretcher in the Co-op. And a gurney too."

"She checked with Mrs. Woo, and they both believe these will be impossible to transport to this location."

Leah sat back, and Rayford saw her scan the hills above her leading to Petra. "She may have a point. What's number two?"

"She says Micah is on GC television and that we might want to tune it in."

"Do you have a TV, Mr. Smith?"

"Of course."

"Well, the captain is as stable as I can make him, and we may be here a while. Let's have a look."

Abdullah pulled a small TV from a leather bag attached to his bike.

"You want to see this, Captain?" Leah said.

Chang was glued to his monitor, but he asked Naomi to gather around him the rest of the techies on duty.

"Check this out, people," he said. "Look at the counter in the upper left of the screen."

Whistles and back slaps and exultations followed the speeding numbers, racing upward by the tens of thousands a second but having already surged far past the largest television audience in history. Nothing Carpathia ever broadcast had come close; in fact, the previous three records had all been held by Tsion Ben-Judah.

"Dearly beloved," Chaim had begun, "I speak to you tonight probably for the last time before the Glorious Appearing of our Lord and Savior, Jesus Christ the Messiah. He could very well come during this message, and nothing would give me greater pleasure. When He comes there will be no more need for us to fight Antichrist and his False Prophet. The work will have been done for us by the King of kings.

"But as He did not return seven years to the minute from the signing of the covenant between Antichrist and Israel, many are troubled and confused. I wish to speak to that here, but mostly I need to be brief, for as you know, we commandeer these airwaves against the wishes of our archenemy, and you must believe that he is doing everything in his power right this very instant to bump us.

"More important than discussing the timing of Messiah's return, however — which I can summarize in a sentence: I believe He will be here before midnight, Israel Time — is the spiritual state of my fellow Jews around the globe. If you have never listened before, lend me an ear this day. This is your last chance, your final warning, my ultimate plea with you to recognize and accept Jesus as the Messiah you have for so long sought.

"You have heard many times the proclamations of my dear friend and colleague, Dr. Tsion Ben-Judah, who outlined the numerous prophecies that soon came to pass. If these never persuaded you, hear me now and know that it is likely this very day that you will see the signs in the sky heralding the Glorious Appearing of Jesus.

"The Bible says in Matthew 24:29 and 30 that 'immediately after the tribulation of those days the sun will be darkened, and the moon will not give its light; the stars will fall from heaven, and the powers of the heavens will be shaken.

" 'Then the sign of the Son of Man will appear in heaven, and then all the tribes of the earth will mourn, and they will see the Son of Man coming on the clouds of heaven with power and great glory.'

"This *is* the last day of the Tribulation that was prophesied thousands of years ago! Today is the seventh anniversary of the unholy and quickly broken covenant between Antichrist and Israel. What is next? The sun, wherever it is in the sky where you are, will cease to shine. If the moon is out where you are, it will go dark as well because it is merely a reflection of the sun. Do not fear. Do not be afraid. Do not panic. Take comfort in the truth of the Word of God and put your faith in Christ, the Messiah.

"What does it mean that the powers of the heavens will be shaken? I do not know, but beloved, I cannot wait to find out! The Bible says God 'will show wonders in heaven above and signs in the earth beneath: Blood and fire and vapor of smoke. The sun shall be turned into darkness, and the moon into blood, before the coming of the great and awesome day of the Lord.'

"I expect a show like I have never witnessed, but I will be safe as He has promised. Will you be safe? Are you ready? Are you prepared? Do not put it off another second.

"What is the sign of the Son of Man? Again, I do not know, but I know who the Son of Man is: Jesus, the Messiah. His sign could take any form. Might it be a mighty dove, as descended upon Him when John baptized Him? Might it be the form of a lion, as He has also been called the Lion of Judah? Might His sign be a lamb, as He is also the Lamb of God? The cross upon which He died? The open tomb, in which He conquered death? We do not know, but I will be watching. Won't you?

"Who are these tribes of the earth who will mourn when they see Him coming? Those who are not ready. Those who have lingered in their rebellion, their disbelief, their sloth.

"Zechariah, the great Jewish prophet of old, foretold this thousands of years ago. He wrote, quoting Messiah: 'I will pour on the house of David and on the inhabitants of Jerusalem the Spirit of grace and supplication; then they will look on Me whom they pierced. Yes, they will mourn for Him as one mourns for his only son, and grieve for Him as one grieves for a firstborn.'

"Imagine that, people! Historians tell us Zechariah wrote that prophecy well more than four hundred years before the birth of Christ, and yet he quotes the Lord referring to Himself as 'Me whom they pierced.'

"Zechariah goes on: 'In that day there shall be a great mourning in Jerusalem. . . . And the land shall mourn, every family by itself: the family of the house of David by itself, and their wives by themselves . . . all the families that remain, every family by itself, and their wives by themselves.

" 'In that day a fountain shall be opened for the house of David and for the inhabitants of Jerusalem, for sin and for uncleanness. And it shall come to pass in all the land . . . that two-thirds in it shall be cut off and die, but one-third shall be left in it.

" 'I will bring the one-third through the fire, will refine them as silver is refined, and test them as gold is tested. They will call on My name, and I will answer them. I will say, "This is My people"; and each one will say, "The Lord is my God." '

"Can there be any doubt, friends, that He is who the Bible says He is? If you can still reject Him after seeing the sun snuffed out, the heavens shaken, and His sign appear, surely you are past hope, past saving. Do not wait. Be part of that one-third whom the Lord God has promised to bring through the fire.

"One of our first-century Jews, Peter, said, 'It shall come to pass that whoever calls on the name of the Lord shall be saved.' I cannot choose more appropriate words than his when I speak to fellow Jews, saying, 'Men of Israel, hear these words: Jesus of Nazareth, a Man attested by God to you by miracles, wonders, and signs which God did through Him in your midst, as you yourselves also know — Him, being delivered by the determined purpose and foreknowledge of God, you have taken by lawless hands, have crucified, and put to death; whom God raised up, having loosed the pains of death, because it was not possible that He should be held by it.

" 'For David says concerning Him: "I foresaw the Lord always before my face, for He is at my right hand, that I may not be shaken. Therefore my heart rejoiced, and my tongue was glad; moreover my flesh also will rest in hope. For You will not leave my soul in Hades, nor will You allow Your Holy One to see corruption. You have made known to me the ways of life; You will make me full of joy in Your presence."

" 'Men and brethren, let me speak freely to you of the patriarch David, that he is both dead and buried, and his tomb is with us to this day. Therefore, being a prophet, and knowing that God had sworn with an oath to him that of the fruit of his body, according to the flesh, He would raise up the Christ to sit on his throne, he, foreseeing this, spoke concerning the resurrection of the Christ, that His soul was not left in Hades, nor did His flesh see corruption. This Jesus God has raised up, of which we are all witnesses. Therefore being exalted to the right hand of God, and having received from the Father the promise of the Holy Spirit, He poured out this which you now see and hear.

" 'Therefore let all the house of Israel know assuredly that God has made this Jesus, whom you crucified, both Lord and Christ.'

"Beloved," Chaim raced on, "the Bible tells us that when they heard this, they were 'cut to the heart, and said to Peter and the rest of the apostles, "Men and brethren, what shall we do?" '

"Do you find yourself asking the same today? I say to you as Peter said to them, 'Repent, and let every one of you be baptized in the name of Jesus Christ for the remission of sins; and you shall receive the gift of the Holy Spirit. For the promise is to you and to your children, and to all who are afar off, as many as the Lord our God will call.'

"Oh, children of Israel around the globe, I am being signaled that our enemy is close to wresting back control of this network. Should I be cut off, trust me, you already know enough to put your faith in Christ as the Messiah.

"Not knowing when this signal shall fade, let me close by reading to you one of the most loved and powerful prophecies concerning Messiah that was ever written. And should my voice be silenced, you may find it and read it for yourself in Isaiah 53. And remember, this was written *more than seven hundred years* before the birth of Christ!

" 'Who has believed our report? And to whom has the arm of the Lord been revealed? For He shall grow up before Him as a tender plant, and as a root out of dry ground. He has no form or comeliness; and when we see Him, there is no beauty that we should desire Him. He is despised and rejected by men, a Man of sorrows and acquainted with grief. And we hid, as it were, our faces from Him; He was despised, and we did not esteem Him.

" 'Surely He has borne our griefs and carried our sorrows; yet we esteemed Him stricken, smitten by God, and afflicted. But He was wounded for our transgressions, He was bruised for our iniquities; the chastisement for our peace was upon Him, and by His stripes we are healed. All we like sheep have gone astray; we have turned, every one, to his own way; and the Lord has laid on Him the iniquity of us all.

" 'He was oppressed and He was afflicted, yet He opened not His mouth; He was led as a lamb to the slaughter, and as a sheep before its shearers is silent, so He opened not His mouth. He was taken from prison and from judgment, and who will declare His generation? For He was cut off from the land of the living; for the transgressions of My people He was stricken. And they made His grave with the wicked — but with the rich at His death, because He had done no violence, nor was any deceit in His mouth.

" 'Yet it pleased the Lord to bruise Him; He has put Him to grief. When You make His soul an offering for sin, He shall see His seed, He shall prolong His days, and the pleasure of the Lord shall prosper in His hand. He shall see the labor of His soul, and be satisfied. By His knowledge My righteous Servant shall justify many, for He shall bear their iniquities. Therefore I will divide Him a portion with the great, and He shall divide the spoil with the strong, because He poured out His soul unto death, and He was numbered with the transgressors, and He bore the sin of many, and made intercession for the transgressors.' "

During the broadcast, Chang had superimposed on the screen a Web site where those who were making decisions to receive Christ could let Dr. Rosenzweig know at Petra. Even before the GC reclaimed control of the television network, the Web site was being overrun with such messages. Millions around the world, most of them Jews, were acknowledging Jesus as the Messiah and putting their faith in Him for their salvation.

Mac was always moved by Scripture, and all the more so now to see Nicolae Carpathia, Antichrist himself, and his False Prophet, Leon Fortunato, squirm so.

"I wonder," Nicolae said, "how many died in Al Hillah before we succeeded in pushing the pirates off the gangplank. Who was the next one standing, now in charge?

"Well, let me tell you something. These people can say what they want, preach what they want, believe what they want. But if they have not taken my mark, not sworn their allegiance to the living god of this world, they shall surely die. This man appeals to the Jews, the dogs of society, the ones I have declared my enemies from the first. Meanwhile I have cut them down like a rotted harvest all over the world.

"And while my assassin sits temporarily free, hiding like a coward behind stone walls, my armies are decimating his wretched brothers and sisters in their so-called Holy City. After we have stormed Petra and laid waste to our enemies there, we shall return to complete the taking of Jerusalem. The resistance thinks they own the surface above where we even now reside, but their options are gone. They have nowhere to run, nowhere to hide.

"Let their *Savior* appear! I welcome Him. I will cut Him down like a dog and ascend to my rightful throne."

Mac's thighs ached and quivered with fatigue. The wall behind him had lost its coolness, and he couldn't figure it. Had his body heat finally tempered the subterranean effect? No, something was happening. The temperature was rising. How could that be?

What would cause it?

Even Carpathia, immune to hunger and fatigue and thirst since his resurrection, if the reports could be believed, noticed. He tugged at his collar. "What has happened to the air-conditioning?"

"None is needed, Excellency," Leon said. "We are forty feet below the sur—"

"I know where we are! I want to know why the temperature has risen. Do you not feel it?"

"Of course I do, exalted one. But there is no source of heat here. It has always remained a constant of —"

"*Will* you silence yourself! The temperature has risen, and even our collective body heat should not have resulted in that much difference."

Could it be? Mac wondered. Was there a chance this was a sign of the imminent return? Might Jesus appear even here, in the lair of His enemy? "Lord, please!"

Maybe outside the sun had darkened.

Rayford shielded his eyes and squinted into the sky. Not one cloud. The sun had finally coursed far enough to see the temperature drop, perhaps more than ten degrees, since its brutal noontime peak. Rayford gratefully accepted Abdullah's offer of his cap, which was

113

a little small but served its purpose.

"If we're not going to be able to carry you to Petra," Leah said, "we at least need to sit you up. Can you manage it?"

"I can't imagine," Rayford said. "But I know you're right. I'll need help."

"You're going to be dizzy," Leah said, which proved an understatement. When she and Abdullah sat him up, blood rushed so quickly from Rayford's head that he felt he'd lost his bearings, though he was still firmly planted — albeit on his seat now — in the shallow grave of his own making.

"Whoa," Rayford whispered.

"When you're steady," she said, "tell me what hurts most."

"I can tell you that now. The ankle. Then the shin. Then the hand."

"I'll take them in order," she said, "but it's all going to be temporary and makeshift. It's not what I would want done if I had you in a sterile environment and could do an MRI."

As Leah cleansed and anesthetized the ankle, which had a gaping gash and obvious damage inside, she said, "A surgeon will want to work on the bone before closing this up, but you don't need sand and air in it." She cut away dead and damaged skin that could not be salvaged and sutured it in such a way that it could easily be accessed again.

"This is going to hurt," she said, cutting away his khaki pants below the left knee and examining his shin with both hands. "No doubt you have a fracture, but this is not an easy bone to set. I can give it a try, but only before I numb it. You up to it?"

"I have a choice?"

"No. We may have to try to put you on one of our bikes, and without this set and splinted, you'll pass out from the pain."

"And what about the pain from your trying to set it?"

"No promises."

Rayford had been severely injured before, but he could not remember agony like this. Leah failed in her first attempt to set the shinbone, but she simply said, "Sorry, I can get it," and took another run at it. Despite a wad of gauze to chew on, Rayford screamed loud enough — he feared — to alert the Unity Army. Even once the bone was clearly in place, his leg hurt so badly that it jumped and quivered for more than ten minutes as he fought to keep from whimpering.

"I'll let that settle down some before applying a splint," Leah said.

"You're so kind," he said, and elicited a smile from her.

The splint, fortunately, was inflatable plastic and once in place provided enough stability that the pain finally started to subside. Leah busied herself cleaning and dressing the wounds on the heel of his hand, his chin, and on both arms and both knees.

"I'm going to look a sight," he said. "Better not let Kenny see me until some of this stuff is off."

George Sebastian was relieved to know that Rayford had been found alive, but he had to wonder how busted up his boss must be. More pressing, he was uneasy about what the Unity Army was up to. They had closed the mile gap by half, advancing on his position so slowly that the maneuver had taken hours. And now they were stopped. If it was some sort of psychological warfare, it was working. Sebastian's people were spooked.

It was as if this roiling armada, fronted by the hundreds of thousands of mounted horsemen, was just waiting for one word from Antichrist to either open fire or charge. Bothering Big Dog One most was that he now had to turn his head more than 120 degrees just to take in the breadth of the fighting force he faced. And regardless of how high he could place himself, he could never see its full depth. The end of this army literally blotted out the horizon.

★ ★ ★

Mac was as stunned as Leon clearly was when Carpathia said, "I need a chair. Get me a chair!"

Nicolae rarely sat anymore. He was known not to have eaten or slept in three and a half years, persuading loyalists he was the true and living God, and confirming to his enemies that he was indeed Antichrist, indwelt by Satan. His rage was legendary. But no one had seen a weakness or physical frailty in him.

And now he needed a chair?

Leon Fortunato leaped from his own and slid it behind the potentate, who shakily sat. Nicolae tore at his collar and unbuttoned his shirt, feebly fanning himself with his hand. "Allow me, Excellency," Fortunato said, and he knelt and grabbed the hem of his own ostentatious robe, lifted it to his waist, and began fanning the potentate.

Normally Carpathia would quickly tire of such obsequiousness, but he actually appeared panicky and grateful. But when Leon turned to ask Viv Ivins to pour Nicolae a glass of water, his garish fez slipped off and landed in the blousy folds of his skirt. His next tug tightened the fabric and launched the hat into Carpathia's lap.

"Oh!" Leon cried out. "Oh, majesty! Forgive me!" He lurched forward and tried to retrieve the fez, succeeding only in knocking it out of Nicolae's lap and onto the floor on his other side. Leon's momentum carried him over the potentate, and now he was stretched out across the ailing world leader, his ample belly in his boss's lap. He grabbed the hat with both hands, and as he rocked back to his feet he jammed it atop his head again, uttering every apology imaginable.

Mac was certain Nicolae would execute his right-hand man for such a breach of etiquette, but he appeared to have hardly noticed. Carpathia was in trouble. Viv Ivins finally got a glass of water in front of him, but by now his hands were at his sides and his usually ruddy countenance had paled.

Leon grabbed the water and held it to Carpathia's lips as the fez began to tumble yet again. This time Leon angrily batted it away with his free hand and it toppled to the floor behind them. Carpathia could barely manage to open his mouth, water sloshing down his chin.

"Get paramedics in here!" Leon squealed. "Someone, please! Hurry!"

Five

Sweat trickled down Mac's back. The temperature was rising, almost as if there was a fire below the Temple Mount. With Carpathia having his own problems, Unity Army sentries fell out of attention and wiped their brows, tugged at their shirts and jackets, and traded looks as if to ask what was going on.

Mac turned and leaned out the arched opening at the sound of shouts. Whatever this was, it was widespread. And suddenly, the stables were in chaos. Unfettered horses broke free from their handlers, neighing, spooking each other into a stampede that had nowhere to go. Stablemen tossed lassos but found themselves pulled off the ground when the steeds reared, and then thrown to the ground when they took off, horses jostling horses, fighting for space to get through the arches.

Men and women were trampled, some to death, but when a shortsighted soldier fired into the air, things only got worse. More than a thousand full-size Thoroughbreds were manic and terrified. Following their instincts, they tried to flee, crushing anything in their path, including each other.

Mac saw great equine shoulders ripped open as horses were crushed against the stone walls. He heard legs snapping, saw horses nipping and biting each other, and soon it was a free-for-all.

"Where's the fire?" someone shouted. Many must have heard only "fire," for it was repeated and repeated, soldiers screaming it all over the underground. Mac saw no flame, smelled no smoke. But he heard "Fire!" "Fire!" "Fire!" and like the rest, his instinct was to head for the surface.

But a commander nudged him back into the room with the barrel of a nuclear submachine gun. "There is no fire!" he announced. "Every soldier in this room has a job, and that is to protect the potentate. That is what we shall do. No one enters; no one leaves."

"Permission to speak, Commander," came from a corner.

"Granted."

"What is causing the heat?"

"No idea, but let everyone else kill themselves trying to escape a fire that doesn't exist. You're not going to best a twelve-hundred-pound horse that wants your space anyway, so stay here and do your job."

"What's wrong with the potentate?"

"How should I know?"

"Are the paramedics coming?"

"I don't know how they'd get here. But you can bet no one else will get in. If this is a plot against His Excellency, it stops right here. Now come to attention! Weapons at the ready!"

Mac had never liked being underground, but up till now this foray had not brought on claustrophobia. The sheer size of the area had given him room to move and breathe. But now, outside the only room where everyone remained still, pandemonium reigned. There would be no escape, no freedom, no daylight, no air, no lessening of the heat, even if he opened fire and killed everyone around him and made a break for the surface. What was happening on the dirt ramp and the wood stairs dwarfed mass tragedies due to fire in crowded buildings. Even without an actual fire, this was going to be catastrophic.

With his safety turned off and his firing

finger on the trigger, Mac fought to maintain his composure, remaining at attention, staring straight at Carpathia, sweat running freely now inside his uniform.

Nicolae looked wasted. His formerly full head of hair appeared somehow sparse now. His clear, piercing eyes were bloodshot and droopy. His face was sallow, and though it made no sense, Mac believed he could see veins spidering across the man's face, framing his hollow eyes.

Carpathia's fingers looked thin, his skin papery, his shoulders bony. It was as if he had lost fifty pounds in minutes. His pale, bluish lips were parted, and his teeth and gums showed . . . the mouth of a dead man.

"You must drink, Excellency!" Fortunato whined.

"I am spent," Carpathia said, and though Mac could barely hear him, his was clearly not the voice Mac had come to recognize. His words seemed hollow, faint, echoey, as if he spoke from a dungeon far away. "Hungry," Carpathia said flatly. "Exhausted. Dead."

No doubt he meant that last as a figure of speech, but to Mac he did look dead. Were his skin any worse he could have passed for a decomposing corpse. Even his ears had lost color and appeared translucent.

In the next instant, Mac found himself on his knees, shielding his eyes from the brightest light he had ever experienced. It reminded him of a science experiment in junior high more than fifty years before when he and his classmates wore heavily tinted goggles as they ignited magnesium strips.

Mac peeked to find that he was not the only soldier on the ground. Most had pitched forward onto their stomachs, weapons rattling to the floor. Whatever the source radiating from the middle of the table, it lit the room like the noon sun.

"Beautiful! Beautiful!" people whispered, interlaced with the *ooh*s and *aah*s associated with fireworks displays. All the dignitaries had thrust their chairs back from the table and covered their eyes, peeking through fingers to gaze on this magnificent appearance, whatever it was.

Mac pushed himself up and rocked back on his haunches, his eyes gradually becoming accustomed to the initially blinding radiance. As he squatted there, hands on his weapon again, it was clear why so many thought this . . . this apparition was so striking. It seemed to hover inches above the table, directly in the center, such a bright gold-tinged white that you could not take your eyes from it. It shone with such brilliance that no detail was clear, from the bottom to the top of what appeared to be a roughly six-foot human form. There was no way to tell whether it — if it was a humanoid being — wore shoes or clothes or was naked.

Gradually Mac realized he was looking at the back of a being that faced Carpathia and Fortunato. Flowing blond hair came into view, but it appeared that the rest of the body would remain a mystery to the human eye. Clearly, this was not the Glorious Appearing of Christ, as Mac knew He was to return on the clouds with His faithful behind Him.

Viv Ivins's chair was empty, but Mac could hear her moaning in ecstasy on the floor.

Leon was also on the floor, head buried in his hands, rocking, weeping.

Carpathia had fallen forward in his borrowed chair, his cheek on the table, arms outstretched, palms flat. "Oh, my lord, my god, and my king," his death-rattle voice repeated over and over.

From outside the room Mac heard the awful, terrifying sounds of death. Panic, screams and screeches, pleading, bones being crushed, air pushed from lungs, horses snuffling and caterwauling as other, smaller creatures might do.

Pitiful, lonely cries could be heard from grown men and women. "Save me! Oh, God, save me! I don't want to die!"

And yet die they did. Without even being able to see, it was clear to Mac that the carnage between him and the exit would be unlike anything he had ever encountered. Shooting began, and he could only guess it was the few remaining soldiers putting horses or comrades out of their misery and trying to pave themselves some macabre exit route over dead bodies.

Carpathia raised his pathetic head, his Zorro getup hanging as if on a cadaver. "Lucifer," he managed in that rasping, hollow voice, appearing to squint into the eyes of the being. "My lord king, why have you forsaken me? Why have you withdrawn your spirit from me? Have I not given myself wholly to you, to serve you with my entire heart and being?"

"Silence!" came the response in a voice so phantasmagorically piercing and awful that it made Mac recoil and want to cover his ears. "You disgust me! Look at you! You dare suggest you have anything to offer *me* besides your pathetic frame?! You are drunk with a power whose source is far beyond your own! You are merely a vessel, a tool, a jar of clay for my purposes, and yet you pa-

125

rade yourself as if you had a shred of value!"

"Oh, my king!" Carpathia gasped. "No! I —"

"You do not even understand the meaning of the word *silence!* You are nothing! Nothing! You had no power to rise from the dead! You were a carcass, stiff and decaying. Look at you now. Aside from my grace, you would return to the earth, ashes to ashes and dust to dust."

"Spare me, oh, my lord! I love you and long to serve you! I will do anything for —"

"Oh, spirit of nothingness, mere speck of my imagination. I will borrow your otherwise worthless skeleton yet again. But you must know, and if you cannot fathom it, I must myself remind you who you are and who you are not. You are not me! I am not you! You are mere inventory, goods and services. You are a piece of equipment, and you must never dare imagine otherwise."

"I have never, divine one! Never! I am humbly at your serv—"

"I am the lord your god, and I will not share my glory!"

"Absolutely," Carpathia said, panting. "O king of heaven and earth."

"Do not think it was by accident that my Adversary, in His own words, acknowledged that I originated in heaven and called me the son of the morning! Do you not know, as He knows, that it is I who have weakened the nations?"

"I know," Carpathia sobbed. "I know!"

"I, not you, not anyone else in all of the evolved world, am the one who shall ascend into heaven. I will exalt my throne above the stars of God; I will also sit on the mount of the congregation on the farthest sides of the north; I will ascend above the heights of the clouds. I will be like the Most High."

"Yes, precious master. Yes!"

"Yet my Enemy claims I shall be brought down to Sheol, to the lowest depths of the pit."

"No, lord, no!"

"He claims that those who see me will gaze at me and consider me, saying, 'Is this the man who made the earth tremble, who shook kingdoms, who made the world as a wilderness and destroyed its cities, who did not open the house of his prisoners?'"

"May it never be so, my sovereign!"

"Oh yes, my Enemy derides me! He claims all the kings of the nations, all of them, die in glory, every one in his own grand tomb, but that I — *I* — shall be cast out of my grave like an abominable branch, like the garment of those who are slain, thrust through with a sword, who go down to the stones of the pit, like a corpse trodden underfoot. *I* will be buried like a common soldier killed in battle?"

"Never!" Carpathia sobbed. "Never! Not as long as I have breath!"

"Are you so thick you do not understand? It is *I* who give *you* breath!"

"I know! Yes, I know!"

"And what shall be your contribution, knave, when the Enemy attempts to make good on His promise that no monument will be given me, for I have destroyed my nation Babylon and slain my people? He taunts me that my son will not succeed me as king."

"Oh, let me be your son," Carpathia blubbered. "And you shall be my father!"

"But *no!* The Enemy derides me. He says, 'Slay the children of this sinner. Do not let them rise and conquer the land nor rebuild the cities of the world. I, myself, have risen against him,' and He has the audacity to call Himself the Lord of heaven's armies."

"But that is you, O beautiful star! It is you alone!"

"He has already destroyed my beloved Babylon, but He will not be content until He makes her into 'a desolate land of porcupines, full of swamps and marshes.' He promises to 'sweep the land with the broom of destruction,' this so-called Lord of the ar-

128

mies of heaven."

"We shall never let that happen, Your Grace."

"But He has taken an oath to do it! He says this is His purpose and plan. He has decided to break the Assyrian army when they are in Israel and to crush them on His mountains, saying, 'My people shall no longer be their slaves. This is My plan for the whole earth — I will do it by My mighty power that reaches everywhere around the world.' "

"But His power is nothing compared to yours, conquering king! We will prove it even today, will we not?"

"We? *We?*"

"You! You, exalted one!"

"Who are you to speak? What have you to offer me when the Enemy, who calls Himself the Lord, the God of battle, has spoken — who can change His plans? When His hand moves, who can stop Him?"

"You can, all-powerful one. I believe in you."

"I can. And do not forget it. Who does He think stood up against Israel and moved David to number Israel, when clearly his God had forbidden it?"

"He knows. I know He knows!"

"Of course He knows! It is I who have

gone to and fro in the earth, walking up and down in it. It was I who tested and tempted Job to nearly abandon and curse his God. When Joshua the high priest stood before the Angel of the Lord, it was I who stood at his right hand to oppose him. It was I who tempted the Enemy's own Son in the wilderness."

"And you nearly succeeded."

"Success comes today."

"I believe it, my lord."

"I am the one who took the Enemy's Son up into the Holy City and set Him on the pinnacle of the temple. I said to Him, 'If You are the Son of God, throw Yourself down. For it is written: "He shall give His angels charge over You" and "In their hands they shall bear You up, lest you dash Your foot against a stone." ' But He would not! He Himself did not believe! He countered as a coward, with mere words. He tried to tell me, as if *I* did not know, that 'It is written again, "You shall not tempt the Lord your God." ' Well, He is not *my* Lord or God!"

"Nor mine, prince of the power of the air."

"It was I who took Him up on an exceedingly high mountain and showed Him all the kingdoms of the world and their glory. I offered Him all of these if He would but fall down and worship me. But He would not."

"He was a fool."

"But I did not bow to Him either."

"And you never will."

"I never shall. He spoke the truth and told it well when He called his own disciple Satan. I had hold of Peter for a time then. The Enemy's Son rightly accused him of not being mindful of the things of God, but of the things of men."

"May it ever be so!" Carpathia gushed.

"Oh, the Son knew well that when men heard His message, it was I who came immediately and took away the word that was sown in their hearts."

"That has always been your strength."

"It was I who entered Judas, who was numbered among the Son's disciples. And it was I who asked for Simon Peter yet again, that I might sift him as wheat. He was so weak that night."

"I will not be weak in your hour of need, master."

"I do not need you! I will not be weak! You, sad one, are unteachable."

"Forgive me, lord."

"It was I who filled Ananias's heart to lie and keep back part of the price of his land for himself."

"A masterpiece!"

"Silence! I am wearying of you. I am preparing for battle with the One who calls Himself the God of peace and claims He will crush me under His feet. I, the one who takes advantage when men are ignorant of my devices. I am the god of this age, able to blind the minds of those who do not believe — as I do not — in what my Enemy calls the light of the gospel of the glory of Christ, who is the image of God. I am more than His image. I am His superior and shall be His conqueror. I was crafty enough to deceive Eve, His second creation. Am I not up to this task?"

"You are, and the universe shall sing your praises and call you blessed."

"You have well said that I am the prince of the power of the air. I am the spirit who now works in the sons of disobedience toward the Enemy. I work among them to fulfill the lusts of their flesh, fulfilling the desires of the flesh and of the mind. None shall stand against my wiles. They do not wrestle against flesh and blood, but against my principalities, against my powers, against my rulers of this age, against spiritual hosts in the heavenly places."

"That is you, O blessed one."

"I have fiery darts that cannot be quenched."

"Amen and amen!"

"I hindered even the Enemy's favored servant, Paul, thwarting his plans time and again. And in his absence from his followers, I tempted them from their faith. I was their adversary, and they referred to me as akin to a roaring lion, seeking whom I might devour."

"Today shall be a feast for you."

"The Enemy who calls Himself God has decreed that His Son was manifested, that He might destroy my works."

"Blasphemy!"

"He called me the great dragon, called me that serpent of old, called me the devil and Satan, and acknowledged that it is I who deceives the whole world. But He erred when He cast me to the earth and my angels with me."

"He made an eternal blunder, lord. How excellent is your name in all the earth! Be exalted above the heavens. Let your glory be above all the earth. You, my lord, are high above all nations, and your glory above the heavens. Who is like unto you who dwells on high?"

"I have need of your shell again for a brief season."

"I am yours," Carpathia said.

And with that the light disappeared and

Nicolae stood, chin lifted, arrogance restored. His color returned as he buttoned his shirt and straightened his clothes. It was as if he had come back to life, his voice again crisp and sure.

"Return to your seats, ladies and gentlemen, please. Ms. Ivins, please. Reverend Fortunato." He deliberately moved the chair Leon had provided for him and held it as the holy man awkwardly disentangled himself from his garments and stood, then sat.

"Sub-potentates, generals, assistants, sit, please. Soldiers, return to attention."

It was plain to Mac that the room was full of shocked and shaken people. Their eyes shone with fear. Their bodies were hesitant and unsure. They returned to their places fearful and stunned.

"Your discomfort will soon cease," Nicolae said. "When you are all in place, I shall tell you what you just witnessed and what you will remember."

An Asian dignitary raised a hand, consternation on his face.

"Please hold all questions, just for a moment."

An African stood, hand also raised.

"Please honor my request, sir," Carpathia said. "I will get to you in a moment if you will extend this courtesy."

The African sat, clearly troubled. Others looked at each other, eyes narrow, shaking their heads.

"Ladies and gentlemen and soldiers," Carpathia began, but he was interrupted by a man at the door. "What is it?"

"Because of the carnage outside, Excellency, we have been unable to find a paramedic unit for this room."

"Thank you. No longer needed."

"And, your grace, neither have we been able to determine the source of the heat that caused the stampede."

"I believe that issue is moot now, is it not? Anyone uncomfortable?"

"Not from the heat," an Aussie said, "but I have some serious questions about what just —"

"I shall ask you too, sir, to hold all questions and comments for another moment. Thank you. And, sir?" he added, addressing the one in the archway. "Would you mind staying as I offer an explanation?"

The man moved past Mac and stood behind those seated at the far end of the table from Carpathia.

"Ladies and gentlemen," Nicolae began in his most mellow, persuasive tone, slowly scanning the room and looking briefly but directly into the eyes of everyone. "Do not feel obligated to look away this time. I am choosing to connect with you visually. You have just been privileged to enjoy a unique experience. You were present when I left this mortal body and took on my divine form. I charged you with all the rights and privileges that attend your station as loyal followers and encouraged you in the battle to come.

"You shall become aware as we leave this place and mount up to ride into our glorious victory that the enemy has succeeded in penetrating the ground above, essentially our ceiling. I divinely protected myself, you included, but they caused a stampede that has caused many casualties among our troops and our livestock, which, as you know, we value as highly as our human resources. But do not be alarmed. Do not fear. Our resources are limitless. I shall lead you up and out, and there will be enough mounts for all. Now, there were some comments and questions?"

The Asian stood, bowing. "I just wanted to thank you, Excellency, for the privilege you have extended to me and my party. To have been here for this most momentous and historic moment will become the memory of a lifetime, and we are most grateful."

"Thank you. Yes, sir?"

The African stood. "I would like to echo that sentiment, your holiness, on behalf of my staff. You are most worthy to be praised, and we look forward to joining you in your ultimate victory, after which the world shall see you for who you truly are."

Mac wanted to shout an amen. If he was the only believer in the room — and he couldn't imagine otherwise — he was the only one not hypnotically hoodwinked by Carpathia.

The exit to the surface was surreal. The men and women were led and followed by contingents of the soldiers, giving Mac a perfect view of their response to what had befallen everyone else. The place was worse than any war zone. Hundreds of horses and even more men and women lay dead in hideous repose, broken, trampled, crushed, torn to pieces. The stench of the stables was nothing compared to the steaming entrails of human and beast, and yet the men and women from the meeting room stepped on and over the remains as if traipsing through a meadow.

No one made a face, held his nose, or had a comment. It was as if they could not see the slaughter that soaked their shoes and caused dirt to adhere to the blood. As they reached the surface they blithely stamped their feet and thanked the soldiers for their assistance. The mood was festive as great steeds were moved into line for them and each was helped into the saddle.

Bound for Armageddon, they smiled and laughed and chatted as if on their way to a day at the races. Mac noticed for the first time that day that puffy, fluffy clouds had begun to dot the sky. The sun was still visible, turning orange on the horizon. All he wanted was to slip away and be with his brothers and sisters in Christ when the end came.

Rayford had his misgivings about both the vehicles. There was room on Abdullah's for the both of them, but not much. And it was a thin, whiny, violent machine built for speed, hardly comfort. Leah's ATV was wider and sturdier and slower, but unless they left her supplies behind there would not be room for two people. As the second rider, Rayford needed stability. And speed would be his enemy. The angles, the inclines, the acceleration, the turns and bounces and jostling would be torture.

The alternative was not acceptable. He didn't want to stay in the barren, rocky hills any longer. Who knew what the global earthquake would do out there? He didn't expect to die in it, but he hadn't expected to be pitched off his ATV either.

His ATV. Now there was a solution. Not his, of course. It lay in ruins. But there were more where that came from. They called Sebastian.

"Camel Jockey to Big Dog," Smitty said.

"This's Dog, Jockey. Go."

"Can you get us an ATV to transport Captain Steele to Petra?"

"If I can drive it."

"Affirmative, but should you leave your troops?"

"Kidding, Smitty. I'll send Razor."

"You know our position?"

"Affirmative. Chang zeroed you in for me. Rayford going to make it?"

"If he survives the trip. How does Mr. Razor drive?"

"I think he knows what's at stake. What do you make of the clouds?"

"First ones all day, Big Dog. I think Somebody's coming."

"I've got to get out of here," Chang said, rubbing his eyes.

"That's all I need to hear," Naomi said, virtually lifting him from his chair.

"Let me log off first," he said, resisting.

"Not on your life. Now let's go. Nobody's going to suffer if you don't log off. This is supposed to be a spectacular sunset."

"With no clouds? How do you figure?"

"You'll see. You've been so busy, you don't even know what's going on."

When they got outside, Chang was stunned. The sun was dropping, big and wide, and there were indeed clouds. They seemed to appear from nowhere, more and more by the minute. There was something festive about them — bouncy, fleecy, and yet moving quickly as if there were strong winds high in the atmosphere. Before long they were joining each other, making shadow-forming canopies south of the sun while individual clouds continued to form to the north.

These, too, soon began to join. Chang and Naomi went to their favorite high spot and lay on their backs, hands behind their heads. "I've never seen that before," Chang said, pointing straight up. Clouds seemed to be forming directly above, not on the horizon as usual. They began as long, narrow formations in the stratosphere, quickly forming into stratocumulus.

"We're getting high-, mid-, and low-level formations all at the same time," Chang said.

"They're gorgeous."

"Yeah, now. Wait till they start developing vertically. They can reach heights of more than seven miles and generate incredible energy."

"How do you know all this?" she said. "All I know is computers."

"I know everything," Chang said.

Naomi punched him. "Hey," she said, turning on her side and gazing at his face. "You're going to fall asleep."

"Not likely," he said. "Too much happening up there. Too much to look forward to."

Six

"Brother Enoch," a Hispanic man said, "if you can concentrate, we can concentrate."

"I don't follow," Enoch said, again looking through trees and windows at the edge of the mall's courtyard to be sure the GC had not found them out.

"You seem distracted, brother. I mean, we're all waiting for the same thing. We want to be ready. We want to be here when Jesus comes. But in the meantime we want you to teach us. You keep saying you're no scholar, but you've been our pastor for years. Something's working."

"Yeah," another chimed in. "I don't feel like I've got a handle on what all's happened and what's going to happen. I know we'll soon be with Jesus — or anyway, He'll be with us — but I wouldn't mind going into all this with more understanding. You got more for us?"

Enoch had to smile. "I do," he said. "I just didn't expect to have the time to cover it, and I certainly didn't expect you to have the patience for it."

"Beats waitin' around. I can't wait till Jesus gets here, but the clock moves slow when nothin's happening."

"Fair enough. I've got my Bible and my notes, if you're game."

"We're game. But, Pastor, have you looked up lately?"

It was coming up on noon in the Midwest, and the sun was riding high. Enoch shielded his eyes. "Clouds," he said.

"Clouds that weren't there an hour ago. If I'm not mistaken, we woke up to blue skies."

"Totally blue."

"They're not threatening clouds," Enoch said. "I don't expect we'll get rained on."

A woman laughed. "I just wanna see clouds Jesus can ride in on."

Razor showed up on a 750cc ATV plenty big enough to accommodate Rayford if he were healthy. But he had not been sitting up long, let alone standing or bouncing along on a vehicle.

"You didn't happen to bring any food, did you?" Rayford said.

"Sir, yes, sir," Razor said in the maddening military formality of which Rayford had been trying to break him.

"Miz Leah here didn't care if I starved to death."

"Hydration was most important," she said. "And I didn't expect you to be stuck here this long."

"I'm kidding, Leah. You saved my life. Now what've you got, Razor?"

"An energy bar, sir."

"One of those Styrofoam jobs that tastes like cardboard?"

"One and the same."

"Flavor?"

"Corrugated chocolate, I believe, sir."

Kidding aside, Rayford was famished. He tore open the wrapper and took a huge bite.

"Easy there, cowboy," Leah said. "Your system's been traumatized."

"Well, this ought to help," Rayford said, following orders and slowing down. He was stalling. Climbing aboard an ATV was going to be an ordeal, but that would be the least of it. The path back to Petra, such as it was, looked like a sheer cliff from his vantage point. "It's going to be a beautiful sunset," he said idly.

"And probably the last one before Jesus comes," Leah said.

Sebastian sat on the hood of a Hummer that had been idle for hours, but whose metal had only just cooled enough to allow him there. The Unity Army seemed distracted, if that characteristic could be applied to such an expansive gathering. Ever since they had advanced half a mile and stopped, they had sat staring menacingly at him and his troops.

George had decided not to antagonize them with directed energy weapons or fifty-caliber fire, and in the last half hour they had grown, well, somehow less threatening. It was as if they had lost focus. Earlier, the hundreds of thousands of mounted troops alone had seemed to act in concert to stare him down, and now he heard their squeaky saddles in the distance. They had stopped staring and had begun wheeling in their saddles, chatting with each other.

Was it possible the rumors had reached the battlefield? Did these soldiers know that they might not be spelled by reinforcements or that, even if they were, it was unlikely they would be paid on time, if at all? The grapevine was remarkably accurate, quick, and — if this proved true — resilient enough to reach across the desert sands.

Could Big Dog One take advantage of this lapse? He couldn't imagine how. A volley of shells or DEW rays would succeed only in getting the enemy re-engaged, setting them back on course. For now, hopelessly out-numbered as he was, Sebastian liked his adversary just the way it was. If he could choose, he'd have moved them back about a mile and a half. But they couldn't pull that off even if they wanted to, even if they were ordered to. Backing up the front lines meant backing up the rear, and coordinating that would take weeks. This was a fighting force that could go only one way, and Sebastian and his excuse for a defending force were directly in their path.

He got on the phone. "Chang, what're you doing right this instant?"

"You don't want to know."

" 'Course I do."

"I'm lying on my back, watching the clouds."

"And you're not alone, are you?"

"Of course not," Chang said.

"Priscilla and I are going to be apart when Jesus comes," Sebastian said.

"You want me to send her and Beth Ann to be with you?"

"Hardly. We've arranged a meeting spot

for when this is over."

"I hope Captain Steele will be up to watching all this when he gets here and the time comes," Chang said.

"Oh, he will be. Just hope the time doesn't come before Razor gets him there."

"As you know," Enoch told his people, "the whole theme through my teaching of the events of the end times has been the mercy of God. To many of you this seemed inconsistent with what was prophesied and what came to pass. But as I have said, all of this, all twenty-one judgments that have come from heaven in three sets of seven, have been God's desperate last attempts to get man's attention. Make no mistake about it, however; the last seven judgments in particular also evidence His wrath.

"In fact, the angels who carry out these judgments are depicted as turning over and emptying out bowls or vials, so that every drop of judgment is poured out on the various targets of God's anger. Notice the focus of these judgments:

"The first bowl was poured out on the *earth* in the form of horrible malignant sores on the bodies of those who had taken the mark of the beast.

"The second was poured out into the *sea*,

turning the water to blood and killing every living thing in it.

"The third was poured into the *rivers* and *springs* so that all remaining freshwater was turned to blood. You'll recall that this was God's initial and partial response to the martyrs' prayers in Revelation 6:10 that their deaths be avenged: 'And they cried with a loud voice, saying, "How long, O Lord, holy and true, until You judge and avenge our blood on those who dwell on the earth?" '

"The fourth bowl was poured out on the *sun* so that it so increased in power that extraordinary heat burned men with fire. And how did those who survived respond? Revelation 16:9 tells us they 'blasphemed the name of God who has power over these plagues; and they did not repent and give Him glory.'

"The fifth bowl was poured out on the *throne of the beast.* Who knows what that means?"

"New Babylon."

"Yes! And we know that mighty city was plunged into a darkness so great that it caused physical pain so severe that men and women gnawed their own tongues. And once again, what was their response? 'They blasphemed the God of heaven because of

their pains and their sores, and did not repent of their deeds.'

"The sixth bowl was poured out on the
great river, the *Euphrates,* and it dried up.
That allowed the leaders from the east to
bring their armies to the mountains of Israel
for the battle of Armageddon. Here God
was clearly luring Antichrist into His trap.
Joel 3:9–17 prophesies this, and though
scholars disagree about when the book of
Joel was written, it is generally agreed that it
was more than eight hundred years before Christ:

" 'Proclaim this among the nations: "Prepare for war! Wake up the mighty men, let
all the men of war draw near, let them come
up. Beat your plowshares into swords and
your pruning hooks into spears; let the weak
say, 'I am strong.' "

" 'Assemble and come, all you nations,
and gather together all around. Cause Your
mighty ones to go down there, O Lord.' Let
the nations be wakened, and come up to the
Valley of Jehoshaphat; for there I will sit to
judge all the surrounding nations. Put in the
sickle, for the harvest is ripe. Come, go
down; for the winepress is full, the vats over-
flow — for their wickedness is great."

" 'Multitudes, multitudes in the valley of
decision! For the day of the Lord is near in

the valley of decision. The sun and moon will grow dark, and the stars will diminish their brightness. The Lord also will roar from Zion, and utter His voice from Jerusalem; the heavens and earth will shake; but the Lord will be a shelter for His people, and the strength of the children of Israel.

" 'So you shall know that I am the Lord your God, dwelling in Zion My holy mountain. Then Jerusalem shall be holy, and no aliens shall ever pass through her again.' "

Enoch continued, "The seventh bowl judgment, the one we still await, will be poured out upon the *air* so that lightning and thunder and other celestial calamities announce the greatest earthquake in history. It will be so great it will cause Jerusalem to break into three pieces in preparation for changes during Christ's millennial kingdom. It will also be accompanied by a great outpouring of hundred-pound hailstones.

"And what will the general response be from the very ones God is trying to reach and persuade? Revelation 16:21 tells us that 'men blasphemed God because of the plague of the hail, since that plague was exceedingly great.' "

"And this is what's coming next?" someone said.

"In advance of the Glorious Appearing," Enoch said. "Yes."

"And you believe this?"

"Without question."

"Then what are we doing outside while the clouds gather?"

"Do you not recall that believers have been spared injury under all these judgments? I rest in that."

"Amen!"

"Praise the Lord!"

"Come, Lord Jesus!"

"I rest in something else, beloved," Enoch said. "One of the most beautiful and reassuring passages in Scripture is John 14:1–6, where Jesus is comforting His disciples. I believe we can take these promises for ourselves and stand secure, knowing they were made by One in whom there is no change, neither shadow of turning. Let me read them to you.

" 'Let not your heart be troubled; you believe in God, believe also in Me. In My Father's house are many mansions; if it were not so, I would have told you. I go to prepare a place for you. And if I go and prepare a place for you, I will come again and receive you to Myself; that where I am, there you may be also. And where I go you know, and the way you know.'

" 'Thomas said to Him, "Lord, we do not know where You are going, and how can we know the way?"

" 'Jesus said to him, "I am the way, the truth, and the life. No one comes to the Father except through Me." ' "

Rayford noticed a lull in the activity and assumed it was because both Razor and Leah needed Abdullah's help to load him aboard the big ATV. And Abdullah was fifteen feet or so down the rocky slope with his back to them, on the phone. When it appeared he was finished, he called someone else.

The energy bar, distasteful as it was, had its desired effect, and Rayford was ready to get going. He'd felt better in his day, but despite numerous ailments, he had a renewed sense of purpose and drive. *Let's go; let's go!* he thought, but he said nothing.

Presently Abdullah returned. "Many people worry about you, Captain," he said. "Ree Woo for one, but especially Chaim himself. He wonders what your plans are."

"My plans? To keep breathing. To survive the trip."

"He is wondering if you would be up to his visit at your quarters when you arrive."

"Of course," Rayford said. "Know what he wants?"

"Again," Leah said, "let's not get ahead of ourselves, shall we? You joke about surviving the trip, and frankly I am quite worried about that. You have no idea how you'll feel when you arrive. You likely have a broken rib on top of everything else, maybe more than one. It's nearly impossible to tell without an X-ray or MRI."

"What're you saying, Doc?"

"I'm just a nurse, but moving you the way we're planning is just about the worst possible scenario for you right now."

"Just about?"

"Staying here would be worse, but at least you're stable."

Mac gingerly climbed aboard the biggest, blackest, most powerful horse he had ever seen. It had been years, but he knew enough to plant his left foot firmly in the stirrup before swinging his right leg up and over. If anyone was looking, he might appear to have a clue.

Unfortunately, he was more concerned with mounting than he was with his dangling Uzi, and before he settled firmly in the saddle, the barrel of his weapon poked the horse in the back, just above the saddle horn at the base of the neck. The beast started and stepped about quickly, causing Mac to panic and stiffen. That made the horse rear. Mac pulled on the reins with all his weight, desperate to hang on and not be chucked off onto his head.

As the steed whinnied loudly and reared higher, spooking other horses and riders, Mac slid out of the saddle and the stirrups slackened. Mac pushed his legs straight as hard as he could, tucked his chin to his chest, and held the reins for all he was worth. That pulled the horse's muzzle down and nearly made him topple backward. Mac was almost upside down, all his weight pulling against the horse, and he could imagine pulling the animal down atop him.

Somehow the horse balanced itself with a few well-placed steps with its back feet, then slammed down to all fours, thrusting Mac hard into the saddle and throwing him forward to where he was now hugging the horse around the neck. The animal still felt unsure beneath him, and Mac knew he had done the opposite of showing it who was in charge. If a message had been sent to the horse, it was that the rider was scared to death and hanging on for dear life.

Mac's "superior" appeared not to have noticed. He cantered up and pointed to several soldiers, Mac included, directing them to position themselves off the flanks of

Carpathia's horse. Leave it to the potentate to have a monster creature that put the rest to shame. His horse was at least two hands taller and a hundred pounds heavier than the others. It had a spot of white between its eyes and four white feet. Its tail seemed to shoot straight up before the rest of it cascaded down in a smart flow. The mane was somehow longer and thicker as well. Mac had heard of the hound of heaven. This was the horse from hell.

It even seemed to have attitude. It snuffled loudly whenever another horse invaded its space, and it nipped and kicked to keep its place. Carpathia appeared to have been raised around horses, deftly controlling the thing with a light grip and decisive hands, knees, and feet. He rode ahead several feet and turned his horse to face the others.

"Let me remind you all," he said, "that we are merely feet from an active battleground. The resistance currently holds the Temple Mount, aboveground, and they are capable of firing from atop the wall. Be vigilant. This is not a press junket or a sightseer's safari. I am most disappointed to tell you that I have just been made aware of an insurgence within our own ranks from both the south in Egypt and below and from the northeast. Ironically, some who pledged their allegiance now call themselves 'Revitalized Babylon' and condescend to assert their independence. These uprisings shall be crushed posthaste. As we speak, portions of our more than extravagantly outfitted fighting force will peel off to these locations to lay waste to the pretenders. They will regret their insolence only as long as they have breath, and then they will be trampled and made an example of.

"Meanwhile, we will figuratively set out for Petra. I say figuratively, because I do not plan to waste the hours it would take to actually ride some sixty miles on horseback. The Global Community media will get what it needs as we strike out from here, leave the occupied Muslim Quarter, and head southwest through the Jewish and Armenian Quarters — both also having been easily taken by our forces — and leave the Old City through the Zion Gate. There you will transfer to ground vehicles capable of covering the distance at well over a hundred miles an hour. I will set out a few minutes later with my generals and cabinet in aircraft that will actually transport us and our horses to the area slightly in advance of your arrival.

"We have mounts similar to those you are on now waiting for you outside Petra, and you shall have the privilege of witnessing my leading our troops to victory over what shall by then be one of only two remaining enclaves of opposition to the New World Order. Smile for the cameras!"

Mac finally felt he had control of his horse, but he had no intention of following Carpathia in one of the ground vehicles. If any portion of the security detail was assigned elsewhere, Mac would find a way to join them, and then peel off to his own helicopter. He wouldn't mind seeing what went down at Petra, though he had been taught that the actual fighting would take place twenty miles north in Buseirah, Jordan — the modern name of the city of Bozrah, ancient capital of Edom — when Messiah chased the Unity Army back toward Jerusalem.

Besides the dizziness that came with trying to stand for the first time in hours, Rayford found himself wholly dependent upon the small but wiry Abdullah Smith and the broader, stronger, and younger Razor. Leah had brought everything, it seemed, but crutches. She did her bit to help too, but she could not support him and mainly directed traffic, trying to keep his most vulnerable injuries isolated.

Rayford could put zero weight on the broken shinbone, splint or not. Hopping was out of the question, so the two men had to bear all his weight as they moved him to the ATV. Even his good foot touching the ground occasionally sent shock waves of pain throughout the rest of his body. The anesthetic in his temple was wearing off, and Leah had decided not to add more.

Straddling the ATV was a delicate operation. Leah rolled up a towel and bunched it under the knee of his broken leg in an attempt to keep his foot from touching the vehicle. That left him able to balance himself only with his good foot and leg, with his painful arms latched tightly to Razor's waist. Rayford dreaded what he knew was coming. At some point his weight would shift to the broken shinbone side, and he would either have to wrestle Razor the other way or plant that foot to keep from flying off the ATV.

Once he was in place, Leah insisted he just sit there and get his bearings. "You okay?" she said.

"Think so," he said, already exhausted. He shut his eyes and rolled his neck, hearing it pop and crack. Then he stole a look at the sky. Clouds covered half the visible canopy now, and they were beginning to roil in all different colors. The sun was half below the horizon, wide and flat and at its most burnt orange, painting the clouds in pinks and reds and yellows. Were he not fearing for his life, he'd have thought it one of the most beautiful skies he had ever seen.

Leah had final instructions for Razor. "I'll lead the way," she said. "Mr. Smith will follow you, should we have a problem and need to lift Captain Steele again. My machine has a lot of weight on it too, so if I can make it through a certain area, you should be able to as well. I'll be trying to avoid ruts, bumps, even the smallest rocks, but of course we can't avoid them all. Try to take the steep areas as slowly as possible, but you'll need some power and momentum. Rayford, you'll just have to hang on and grit your teeth. The first fifty yards or so are pretty clear, so I'll try to keep an eye behind me to make sure you're both doing okay."

Rayford had always considered himself a man's man. Six-four and thickly muscled, he had played sports through pain of all sorts. And since the Rapture, he'd endured his share of serious injuries. But as he sat there, vise-gripping Razor's belt, he wanted to scream like a baby. Everything hurt. It was as if the pain had a life and mind of its own and threatened to kill him itself. It dug deep, mostly in his temple and shin, and it vibrated, throbbed, prodded.

When Razor so much as fired up the engine, the hum alone flashed through Rayford's body and made him instantly lightheaded. Razor would likely be able to tell if he passed out, just from the change in his grip. But Rayford was determined to gut this out.

Leah slowly pulled ahead, the pair of coolers hanging off the sides of her ATV like mismatched saddlebags. Razor turned his head. "Just say the word, and I stop."

"Go," Rayford managed, and the four-wheeler began rolling. "Lord, have mercy."

"Okay?" Razor called back.

"Don't ask, son. I'll let you know. You just keep moving."

Sebastian was struck by the grandeur of the early evening sun casting its glow over the black-clad enemy. Who'd have thought this evil mass of humanity could be seen in an attractive light? He had been joined by Otto Weser, the German who had maintained a small band of believers inside New Babylon until nearly the end.

"Ever dream you'd have this privilege, Otto?"

"Privilege? This is my definition of the awesome and terrible day of the Lord."

"But to be standing here, facing Antichrist's army on the last day of the earth as we know it . . ."

"I'd rather have acted on the truth when I had the chance and be in heaven already, if you want complete honesty."

"Well, 'course," Sebastian said, "but given that we missed it, there's no place I'd rather be right now. I just wish my wife and daughter could be with me."

"You wouldn't want them out here," Otto said, the understatement so obvious that Sebastian could not think of a retort. "You're not bothered by an enemy close enough to look up our nostrils?"

Sebastian shook his head. "If they wanted to kill us and God allowed it, it would have happened long ago. I've been in aircraft that missiles had no business missing. I feel invulnerable standing here. I can't beat this army, I know that, not on my own. But Dr. Ben-Judah and Dr. Rosenzweig and lots of other teachers have me convinced that this whole fighting force is going to make like the Midianites before Gideon and turn tail and run by the time this night is out. I can't wait to see that."

"It's a little hard to believe, though, isn't

it? I mean, looking at their sheer numbers?"

Sebastian turned and studied the older man in the twilight. "God changed a cloudless day into a cloudy one a little while ago. And you. You watched while the entire city of New Babylon was laid to ruins in the space of sixty minutes. And you say something's hard to believe?"

Rayford hated it most when Leah stopped and Razor had to do the same. There was no smooth way to do that, not on these inclines. Sometimes Razor was forced to stop without having found a flat place. There Ray sat, hanging on tight to keep from slipping off the back of the ATV.

"This is where the going gets tough," Leah said.

And the tough get going, Rayford thought. "What do you call what we've been doing so far?" he said.

"Easy street," she said. "From here on out, we can't stop. We can barely slow down. We're going up steep angles and we need to keep moving. You just have to gut it out. Let's go."

She took off faster than Rayford had thought possible or prudent, and while Razor eased into his speed a bit more carefully, he was soon gunning the engine to make the grade. A couple of sharp turns made Rayford cry out, but when Razor backed off the throttle Rayford assured him with a shout that he was okay.

Soon they hit the steepest climb and Rayford felt as if he were hanging upside down. He scanned the area around him and realized if he lost his grip here he would be in serious trouble. He would tumble farther than he had initially. Abdullah's bike whined up beside them and he flashed a thumbs-up. Rayford shook his head. All he needed was to yield to the temptation to let go with one hand and return the gesture, and he'd be a dead man.

He rested his forehead in the middle of Razor's back. Where did these kids get the steel muscles today? In his prime Rayford was never cut like this specimen.

The sun was fast fading, and all three vehicles' automatic lights came on at the same time. They finally rounded a curve that put them on an actual path, and Rayford realized the rest of the way would be relatively easy.

What he was not prepared for, however, was the welcome he received. Tens of thousands of residents were out gathering the evening manna and watching the heavens. Word must have passed far and wide about his predicament, because everyone seemed to know the makeshift motorcade was his transport home.

People waved and shouted and whistled and raised their hands. He could not acknowledge them except to nod. Meanwhile, Smitty was waving as if it were his own ticker-tape parade.

Rayford could only imagine the welcome Jesus would receive.

Seven

The sun had dipped below the horizon, leaving a bright, nearly full moon to illuminate an otherwise inky, cloud-scattered sky. The cloud colors had seemed to change in an instant, pastels giving way to deep blues, purples, lavenders, and traces of a fast-fading burnt orange.

Abdullah, Razor, and Leah helped Rayford to his quarters. He insisted on waiting, uncomfortably, in a side chair, while they moved his bed to face the open window. That way, on his back, he could take in the entire vista of the beautiful night sky. Something was brewing and, of course, he knew what it was.

Razor appeared eager to get back to his post and was quickly gone. Leah said she would be close by in the infirmary and that either she or Hannah would be available at a moment's notice with just a call.

Abdullah said he was worried about Mac, then looked as if he shouldn't have said anything.

"Where *is* Mac, Smitty?" Rayford said.

Abdullah told him.

"If anything's happened to Buck," Rayford said, "I don't want Kenny knowing. And I don't want him seeing me this way. Can you confirm Kenny's still with Priscilla Sebastian?"

Abdullah got on the phone, updated Priscilla on Rayford, and nodded to Ray. "Kenny is about to go to sleep for the night," he said.

"That'll be one to tell his grandchildren," Ray said. " 'I slept through the Glorious Appearing.' "

Rayford was grateful to be off the four-wheeler and in his own bed, but he had not realized how much the day had taken out of him until he was lying flat. "I may sleep through it myself," he said. "Would you keep me company, Smitty? Keep me awake?"

The Jordanian looked ill at ease. He had never been one for confrontation, but it was obvious he didn't want to accede to Rayford's request.

"Hey, it's all right, man," Rayford said. "You've got stuff to do, places you need to be."

"It is not that, Captain. But Dr. Rosenzweig is due soon —"

"Oh, that's right!"

"And, yes, I would like to be in the air when all these things come to pass. If you do not mind."

"You kiddin'? You know that's where I'd love to be if I could. You go right ahead, buddy. Really. I'll be fine."

"Oh, there is no way I would leave you alone. I can stay until Dr. Rosenzweig arrives."

Rayford carefully put his hands behind his head and folded his pillow double to prop his head a bit more. From his vantage point he had a wide view of the heavens, with the moon far to his left and the rest of his field of vision filled with heavy, colorful, moving clouds. As the sky grew darker, the moon seemed brighter, the clouds denser, and the stars clearer. As usual, when his eyes grew accustomed to the night sky, a deeper layer of stars came into view. But as he studied them, they disappeared and he had to search between clouds for more.

Chaim arrived with a small entourage, and Rayford was surprised when he dismissed all of them. "I will call if I need you," he said.

And as Abdullah Smith left, Rayford exacted from him a promise that he would call with anything new about Mac or Buck.

"Are you sure you want to know?" Abdullah said.

"Of course. Don't protect me. Even if it's the worst, we'll reunite with them soon."

Chaim settled into a tilting chair next to Rayford's bed and leaned back. "Magnificent," he said. "Like a front-row seat to eternity."

It wasn't like Chaim to stall. Though well past seventy now, he was a brilliant man of seemingly unbridled energy, and no one knew him to waste time. Yet here he sat, studying the skies of Israel, with apparently nothing to say.

"Something on your mind, Doctor? I mean, more than a million people here would give anything to spend this night with you. To what do I owe the pleasure?"

Global Community news-media cameras were trained on the Carpathian cavalry that emerged from the Dung Gate. Mac was relieved to discover he was not nearly the only member getting used to his steed. An equal number of men and women, most representing other sub-potentates, overreacted to their horses and wound up steering them in circles or being nearly chucked off. At first this was greeted with smiles all around, but it quickly became obvious that Carpathia was no longer amused. He dismissed the press and urged his generals to get everyone to their various means of conveyance to Petra.

Mac watched for his opening and was disappointed when his commander chose him as one to accompany Carpathia's cargo plane, big enough for several horses and vehicles. If those in charge only knew that Mac was once Nicolae's chief pilot . . .

Mac had once prided himself on keeping cool in a crisis, particularly when undercover. But as he dismounted and went through the motions of turning his horse over to a swarthy young man in a loud T-shirt who would walk it aboard the plane, he could think of nothing more creative than to simply try to talk his way out of it.

"Say, I've got a problem here, sport," he said.

"Yeah? What might that be, *sport?*" the young man said, his accent that of a New Zealander.

"Got myself in the wrong group. Is it too late to catch up with the others?"

"You mean the ones being carried by Hummers and such?"

"Right."

"I don't know, but you'd better try. You get on board this plane when you're not supposed to, and there'll be blood to pay. Anyway, I got no room for even one extra horse."

Mac took the horse back and mounted, and when someone called after him asking what he thought he was doing, he hollered, "Following orders! Going where they point me!" He looked over his shoulder to confirm that the voice was not that of his commander. He was otherwise engaged, which Mac found comforting. He didn't want to have it out with anybody in the GC this close to the return of Jesus. All he needed was to be arrested or shot just before the end.

The animal beneath him seemed to respond to Mac's sense of purpose. Mac knew where he was going now, and he wanted to get there fast. The first thing he wanted to do, once out of anyone else's sight, was to call in the news about Buck and about Carpathia's plans and see if there was any word on Rayford. Then he wanted to get into his own chopper and out of this infernal Global Community Unity Army uniform.

His own plain and baggy clothes had never seemed so inviting.

Sebastian felt the fatigue, not of boredom but of inactivity. Tension and anticipation would carry him until midnight or even dawn, if necessary. He hoped it wouldn't come to that.

He was grateful for the International Co-op and the job Lionel Whalum had been doing with it since Chloe Steele Williams's death. Behind Sebastian stood three gargantuan searchlights, equipment only the Co-op could have located and transported. Without the lights, Sebastian's eyes could play tricks on him. In the moonlight alone, he might have imagined the Unity Army beginning to advance again. He sensed the rumble, felt the vibration, knew something was happening, but all he needed was to flip the switches, train those gigantic beams toward the enemy, and determine that they were merely holding their ground half a mile away.

Razor's ATV came skidding up behind him in a cloud of dust. Razor approached with a salute and stood at attention.

"You've really got to quit that, boy," Sebastian said. "I'm as military and gung ho as the next guy, but what am I going to do

171

with you? Court-martial you and put you in the brig for what — an hour or two?"

"Sorry, sir," Razor said, fully reporting on what he called his Captain Steele detail.

"Well, I'm just glad to know it was only you making the ground rumble. Had me thinking the enemy was on the move again."

"Oh, they are, sir."

"They are?"

"Yes, sir. From up on the slopes I could see them advancing. You can't see them at this level, but they've moved a good bit, sir. They surely have."

Sebastian dispatched Otto Weser to flip the switches on the big lamps. "I'd trust my night-vision goggles, but I don't mind the Unity boys seeing what we've got. Anyway, their horses can't be accustomed to this."

"Standing by, Big Dog One," Otto called in.

"Fire 'em up," Sebastian said, and the high beams ripped across the desert sand. "Mercy."

The enemy had advanced at least eight hundred yards in the darkness, and the front line of their seemingly endless mounted troops now stood silently about eighty yards away. It was plain they were merely waiting for orders to attack.

"We should attack them, sir," Razor said.

"Say again?"

"We should —"

"I heard you, Razor. I just can't believe I heard you. In any other situation, that would be brilliant. Seriously. Sucker punch them. Like taking the first swing at the bully. You know they wouldn't be expecting it."

"But?"

"But two things: First, if everything we threw at them found its mark, we'd cause a ministampede, kill a few soldiers and horses, then get massacred. Second, we're invulnerable where we stand, as far as we know. We may not be out there."

"There is one other thing," Razor said.

"I'm listening."

"This battle's already been won, and without us lifting a finger."

"Well, there is that, yes."

Sebastian's phone chirped. It was Mac. "Yes," George said, "Rayford's back in his quarters with Chaim and will apparently pull through. And Buck? . . . I'm sorry to hear that. You talked to Chang? . . . Probably monitoring the world. We'll spread the word."

"I sense we are a lot alike, Captain Steele," Chaim said.

That drew Rayford's gaze from the window for a second. He couldn't imagine many people he was more different from than Chaim. They were Jew and Gentile, old and not so old, Middle Eastern and American, botanist and aviator, leader of a million people and leader of a small band.

"I sense," Chaim said, "despite our cultural and professional differences, that we are both normal men thrust into decisions and roles not of our own making. Am I right?"

"I guess."

"It may be even more surprising that I am a believer in Messiah than you are. But both of us took the long way to get here, didn't we?"

"We did."

"As you know, in my current position I have more company — more friends and associates and elders and advisers — than anyone would ever need. True, I had no shortage of options as to with whom I would spend this evening. Frankly, if I could have chosen from the whole universe, I would have chosen your son-in-law. We go back a long, long way. I knew him before he was a believer, and he knew me so long before I was that I daresay he still finds it hard to fathom. My hope is that if Cameron returns tonight, he will join us and feel welcome."

Chang was, in fact, monitoring the world. He had seemed to catch his second wind. He knew he should be in bed, but who could sleep at a time like this? He sat at his computer, staring at the reports coming in from all over the world about people, especially Jews, putting their faith in Jesus Christ as their Messiah. Tens of thousands every few minutes were totaling in the millions now, and Chang had the feeling it wouldn't stop until the Glorious Appearing. There were to be signs in the heavens before that, and more were prophesied to come to Christ.

Rayford and Chaim got the news about Buck from Sebastian a few minutes later. Rayford didn't know what to feel. He knew Buck was fine, better than he had ever been, and that he would see him soon. But he hated the thought that the young man, the father of Rayford's grandson and the husband of his daughter, had suffered so. Rayford had lost many friends and loved ones, none so close as his daughter and now son-in-law. But in the past he had somehow been able to come to terms with the losses, to tell himself it was the price of war, the inevitable result of what they had been called to do.

It was not so easy now, not when it struck so close to home. He called Mac.

The clouds parted and the moon shone brightly, all the way to the Dead Sea, directly beneath Mac.

"I'm not gonna lie to you, Ray. Yeah, it looks like Buck came to a rough end. But he was doing what he wanted to do. He worked at it, trained for it, and if you remember the first reports we got from him, he and Tsion got done what they hoped to."

"How's the resistance?"

" 'Bout finished. Unity's got 'em pushed into the Temple Mount, and it's clear the GC has hardly scratched the surface of their resources yet. They could take the whole city anytime they wanted."

"You're heading back, I assume."

"Not all the way," Mac said. "I want to see what happens on the Petra perimeter from the air. Then I want to head back up to Buseirah and see how that plays out."

"You know I'd give anything to be there with you."

"Holy mackerel! You see that, Ray?"

"I see it. I'll let you go. Time to watch the show."

★ ★ ★

A cloud had now covered the moon. It was bright and nearly full and had been highlighting the dancing clouds. Suddenly, it had seemed to disappear, as if someone had turned it out like a light. Rayford knew the moon merely reflected the sun anyway, thus it was the sun — far below the horizon now — that had lost its light. The sky was pitch.

Rayford asked Chaim to douse all the lights.

"We will see nothing, Captain," Chaim said. "Nonetheless, the better to see what is coming."

Once the lights were off, Rayford could tell Chaim stood by the window only by the sound of his voice.

Rayford said, "Have you ever seen blackness so thick?"

"I have seen many wonders in the last seven years," Chaim said. "This is like seeing nothing. But the mere anticipation it engenders causes a buzz from the top of my head to the soles of my shoes."

Lightning ripped through the sky, and Rayford was stunned to see the clouds briefly again. "I think I saw a shooting star," he said. "I love those."

"That was more than a shooting star,"

Chaim said, "which, as you know, is not really a star anyway. What you saw was truly a falling star, maybe a meteor. Soon stars and meteors will fall, but you will only hear them. Isaiah foretold that the stars of heaven and their constellations would not give their light. The sun will be darkened and the moon will not shine.

"God is saying, 'I will punish the world for its evil, and the wicked for their iniquity; I will halt the arrogance of the proud, and will lay low the haughtiness of the terrible.

" 'I will shake the heavens, and the earth will move out of her place, in the wrath of the Lord of hosts and in the day of His fierce anger.

" 'Everyone will flee to his own land. Everyone who is found will be thrust through, and everyone who is captured will fall by the sword.' "

Rayford shook his head. "There's another difference between us, Chaim. I've never been able to memorize like that."

"What else have I to do, Rayford? As I say, I was thrust into this position, and the teacher became the student. My former protégé, Dr. Ben-Judah, would not hear of my giving short shrift to the Scriptures. He discipled me, pushed me, grounded me in them. Most of all, God gave me a love for

His Word. Now there is nothing I would rather do than study it every spare moment and commit as much of it as possible to memory."

Enoch's people leaped to their feet and cried out when the early afternoon sun disappeared from the suburban Chicago sky. Though he knew it was coming, Enoch himself was spooked when the light of day turned into the darkest night and the temperature immediately dropped.

He heard a roaring, whistling sound and thought of the cliché that people always used when recounting a tornado: "It sounded like a freight train." Well, this sounded like a plane about to crash. They were close enough to the airport that it could have been, but Enoch did not recall hearing a jet.

Something was coming, and it was getting closer.

"Don't be afraid!" Enoch called out, but he couldn't hide the fear in his own voice. "This was prophesied. We just talked about it. It's all part of God's plan."

But when whatever was falling finally crashed into the main road on the other side of the mall, there was no stopping the gathering from bolting to take a look. Enoch jogged along behind them, grateful for the light-sensitive streetlights that began popping on all over. A meteor about three feet in diameter had bored a ten-foot-wide hole twenty feet deep in the road.

And here came another.

People screamed and scattered, but Enoch held his ground. "I believe we're protected!" he said. "None of the judgments from heaven harmed God's people! We bear His mark, His seal! He will protect us!"

But his body of believers had taken flight. Enoch smiled. He would chide them tomorrow when all were unscathed. How strange it seemed to be walking around in midnight darkness early in the afternoon. The next meteorite, which Enoch guessed was twice the size of the first, obliterated one of the former anchor stores in the deserted mall. It caused such an explosion he had to cover his ears. While he truly believed he would not be hurt, he found himself ducking and expecting debris to crack him on the head.

Enoch ran back to where he had met with the people, but he was alone now. He sat on a concrete bench and watched the show. Mostly he listened. Had he been a caveman, he would have believed the sky was falling, that the stars would all eventually hit the earth.

★ ★ ★

If anything, the rate of incoming reports of Jewish people turning to the Messiah increased dramatically over the next half hour. Chang beckoned Naomi to his side and sat with his arm around her waist as she stood. They couldn't decide what was more entertaining — the myriad camera feeds from all over the dark world, or the racing meter giving evidence of the fulfilling of the prophecy that a third of the Jewish remnant would come to believe in Jesus as their Messiah by the time of the end.

Chang could only think back to the horrific scenes he had monitored when Carpathia was at the height of his murderous fury against the Jews. He had had them rounded up, put in death camps, starved, tortured, beaten, humiliated with psychological warfare — you name it. That any survived was a miracle. That many became believers was something else.

"This is sure different from the last time Jesus came," Naomi said. "Besides that we weren't ready, it happened in the twinkling of an eye. Apparently God's going to play this one out for all it's worth."

Mac had the strangest sensation. He had been trained to fly by instruments, of

181

course, but still he found it disconcerting to see nothing above. And the only light on the ground was man-produced. Gradually he picked up boat lights, lights on other planes, headlights of cars and trucks and military vehicles. He heard the scream of falling meteorites over the usually deafening *thwock-thwock-thwock* of the blades and even heard the explosions when they blasted the earth. That was new. Mac had never been able to hear anything inside the chopper cockpit, especially with his earphones on.

Now, even above the cacophony of GC aviators demanding to know what was going on, the earth resounded with the wrath of God, with the literal falling of the heavens. A meteor at least ten feet in diameter fell within a hundred feet of Mac's helicopter. His lights picked it up, and he followed it until it hit a building, sending a shower of fire and sparks into the air. He had no idea what the building might have been, but it gave him pause. Was he protected from these free-falling monsters of stone or metal? Even a small one would demolish a chopper, and now they began to fall all around him. People on the ground, particularly Unity Army troops, had to be terrified. Mac wondered how many wished they could change their marks of loyalty now.

He was fairly certain he would be protected, as believers had been since the judgments began seven years before. But *fairly* certain wasn't enough for him to follow through with his plan. Mac made for Petra, knowing that airspace was secure. He could have been killed there many times over, but he had been miraculously spared every time.

Rayford was having the time of his life. The news about Buck had set him back, of course, and despite what he knew about the future, it gave him that ache in the pit of his stomach, as had his loss of Chloe. But to lie in his bed watching the heavens shake as they had been prophesied to do thousands of years before . . .

And to have his old friend, Chaim Rosenzweig, the one God had chosen to be a modern-day Moses, standing there quoting those prophecies from memory, well, it almost made him forget his grief and his wounds.

" 'I saw another angel coming down from heaven,' " Chaim said, " 'having great authority, and the earth was illuminated with his glory. And he cried mightily with a loud voice, saying, "Babylon the great is fallen, is fallen, and has become a dwelling place of demons, a prison for every foul spirit, and a cage for every unclean and hated bird! For all the nations have drunk of the wine of the wrath of her fornication, the kings of the earth have committed fornication with her, and the merchants of the earth have become rich through the abundance of her luxury." '

"That is what has Carpathia so enraged today, Rayford. It was one thing to lose his beloved city and to see the rest of the kings of the earth and the merchant moguls weeping crocodile tears over her. But to have it rubbed in like this, to have an angel pronounce it, to know that it was the fulfillment of an ancient prophecy by his arch-enemy . . . no wonder he is on the rampage now. He has a plan, a scheme he thinks is foolproof, even though he is no fool and has read the Book. But he will fail, and we will witness it."

"I so wish I could be out there right now," Rayford said. "Why did this have to happen today, of all days?"

He could not see Chaim, but he heard the smile in his voice. "The leader of the Tribulation Force is not going to start questioning God now, is he? You of all people. You have been delivered by His hand as many times as I have. You walked through the fire just like Shadrach, Meshach, and Abednego when the GC launched their bombs on Petra, and you are going to whine about having to play inside on a rainy day?"

Rayford had to laugh.

"Listen to this from the prophet Joel," Chaim said. " 'I will show wonders in the heavens and in the earth: blood and fire and pillars of smoke. The sun shall be turned into darkness, and the moon into blood, before the coming of the great and awesome day of the Lord.' "

"I saw that," Rayford said. "When the moon was turned to blood. That was not long before I lost Amanda."

"I know," Chaim said after a pause. "We have all lost so much. And yet so much will be restored. Here is the best part, also from Joel: 'And it shall come to pass that whoever calls on the name of the Lord shall be saved. For in Mount Zion and in Jerusalem there shall be deliverance, as the Lord has said, among the remnant whom the Lord calls.

" 'For behold, in those days and at that time, when I bring back the captives of Judah and Jerusalem, I will also gather all nations, and bring them down to the Valley of Jehoshaphat; and I will enter into judgment with them there on account of My people, My heritage Israel, whom they have scattered among the nations.' "

All Rayford could do was grunt. Sometimes Scripture had that effect on him. There was nothing more to say. At least not by him.

"We are those captives," Chaim said. "My brothers and sisters, the children of Israel."

"Makes me wish I were," Rayford said.

"Oh, you *are*, of course, by adoption. Gentile believers are His adopted sons and daughters."

"But you all are His chosen people."

"Not that we have proved worthy. Maybe that is why we are always referred to as the *children* of Israel."

"What's that reference to the Valley of Jehoshaphat?"

"Oh, that is where the judgment will take place, in a valley created by the splitting of the Mount of Olives when He sets foot on it. Jesus Himself will judge all men, and prophecy states it will be right there. The Bible says more about Him than that He is just the returning King and victorious Warrior. It also calls Him the Judge. The Gospel of Mark says, 'Then they will see the Son of Man coming in the clouds with great power and glory.' And Revelation says, 'Now I saw heaven opened, and behold, a white horse. And He who sat on him was called Faithful and True, and in righteousness He judges and makes war.' "

Sebastian stood next to his Hummer with Otto and Razor, straining his eyes to see what he could see. Meteors were raining upon the enemy, and the sounds of panicking soldiers and horses washed over him. Was it possible the hundreds of thousands of steeds would stampede, and what would that do to the plans the Unity Army had for Petra?

Vehicles were smashed, exploding into flames and offering the only light to give him a clue how far back the front lines had been driven. It seemed they were still virtually atop him, but Sebastian needed to know.

Eight

"Do we know the timing?" Rayford said. "I know we know *what* comes next, but do we know when?"

"We never have," Chaim said. "I was one who thought the Glorious Appearing would be exactly seven years from the signing of the covenant between Antichrist and Israel, but clearly we were wrong about that. We know that following the phenomena in the sky comes the sign of His coming, but nothing tells us whether that will be immediate. God has His own timetable."

"A thousand years is as a day, and all that," Rayford said.

"And vice versa."

The booming of the meteorites shook Rayford's little shelter, and as they increased in frequency, his bed moved. He felt every injury. The anesthetic in his temple had long since worn off, and the pain pierced and throbbed. His chin bothered him too, though he had considered that the least of his wounds. Every nick and scrape and gash was sensitive, and the aching ankle, which had caused his foot to swell, made his muscles tense. He felt it in both legs, all the way to his hip.

Rayford spread his pillow flat and laid his head back, stretching. He had no idea what was keeping him awake. On the other hand, of course he did.

Mac overflew Buseirah, where he saw little but scattered lights on the ground, and was soon at the edge of Petra. He checked in with Chang to let him know he would be putting down. The last thing he wanted was to be mistaken for enemy aircraft and be fired upon by Big Dog One and his own people. Would God protect him even from them?

"Hey!" Mac shouted into the phone. "What's that? What's Sebastian doing?"

"Using his big torches to light up the sky," Chang said. "He wants to know how much damage the meteorites are doing to the Unity Army."

"Looks like he's more fascinated with the clouds."

"So am I."

"I hear you, Chang. Me too. If you're in touch with Sebastian, tell him to leave those babies pointing straight up."

Sebastian wouldn't have dreamed of doing anything else. The searchlights had the enemy looking up too. The clouds blanketed the entire sky, bubbling and roiling and joining one another to form a ceiling unlike anything anyone had ever seen. Far in the distance Sebastian heard the low rumble of long, echoing explosions and finally deduced it was thunder. Did that mean lightning was striking somewhere? Or was it just streaking through the heavens among the clouds?

"Cut the lights a minute," he radioed, eliminating the possibility that they would cost him a view of the lightning. Sure enough, above the clouds — and who knew how thick they were? — tiny pulsating bursts of light seemed to try to peek through. Suddenly the artificial light lost its allure. If a storm was coming his way, Sebastian wanted to see it in all its natural glory.

Mac landed and hurried to Rayford's

quarters, surprised to find them dark as midnight. He considered refueling and heading out again. Regardless of Rayford's view, if he was here after all, nothing would compare with watching from overhead when the Antichrist got his due.

He knocked lightly. "Anybody in here?"

"Mac!" he heard. It was Rayford, but Chaim greeted him when the door opened.

After embraces all around in the dark and a quick retelling of both men's day, Rayford told Mac there was another chair in the other room. Feeling about, Mac noisily banged his way back with it and sat himself in front of the window. "Nice show," he said. "But you ought to see it from a chopper."

"You're breaking my heart," Rayford said.

"Sorry."

"No, I want every detail. You going back out?"

"Thinkin' about it, pardner. Seems risky."

"I'd think you'd be throwing caution to the wind at this point."

"I want to be alive when it happens, Ray. That's all."

"I'll bet old Chaim here would even be tempted to go with you, once the sign appears in the sky."

"Oh no, gentlemen," Chaim said, chuckling. "My place is here. I want the entire remnant out in the high places, watching for the return. We must all be in place, singing, praying, ready to worship Him in spirit and in truth, and best of all, in person."

"I've at least got to be *there*," Rayford said. "Mac, can you make sure of it?"

"Unless you talk me into getting back in the air, sure." All three men jumped when lightning shot from straight overhead to the ground, followed by an immediate resounding roar. The strike had to be less than half a mile away. It shook the dwelling and echoed for half a minute among the surrounding mountains and hills.

"Here we go," Chaim said. "Keep your eyes on the heavens."

"Don't need to tell me that," Mac said.

"Supposed to rain?" Sebastian said. "Looks like it might, but I didn't count on that."

"Don't think so," Otto said. "I don't recall hearing that in any of the teaching, but that may say more about my attention span than the prophecies."

"I don't want my guys out here in a downpour," Sebastian said. " 'Specially if we have a choice."

"What's the choice?"

"Got me there. We don't have nearly

enough vehicles, and no one wants to be back in Petra when everything goes down."

"Speak for yourself, Big Dog," Otto said. "I'm into creature comforts. I mean, I want to see what there is to see. But I have nothing against a poncho and an umbrella."

Sebastian threw his head back and guffawed. " 'Here am I, Lord,' " he mocked in a bad German accent. " 'Put galoshes on me!' "

That made even Razor laugh, but he quickly recovered. "Begging your pardons, sirs," he said. And soon all three were howling.

After leaving Rayford's quarters, Abdullah had taken a small jet with a large Plexiglas hood over the cockpit, giving him a panoramic view. He flew over the masses assembled near Petra, then rocketed north, all the way to Jerusalem, nearly overcome by the expanse of the Unity Army. He knew. He'd heard. He'd been taught. But to see it for himself made it hard to breathe.

How far he'd come in just a few years! He'd made it a practice not to show his emotions in public. It was his culture, the way he was raised. Oh, he had been amused, mostly by Mac, and he had been prodded to anger — also by Mac. But to ride above the elements that made up the final chapter of history and realize how easy it would have been to miss it all, Abdullah couldn't stem the tears.

He had been raised in another religion altogether, and to convert to Christ was to turn his back on his family and, it seemed, his country. Yet the truth had pressed in upon him. His decision for Jesus was a towering leap of faith, yet from the beginning the rightness of it, the truth with a capital *T,* had become clear. He had always been a student, after all.

Abdullah had been amused that his friends, particularly the Americans, seemed to think him intellectually limited because of his broken English. Something about his speech patterns, with his Jordanian accent, rendered his sound childlike to Americans. He could tell in how they looked at him, how they responded to him. Sometimes, he admitted, he played to it. One could garner more information by sounding young and innocent.

He was anything but, however. Abdullah had been put through the rigors of military training to where he was certified to fly jets of almost any type. Did his friends really think all Jordanians were so childlike and stupid that they would entrust a young man of limited mental capabilities to pilot fighter-bombers worth tens of millions of dinars? It was laughable. He had been a celebrated pilot, eventually a trainer himself.

Abdullah wondered what Rayford and the others thought of his serious study of prophecy under Tsion Ben-Judah and Chaim Rosenzweig. Unlike the others, he was mostly quiet and didn't ask many questions. But he put to use the same gray matter that allowed him to understand the myriad technical specifications of sophisticated modern aircraft and had made him an accomplished pilot.

Perhaps because they were humble Middle Easterners themselves, neither Dr. Ben-Judah nor Dr. Rosenzweig acted surprised at Abdullah's intellectual proclivities, evidenced in private e-mails and conversations. And while the teaching could be heavily theological and deep, the most persuasive parts of all were the almost daily fulfillments of prophecy.

Abdullah had no doubt that the ancient Scriptures were authentic, penned thousands of years before the birth of Christ. Hundreds and hundreds of prophecies had been fulfilled, many before his eyes. In spite of his grief over the loss of his family, in the midst of constant fear of being discovered without the mark of Carpathia, and yes, even with his private offense over his friends' clearly assuming he was not as bright as they, Abdullah's fledgling faith had grown more solid every day.

He knew Mac and Rayford and Buck and the rest really loved him. Perhaps he could educate them in the next chapter of this unfolding of history and then they would see that, while they no doubt did not even realize they were doing it, there was no reason to condescend to him.

The lightning had increased, and Abdullah loved it. It cast eerie, intermittent bursts of light upon the restless troops below. And it lit up the clouds, which he otherwise could not see due to the absence of moon and starlight. Oh, what a glorious, frightening scene!

Abdullah prayed, thanking God for how far he had come, for allowing such an unlikely prospect into His kingdom, for protecting him even now from the killing power of the enemy.

Over Jerusalem Abdullah noticed tiny campfires dotting the city, many at the Temple Mount. The lightning revealed Unity troops surrounding that area, which he now knew was the last stronghold of the stubborn resistance. He had to chuckle. If only they could see their plight from his vantage point. It was as if a parakeet believed he had commandeered his own cage. Still, he admired them. He was on their side. They were God's chosen people, and in the end, Jesus Christ would give them the victory.

Oh, Jerusalem was to fall, Abdullah knew. But because every one of the other prophecies he had ever studied had literally come true as it was spelled out, he also had zero doubt that Jesus would make things right again. With a full fuel tank and a lightning show to illumine the playing field, he felt he was in the prime spot for the greatest show on earth.

With a steep left bank and a flyover of the millions of troops in the great Valley of Megiddo, Abdullah turned his screaming craft back to the south. Next on the agenda was Carpathia's showing up in Edom to lead a third of his forces against Petra. Unity Army searchlights from the ground crisscrossed the sky and occasionally locked onto Abdullah's craft. But he was fearless. "Launch your surface-to-air missiles," he whispered. "They will bounce off this plane like shuttlecocks."

Rayford was speechless. He'd never been considered particularly quiet, but among

197

this trio, he might have been a church mouse. Chaim had always loved to talk everything to death — every truth, idea, or concept. It was his way. And Mac was his Texan counterpart, maybe not as articulate and intellectual but always prepared to weigh in with a homespun opinion on everything.

But now it was eerie. All three were silent. The lightning had become almost constant; long, thick streaks of gold fired from cloud to cloud, cloud to ground, and — Rayford knew — though beyond detection of the human eye, often from ground to cloud.

The length and severity of the bolts varied, but they snaked through the heavens with such speed and abundance that the air crackled and snapped. *Boom! Boom! Boom!* came the deafening crashes of thunder that rattled the walls of Rayford's flimsy quarters.

The flashes lit up the clouds. Rayford could not have imagined them getting larger or more active, and yet they had. They seemed miles wide and deep now, gray and black and pregnant with moisture, as if about to burst. And these blotted out everything above. Were it not for his faith, this would be a horrifying scene. Indeed, the power and wrath of the God of the universe were being unleashed, and those without confidence in His love had to be terrified.

"Astounding," Rayford whispered, but the other two men, silhouetted in the constant flashes, neither moved nor responded. His lame summary must have hit them as feebly as it had him.

Sebastian trained his night-vision goggles on the skies, reminding himself to breathe. He felt Otto pressing in on one side and Razor on the other, and strange as that might seem in any other circumstance, it reminded him of his childhood when he and his younger brother hugged each other in fear while watching a thunderstorm from their bed, a storm a thousandth the size of this.

And just when Sebastian believed the sky could contain itself no longer, the lightning seemed to ratchet up to a ridiculous speed. Hundreds, thousands of bolts crashed to the desert floor every second, deafening roars of thunder piling atop each other in such an overwhelming invasion that he was forced to let the goggles drop and dangle from his neck as he covered his ears with both hands. The sky from east to west and north to south was ablaze, blinding streaks firing every which way. The ground heaved and rolled, and Sebastian knew that had to be from a combination of the lightning, the thunder, and the thorough panic of Antichrist's mounted forces.

He sent Otto to check on Ree Woo's troops on the other side of the perimeter and Razor to check his own on this side.

Enoch sat in Illinois with his Bible tucked under his arm, trying to protect it should the rain come. But when the lightning seemed to lose all sense of proportion, all he could do was stand, thrusting the Bible over his head in both hands, offering it to God as a form of worship. What a show! The awful and terrible wrath of the Lord on display for the whole world!

Enoch thought of Old Testament Scriptures he had bookmarked and quickly sat again, riffling through the pages and reading them by the almost constant light of the electrical extravaganza, shouting them to the heavens.

" 'Enter into the rock, and hide in the dust, from the terror of the Lord and the glory of His majesty. The lofty looks of man shall be humbled, the haughtiness of men shall be bowed down, and the Lord alone shall be exalted in that day. For the day of the Lord of hosts shall come upon everything proud and lofty, upon everything lifted up — and it shall be brought low.

" 'They shall go into the holes of the rocks, and into the caves of the earth, from the terror of the Lord and the glory of His majesty, when He arises to shake the earth mightily.' "

Finding the prophetic warnings in the books of Hosea and Joel, Enoch read of the enemies of the Lord. " 'They shall say to the mountains, "Cover us!" and to the hills, "Fall on us!" '

" 'The Lord gives voice before His army, for His camp is very great; for strong is the One who executes His word. For the day of the Lord is great and very terrible; who can endure it?' "

I can endure it, Enoch thought, *just like anyone who sees past His wrath and trusts God's mercy.*

He read from Joel 2:12: " 'Now, therefore,' says the Lord, 'turn to Me with all your heart, with fasting, with weeping, and with mourning.' "

Turning to Nahum 1:6, Enoch read: " 'Who can stand before His indignation? And who can endure the fierceness of His anger? His fury is poured out like fire, and the rocks are thrown down by Him.' "

The very next verses offered hope and yet

another dire warning: " 'The Lord is good, a stronghold in the day of trouble; and He knows those who trust in Him. But with an overflowing flood He will make an utter end of its place, and darkness will pursue His enemies.' "

Near the end of the Old Testament, Enoch came to Zephaniah and read from chapter one, verses 14 to 17: " 'The great day of the Lord is near; it is near and hastens quickly. The noise of the day of the Lord is bitter; there the mighty men shall cry out.

" 'That day is a day of wrath, a day of trouble and distress, a day of devastation and desolation, a day of darkness and gloominess, a day of clouds and thick darkness, a day of trumpet and alarm against the fortified cities and against the high towers.

" 'I will bring distress upon men, and they shall walk like blind men, because they have sinned against the Lord; their blood shall be poured out like dust, and their flesh like refuse.' "

Beyond all comprehension, Chang thought, the Global Community News Network ignored the nature show. He knew from pirating the feeds from all over the globe that the constant lightning was a universal phenomenon. From Sri Lanka came visual feeds of a metropolitan area ablaze, the downtown having been ignited by thousands of lightning strikes. People rioted, trampling each other, screaming, pleading for mercy.

A GCNN cameraman, or his brave producer, transmitted images of a tiny band of anti-Carpathia Jews kneeling amid the lightning flashes beneath an ancient Israeli flag, a Star of David, and a rough-hewn cross. They were thumbing their noses at the god of this world, boldly showing that they had never received the mark of loyalty to the supreme potentate, but had now staked their claim with Messiah.

From South America came the same. Regardless of where the feed originated, it came as if at midnight. The only light came from the lightning and artificial sources. Citizens were hysterical. Even many with Carpathia's mark screamed obscenities at him through the cameras and demanded to know where he was and what he was doing about this. Chang asked a Hispanic coworker to translate what the South Americans were shouting.

"They are saying," she said, "that this is obviously an offensive from God Himself, and so what does the potentate have to say about that? Who will win? They want to know, who will win?"

Even the producers, who worked directly for the GC, sent in harshly worded demands to know why GCNN was ignoring their feeds. What, they asked, was more important than a cosmic disturbance like this, one that saw global panic and devastation? People were being killed, committing suicide, looting, rampaging. Yet GCNN ran wall-to-wall coverage of the war effort.

"Unity Army troops assigned to Egypt are already on their way back to the Valley of Megiddo," intoned an anchorwoman, showing clips of overwhelming victories for the GC. "Reports from the northeast mirror these, and Unity generals report they will have their platoons back to Israel in plenty of time for the siege on Jerusalem."

An interview with Carpathia himself showed the folly of the so-called objective coverage. The potentate was shown mounting his enormous horse, just outside the cargo plane that had delivered him and his generals to Ash Shawbak, about halfway between Petra and Buseirah. That put Carpathia and his people about ten miles east of the edge of his massive Unity Army that extended to the border of Petra.

"I am pleased with the reports from the south and from the northeast," he said.

"And now we are about to embark on one of our most strategic initiatives. A third of our entire fighting force will advance upon the rebel stronghold cowering in Petra. Intelligence tells us that a paltry defensive unit has rung the city round about, but they are hopelessly outnumbered and have already offered to surrender."

Carpathia was interrupted by nearly continuous crashes of thunder, which he and the reporter appeared to ignore.

"Was this enclave not attacked twice before, Excellency?"

"*Attacked* would not be the proper term," Carpathia said, making Chang laugh aloud. The first failed attempt saw the GC bring huge numbers of troops and weapons, only to see them miraculously swallowed up by the earth. The second was a double bombing that produced a spring of water that provided sustenance for the people to this day, and which also resulted in the inhabiting Jewish remnant and a few of the Tribulation Force being supernaturally protected from the ensuing firestorm.

"In fact," Carpathia continued, "we made peaceful overtures to the leadership, offering amnesty for any who would voluntarily leave the stronghold and take the mark of loyalty. Our understanding is that many wished to make this move, only to be slaughtered by the leadership. Many will recall that it was this very leadership who assassinated me, serving only to give me the opportunity to prove my divinity by raising myself from the dead.

"Well, this time around, there will be no negotiating. Loyalists to our New World Order have either been murdered or have escaped, so intelligence tells us Petra is now inhabited solely by rebels to our cause, murderers and blasphemers who have thumbed their noses at every attempt to reason with them."

The cameras homed in on the potentate as he was handed an almost cartoonishly oversized silver sword with gold rococo inlays and a garishly overdone handle. He strapped it around his waist, then theatrically unsheathed it with a long, slow, metallic screech. He pointed it skyward.

Chang couldn't help praying silently that just one of those bolts of lightning would find that tip and roast the enemy where he sat.

"Therefore," Carpathia said, "our plan is annihilation. I shall personally lead this effort, with the able assistance, of course, of my generals. We shall rally the troops as soon as we arrive, and the siege should take only a matter of minutes."

As Carpathia yanked the reins and turned his mount to the east, racing off at a gallop, the reporter called after him, "All the best to you, holy one! And may you bless yourself and bring honor to your name with this effort!"

Chang called Mac and filled him in on the lunacy. "You guys ought to turn this on," he said. "Things are coming to a head."

Abdullah had heard the broadcast over the radio and flew over Ash Shawbak. Carpathia's planes and rolling stock were visible, but Abdullah was a little high to make out individuals or horses. He could, however, see the Unity Army to the west and knew it wouldn't take Nicolae long to get there.

The lightning exposed an army in disarray. The horses, naturally, were spooked by the light show and thunder, and it appeared to Abdullah that riders were fighting to keep their mounts from heading for the hills. What Carpathia thought he could do with this mess was a mystery.

And just like that, the lightning ceased.

As before, the sky was as black as coal. Unity searchlights looked pathetic, peering feebly into the murky blackness. They reached the thick, stewing clouds that hovered menacingly over the whole earth.

The cessation of the rolling thunder made the relative silence of the cockpit unearthly. Abdullah looked all around for what was to come next. And the longer he looked, the more he wondered how long the Lord would tarry. Those horses would be controllable now. Carpathia would surely believe victory was at hand.

Rayford directed Mac to find his radio in the other room. Mac brought it in, feeling his way in the utter darkness.

"You could turn on a light," Rayford said, the ghostly silence unnerving him.

"Oh, please don't," Chaim said. "This darkness is of the Lord. Can you not feel it?"

"I feel it all right," Rayford said. "Every part of me wants to be out in it. I would give anything to be at Carpathia's side right now. I'd love to see the look on his face when he is chased back to Buseirah and then to Jerusalem."

"How would you see anything at all?" Mac said.

Chaim said, "This is just a preliminary. At some point this darkness will turn to daylight. Carpathia will turn tail and run from the Son of Man, who will be the only source of light. Anyone near Nicolae will be able to see him, all right, and I am with Rayford in wishing I could be there. But I will be here, watching, worshiping, singing. And then we will all follow, tracing the route that brought us here. We will sweep across the great expanse and join Messiah when He triumphs in Jerusalem and then ascends the Mount of Olives, from which He was transfigured so long ago."

"I've got to be on that trip," Rayford said.

"Not in your condition," Mac said.

Rayford shook his head in the darkness. "It's going to be mighty lonely here."

The sudden silence and abject blackness made Enoch fear rain again, and it sent him searching for his car. His ears still rang from the cacophony of the last hour, and as he staggered along, feeling his way with his toes, he finally picked up the faint glow of a few streetlights. He drove toward home, planning to drag a chaise lounge out of the cellar and enjoy the rest of the show from the yard.

Somehow Enoch had to find a way to get to the Holy Land as soon as possible after Jesus returned. He was confident he would see it in the sky — the return and all — but Jesus would apparently confine Himself to an earthly body once again, and believers from around the world would want to see Him. He would govern from Jerusalem, and the pilgrimages would begin immediately. He and the people from The Place would have to start raising money to finance this trip.

Sebastian was up to speed and debating what to do. His night-vision goggles were virtually worthless in this kind of darkness. That meant it had to be supernatural, because he had successfully used these underground where there was no source of light. He could make out nothing of the clouds now, and only the occasional vehicle light in the Unity Army ranks provided visual clues.

What was he to do if Global Community forces attacked before Jesus returned? He knew he and his people, and the entire remnant at Petra, were prophesied to be delivered in the end. But what about in the meantime? Was he to fight? to retaliate? to shoot? He knew he could do some damage because he and his forces already had. Would his people take fire, and would they be wounded or killed?

He was a military man, but this was as much a theological decision as a tactical one. Sebastian could consult with Dr.

Rosenzweig, but the old man had enough on his mind. His purview was the remnant. Sebastian's was the defense of the perimeter. Might it be as effective strategically to let the Unity Army overrun his position, knowing they were advancing into a trap of cosmic proportions?

It wasn't the way he was trained, but then it wasn't as if he had much of a choice anyway. Sure, he could stall them, slow them with surgically designed strikes from his directed energy weapons and fifty-caliber rifles. But no one could tell him whether that would do any good, or for how long he should try to hold them off.

Clearly there would be no holding back a force of that size for long. Ten minutes? Twenty? Surely no more than that. He could do some damage. But once the Lord arrived, Sebastian's puny efforts would be meaningless. The question was, were they meaningless regardless?

Nine

Coming up on the two-hour mark of the utterly silent blackness covering the face of the earth, Rayford sensed a restlessness in Chaim.

"I had better get to the elders," the older man said. "This cannot go on much longer, and once the sign of the Son of Man appears, who knows how long it will be before the event itself?"

" 'Who knows' is right," Mac said. "Once that comes, I think I've talked myself into goin' back out. You don't mind, do ya, Ray?"

" 'Course I mind, but I wouldn't deprive you of that. I can handle the loneliness. It's the jealousy that'll be the issue."

"You'll forgive me," Mac said.

"I will."

"Want me to send Leah or Hannah or

somebody to keep you company?"

Rayford pondered that. "Don't think so," he said. "Anybody else here might just prove to be a distraction."

"I am going," Chaim said. "This has been a wonderful memory."

"Suit yerself, Doc," Mac said. "I could take you for the ride of your life, you know."

"I know. I am grateful. But until Messiah appears, I have responsibilities."

Rayford heard him approach in the darkness and reached for his hand. Chaim took Rayford's in both of his. "Mr. McCullum," Chaim said, "join us, won't you?"

Mac stepped close and Rayford felt a hand on his shoulder and assumed the other was on Chaim's. "Revelation 1:3 says this," Chaim said. " 'Blessed is he who reads and those who hear the words of this prophecy, and keep those things which are written in it; for the time is near.' Amen."

Rayford and Mac repeated the amen.

"Let me pray for us," Chaim said, but before he could, Rayford's eyes popped open, first at the sound, then at the light of something new in the sky. Rayford could compare the sound only to a downed high-tension power line he'd once seen bouncing and popping.

"O God, O God," Chaim prayed as he too

turned to look. Rayford could only stare.

He rocked up into a sitting position and leaned forward, peering out at what appeared to be lightning but was like none he had ever seen. Thick, jagged, and pulsing, a vertical yellow streak extended from about a hundred feet above the horizon to what he estimated was at least ten miles into the sky. Two-thirds of the way up it was crossed by a horizontal streak of the same thickness and half its length.

Rayford could not speak. He could barely breathe. Here, clearly, was the cross of Christ, emblazoned in the heavens in lightning that lingered, crackling with unbridled energy, yet striking nothing. He squinted at its brightness but could not turn his eyes from it. He felt full of awe, of wonder, of the love of God Himself. This was the sign of the Son of Man, and it was there for the whole world to see. But it was also personal, burning into his heart.

The blazing radiance of it lit the room. Chaim finally pulled away and left without another word.

Rayford stole a glance at Mac and nearly fell off the bed. Mac was black! And he appeared to be trying to say something. "Well, I'll be," was all Mac could manage, then, apparently noticing Rayford's reaction, said,

"It's me, Ray. Zeke's handiwork."

"Mac, something's happened to me."

"Me too, buddy. It's a-standin' there plain as day."

"No, something's happened."

"What're you goin' on about?"

Rayford slipped quickly off the bed and stood next to Mac at the window. "I'm standing," he said.

Mac turned. "Don't get ahead of yourself there, Ray. Let's take this one step at a time."

"I'm fine," Rayford said.

"Are you sayin' — ?"

"That's what I'm saying, Mac. No pain. No wounds. Look at me."

Rayford tore off his bandages. Even the hole in his temple was gone, though where Leah had shaved around the stitching, he still had no hair. He bent and yanked at the ankle wrap. Not even a scar. He jumped up and down, then loosened the plastic shin splint and kicked it free.

"You don't say."

Rayford whooped and hollered. "I do say! Let's get out there, Mac! Get me into the air."

"Now I don't know about that, Ray."

"Then sit here and watch, man, because I'm going!"

Enoch was cozy under a light blanket in

215

his chaise lounge in the backyard when the sign appeared. He burst into tears and lifted his arms. "Praise God, praise God," he said, and began singing every worship song he knew. The cross that extended from sky to sky towered, as the hymn writer had put it, "o'er the wrecks of time." Something about the overwhelming majesty of it simply communicated victory.

For how long had he prayed and carried a burden for the inner-city people to whom God had sent him to minister? And for how long had he preached and taught and warned of this very day, this very event? He'd had no idea what form it would take, but this was perfect. "In the cross of Christ I glory," he said, his voice thick.

Enoch slid off the cheap, rickety lounge chair and onto his knees, bowing before God. Though he lowered his head and closed his eyes, still the image of the cross in the sky stayed with him, as if burned onto the insides of his eyelids.

As soon as Chang saw the cross on every screen in the bank of monitors before him, he shouted for Naomi and she came running. Hand in hand they raced outside and up to their favorite spot. They didn't speak. There were no words for this. They stretched out on their backs and stared and stared.

"Thank You! Thank You, God!" Abdullah exulted. At the first appearance of the sign he had pointed the jet directly at the cross and throttled to full power. Was it there, right in front of him, as 3-D objects had appeared to be in movie theaters when he was a child? It was as if he could reach out and touch it, but though his craft reached top speed in seconds, the cross never appeared to grow closer. Its horizontal arms, like those of Jesus Himself, seemed to welcome the entire world into its embrace.

The only logical follow-up was the Lord Himself, and Abdullah couldn't wait.

For two hours Sebastian had not known what the enemy was waiting for, and maybe the enemy didn't either. But the sign became an impromptu trigger, and suddenly the frisky horses of the Unity Army were on the move. Their riders, now clearly visible because of the pulsating cross in the sky, urged their mounts to full gallop.

And here they came.

"Big Dog One to all units," Sebastian intoned into his radio. "Hold your fire. Wait. On my command."

Protests from every side crowded his ears.

217

"Hold, hold, hold," he said, though platoon leaders from all around the perimeter reported the enemy literally yards away.

"Have you lost your mind?" Otto squealed from a quarter mile to Sebastian's left.

"Have you lost your faith, Otto?"

"Ree Woo to Big Dog: It's time, sir."

"Hold."

"Permission to speak my mind, sir," came an urgent transmission from Razor.

"Denied. Follow orders."

The front line of the Unity Army closed the gap in seconds. Sebastian stood his ground, facing horsemen with rifles pointed at him and others with swords drawn. He knew he was as visible to them as they were to him, the Petra perimeter suddenly bright as day. Only the sky behind the rugged cross was black with cloud cover.

The Unity Army opened fire and Sebastian winced, but he did not turn or seek shelter. A couple hundred of his own troops stood between the army and the hillside that led almost straight up to the rose-red city of Petra, and all were fired upon. Shooting from a galloping horse was no small chore, but surely some of the bullets should have found their marks.

The *pings* of shrapnel ricocheting off rocks filled the air, and the looks on the faces of the horsemen were priceless. Swordsmen steered their horses behind the mounted riflemen and one, clearly troubled but determined, came straight for Sebastian. George raised a hand and wiggled his fingers as if in greeting — or farewell — and the blade-wielding soldier swung his rapier in a wide arc while brushing past. It was as if the blade went right through Sebastian at the waist.

Sebastian was now adrift in the middle of the Unity Army, and horseman after horseman rode straight at him — some shooting, some hacking with their swords. None so much as jostled him. One stopped and spun his horse around to try again, only to be overrun by a wave of his own comrades who had nowhere to retreat to.

George turned and watched the assault on the hillside leading to Petra. The army had apparently underestimated the riders' ability to stay aboard their mounts as the horses managed the steep terrain, and everything slowed to a halt. Those on the plain below kept coming, causing a traffic jam of biblical proportions. Soldiers shouted at one another. Commanders screamed orders that could not be followed.

Meanwhile, Sebastian and his people blithely walked through the midst of the enemy, unscathed.

★ ★ ★

Chang ignored his phone as long as he could. He had considered turning it off, deciding his work was finally over. But a sense of duty prevailed. He tore away from the magnetic sign in the sky, shot Naomi an apologetic smile, and answered.

It was his assistant. "You'll want to see this," he said.

"I'm already seeing what I want to see," Chang said.

"But you're still interested in the Jewish question, right?"

"The Jewish question?"

"What Dr. Rosenzweig called the 'worldwide turning to Messiah'?"

"Of course, but that's been going on since Chaim's broadcast."

"And it picked up with the lightning storm."

"Exactly," Chang said. "So what's new?"

"You must come and see. *Massive* doesn't begin to describe it. There must have been millions still undecided, but no more. They're all coming to the Lord, and it seems every one of them is letting us know."

Rayford had never thought about what one wears to meet Jesus. He dug through his closet, finding — also as prophesied —

three-and-a-half-year-old but good-as-new khakis, socks, and boots. He was dressed in seconds.

"You thinkin' what I'm thinkin', Ray?"

"What?"

"That we got no business skedaddlin' out of here if you're healthy enough to fight. There's a battle comin', and the both of us were supposed to be in it."

"Don't do this to me now, Mac."

"I don't want to be here any more'n you do, Ray. But Sebastian and Razor and Otto and them are all tryin' to hold the perimeter."

"Oh, man! Well, Abdullah's gone." Rayford was transported back to his childhood when he would plead his case with his parents. "Why does *he* get to do it?"

"Abdullah can answer to his own conscience."

"And I've got to answer to yours?"

"Just do the right thing, Ray."

"You staying, either way?"

"Got to. It's the way I'm made."

"You *would* have to get parental on me all of a sudden."

"Do what you got to do, Ray. I'll understand."

"I'm not flying without you, Mac. You really think God healed me so I can help in a battle He's already promised to win?"

Mac shook his head. "I didn't say it made sense. I just told you what I thought."

"I'm calling Sebastian."

"This is Big Dog One!" Sebastian shouted. "Talk to me!" When he heard Rayford's question he laughed loud and long. "You and Mac get yourselves in the air right now, and if you don't I'll come up and shoot you myself."

He told Rayford where he was and what was happening.

"Then you'll believe it when I tell you that when the sign appeared, God healed me."

"I'd believe anything right now, buddy. If it didn't mean leaving my people, I'd go with you. So you remember every detail, hear?"

Chang had been told enough, by Naomi — whose love for him made him wonder about her objectivity — and by the leadership, that he had served a crucial function not just for the Tribulation Force, but also for the entire remnant in Petra. He was gratified to hear it, and while he was re-lieved to be out from under the daily pres-sure of living as a mole in the Antichrist's own lair at New Babylon, he had found Petra an unusual challenge.

Naomi had been the bright spot, of course. But his work, sometimes fourteen to sixteen hours a day, could be both a grind and invigorating. It motivated him because he was — he couldn't deny it — somewhat of a prodigy in technical things. Associates told him that was an understatement, and some even held that he might be the leading computer expert in the world, despite his youth.

All well and good, but when he examined himself and tried to decide what was troubling him about his current work, it was the old real-estate agent's adage: location, location, location.

Computers had come a long way in his lifetime alone, but they still largely had to be housed inside, out of the weather. It seemed to Chang that he was still a mole, living mostly underground — or at least indoors. His forays out were always on breaks or at the end of the day, or when he was stealing a moment or two with Naomi, as he had just done.

Now here it was, just before the Glorious Appearing of Christ, and he was back inside, sitting before a bevy of screens, keeping tabs on the whole world. It was a privilege, sure. Who else was doing it or knew how? And he knew he brought a lot to the table, like the ability to hack into the en-

223

emy's transmissions, both computer and television. And while he would rather be with the rest of the remnant, marshaling outside and being directed to various high places, Chang knew this was where he would sit for the end of the world.

He could cry and moan or he could do his job, and he would do the latter. There would be time to be a frontliner, able to take in every detail of the millennial kingdom. For now he would monitor and coordinate the activities of his compatriots. They had to be kept in touch with each other.

Sebastian was in the midst of the Unity Army's attempted invasion, as were Razor and Otto and Ree.

Abdullah was in a jet, who knew where?

Chaim was working with the elders to coordinate the people.

Last word Chang had heard was that Rayford had been healed and that he and Mac were looking for four-wheeled ATVs so they could rejoin the fray.

Lionel was in Chang's same situation, tied to a desk, still managing the far-flung exploits of the International Co-op from Petra with the help of Ming Woo.

And Leah and Hannah were running the infirmary, a polite term for a medical facility as large as most hospitals.

More fell to Chang than he felt should be under his purview, but with the leadership otherwise engaged, he would have to make some executive decisions. Abdullah had radioed in, asking permission to rejoin the masses at Petra.

"I understand the resistance to the Unity Army on the perimeter has already been overrun," he said. "But they are still safe and protected, and we know extra help is not needed there."

Chang couldn't blame Abdullah for asking. It was the very thing he wanted to do and to be — a camper instead of a counselor, for lack of a better description. "Come on ahead," Chang told him. He also explained why Abdullah was having trouble reaching Rayford and Mac, but a minute later that all changed too.

"Chang," Rayford said, "Sebastian doesn't need us and can't use us. I've instructed him to bring his troops in to join the remnant. Their work is done."

"But won't they have to come through the Unity Army to get here now?"

"They're in the middle of 'em already, and the enemy has no power over them. Once Chaim and the elders get everyone in place, the population here can look down on the plains all around Petra. They'll have a perfect view of the sky and the earth."

"And you and Mac?"

"Mac's going to take his chopper and I need an ATV."

"You sure you want to go back out on one of those?"

"What are the odds, Chang? Gotta climb back on the horse, as they say."

Chang checked his records and told Rayford where Lionel Whalum kept the best units, "full of fuel, charged up, and ready to go. And where will you go, or do I want to know?"

"I'm going to go where Mac tells me. He'll be hovering over the Unity Army, trying to spot the leader himself. I want to be close enough to see and hear Carpathia. He's got to be somewhere out there behind the horde that has swept past Sebastian's position and is on its way up to our western border."

Chang filled Rayford in on what everyone else was doing, including Abdullah. "And you know where I'll be."

"We couldn't survive without you, Chang."

"Yeah, yeah."

Enoch got on his phone, shaking his head. He couldn't blame his little flock for cutting and running. He'd been scared too, but there was nowhere to go and, really, nothing to fear. That was easy to say but quite another thing to act upon when the powers of heaven had been shaken. But it didn't seem right to be apart from his people, not now.

How surreal it felt to be stretched out on a chaise lounge in a suburban backyard, trying to reach parishioners on the phone while a cross of lightning miles tall and wide vibrated in the sky. He finally reached Florence, a late middle-aged black woman who seemed to have the most influence with the congregation.

"Florence, where is everybody?"

"About half of us are right here, Pastor. A little embarrassed, but okay."

"And where's *here?*"

" 'Bout three blocks from you, I reckon. We came back to the mall, but your car was gone, so we figured you was at home."

"I'm home. Why don't you all come here and be with me when the Lord returns."

"You told us never to give away your hideout. How we all gonna fit in your cellar, anyway?"

He told her where he was. "Of course we don't want to draw the attention of the neighbors or the GC, but don't you think they're preoccupied with the sky right now?"

"Watch for us. We'll be comin'. Only a few of us have cars, and we'll leave those here."

Mac stood talking with Lionel Whalum while refueling the chopper. "Haven't been outside all day," Lionel told him, hands on his hips, studying the cross in the sky. "Except to get Captain Steele his ATV, of course."

"Not even for the lightning storm? That was something."

"Heard it. Saw it on a monitor. Tell ya, Mac, you'd think Co-op stuff was over now, but we've never been busier."

Chaim missed Tsion in the worst way. The younger man commanded respect, maybe because he was a rabbi, maybe because he simply exuded a walk with God that was newer to Chaim. It wasn't that Chaim couldn't get his elders' attention. It was just that he had to raise a hand and ask for the floor. Tsion never had to do that. Merely leaning forward or taking a breath or opening his mouth seemed to draw attention to him and quiet everyone else.

Eleazar Tiberius, not that much older than Tsion had been but a much bigger, rotund man, had become a wonderful ally. Twenty years younger than Chaim, his deep bass voice and the gray invading his sparse rim of black hair and beard lent him an air of authority. And he was appropriately deferential to Chaim's leadership, frequently calling for order and requesting — demanding, really — that his colleagues listen to Dr. Rosenzweig.

That was crucial now when the elders were about to split up and coordinate the various group leaders for all the Petra citizens in their respective areas. "We must have order," Chaim said. "We must keep people moving and under control. Notice the chart here. Gentlemen, please. Notice the chart where the groups are to go. Please! Each of you is responsible for undershepherds who will have a total of a hundred thousand men, women, and children in their charge."

Chaim stopped and looked down. He feared the elders were not listening. He could understand that they wanted to get back outside so as not to miss the Glorious Appearing. But that was what this was all about. He didn't want anyone to miss it. He looked at Eleazar, who used his voice to fix the matter.

"Gentlemen! If you do not at least glance at the chart, you will not know where to tell your group leaders to go! Group number one, as you can see, you are taking the southern route to the high places on the western border. Our engineers have determined there is enough room for everyone, if all cooperate. The first forty groups of a thousand each can move to within ten feet of the edge, but they must all be willing to sit once they get there. And it is of crucial importance that the sixty groups behind them not press forward or we could lose tens of thousands over the side. Understood?"

Chaim was pleased to see Abdullah rush in. As Eleazar continued the instructions to the other elders, Chaim pulled the Jordanian aside and embraced him. "How is my prize student?"

Abdullah told him where he had been and what he had seen. "As you know, Doctor, I am not a man of outward emotion, but I do not mind telling you, I was moved to tears by what the Lord showed me. It was such a privilege."

"I cannot imagine your wanting to leave the sky."

"I had an overwhelming desire to be with you and the people for what comes next. I have the strangest feeling that it could be any second, even before we get everyone assembled."

"We fear the same," Chaim said. "The

Unity Army is at our doorstep, and the only reason our people have the confidence to look down over the sides into their gun barrels is that we saw them swallowed up by the earth the first time they dared approach, and we danced in the fire they sent us the second time."

Rayford loved the feel of the monster ATV. Any fear that he would be tentative had vanished when he took it for a spin inside Petra, leaning this way and that as he gradually accelerated and made right and left turns, eventually at high speeds. He didn't plan to be careless. He would use the headlights, even with the illumination from the cross above, and keep his eyes on the ground to avoid ruts and rocks.

The loud, staticky humming in the sky both thrilled and unnerved him, because while he knew the portent of it, he also believed Jesus could appear at any time. The only thing better than being here when that happened was to be close enough to Carpathia to see his response. In truth, Rayford assumed he himself might be so overwhelmed that he would no longer give a rip about Carpathia.

Having given Lionel Whalum a thumbs-up, he pointed the vehicle toward the steep grade that led to the western flats. He would accelerate for as long as he felt in control, and at the first sign the bike was getting squirrelly, Rayford would ride the brake.

Mac ascended vertically several hundred feet before leaning the helicopter away from Petra airspace and swooping directly over Unity Army forces. He had to watch for their own aircraft, but it appeared no one on the ground paid him any mind.

He knew Carpathia and his entourage had come from the east, so he flew to the eastern edge of the massive army. There, perhaps a quarter mile from the mounted troops, was an encampment of vehicles and horses and what appeared to be comfortable chairs. Dignitaries sat watching the action on television. He'd have liked to have been there when the cross first appeared, because he imagined it quickly drew their attention away from the TVs.

But they now appeared to have grown used to the ominous sign and were apparently trying to follow the exploits of their leader. Wait till they saw what was coming next in the sky.

Meanwhile, Mac wondered how he was supposed to locate Nicolae Carpathia in the sea of black below.

Ten

Leah Rose had thought she was past impressing. She had been with Rayford, after all, when the judgment of 200 million demonic horsemen had invaded the earth and wiped out a third of the remaining population. And she had seen and endured, firsthand, all the judgments that followed.

Leah and Hannah Palemoon, the younger nurse who had become such a close friend, were the first to run from the infirmary when word came that the sign of the Son of Man had appeared. It was not the first time they had ventured out that evening. They had also seen the lightning show.

They had been discussing their collective guilt over leaving Lionel Whalum to handle things at the Co-op. He had help, sure, but they had been his assistants for months and

233

were only recently pressed back into nursing duties because of various ailments, injuries, and illnesses throughout Petra. These maladies were solely among the spiritually undecided, which Leah thought should be a lesson to all.

But if there was one thing she had learned since becoming a fugitive from the Global Community, it was that people learned slowly. She had been taught and had heard over and over that mankind would be blind to the acts of God: they would see His mighty works and yet still reject Him and choose their own path. It was no longer a matter of unbelief. That was clear. No one in his right mind could see all that had gone on over the last seven years, starting with the Rapture, and still claim not to know this was the ultimate battle between good and evil, heaven and hell, God and the devil.

So if it was not unbelief, as had been Leah's own problem in the pre-Rapture world, what was it? Were people insane? No, she decided, they were self-possessed, narcissistic, vain, proud. In a word, *evil*. They saw the acts of God and turned their backs on Him, choosing the pleasures of sin over eternity with Christ.

God had, in the meantime, hardened many hearts. And when these unbelievers changed their minds — or tried to — they were not even capable of repenting and turning to God. That had seemed unfair to Leah at first, but as the years rolled by and the judgments piled up, she began to see the logic of it. God knew that eventually sinners would grow weary of their own poverty, but His patience had a limit. There came a time when enough was enough. People had had way more than enough information to make a reasonable choice, and the sad fact was they had made the wrong one, time and time again.

Well, today was really the end. No question God's mercy still extended to His chosen people. He, through His servants like Tsion and Chaim and the 144,000 witnesses, still pleaded with unbelievers in the final remnant to come to Him. And to hear it from Chang's sources, millions were doing just that.

But Leah was intrigued to see that she was not, after all, unable to be further impressed. For when she and Hannah finally returned to the infirmary, she was staggered to find that everyone there had been healed. Everyone. No one was sick, hurt, or lame. All were up and about, congratulating each other, getting dressed, and leaving without even checking themselves out.

Best of all, many of the formerly undecided were on their knees, crying out to God
to save them. And all around them were
remnant volunteers, counseling them,
praying with them.

"We, Hannah," Leah said, "are out of
work."

She called Rayford, only to find that he
was already up, dressed, and looking for action.

When he came within striking distance of
the slowly advancing Unity Army, Rayford
applied all three brakes to his ATV — the
ones on each handlebar and the one under
his right foot. He had been merrily cruising
down the side of the rocky hill, hearing the
advance. But when he swung around some
underbrush and realized the army could see
him, his eagerness was checked.

Many of the soldiers were on foot, vainly
urging their horses upward. Those still
mounted struggled to keep their animals
pointed in the right direction. The soil was
loose, the going rough. They didn't look
happy, but they sure looked intrigued to
have a target.

"Identify yourself," one barked, reining
his horse and stopping ten feet in front of
Rayford.

"Citizen of Petra," Rayford said, his voice not as confident as he had expected.

"You're now a prisoner of war."

"You're taking prisoners? There are more than a million of us."

"Only you. You can be of help to us. We need to know where everyone is, the best way in, all that."

"And then I can go?"

"Don't be smart."

"Well, as for where almost everyone else is, they're inside. But you knew that. The best way in is all the way around the other side from where you are, but of course you're not allowed. I'm curious, though. Why didn't you take one of the perimeter guards hostage and ask these questions?"

"Massacred them all."

"That so?" Rayford pulled a walkie-talkie from his belt and mashed the button. "Big Dog One, this is your captain. Over."

"One, here. Hey, Rayford."

"How're we doing? Any casualties?"

"Not a one."

"Then if I wanted to thumb my nose at the Unity Army, I should be confident that —"

"Where are you, man?"

"About a mile south of the western border."

"I'm about a half mile down from you and on my way up."

"In the middle of the enemy, Big Dog?"

"Exactly. Their bullets are no good here. Their blades either."

"Kill him," the soldier said, and half a dozen weapons opened fire.

Except for a ringing in his ears, Rayford did not suffer. "Maybe you all can tell me something," he said. "I'm looking for your leader, the big man, the top guy. Where's Carpathia?"

But the soldiers had paled. It was as if they were wondering what was the use. If they could not kill the rebels, what was the sense of storming their fortress? And what did the rebels need a fortress for, anyway?

"That's all right," Rayford said. "I have my sources. 'Scuse me," he said as he let the ATV roll on down the way. " 'Scuse me." A few more soldiers shot at him and a couple of others thrust swords at him, but soon commanders were instructing personnel to save their ammunition for the siege of the stone citadel.

Finding Carpathia was not as difficult as Mac had feared. In the middle of the churning mass of humanity that pushed its way across the flatland toward the gridlock on the hill was a circle of lights pointed at a man on a bigger-than-average black stallion. Only Carpathia needed lights shined his way, so the worldwide television audience could see him in action.

As Mac watched from his chopper, Nicolae spent a lot of time holding his sword aloft and appearing to shout commands. Then he would sheath the weapon and engage in angry conversation with those around him, presumably his generals. He was clearly not happy with the slow pace, but when the sword was unsheathed again, he worked up a determined expression.

Mac called Rayford and gave him the coordinates where he might find the potentate.

"Thanks, Mac. I expect to run into Sebastian and some of his people first."

As Rayford picked his way through the Unity Army, he found more and more soldiers who must have learned the futility of trying to attack their enemy outside Petra. They looked at him, raised weapons, then wearily moved on.

But soon there was a new development. Word came through the commanders that all personnel on the hill were to execute an immediate right-face and clear the area. Some grumbled, but most looked relieved.

"About time," Rayford heard one say.

As the thousands of horses and riders cleared the area, the rest of the Unity Army stopped at the foot of the hill. An area fifty feet wide was cleared in the middle of them, and Mac told Rayford that was the avenue Carpathia and his people would use.

"Looks like they're planning to take over this operation themselves," Mac said, "and it's gonna happen as soon as he's in place at the head of the line."

"Their horses won't have any more luck on this incline than the others did," Rayford said.

"They're gonna get rid of the horses, I think," Mac said. "Nick himself is in the big Humvee, but they've also got the smaller Hummers, SUVs, and armored personnel carriers. Uh-oh, somethin' else too. Grenade and missile launchers are comin'."

"What do you mean, 'uh-oh'? Why should those work any better here than bombs?"

"Good point. I'm just sayin' —"

Rayford came upon a Hummer carrying Sebastian, Weser, and Razor. It had little trouble managing the ascent, especially now that the Unity Army had abandoned the area. Rayford pulled up to the driver's side and shut down his engine.

Sebastian lowered the window. "How exciting is this?" he said.

"You know you're showing the enemy how to handle the terrain."

"So it'll be my fault if they crash through on top and kill everybody, and all the prophecies are proved wrong?"

"I'll hold you responsible," Rayford said. "Wanna have some fun? Follow me down and around. I'm going to settle in behind Carpathia's mobile command center and tag along."

Sebastian sighed. "I'm tempted," he said. "Make it an order so I don't have a choice."

"What's your best assessment of what you should be doing, George?"

Sebastian looked at Weser and Razor, then back at Rayford. "What I'm doing right now. I want to get all of my people back up there and inside so they have the best view of what's next. I can't abandon them now."

"Then that's what you ought to be doing." Rayford slapped the hood of the Hummer. "Carry on."

Abdullah was back on his dirt bike, noisily picking his way through tens of thousands of people. He supervised and advised elders as they directed undershepherds and group leaders in getting more than a million people to their places. The going was slow, but it was getting done.

Abdullah had scouted an area to the northeast and decided that was where Chaim and the elders should stand when everyone else was in place. At least 80 percent of the populace would be able to see Chaim from there. And in case he had any last words for the citizens, he had access to the public-address system. "But I expect all attention will be on the sky anyway," he said.

Chaim could not hide his apprehension from Eleazar. "What is it?" the younger elder said.

"Lack of faith," Chaim said.

"Surely not. Not you. The Lord has brought us too far, showed us too much. Can there be any doubt that He will appear and rescue us at the appointed time?"

"But what is that time, brother? Chang's people tell me the Unity Army has cleared the western slope for a rolling armada with Carpathia himself in charge."

"All the more reason to believe Messiah is coming soon. He will not fail us, will not break His promises. Antichrist cannot prevail, and the closer he comes, the sooner we shall be delivered."

"I believe that, Eleazar."

"Of course you do. So what troubles you?"

"Things have been left unsaid."

"By you?" Elder Tiberius said with a twinkle. "I cannot imagine it."

"I wanted to explain the imagery of the Glorious Appearing. Tsion and I both have spent so much time insisting on a literal approach to the Scriptures that I fear I have neglected some of the clearly symbolic references in the Glorious Appearing passages."

"Perhaps there will still be time," Eleazar said, "but why don't we discuss it outside? The Lord may get here before you do!"

"But I must make notes."

"Do you want to be in here scribbling when it happens? Bring pen and paper with you, Chaim, but come, please!"

For months Enoch had hidden his car a few blocks from the home where he lived in the cellar. He never turned on lights upstairs, and the basement windows were boarded over. The neighbors in Palos Hills never saw him out in the light of day because he would have been unable to hide the fact that he did not bear the mark of loyalty to the potentate. He sneaked in and out of the seemingly abandoned house in the wee hours of the morning.

But now here he sat in the high-fenced

backyard, hearing neighbors quizzing each other, discussing the astronomical phenomena in panicky tones. What would they think of strangers invading, gathering in his yard? Would they take the time and trouble to check and see if he and his friends were renegades, fugitives, outlaws? Would there be time for the neighbors to put them to death?

Since the neighbors had to assume his place was uninhabited, nothing else would arouse suspicion in the dark. Why would they have to assume anything about him or his people? *Ah,* he thought, *that's naïve. What would we all be doing here?*

Mac had a clear view of the latest Unity Army maneuver, and he had to hand it to the leadership. Someone knew how to fix a problem. Whether it was Carpathia or one of his henchmen, the plan was working. The thousands from the front lines who had begun storming up the western slope found the going impossible and had already moved south, then west, then back northeast again, and had begun reinserting themselves into the ranks.

Meanwhile, the quarter-mile-long and fifty-foot-wide corridor had opened before Carpathia's private unit — and also about fifty yards behind it. He and his people were transferring to rolling stock. A convoy of ten vehicles was maneuvered into position, trailed by two carriers of heavy armaments. If Mac had to guess, he would say Carpathia would lead the charge, the munitions right behind, and that the rest of the army — other than those on horseback — would bring up the rear.

From where Mac sat, it was obvious that under other circumstances Petra wouldn't have had a chance. They were unarmed and outnumbered three or four to one by only a third of Carpathia's total fighting force. Unity Army vehicles could easily traverse the terrain, and the front line of this new unit could be on the other side of the walls of Petra in less than half an hour.

Mac called Chang. "You able to crack into Carpathia's communications yet?"

"Almost. I can pick up everybody but him, but I've got a rapid decoder screaming through it, so it shouldn't be long."

"Patch it through to me as soon as you get it, hear?"

"You got it. Rayford wants the same."

"Roger."

Rayford waited at the base of the hill, facing the Unity Army about ten degrees south of the opening that had been left for Carpathia's unit. Rayford was virtually ignored as the rest of the troops had quickly become aware of the VIP in their midst. All eyes were on Nicolae.

Rayford's plan was to fall in with Carpathia as he swept past, hoping not to attract attention. That would have been sheer folly aside from what had already occurred. The Unity Army had finally seemed to concede that they had no power on the perimeter against the meager defense. Why they thought they had a prayer inside Petra itself, given their futile history against God's people, was a mystery. Carpathia's ego knew no bounds.

Enoch's fears proved unfounded. His people were sly enough to appear silently in twos and threes, and they found their way to the backyard without drawing notice. The neighbors drifted to their own homes eventually anyway, and Enoch was left in the yard with more than forty of the hundred or so that had joined him at the mall that morning.

They gathered around his chair and sat in the grass, no one seeming to grow tired of gazing at the cross adorning the horizon. "Come, Lord Jesus," several whispered, and others joined in. "Come, Lord. Come soon."

"Everything that's gonna happen is going to be over there, right, Pastor?" a young man said.

"Over there?"

"In the Holy Land. You said Jesus was going to fight for the Jews in Petra first, then save Jerusalem. How we gonna know when He's come?"

"Well," Enoch whispered, "the Bible says the whole world will know when He comes. Revelation 1:7 says, 'Behold, He is coming with clouds, and every eye will see Him, even they who pierced Him.'"

"How's He gonna 'complish that? Holy Land's on the other side of the world."

"Don't you think they're seeing what we're seeing now?"

"I guess, but like when the moon is out, people over there see the other side of it, right?"

"They could be seeing the other side of this cross too. We have no idea how massive it is."

"Or if there's more than one," someone said.

"How's that?" Enoch said.

"God can do what He wants, right?"

"Right."

"He could put ten crosses in the sky to make sure ever'body sees one."

"But there's only one Jesus."

"Yeah, but He can show up anywhere He wants, all at the same time. Just like He was only one man but He died for everybody, He can appear to everybody too."

"Now you're talking," Enoch said.

"Is He gonna kill a bunch of people here, like He is over there?"

"I'm afraid He is. If they're working for the Antichrist, they're in serious trouble."

"Rayford, you should see this from where I'm sittin'," Mac said.

"I kind of like where I am," Rayford said.

"Yeah, but it's pretty. The red-stone city is lit from the cross above, and I feel like I'm in one of those blimps that used to hover over the football stadiums at night. Everybody's just about in place, ringing the top of Petra. In front, people are sitting so the ones standing behind them can see. Most of 'em'll be able to see the Unity Army attacking and the Lord returning. I hope He gets here soon."

"I imagine He'll be right on time, don't you?"

"I imagine. I can see Chaim and the elders makin' their way to a spot where most

248

everybody can see them. You gotta wonder if anybody is scared to death out there on the edge."

"I would be, and I've lived through it all."

"Me too, Ray. Guess it's human nature to feel like you're testin' fate one time too many. Hey, looks like Chaim's addressin' 'em. I'm gonna see if Chang can patch us in — oh, he's way ahead of us. Here it is. Talk at you later."

". . . and sisters in the Messiah," Chaim was saying. "We gather here in this historic place, this holy city of refuge provided by the Lord God Himself. We stand on the precipice of all time with the shadow of history behind us and eternity itself before us, putting all our faith and trust in the rock-solid goodness and strength and majesty of our Savior.

"May the Lord appear as I speak. Oh, the glory of that moment! We stand gazing into the heavens where the promised sign of the Son of Man radiates before us, thundering through the ages the truth that His death on the cross cleanses us from all sin.

"Within the next few minutes, you may see the enemy of God advancing on this fortified city. I say to you with all the confidence the Father has put in my soul, fear not, for your salvation draweth nigh.

"Now many have asked what is to happen when Antichrist comes against God's chosen people and the Son intervenes. The Bible says He will slay our enemy with a weapon that comes from His mouth. Revelation 1:16 calls it 'a sharp two-edged sword.' Revelation 2:16 quotes Him saying that He 'will come to you quickly and will fight against them with the sword of My mouth.' Revelation 19:15 says that 'out of His mouth goes a sharp sword, that with it He should strike the nations.' And Revelation 19:21 says the enemies 'were killed with the sword which proceeded from the mouth of Him who sat on the horse.'

"Now let me clarify. I do not believe the Son of God is going to sit on His horse in the clouds with a gigantic sword hanging from His mouth. He is not going to shake His head and slay the millions of Armageddon troops with it. This is clearly a symbolic reference, and if you are a student of the Bible, you know what is meant by a sharp, double-edged sword.

"Hebrews 4:12 says the Word of God 'is living and powerful, and sharper than any two-edged sword, piercing even to the division of soul and spirit, and of joints and marrow, and is a discerner of the thoughts and intents of the heart.'

"The weapon our Lord and Messiah will use to win the battle and slay the enemy? The Word of God itself! And while the reference to it as a sword may be symbolic, I hold that the description of the result of it is literal. The Word of God is sharp and powerful enough to slay the enemy, literally tearing them asunder."

Anticipation surged through Rayford. He turned to look up at Petra when the cheering and applause drowned out Chaim, who was apparently finished. Emotion swept over Rayford as he took in the scene. Rimming the very top of the fortified city was the remnant of God, slowly turning from Chaim to face the sky and then the enemy below them.

From that distance they were mere specks, but there were so many that Rayford could tell they were raising their hands and clasping them together. He heard the strains of hymns from their collective voices, faint at first, then with growing volume. First they sang "I Sing the Mighty Power of God." Moments later they sang "A Mighty Fortress Is Our God."

When they broke into the "Hallelujah Chorus," Rayford wished he could stand

and join in. And when the echoing truths washed down the mountainside — "For the Lord God omnipotent reigneth" — he thought he would shed his skin.

At that moment Chang apparently solved the encryption coding of the potentate's audio transmission, and it came crackling through the earphone in Rayford's left ear. So at the same time he was hearing the magnificent *hallelujahs* in one ear, he heard Antichrist in the other.

And Nicolae was not happy. "Let us roll! The fools are singing!" He cursed and cursed again. "They sing in the face of their own deaths!"

The caravan began rolling, the cross above it bouncing waves of light off the dust that ensued. "Take me to the highest and closest point," Nicolae ordered, "with our munitions settling in behind where the angle is optimal. I shall stand on the roof of the vehicle so all can see me: my troops to be inspired, and the enemy so they know the author of their doom."

At the mention of Carpathia's intended destination, Rayford glanced again up the slope to where hundreds of thousands swayed and sang and looked down. The immense cross shone on the entire hillside, as if pointing the enemy to the spot where God

Himself wanted them.

Rayford had to wonder if any in Petra had second thoughts, doubts. He was happy to say he had none. He had come too far. His own pride and laziness had cost him his wife and son at the Rapture. He'd felt responsible for the fact that his own daughter had shared his jaded view of people of faith and had followed his example, thumbing her nose at God.

And while he was grateful beyond expression for his own salvation and Chloe's, seeing her and her husband martyred was merely the capstone of the tragedy that resulted from his having missed the truth in the first place. So many friends and loved ones had suffered over the past seven years. New friends, old friends, a new wife, spiritual mentors, dear compatriots had been injured, killed, tortured for their faith.

Yet God had proved faithful and true to His Word. Every prophecy had been fulfilled. While there had to be those who wondered why the Lord tarried even now and whether there was any sense or logic to allowing Antichrist to reach the very boundary of the city of refuge, Rayford found himself simply trusting. God had His plans, His ways, His strategy. Only when Rayford stopped questioning God had he finally come to grips with the confusing, sometimes maddening, ways of God — which the Scriptures said were "not our ways."

Some things still didn't make sense, and many would not become clear, he knew, until he saw Jesus face-to-face.

The evil motorcade thundered within yards of Rayford. He gunned his ATV engine and joined them, a couple of vehicles behind Carpathia's and ahead of the rumbling armament carriers. A general tried to wave him off. Rayford smiled and waved back. The general reached for a weapon from an aide and aimed it out the window. Rayford winked at him, and the man opened fire.

The general blanched when the burp of bullets he'd fired at point-blank range seemed to go right through Rayford.

"No shooting!" Carpathia screamed. "Ignore any enemy outside the walls of the city!"

Abdullah studied his copy of the location charts and slowly picked his way through narrow pathways and crowds until he found the area where George Sebastian's wife, Priscilla, should be with her daughter, Beth Ann, and Rayford's grandson, Kenny

Bruce. Once there, he had to ask several people, but finally he found them.

Priscilla had Beth Ann next to her, holding her hand, and her free arm held a lanky, incongruously sleeping Kenny, draped over her shoulder.

"Let me take him," Abdullah said.

"Oh, would you, Mr. Smith? He's getting so heavy."

"Come here, big boy," Abdullah said, taking him in his arms. He gently put Kenny's head on his shoulder and began to rock him, but when Abdullah also tried to quietly join in the singing, the boy roused.

"Uncle Smitty," he said.

"Hi, Kenny."

"Jesus comin'," the boy said.

"Yes, He is, buddy. He sure is."

Eleven

At long last, there was nothing more Chang could do. It seemed likely that he and Zeke were in the same boat. Both might have to find a new trade or be out of work for the next thousand years of Christ's rule on earth.

Chang knew where everyone was, had them all in place.

Abdullah was back in the fold.

Chaim and the elders were with the people, waiting and watching.

Hannah and Leah had shut down the empty infirmary and were outside, as were Lionel and Ming — the Co-op finally dark.

Mac was in the air, Rayford on the ground, and Sebastian, Otto, Razor, and Ree should be entering Petra at that very moment, joining their own people and urging the rest of the rebel soldiers to do the same.

Chang had patched the enemy's radio transmissions to Mac and Rayford and wore an earphone himself so he could stay posted. He sat back and sighed, then stood quickly. It was time to find Naomi and get outside where they belonged.

"Taking the rest of the day off?" she said, taking his hand when Chang found her.

"The rest of my life," he said.

Mac kept an eye on Sebastian's vehicle and the hundreds of remnant rebels following him into Petra. "Looks like they're all safe, Ray," he reported. "Ever'body's home and accounted for but you and me."

"Wish I could be with Kenny right now," Rayford said. "Priss says he was asking for his dad earlier, and all she could think to tell him was that they'd see him tomorrow."

"Good thinkin'. Hey, Ray, ol' Nick's leaving nothing to chance."

"How so?"

"He's got the rest of the troops fanning out to surround the city."

"I didn't hear that order, Mac."

"Musta been something he decided on before we could hear him."

"The mounted troops must just be in the way. Not to mention all the meteor craters."

"Some of the trails on this side are navigable. Remember they used to have donkeys bring tourists in."

"Rally the planes," Rayford heard. Carpathia's voice.

"What's he doing, Mac?"

"I'll watch, but it looks like he's bringing everything he's got in this region."

"A third of the total, just like the Bible says."

"He can't get out from under the prophecies, can he, Ray?"

As Rayford surged up toward Petra in the evil procession, he heard jets screaming. "Fighter-bombers?"

"Nah," Mac said. "Fighters but not bombers. Guess they know better than that. He'll have to learn the hard way that the guns don't work here either."

When Carpathia's Humvee reached the last particularly steep stretch, it was nearly pointed to the sky. "Find me a place," he told the driver, "where I can stand on the roof and see all my troops on this side and can also see the enemy."

"I believe we're almost there, Excellency."

Rayford left the formation and shot right about twenty yards to where he had a good view. He shut down his engine and swung his left leg over the seat, using the ATV as a bench. "Attack, you coward," he whispered,

258

hoping that would bring Jesus from heaven. *Yeah, I know. He'll be here in His own time.*

"How's this, Your Highness?"

Rayford heard the squeak of Carpathia's leathers as he moved to look this way and that. "Perfect."

His door opened and simultaneously generals opened their doors and piled out the back. One held Carpathia's door and offered his hand so the potentate could mount the hood. But Nicolae ignored him. He leaped onto the front of the truck and stepped atop the roof. The vehicle was at such an angle that he began sliding. He caught himself, loudly drew his sword, and raised it above his head. "Lights!"

A beacon pulled by a Jeep lit him with a harsh, garish beam that cast a one-hundred-foot shadow on the rocks behind him.

"Loyal soldiers of the Global Community Unity Army, observe your commander in chief!"

The singing inside Petra ceased and the people peered down at him.

"You are privileged to be part of the greatest fighting force ever assembled on the face of the earth! You will be lauded for time immemorial for the victory we are about to win. The plan is foolproof, our resources unlimited, your leader divine. Once we have crushed the resistance here, you will occupy the city and enjoy the spoils while I proceed to Jerusalem to lay siege to it.

"And if there really is a God of Abraham, Isaac, and Jacob, and if He truly has a Son worthy of facing me in combat, I shall destroy Him too! When I have been informed that all elements are in place and at the ready, be prepared to advance upon Petra on my command. Leave no man, woman, or child alive. The victory is mine, says your living lord and risen king!"

From out of the back of Carpathia's vehicle stumbled Leon Fortunato, still in his ridiculous regalia. He failed in his first attempt to climb the hood, then finally hiked his skirts and clambered aboard. Stepping onto the windshield to mount the hood, he stepped on the hem of his robe and had to back down and take another run at it.

When he was finally sharing the roof with Carpathia, Leon reached under his robe and produced a small decanter and began sloshing it about. "Praise to the resurrected lord," he chanted, and then began to sing, "Hail Carpathia, our lord and risen king."

"Leon, what *are* you doing?" Carpathia demanded.

"Leading the assembled in worship, Highness."

"This is a battle, man! And lose the holy water!"

Leon bowed and apologized and loudly stepped down to the hood, then slid off the side onto the ground. "Oh yes!" he said. "Almost forgot. I was to tell you that everyone is in place and at the ready."

"Get in the car, Leon."

"By your grace, Excellency."

As soon as Leon's door was shut, Carpathia stomped twice on the roof. Nothing happened. He stomped twice again. Still nothing. "Go!" he shouted. "Go!"

"You want me to drive with you on the roof, Potentate?" the driver said. "I thought I was supposed to stay —"

"Go! Now!"

The vehicle's engine raced, and when it began virtually climbing the wall, it was all Carpathia could do to keep his balance. "Attack!" he screamed. "Attack! Attack! Attack!"

Rayford watched Carpathia's vehicle bounce up and over while planes let fly their bullets. As far as Rayford could see, the Unity Army surged while the remnant peering over the wall stood in silence, holding hands.

The siege was deafening. Jet engines, Jeeps, cars, trucks, Hummers, transports, armaments, munitions, rifle fire, machine-gun fire, cannons, grenades, rockets — you name it. But when the panoramic cross disappeared from the sky, the world went black again. It reminded Rayford of what he had heard about the darkness that had descended upon New Babylon. The only sound was the clicking of weapons that would not fire. Nothing produced light. No headlights. No matches or lighters.

"Light!" Carpathia screeched. But everything was dark. "Fire!" he raged. Still nothing. "Take the infidels by hand!"

But the soldiers could see nothing and would not know whether their victim was friend or foe. The clicking tapered and then quit. All Rayford heard were frustrated shouts and the nickering of thousands of horses waiting below.

And then, as if God had thrown the switch in heaven, light.

But that wasn't enough of a word for it. This was not light from above that cast shadows. This was a brightness that invaded every crevice and cranny. Rayford had to shield his eyes, but it did no good, as the light came from everywhere.

It exposed a Unity Army in chaos. On the

plains, horses bucked and reared, whinnying and throwing riders. On the hillsides leading to Petra, soldiers examined weapons that did not work. On the border of the city, Carpathia stood exposed atop his personnel carrier, sword at his side, stared at by saints standing side by side.

"You can see them now! Charge! Attack! Kill them!"

But as his petrified, lethargic soldiers slowly turned back to the matter at hand, the brilliant multicolored cloud cover parted and rolled back like a scroll from horizon to horizon. Rayford found himself on his knees on the ground, hands and head lifted.

Heaven opened and there, on a white horse, sat Jesus, the Christ, the Son of the living God.

Rayford could not explain how he could see his Savior so clearly. It was as if He appeared within inches of Rayford, and he knew that had to be the experience of everyone everywhere.

Jesus' eyes shone with a conviction like a flame of fire, and He held His majestic head high. He wore a robe down to the feet so brilliantly white it was incandescent and bore writing, something in a language wholly unfamiliar to Rayford and something else he easily understood. On His robe at the thigh a name was written: KING OF KINGS AND LORD OF LORDS. Jesus was girded about the chest with a golden band. His head and hair were white like wool, as white as snow. His feet were like fine brass, as if refined in a furnace.

Jesus had in His right hand seven stars, and His countenance was like the sun shining in its strength.

The armies of heaven, clothed in fine linen, white and clean, followed Him on white horses.

An angel appeared in the light and cried with a loud voice, saying to all the birds in the midst of heaven, "Come and gather together for the supper of the great God, that you may eat the flesh of kings, the flesh of captains, the flesh of mighty men, the flesh of horses and of those who sit on them, and the flesh of all people, free and slave, both small and great."

"I am the Alpha and the Omega," Jesus said, "the First and the Last, the Beginning and the End, the Almighty."

When Rayford first heard the voice of Jesus, he understood what John meant in Revelation when he compared it to both a trumpet and the sound of many waters. It pierced him, reaching to his heart. It was as if he was not hearing with his ears but rather that the voice came alive within him and communicated with his very soul. Rayford was certain every believer on earth heard Jesus in the same way, deep within his or her own being.

This was the One who is and who was and who had finally come, "the faithful witness, the firstborn from the dead, and the ruler over the kings of the earth. This was Him who loved us and washed us from our sins in His own blood, and has made us kings and priests to His God and Father, to Him be glory and dominion forever and ever."

And with those very first words, tens of thousands of Unity Army soldiers fell dead, simply dropping where they stood, their bodies ripped open, blood pooling in great masses. "I am He who lives, and was dead, and behold, I am alive forevermore. Amen. And I have the keys of Hades and of Death."

With that Carpathia scrambled down from his perch and slid in the passenger-side window. "Retreat! Retreat! Retreat!" he shouted, but the driver must have been dead. "Leon, drive! Get this carcass out!" The driver's door opened and a body flopped out. Soon the vehicle was bouncing down the hill toward the desert.

"I am the Son of Man, the Son of God, the

Amen, the Faithful and True Witness, the Beginning of the creation of God. I am the Lion of the tribe of Judah, the Root of David, the One who prevailed to open the scroll and to loose its seven seals."

With every word, more and more enemies of God dropped dead, torn to pieces. Horses panicked and bolted. The living screamed in terror and ran about like madmen — some escaping for a time, others falling at the words of the Lord Christ.

"I am the Lamb that was slain and yet who lives. I am the Shepherd who leads His sheep to living fountains of waters. I am the God who will wipe away every tear from your eyes. I am your Salvation and Strength. I am the Christ who has come for the accuser of the brethren, who accused them before our God day and night, the one who has been cast down."

For miles lay the carcasses of the Unity Army. The manic, crazed survivors ran and staggered and drove over and through them, fleeing for their lives.

"I am the Word of God. I am Jesus. I am the Root and the Offspring of David, the Bright and Morning Star."

It was hard to kneel and look up, but

somehow Enoch found a way. And all his parishioners did the same. He couldn't articulate his feelings, even in the quietness of his own heart and mind. To see Jesus, clad in white, riding the white horse, and speaking with the authority of the ages, and knowing that He was slaying the enemy in the Holy Land at the same time . . . it was just too much to take in.

Enoch believed that Jesus was the lover of his soul, and seeing Him return on the clouds, knowing He was there to set up His thousand-year kingdom reign, completed Enoch somehow. The psalmist said that as a deer pants after water, so the soul pants after God. Enoch somehow knew that his panting was over. His Savior had come.

He was only vaguely aware that neighbors had burst from their homes in terror, screaming and calling to each other. The light blinded them and they ran to and fro, some jumping in cars and careening down the street. Enoch knew that the news the next day — if there would be news — would report hundreds of thousands of employees of the ruler of this world having mysteriously been slain at the time of the phenomenon in the sky.

And the ruler of this world was himself now running for his life.

★ ★ ★

The all-encompassing, pervasive light that preceded the opening of heaven had fully awakened Kenny Bruce, and Abdullah quickly turned him to face the sky. When Jesus appeared, Abdullah awkwardly knelt, careful not to drop the boy.

"Me too, Uncle Smitty," Kenny said. And he too knelt, first intertwining his tiny fingers as if to pray, then reaching out to Jesus.

"My Lord and my God," Abdullah said, and Kenny repeated him.

"Jesus!" Kenny cried, standing and waving. "Jesus!"

Rayford stood atop the seat of his ATV, his attention divided between the Lord on the clouds and the Unity Army breaking for cover across the sandy plains. But there was nowhere to run, nowhere to hide. As the words of Jesus trumpeted throughout the earth, they could not be avoided. He could not be ignored.

Something about Jesus' appearing struck Rayford so deeply that he was glad no one else was around. He would not have been able to utter a sound. There were no words for the thrill, the magnetism, the overwhelming perfection of the moment. Jesus was the culmination of his whole life, and not just since he had been regenerated. Rayford realized that Jesus was whom his soul had been seeking since he was old enough to think and reason. Jesus was the source and the point of all life.

Rayford knew that somewhere in that heavenly band of white-clad saints behind Jesus were his wife and son, and that his daughter, his second wife, and many friends and loved ones would soon be brought forth to join them. How sweet those reunions would be, and yet how the very thought of them paled next to his fulfilled devotion to Jesus.

As the Global Community minions threw miles-long clouds of dust as they scattered, Jesus continued to speak. And the enemies of God continued to die.

"I am able to save to the uttermost those who come to the Father through Me! I live to make intercession for them. I come from above and am above all. My Father has delivered all things to Me. He put all things under My feet and gave Me to be head over all things. I am the anchor of your soul, sure and steadfast. I am the Lord's Christ."

As Rayford slowly made his way down to the desert plains, though he had to concentrate on missing craters and keeping from hitting splayed and filleted bodies of men and women and horses, Jesus still appeared before his eyes — shining, magnificent, powerful, victorious.

And that sword from His mouth, the powerful Word of God itself, continued to slice through the air, reaping the wrath of God's final judgment. The enemy had been given chance after chance, judgment after judgment to convince and persuade them. To this very minute, God had offered forgiveness, reconciliation, redemption, salvation. But except for that now-tiny remnant of Israel that was seeing for the first time the One they had pierced, it was too late.

"I am the vine, you are the branches. He who abides in Me, and I in him, bears much fruit; for without Me you can do nothing. If anyone does not abide in Me, he is cast out as a branch and is withered; and they gather them and throw them into the fire, and they are burned.

"I am the Apostle and High Priest of your confession, God manifest in the flesh, justified in the Spirit, seen by angels, preached among the Gentiles, believed on in the world, received up in glory.

"I am the Son whom God has appointed heir of all things, through whom also He made the worlds; who being the brightness of His glory and the express image of His person, and upholding all things by the word of His power, when I had by Myself purged your sins, sat down at the right hand of the Majesty on high, having become so much better than the angels, as I have by inheritance obtained a more excellent name than they."

Rayford saw soldiers kill themselves at the sight of their slain comrades. Others looked like cartoon characters on speed, using any implement they could find to dig holes and bury themselves, trying to hide from the piercing light and convicting words of Christ.

Carpathia was radioing ahead to generals and commanders in the middle of his army that still extended miles from Petra to the north. "Reinforcements! Reinforcements! Spare no expense or equipment! Meet us at Buseirah!"

The royal Humvee, with the ubiquitous Leon at the wheel, far outraced Rayford's ATV until it ran into the rest of the army trying to flee on horseback and on foot. About half the original caravan trailed the Humvee, minus the munitions carriers that remained inoperative just outside Petra.

Rayford raced up behind the fleeing potentate and his panicked entourage, and turned to see what was happening with the rest of the Unity Army that had been encircling Petra. All he could see for miles were craters; overturned vehicles; clouds of dust; dead and dying soldiers and horses; personnel walking in a daze, running, staggering. And above them great clouds of ravenous birds, getting their fill of man and beast. Strangely, though, the swarming flocks that would have otherwise blocked out the sun cast no shadow on the ground. The light of Christ permeated everything.

"How we doing up there, Mac?"

"Oh, Ray! I can hear every word, and it's like God's in the cockpit with me, looking right into my eyes."

"I know the feeling."

"Listen, I'm going to head to Buseirah, 'cause that's where what's left of the front lines here seem to be headed. From up here it looks like the worst of the damage and casualties is within five miles of Petra. The rest of the one-third is steering toward Buseirah, and farther north the other two-thirds is pretty much intact and trying to regroup."

One of the women told Enoch, without taking her gaze from the sky, that it seemed "as if Jesus is lookin' right at me."

"Me too," another said, and another.

"Just fellowship with your Savior," Enoch

said quietly, not wanting to speak while Jesus was speaking. It should have been no surprise, he decided, that Christ would supernaturally make personal to every believer the truth of His coming, as if He had come for each individually. Enoch had once heard an old saint say, "He loved us every one, as if there were but one of us to love."

Jesus said, "Look unto Me, the author and finisher of your faith, who for the joy that was set before Me endured the cross, despising the shame, and sat down at the right hand of the throne of God.

"God now commands all men everywhere to repent, because He has appointed this the day on which He will judge the world in righteousness by Me, the Man whom He has ordained. He gave assurance of this to all by raising Me from the dead.

"I am Jesus Christ the righteous, your Advocate with the Father. And I Myself was the propitiation for your sins, and not for yours only but also for the whole world. I am the Prince of life, whom God raised from the dead. I am the Word that became flesh and dwelt among you, and you beheld My glory, the glory as of the only begotten of the Father, full of grace and truth.

"I, being in the form of God, did not consider it robbery to be equal with God, but made Myself of no reputation, taking the form of a bondservant, and coming in the likeness of men. And being found in appearance as a man, I humbled Myself and became obedient to the point of death, even the death of the cross.

"Therefore, Enoch, God also has highly exalted Me and given Me the name which is above every name, that at the name of Jesus every knee should bow, of those in heaven, and of those on earth, and of those under the earth, and that every tongue should confess that Jesus Christ is Lord, to the glory of God the Father."

Enoch's jaw dropped. Sitting there in the brilliance of God's glory, his Savior Jesus had spoken directly to him by name. "Did you hear that?" he said, and the three dozen plus kneeling around him dissolved into tears. "He used my name."

"He used *my* name," a young man said.

"He called me by name," a woman said.

"Me too."

"Me too."

Rayford sat in the middle of the carnage surrounding Petra, his heart bursting, the love and adoration he felt for Jesus coming right back at him from the clouds. Christ had called him by name, and as Rayford gazed at Him he had the feeling that it was true that the very hairs on his head were numbered, that Jesus knew everything there was to know about him. It was as if He had returned just for Rayford.

"Ray, this's Mac."

"Yeah, Mac."

"You're not goin' to believe this, but —"

"I know."

"You too?"

"Everybody, I think, Mac."

"Incredible."

Even knowing that the same phenomenon had happened to others, Rayford longed to hear Jesus say his name again. It came with such love, compassion, and knowledge that it was as if no one had ever uttered it before or would again.

"Rayford —" there it was again — "you know My grace, that though I was rich, yet for your sake I became poor, that you through My poverty might become rich."

"I know, Lord," Rayford said, tears streaming. "I know."

"I have delivered you from the power of darkness and conveyed you into the kingdom of the Son of God's love, in whom you have redemption through My blood, the forgiveness of sins. I am the image of the invisible God, the firstborn over all creation.

"For by Me all things were created that are in heaven and that are on earth, visible and invisible, whether thrones or dominions or principalities or powers. All things were created through Me and for Me. And I am before all things, and in Me all things consist.

"I am the head of the body, the church, the beginning, the firstborn from the dead, that in all things I may have the preeminence. For it pleased the Father that in Me all the fullness should dwell, and by Me to reconcile all things to Himself, whether things on earth or things in heaven, having made peace through the blood of My cross."

Again Rayford slid to the ground, raising his arms. "My Lord and my God, I am so unworthy."

"And you, Rayford, who once were alienated and an enemy in your mind by wicked works, yet now I have reconciled in the body of My flesh through death, to present you holy, and blameless, and above reproach in God's sight."

"Unworthy, unworthy!" Rayford cried.

"Justified by faith," Jesus said. "Justified."

It seemed to Abdullah that all in Petra were on their faces and yet still somehow able to see Christ. And when the Savior had called Abdullah by name, he could tell from the response around him that Jesus had called each person by their own name. Even better, Jesus had spoken to Abdullah in his native Arabic.

Kenny shouted, "He *knows* me!"

And Beth Ann wrapped her arms around George's neck and squealed, "He said my name!"

From that moment, Abdullah heard everyone conversing with Jesus as if He were speaking to each of them alone.

Twelve

Mac looked down on Bozrah, the modern-day Jordanian city of Buseirah. It lay thirty miles southeast of the Dead Sea and about twenty miles north of Petra. He told Rayford, "It's a remote village in the mountains here, and access is gonna be difficult."

"Especially if the Lord doesn't want the Unity Army to get there safely."

"And He doesn't."

"Mac, didn't Chaim say the remnant is supposed to go with Jesus to Jerusalem?"

"I believe so."

"How're we going to get a million people sixty miles in one day? We don't have enough vehicles or planes."

"I don't guess it's our problem, Ray."

"So the question remains."

"Look up, brother. Look up. Hey, you're

not gonna try to chase Nicolae all the way to Jerusalem on that little buggy, are ya?"

"I've been reconsidering that, Mac."

"I've been in touch with Chang and Lionel. I don't want to be this far from the action myself. What say we get back to Petra and commandeer us a Hummer?"

"We'd better hurry. I don't want to miss what happens in Bozrah."

"You're drivin', Ray."

"No you don't. You're driving."

"Let's get Smitty. He loves to drive. Plus I'll bet he'd love to be along."

By the time Rayford had scooted back up to Petra, Mac had already landed the chopper and found Abdullah. The three embraced. "What do you call it again," Abdullah said, "when someone states the obvious?"

"I call it statin' the obvious," Mac said. "And it's usually done by a Jordanian. You about to state somethin' obvious, Smitty?"

"I am, sir."

"Well, let 'er fly."

"This is the greatest day of my life. How about you?"

Chaim was nearly overrun with people peppering him with questions. He wanted to give them his full attention, but how could he with his Savior in the clouds? The people were preoccupied with Jesus too, of course, but until they could talk with Him face-to-face, they asked Chaim for answers while looking past him into the heavens.

"Why are the saints behind Him wearing white? To signify their purity?"

"I believe so," Chaim said. "And also because they are not really going to be involved in the war at all. Jesus will do all the work, and the battles — three more following this one — will not really be battles at all, but rather one-sided slaughters."

Rayford longed to see Kenny, but he didn't want to upset him by then pulling away again so quickly. He also wanted to talk to Priscilla Sebastian about how she planned on keeping the kids, her daughter and his grandson, from seeing the horror outside the walls. Abdullah assured him that Kenny was fine for now — he was as enamored of Jesus as they all were — and that Priscilla indeed had a plan.

The million-strong in Petra had fallen far out of their original formation by now and were milling about, most with their necks craned toward the sky but somehow also intuitively migrating toward the exits. They knew they were to be delivered by Jesus, not just from the attack of Antichrist, but back to their homeland, their home city, the City of God, Jerusalem.

"Are we free?" someone asked Enoch.

"I think we are," he said. "No way the Lord will allow Antichrist's forces to kill us for not having the mark of loyalty, now that He is here and is to rule the nations. Even ours."

"How will God do that from over there?"

"I have no idea," Enoch said. "But after today, I will simply believe it, won't you?"

"That's in the Bible, Jesus rulin' the nations?"

"It is. Revelation 12:5 says, 'She bore a male Child who was to rule all nations with a rod of iron. And her Child was caught up to God and His throne.' That's Jesus. And He's here now. That rod of iron sounds like He's going to take no baloney from anybody, doesn't it?"

"I heard that."

"Then I think we're free to live and move about without fear," Enoch said.

"I'm gonna fear a little for a while, but that sure sounds good to me."

The only downside of having Abdullah drive the Hummer was that Rayford would have to trade off with Mac for the privilege of riding shotgun. That transported him back to college when he and his fraternity brothers would compete to call the favored seat, sometimes as much as twenty-four hours before a trip. That also reminded him how far he had been from being a believer back then. Had someone predicted where he would be thirty years later and painted this scene, Rayford would have laughed in his face.

The tight, compact, stiff-riding Hummer made its way out of the city under Abdullah's careful control. Tens of thousands of pilgrims filled the pathways and stone stairways, walking arm in arm, hand in hand, singing, praying, praising God, and gazing at Jesus in the sky.

"This had to be what the Exodus looked like," Abdullah said.

Mac laughed long and loud.

"You know," Abdullah added, "the original one. The children of Israel leaving Egypt."

"I know what the Exodus is, Smitty!" Mac said. "You think those people were happy then?"

"Well, no, I guess not. And they would have had children older than seven too, wouldn't they?"

Finally outside Petra, Rayford was impressed that Abdullah was able to find stretches where he could reach speeds of more than sixty miles an hour. Most of the time he had to be careful of rocks and ruts and craters from the meteorites, and he slowly found ways around the carcasses of horses and soldiers. But clearly he was a man on a mission, wanting to get to Bozrah soon after Carpathia did. And from what Rayford had seen of where the former potentate's convoy had stalled, he thought Smitty might just get them there first.

About four miles from Petra and flying along before a huge cloud of dust, the three of them rolled down their windows and gazed into the clouds when Jesus began speaking again.

"I will surely assemble all of you, O Jacob, I will surely gather the remnant of Israel; I will put them together like sheep of the fold, like a flock in the midst of their pasture; they shall make a loud noise because of so many people.

"I am the One who breaks open, and I will come up before you. You will break out of the city of refuge, pass through the gate, and go out by it. I, your King, will pass before you. I, the Lord, will be at your head."

"He's going to lead the people to Bozrah," Abdullah said.

"Statin' the obvious again, Smitty," Mac said.

But within minutes, Rayford and the others understood Jesus' plan. "Look behind us," Abdullah said.

Abdullah was in a particularly slow patch, carefully picking his way through numerous obstacles, but still a great dust cloud followed them.

"What's that?" Mac said.

"No idea," Rayford said, studying it and becoming alarmed. Something was gaining on them. Something huge and ominous.

Seconds later Abdullah found a smooth stretch and hit the accelerator. Soon they were hurtling along at more than seventy miles an hour. Still the great dust ball caught and overcame them, and the three quickly rolled up their windows. The ground trembled and the wind shook the Hummer.

"It's people!" Rayford shouted above the din. "It's the remnant!"

"They're following the Lord!" Mac said. "Running faster than we're driving!"

"Look at them go! Smiling, laughing, singing! Even little kids!"

"We wouldn't have needed the car!" Abdullah said.

"Statin' the obvious!" Mac yelled, laughing.

★ ★ ★

It had been Hannah Palemoon's idea that the Tribulation Force try to stay together on the trek to Bozrah. She feared that with the move from Petra and the reunions of so many with loved ones, they might never be together in the same way again. No one knew how long the trip would take, and she foresaw the possibility of a very long day. All around her people had questions about how they would get all the way to Jerusalem when Bozrah itself was far enough — really too far to walk.

She didn't care. It began as fun, and everyone was so blessed and full of gratitude, looking at Jesus and seeing Him look back, seemingly directly at each one. Leah was there, and the Sebastians with their daughter and Kenny. By staying in the middle of the huge throng, the kids were spared the ugliness of what was left in the desert. And the children seemed preoccupied with Jesus anyway. Razor was along, and Lionel, Chang and Naomi, Zeke, and the Woos.

Hannah didn't know who first got the idea of walking faster, but suddenly a laughing and smiling group was pushing them. They stepped along as quickly as they could, then began jogging, trotting, and soon they were in a full sprint. Hannah felt light as air, and while it wasn't that she was actually off the ground, it felt that way. Each step carried her farther and farther, and soon she was running faster than she ever had.

To her amazement, she was not out of breath. Her strength and endurance remained, and so, apparently, did that of the old and the young alike. Ahead, George Sebastian ran faster than she, and he was carrying Beth Ann! Priscilla kept up though carrying Kenny.

When the group caught and passed a speeding Hummer, Hannah knew they were running at miraculous, supernatural, superhuman speeds. And of all things, the kids wanted to be let down so they too could run. She passed the Sebastians as they slowed to lower the children, but within minutes they had passed her again, the kids running as fast as the adults.

Half an hour later the entire mass of a million was past the Hummer and nearing Bozrah. By the time Abdullah pulled up to a narrow entryway to the mountain village, Unity Army troops had straggled in. They looked defeated before the battle began.

What was left of their vehicles and armaments was pathetic, but Rayford was surprised how many soldiers remained alive. Several thousand horses too. He had to wonder whether any of these, who were part of the original one-third of Carpathia's fighting force, would remain to join the others in the north.

How strange to see the entire remnant gathered again as Abdullah drove around the edges of the great crowd. The Lord and His white-clad heavenly army hovered over them, and despite the trip, everyone appeared fresh and clean and none the worse for wear. No one was even breathing heavily. Which was good, Rayford thought, because they still had another journey ahead of them, twice as far.

"Wonder where ol' Nick is this time," Mac said. "We haven't heard from him in a while, have we?"

"If I were him," Abdullah said, "I would leave this battle to someone else."

"Me too," Mac said. "I don't see him anywhere."

Rayford directed Abdullah to a high place just northeast of the city. From there they could look down upon the remnant and out across the plains, where several hundred thousand troops were aligned and apparently ready for a fresh attack. Rayford studied the horizon through binoculars, and soon he heard radio transmissions from Carpathia's generals.

"Standing by for your word, Excellency." The voice sounded weary, defeated.

There was a throat clearing. "And the southern platoons?" Carpathia's voice.

"Ready, Supreme Potentate." Rayford detected a note of sarcasm.

"Ready, holiness. May we know your position?"

"For whatever reason?"

"So that we avoid the danger of friendly fire, great one."

"Suffice it to say that I and my cabinet are to your northwest."

So much for visibility and inspiration. Apparently Nicolae was fully aware how close he'd come to being bird feed at Petra. "Right behind you, boys," seemed to be his mantra for this skirmish. But it would prove to be more than a skirmish.

"It appears the entire population of Petra is here," a general broadcast.

"If you are addressing me," Carpathia said, "you will take care to use proper approbation."

"I'm addressing those crucial to this operation, *sir*."

"Your commander in chief *is* crucial, General, and you would do well to remem—"

"I will remember that when this begins, you are hiding in the northwest, away from the action."

"Identify yourself, infidel!"

"Front lines, sir, which is more than I can say for the commander in chief."

"Dissension among the ranks!" Mac crowed. "What could be better?"

"We'd better move now, Excellency," another general weighed in. "We do ourselves no favors allowing the enemy to study us."

"They are unarmed!" Carpathia said. "This should be a walk in the park!"

"They were unarmed in Petra, *Commander*," the first general said. "Have you forgotten *their* commander in chief remains overhead? And have you questioned how they got everyone here so fast?"

"Attack!" Carpathia shouted.

And what was left of the southern third of the Unity Army slowly began moving upon Bozrah.

To Rayford it appeared the operation was a suicide mission. As soon as Global Community forces came within range of the remnant of Israel, the soldiers seemed to launch every last projectile in their arsenal. He could not imagine a more earsplitting fusillade, and yet the bullets and missiles and rockets and mortars fell harmlessly, even in the midst of the mass of people. Millions and millions of rounds continued to pour from barrels of all sizes as the army slowly continued to advance.

Yet despite the din, the words of the Lord could be heard clear and plain.

"Come near, you nations, to hear; and heed, you people! Let the earth hear, and all that is in it, the world and all things that come forth from it. For the indignation of the Lord is against all nations, and His fury against all their armies; He has utterly destroyed them, He has given them over to the slaughter."

Rayford watched through the binocs as men and women soldiers and horses seemed to explode where they stood. It was as if the very words of the Lord had superheated their blood, causing it to burst through their veins and skin.

"Also their slain shall be thrown out; their stench shall rise from their corpses, and the mountains shall be melted with their blood. All the host of heaven shall be dissolved, and the heavens shall be rolled up like a scroll; all their host shall fall down as the leaf falls from the vine, and as fruit falling from a fig tree."

Tens of thousands of foot soldiers

dropped their weapons, grabbed their heads or their chests, fell to their knees, and writhed as they were invisibly sliced asunder. Their innards and entrails gushed to the desert floor, and as those around them turned to run, they too were slain, their blood pooling and rising in the unforgiving brightness of the glory of Christ.

"For My sword shall be bathed in heaven; indeed it shall come down on Edom, and on the people of My curse, for judgment.

"The sword of the Lord is filled with blood. It is made overflowing with fatness. For the Lord has a sacrifice in Bozrah, and a great slaughter in the land of Edom.

"Their land shall be soaked with blood, and their dust saturated with fatness."

It was as if Antichrist's army had become the sacrificial beasts for the Lord's slaughter. Carpathia screamed, "Bring me a plane, a chopper, a jet — anything! Get me to the north! Now! Now!"

And Jesus said, "For today is the day of the Lord's vengeance, the year of recompense for the cause of Zion."

"Where's Carpathia's ride going to come from?" Rayford said.

"Ash Shawbak," Abdullah said.

"That's right, Smitty," Mac said. "That your hometown?"

"Hardly. Amman; you know that."

" 'Course I do. Wasn't Ash Shawbak where the dignitaries were, on their 'zecutive safari, sippin' cordials and s'posed to be watching Nicolae bring home the victory?"

"That is the place," Abdullah said. "I would love to see their faces now."

"Lookie there," Rayford said, nodding toward the sky to the southeast. A jet helicopter was screaming to the northwest, at the edge of the decimated army.

Rayford raised the binoculars again and studied the area. "There they are," he said. "That big old Humvee is just sitting there alone. Looks like Carpathia's not going to even risk getting out until he absolutely has to."

"His army's gone," Mac said. " 'Least this part of it. Not a shot bein' fired from anywhere."

It had grown deathly quiet. As Rayford watched, the chopper put down several yards from Carpathia's position. Only he and Leon disgorged from the vehicle. Leon held the hem of his robe at his waist and ran as fast as was possible for him. Nicolae seemed to catch his great scabbard on the way out of the Humvee, and it hung him up for a second before he angrily freed himself.

He dashed to the helicopter, overtaking Leon and elbowing him out of the way to be the first one on.

As soon as Leon was aboard, having been pulled in by assisting hands, the craft lifted off and headed north. Rayford panned left and right with the field glasses and saw no movement among the wreckage of the Unity Army. Bodies were strewn for miles and the desert floor was red with blood.

"Oh, look at this," Rayford said, scrambling to open his door and leap out. Mac and Abdullah followed and the three climbed atop the Hummer, watching as Jesus descended from the sky. His horse gracefully touched the ground in the plains to the west of Bozrah, and as the entire Jewish remnant watched from the mountain, Jesus dismounted. The army of heaven remained perhaps a hundred feet above Him, following as He strode through the battlefield, the hem of His robe turning red in the blood of the enemy.

The saints above Him began a responsive recitation, asking questions in unison that He answered for all on earth to hear. "Who," they began, "is this who comes from Edom, with dyed garments from Bozrah, this One who is glorious in His apparel, traveling in the greatness of His strength?"

And the Lord said, "It is I who speak in righteousness, mighty to save."

"Why is Your apparel red, and Your garments like one who treads in the winepress?"

"I have trodden the winepress alone, and from the peoples no one was with Me. For I have trodden them in My anger, and trampled them in My fury; their blood is sprinkled upon My garments, and I have stained all My robes.

"For the day of vengeance is in My heart, and the year of My redeemed has come.

"I looked, but there was no one to help, and I wondered that there was no one to uphold; therefore My own arm brought salvation for Me; and My own fury, it sustained Me.

"I have trodden down the peoples in My anger, made them drunk in My fury, and brought down their strength to the earth."

And the vast thousands on horseback above Him in the heavens praised Him in unison:

"We will mention the lovingkindnesses of the Lord and the praises of the Lord, according to all that the Lord has bestowed on us, and the great goodness toward the house of Israel, which He has bestowed on them according to His mercies, according to the multitude of His lovingkindnesses."

And Jesus said, "Surely they are My people, children who will not lie. And so I became their Savior."

With that He turned toward the multitude watching from Bozrah. "When you see Jerusalem surrounded by armies, then know that its desolation is near. Then let those who are in Judea flee to the mountains, let those who are in the midst of her depart, and let not those who are in the country enter her.

"For these are the days of vengeance, that all things which are written may be fulfilled. . . . Now look up and lift up your heads, because your redemption draws near."

"What do you think is happening right now, Brother Enoch?"

Enoch wasn't sure, but he had an idea. In Illinois, as he knew was true everywhere, regardless of the hour, the day was as bright as noon without so much as a shadow. The glory of the Lord was the light of the world. But Jesus was no longer visible in the sky.

"Will we see Him again? Or do we have to go there for that?"

"I believe we *will* see Him again," Enoch said. "Even today. He is probably fighting one of the battles that precede the fall of Jerusalem and His delivering of the Jews there. But the prophecies say that when He delivers Jerusalem and ascends the Mount of Olives, every eye shall see Him. Obviously, that includes us."

"But pretty soon, like after today, we're going to have to get ourselves over there, right?"

"I sure want to," Enoch said. "But it won't be cheap."

"Well, look at it this way: we got us a thousand years to raise the money."

"I don't want to wait that long."

"Me either. How about a car wash?"

"Head west of the Dead Sea and south of Jerusalem," Rayford told Abdullah. He settled into the backseat of the Hummer, letting Mac have the front. "Carpathia's not happy, Mac. You been listening?"

"Yeah," Mac said. "Guess he expected the northern two-thirds of his army to be ready. Sounds like they'd rather cut and run."

"He could lose a bunch of them and still have plenty. He's trying to get them organized to annihilate the Jews at Jerusalem."

"But Jesus won't let them get that far, will He?"

"Actually, He will," Rayford said. "At least a lot of them. But many soldiers are going to die between here and Mount Megiddo. If I read it right and Tsion and Chaim were correct, that's next."

As they traveled, they followed Jesus now riding horseback on the ground, His army above and behind Him, and the Jewish remnant running along en masse. Again, they covered more than seventy miles in an hour, and the whole way Jesus spoke to them as if to each individually.

"I am the King who comes in the name of the Lord," He said. "I am the Mediator of the new covenant. I am the one who bore your sins in My own body on the tree, that you, having died to sins, might live for righteousness — by whose stripes you were healed.

"I am the Bread of God who came down from heaven and gives life to the world. Therefore keep the feast, not with old leaven, nor with the leaven of malice and wickedness, but with the unleavened bread of sincerity and truth.

"I created all things in heaven and on earth, visible and invisible, whether thrones or dominions or principalities or powers. All things were created through Me and for Me. I have come to do the will of God. I came into the world to save sinners, not to be served, but to serve, and to give My life a ransom for many."

Rayford had been taught over the past seven years that the Word of God was quick and powerful and sharper than any two-edged sword. He had also learned that the Word would never return void. Now, as it was being burned into his heart and soul by his Redeemer, he felt filled to overflowing and ready to burst.

What a privilege to hear the Word *from* the Word! He and his friends rolled through the desolate land, hearing what everyone else in the world was hearing, and yet Rayford knew each was taking it as if for him or herself. He certainly was. And just about the time he forgot that truth, Jesus would refer to him by name.

"Rayford, for this cause I was born, and for this cause I came into the world, that I should bear witness to the truth. Everyone who is of the truth hears My voice. I can do nothing of Myself, but what I see the Father do; for whatever He does, I also do in like manner. I am the stone the builders rejected, yet I have become the chief cornerstone, having been built on the foundation of the apostles and prophets."

"Lord, I worship You," Rayford whispered, hearing Mac also praying. Abdullah drove along with tears pouring down his face.

Thirteen

Rayford had to smile. Here were the southern flanks of the remaining two-thirds of Antichrist's Global Community Unity Army all right, but they looked little more organized and ready to fight than did the corpses left in Edom. Perhaps that's why Carpathia was nowhere to be found, and from the transmissions they could hear, he was on his way farther north to the center of his fighting force in Megiddo.

Both Tsion Ben-Judah and Chaim Rosenzweig had been telling Rayford for years that of all the prophetic passages in Scripture, the final four battles between Jesus and the Armageddon armies were the most difficult to understand and put in sequence.

"Our best bet is to follow Jesus," Rayford said.

"There's a sermon if I ever heard one," Mac said.

"These battles are going to take place where they're going to take place, and the only thing I'm sure of is who wins."

"Well," Abdullah said, "I am sure of a little more than that."

Rayford saw Mac shoot Abdullah a double take. "Ya don't say, Smitty. Pray tell."

"I have been studying."

"Studyin' what?"

"Geography mostly. On my own."

"That can be dangerous."

"I have found it most informative."

"And I'd like to hear it, Abdullah," Rayford said.

Mac shook his head and settled back. "Oh, boy. Here we go."

"I had been most curious," Abdullah said, "why all of history pointed to Armageddon for the end. I mean, what is Armageddon? It is a place with many names and actually covers a lot of ground."

"You shoulda been a perfessor, Smitty," Mac said.

"Hush, Mac. Teach on, Abdullah."

"Well, you are both fliers, and you have many times seen the mountain ranges that run the length of Palestine."

"Sure, off the Mediterranean coast."

"You know the break where the mountains all of a sudden drop to altitudes of about three hundred feet or less?"

"Up there where the highlands split off from the northern hills of Galilee?"

"Exactly. That is the Jezreel Valley."

"I always thought that was the Plain of Esdraelon," Mac said, "or however you say it."

"Very good, Mac," Abdullah said. "Gold star for you. *Jezreel* is the Hebrew word for it. *Esdraelon* is the Greek."

"Well, I'll be. You have been studyin'."

"There's more. Some people call it the Plain of Megiddo, because of the city immediately to the west of it. And that's where we get the word *Armageddon*."

"Where?" Mac said. "You lost me, teach."

"*Armageddon* comes from the Hebrew *Har Megiddo,* which means Mount Megiddo."

"You have been doin' your homework, boy."

"Experts say Megiddo has been the site of more wars than any other single place in the world because it is so strategically located. Thirteen battles by the end of the first century alone. Some say Megiddo has been built twenty-five times and destroyed twenty-five times."

"Isn't Jesus' hometown up there somewhere? Nazareth?"

"On the northern side of the valley," Abdullah said. "Imagine how it will feel for Him to fight an entire army that close to home."

Indicative of the uncertainty of the Unity Army forces, their Hummer was virtually ignored. The army seemed to have its eyes trained on Jesus, just like everyone else, warily watching Him with His saints behind Him. The way news traveled on battlefields, no doubt these troops were also aware of the slaughters in Edom.

Rayford advised Abdullah to steer clear of the army. Though he remained confident that they were invulnerable now, nothing would be gained by drawing fire.

"I'm probably gonna regret askin' this, Smitty," Mac said, "but what'd you learn about Megiddo and all that, besides the names? I mean, what *is* so strategic about it?"

Rayford was amused at how Abdullah warmed to the topic. Mac had to be even more surprised than Ray. It wasn't often that Abdullah was in a position to teach his elders. But he seemed to have this down well.

"It is the perfect stage of history," Abdullah said. "Mount Megiddo is really not much more than a hill. For centuries it was the place from which the strategic pass was guarded — the international highway that went from the east all the way down to Egypt.

"Over the last several months, the enemy armies have been amassing into one, as you know. The ones that came from the west, from the revived Roman Empire, landed at Haifa and went directly up to the Valley of Megiddo.

"The armies from the east came through the dried-up Euphrates and straight down to the same place. It is the perfect staging ground. The armies from the north swept past Mount Hermon and down into the land of Israel, ending up in the Jezreel Valley at Mount Megiddo."

"Makes sense," Mac said. "Boy, you missed your callin'."

Chaim could not keep from grinning. Tsion Ben-Judah, first his protégé and eventually his mentor, once told him that prophecy was history written in advance. Here he was, in his seventies, living out that history.

No manna had fallen since Jesus appeared

in the clouds. While Chaim knew that eventually he and all the other mortals would have to eat, he was certain no one felt any more twinge of hunger than he did. The Bread of Life was here.

It was as if fifty years had melted away. Chaim knew he looked the same, but he did not feel fatigue, aches, or pains. He had no serious maladies that had to be healed, but if Rayford was made whole despite his wounds and the infirmary had been closed in an instant, it only made sense that Chaim himself had been delivered from the ravages of age.

He was impressed enough that he had been able to get out of Petra and on the way to Bozrah under his own steam. But when he had begun hurrying, then running, then virtually flying over the terrain, Chaim knew this was no longer of himself. He had neither grown weary nor suffered from joint pain. If he had not had his full attention on his Savior, he might have been tempted to try his favorite childhood game: soccer. *Imagine,* he thought, *an old man cavorting with children.*

As the remnant from Petra followed the Lord and His army north toward Jerusalem, Chaim felt himself swelling with appropriate pride and gratitude. Though there had been hundreds of thousands under his authority and care over the past three and a half years, many whom he had never even met let alone gotten to know, he felt a love and responsibility for each. God had been faithful, feeding them, providing water for them, protecting them.

Now, what was next? Would they be expected to go with Jesus to the battle at Armageddon, or would they be directed to Jerusalem? Word from the Holy City was that the Unity Army was merely toying with what was left of the resistance, and that whenever it wanted to and was ready, it could storm the Old City and complete the fall of Jerusalem.

That, Chaim knew, was prophesied and would happen, even with Jesus on the scene. But He would quickly avenge the loss and reverse it, and many more remnant Jews would come into the kingdom.

Most thrilling for Chaim was any time Jesus spoke. How He addressed the entire globe and yet made it so personal was a mystery. But somehow it satisfied that soul hunger Chaim felt for a personal audience with his Lord. Even knowing that everyone else was hearing the same thing, to Chaim it was as if Jesus were — every time — saying, "Chaim, come here. Let Me tell you something." And, of course, Chaim heard Him in Hebrew.

It was one thing to have flown over the Unity Army and seen it en masse. It was another to ride along on the outskirts of it, seemingly never to come to the end. Rayford had to be impressed by the sheer accomplishment of outfitting such a fighting force. Millions of uniforms, weapons, munitions, vehicles, and various and sundry pieces of equipment made the whole operation appear perfectly supplied for its task. In human terms, they could not lose. They could have overwhelmed any mortal enemy on the planet.

But they faced one Man, the Son of the living God. And they were defeated before they began.

The remnant on the ground that accompanied Jesus and the heavenly hosts began to sing praises as they ran. But they quickly quieted when Jesus responded.

"For the suffering of death, I was crowned with glory and honor, that I, by the grace of God, might taste death for everyone. I was the Deliverer who came out of Zion, and I turned away the ungodliness from Jacob. I was the seed of David, raised from the dead, the Mediator of the new covenant. I suffered once for sins, the just for the unjust, that I might bring you to God, being put to death in the flesh but made alive by the Spirit."

Amazingly, there was not even a battle transpiring at the moment, yet thousands of Unity Army soldiers were slain simply by the Lord's words as He passed by. They were not fighting, not threatening, not advancing or even moving. But they had long since made their decision. They had pledged their loyalty to the god of this world, had willingly taken the mark of Antichrist and bowed the knee to him. For them there was no recourse.

Rayford thrilled to the powerful words of the Master and was horrified by the carnage that resulted from them. His heart was full and yet he found it difficult to tear his eyes away from the bloodshed on the ground. Oh, what this portended for the army as a whole when the actual fighting ensued! How any of the surviving men and women could see their companions die such horrible deaths — simply from the words pronounced from the sky — and still be willing to stay in the fray was beyond Rayford.

"My enemies have become My footstool," Jesus said. "Not with the blood of goats and calves, but with My own blood I entered the Most Holy Place once for all, having obtained eternal redemption. I am the Son of God who has come to give you an understanding, that you may know God who is true.

"I am the living bread which came down from heaven. If anyone eats of this bread, he will live forever; and the bread that I gave is My flesh, which I gave for the life of the world. I am the Word who became flesh and dwelt among you, and you beheld My glory, the glory as of the only begotten of the Father, full of grace and truth. For in Me dwells all the fullness of the Godhead bodily.

"Rayford, take My yoke upon you and learn from Me, for I am gentle and lowly in heart, and you will find rest for your soul. For My yoke is easy and My burden is light."

Every time Jesus spoke his name, Rayford was touched anew. He glanced quickly at his friends and saw that the Lord had communicated to them in the same way. Mac buried his face in his hands, whispering, "Thank You, Jesus." Abdullah looked as if he wished he could pull over and simply worship God.

Sebastian, who was running with Kenny's hand in his, felt a tug. He bent to listen and

Kenny said, "Jesus's talkin' to me!"

"I know!" Sebastian said. "Isn't it wonderful?"

"We need us a proper church, Brother Enoch."

"Great idea," Enoch said. "Who could stop us now?"

"Is it possible all we have to do is find out what's for sale or rent and go get it?"

"Why not?"

"Can we put a cross on it and call it what it is?"

"If Jesus keeps talking to all of us by name, I don't see why not. Anybody who tried to come against that would be due the same treatment His enemies are getting all over the world."

"Let's do it. Churches are going to be springing up all over the place."

Over the next two hours of driving, the scene changed noticeably. The farther north Rayford and Mac and Abdullah traveled, the more obvious it was that the Unity Army had dug in and was prepared for the battle of the ages.

They had to know what their counterparts had suffered, but either Carpathia's broadcasts of encouragement and bravado had succeeded in making them full of themselves, or they were emboldened with the knowledge that they were twice the fighting force their defeated comrades had been. Even with a third of the entire army reduced to nothing, the remainder represented the greatest military power ever assembled.

Maybe they didn't fully know or understand what had gone on. They could see Jesus and His army, and in the core of their being they had to be unnerved that an enemy on horseback and seemingly unarmed — albeit with the ability to defy gravity and move at incredible speed — could compete at all with a foe such as they.

But Rayford saw organization, might, determination. This was going to be anything but a surrender. And yet nothing in Scripture indicated the result would be any different than what they had seen in Edom.

Chang was intrigued that the path they took from the land of Edom to Megiddo bypassed Jerusalem far to the west. It was as if the Lord knew that the remnant would be most curious about their own hometown. Maybe He wanted them to see what happened at Megiddo.

It was strange, Chang told Naomi, to hear Jesus from the sky and hear Antichrist in his earpiece. At times he simply had to remove it. When Jesus called him by name in Chinese it sent chills through him. When that happened to Naomi, he watched as her eyes grew wide with wonder, and she was speechless for several minutes. Maybe the day would come when they could talk about how intimate that felt, but they avoided the subject for now. To Chang it was just too personal, and he assumed it was the same for her.

Bizarre too was the shadowless light that would apparently exist as long as Jesus was in their midst. Chang found himself trying to make shadows with his hands. An omnipresent light source was something science had never approached. Men who loved darkness rather than light were not going to like the millennial kingdom. The piercing glare of the purity of Christ would make easy His ruling the nations with an iron rod. For believers who loved Him and who loved the truth, His rule would be a marvelous change from the last seven years and, indeed, the millennia before that. But for people interested only in their own gain, still thumbing their noses at God, Jesus' rule would be most uncomfortable.

It was fun for Chang to be able to converse with Naomi, even when they were run-

311

ning at superhuman speeds. They didn't have to shout, weren't panting, and when Jesus was not speaking, they were. Mostly they talked about what it would be like to marry and raise children in such an age. Who would perform the ceremony, and would Jesus Himself attend?

Chang always loved when Jesus began to speak again. The entire remnant fell silent, listening, worshiping their Savior.

"I am He whom God exalted to His right hand to be Prince and Savior, to give repentance to Israel and forgiveness of sins.

"I give you eternal life, Chang, and you shall never perish; neither shall anyone snatch you out of My hand. My Father, who has given you to Me, is greater than all; and no one is able to snatch you out of My Father's hand. I and My Father are one."

"Thank You, Lord," Chang said.

But He was not finished.

"My peace I give to you; not as the world gives do I give to you. Let not your heart be troubled, neither let it be afraid."

Chang could not imagine ever being afraid again.

Mac wanted to be let off to make his way to Jerusalem on foot.

"Are you sure?" Rayford said.

"Unless you order me not to."

"I don't see it. What's the point?"

"I want to know firsthand what's happening there. I'll stay in touch by radio and phone. And the way I understand it, I won't miss a thing the Lord says."

"You know what's going to happen, Mac. Jerusalem falls, but then Jesus saves the day."

"And why wouldn't I want a front-row seat for that?"

"We'll get back in time to see it."

"And by the time you get here, I will have kept you up to date on the details."

"Suit yourself."

"Thanks." And Mac was out of the Hummer heading toward Jerusalem.

"What might the Unity Army do to him if they catch him?" Abdullah said.

Rayford shook his head. "I'd like to think they have no power over him."

"But we don't know for sure."

"No, we don't. He knows how to take care of himself."

"He is unarmed, Captain."

"In a manner of speaking."

When Rayford and Abdullah finally arrived at the edge of the Valley of Megiddo, it appeared the Lord and His hosts had left the remnant of Israel about halfway between

313

there and Jerusalem. Rayford could only assume that Jesus wanted the remnant with Him for the Jerusalem conquest and what followed but for some reason did not wish them to witness what was to take place here.

Mac reported that a mammoth contingent of the Unity Army surrounded all of Jerusalem and simply seemed to be waiting for orders. "There's a lot of unrest among the army here," he said. "Grumbling. Hunger. Rumors of no pay and no reinforcements. A lot of gossip about what happened in the south."

"Interesting," Rayford said. "There is no division between the forces there and here. The immense army is virtually contiguous from west of the Dead Sea to the Valley of Megiddo, so it's possible some of the ones you see will be put to work here, and vice versa."

"That's a huge stretch, Ray. You sayin' this army's as big as it's been since the beginning?"

"Except for the casualties earlier in Edom."

Mac whistled. "How's my man Smitty doin'?"

"Happy as a clam. Loves to hear the voice of Jesus."

"Don't we all? Tell him Mac says hey."

★ ★ ★

George Sebastian mingled with the Tribulation Force contingent at the resting place north of Jerusalem. He couldn't help but recall how far he had come since the escapade in Greece where he almost lost his life and had to kill to stay alive. "Otherwise," he told Priscilla, "I'd be waving at you from beyond the skies."

"We sure didn't know what we were getting into, did we?" she said.

"Not by a long shot."

"Our days of soldiering are over, aren't they?" Razor said.

Sebastian sighed. "I hope so."

"You tired?" Razor said.

"Actually, no. I should be. Up all day and night, and now, with this light, I have no idea what time it's supposed to be. And all this traveling? The running? I ought to feel like I could sleep for a month, but I've got nothing but energy. Wish I could see what's going to happen up north."

"Me too," Razor said. "I can still see Jesus and hear Him. I don't understand why He doesn't sound farther away than He does. He sounds the same to me."

Priscilla said, "I think it's because we're hearing Him in our hearts instead of with our ears."

Razor shrugged. "Could be. Otherwise, how would everybody hear their own name?"

Everyone fell silent as the Lord spoke yet again.

"No one has seen God at any time. I, the only begotten Son, who came from the bosom of the Father, have declared Him. I am called the Son of the Highest, and today the Lord God will give Me the throne of My father David."

Suddenly another voice cascaded from heaven, and Sebastian knew immediately it was God Himself. "Behold!" He said. "My Servant whom I have chosen, My Beloved in whom My soul is well pleased! I have put My Spirit upon Him, and He will declare justice."

Then Jesus again: "The law was given through Moses, but grace and truth come through Me. Now, George, may the God of peace who brought Me up from the dead and made Me the great Shepherd of the sheep, through the blood of the everlasting covenant, make you complete in every good work to do His will, working in you what is well pleasing in His sight. Amen."

On the amen the whole of the remnant fell to its knees, praying and thanking God. Sebastian knew each had again heard his own name in the benediction Jesus had pronounced, yet that made it no less personal.

Rayford climbed atop the Hummer again, Abdullah right behind. They looked out on the vast enemy horde as thousands burst open at the words of Jesus and died before they hit the ground. And the battle at Armageddon had not yet commenced. Rayford heard Nicolae Carpathia trying to encourage and rally the troops.

He barked instructions to the generals and commanders. "This is our true enemy," he said. "Best Him, and victory is ours. Jerusalem will be no obstacle."

How he managed to get so many millions of troops on the same page and pointed in the same direction was beyond Rayford, but somehow Nicolae had pulled it off. Somehow he had orchestrated a half-moon of an army covering hundreds of square miles, all facing Jesus in the sky.

Was he going to have them fire upon the King of kings? How would he determine how far away Jesus was? And if Carpathia's armies had been harmless against mere mortals, what did he expect to accomplish here?

Before a command could be given or a shot fired, Jesus spoke. And while it took only a matter of several minutes, the devastation was enormous.

"Test the spirits, whether they are of God," He said, "because many false prophets have gone out into the world. By this you know the Spirit of God: Every spirit that confesses that I came in the flesh is of God, and every spirit that does not confess that I came in the flesh is not of God. And this is the spirit of the Antichrist."

Rayford heard Carpathia raging, cursing.

And Jesus said, "A mighty king arose who ruled with great dominion, and did according to his will. But his kingdom shall be broken up and divided toward the four winds of heaven, but not among his posterity nor according to his dominion with which he ruled; for his kingdom shall be uprooted.

"Now is the appointed time. The king of this world did according to his own will: he exalted and magnified himself above every god, spoke blasphemies against the God of gods, and prospered until now. But what has been determined shall be done."

The great army was in pandemonium, tens of thousands at a time screaming in terror and pain and dying in the open air. Their blood poured from them in great waves, combining to make a river that quickly became a swamp.

"He regarded neither the true God nor any god," Jesus continued as the soldiers fell and the blood rose, "for he exalted himself above them all. But in their place he honored a god of fortresses; and a god which his fathers did not know he shall honor with gold and silver, with precious stones, and pleasant things. Thus he acted against the strongest fortresses and divided the land for gain.

"Though in the end the king of the South attacked him, and the king of the North came against him like a whirlwind, with chariots, horsemen, and with many ships; he entered the countries, overwhelmed them, and passed through.

"And now he has also entered the Glorious Land, and many countries were overthrown; but these shall escape from his hand: Edom, Moab, and the prominent people of Ammon."

Rayford looked to Abdullah. "Did your geography study tell you where those were? I mean, I know Edom is where Petra is."

"Moab is to the north of there, in Jordan, and Ammon is north of that."

Jesus continued: "He stretched out his hand against the countries, and the land of Egypt did not escape. He had power over the treasures of gold and silver, and over all the precious things of Egypt; also the Libyans and Ethiopians followed at his heels.

"But news from the east and the north troubled him; therefore he went out with great fury to destroy and annihilate many. And he planted the tents of his palace between the seas and the glorious holy mountain . . ."

"He means Jerusalem," Abdullah said.

". . . yet he shall come to his end, and no one will help him."

It seemed to Rayford that the entire Unity Army within his field of vision was dead or dying, and the blood continued to rise. Millions of birds flocked into the area and feasted on the remains.

Carpathia screeched in a frenzy, "I have *not* met my end. I shall take His beloved city and bring it and Him to ruin! Leon, get me out of here!"

Fourteen

"Smitty," Rayford said, "let's follow Carpathia and Fortunato."

"Are you serious, Captain Steele?"

"They won't even notice."

"Something I do not understand, Captain. Why does Jesus not just capture them? He kills almost the entire army with the words from His mouth, and yet He allows them to run free. I know He is not going to kill them, but it seems He is playing a game with them."

"I'm no theologian," Rayford said, "but as you know, God has His own timetable. All this has been prophesied, scripted. It's going to happen when it's supposed to happen."

As Abdullah steered the Hummer toward the valley and Carpathia's bigger Humvee, for the first time since the appearance of Jesus, the sky began to turn. Dark, menacing clouds formed on the horizon and quickly rose, filling the heavens except where the Lord and His army hovered.

"You feel that?" Mac radioed. "Temperature musta dropped ten degrees in the last minute!"

"Something's brewing," Rayford said.

"Now *you're* understatin' the obvious. I'm heading for cover, Ray."

"Keep in touch."

"Don't worry."

Rayford and Abdullah rolled up their windows. "Do you not want me to lose Leon?" Abdullah said, nodding far across the killing grounds to where the Humvee was picking up speed, apparently trying to find a path through the massacre toward Jerusalem.

"Just try to keep an eye on him," Rayford said. "He's going to have a rough time heading that way. Hey, hit the heat."

Abdullah stopped just the other side of a ravine that separated the high country from the valley where thousands of bodies lay. Although they were dead and their blood had ceased flowing, it seemed to ooze from their bodies and quickly filled the lower areas.

Frost appeared on the windshield. "That's the first time I've seen that in this part of the world," Abdullah said. "In America, yes, but not here." He turned on the wipers, but they merely spread the ice crystals and blocked the view.

Rayford played with the controls until he got the heater and defogger blasting, quickly clearing the window. But even with the heater on full, he was chilled. And the sky turned darker. Strangely, there were still no shadows on the ground. The light of Christ continued to permeate, except for the blackness of the sky that ringed Him and His mounted followers.

Suddenly a voice came from the sky, loud and authoritative, but it was not Jesus'. "It is done!"

Lightning burst from the clouds and explosions of thunder followed. And then came hail — if you could call it that. These were not mere ice chips — not even golf-ball or softball size. The first chunk Rayford saw looked the size of a dining-room table, half a foot thick. It landed about twenty feet below the Hummer and embedded itself a couple of feet into the ground. The concussion sounded like a bomb.

The few remaining Unity Army soldiers behaved like madmen, tearing their hair, some shooting themselves, others begging comrades to shoot them. Another chunk of ice hit a grenade launcher and flattened it. Soon hundred-pound blocks of ice began pelting the entire area, smashing bodies, destroying trucks and cars and Jeeps.

The royal Humvee, with Leon driving erratically, narrowly escaped three chunks, one of which caught a running aide squarely atop the head and crushed him to the ground. The gigantic hailstones were soon dropping steadily, and there was no escape. It was as if God were burying the bloody battlefield in a thick layer of ice.

"You getting this hail in Jerusalem?" Rayford radioed Mac.

"Nope. No hail. Looks like it's threatening rain or snow, but so far we're just freezin' our tails off."

Survivors remained only in scattered spots, but instead of trying to find cover or protecting their heads or even falling to their knees and begging for mercy, they lifted their faces to the sky, shouting, apparently railing against God, flashing obscene gestures at Jesus and His army. Soon they were crushed under the monstrous hailstones.

The temperature returned to normal as quickly as it had dropped, and the clouds rolled away and disappeared. The whole of creation seemed bright as day again, and while the sun still had not been seen since before Jesus came, the desert was soon toasty again. Rayford turned off the heat and opened the windows, and he and Abdullah lit out after Leon and Nicolae.

The ice quickly began to melt, and the water mixed with the torrent of blood. "Stop here," Rayford said, as they watched the blood-and-water mixture rise higher than the tires on the potentate's Humvee. The vehicle was soon bogged down in a reddish brown mud. Rayford heard Carpathia shrieking at Leon to get them out of the mess and on toward Jerusalem. But they quickly found all avenues of escape blocked by the rising muck. When it reached the middle of the door of their vehicle, Carpathia ordered Leon out to push while he climbed into the driver's seat.

"But, Excellency, I will drown!"

"You will do no such thing. Do you want your king to get out?"

"No, my lord, of course not. But I-I, ah —"

Leon pushed open the door and the liquid invaded the vehicle. "Hurry, man!" Nicolae shouted. "Shut the door!"

Leon stepped gingerly into the drink, which reached his waist and made his robe balloon out. He had wisely left his fez in the Humvee. "It's freezing!" he squealed. "My legs are going numb!"

"Of course it is freezing! It has ice in it! Now start pushing!"

"It stinks!"

"Push!"

It took Leon a moment to make his way behind the vehicle, and the footing beneath the surface was clearly uneven. Once he nearly plunged all the way under and had to grab the fender to stay upright. His robe was a mess, his hands and face pale, his hair mussed. Rayford could see he was shivering to his core.

When he got behind the Humvee, Carpathia apparently floored the accelerator, for all he accomplished was to kick up a rooster tail of liquid and steam that covered Leon. The Humvee didn't move.

"Try to rock it!" Leon shouted.

"That is what you are there for! Grab under the bumper and lift!"

"Lift a Humvee!?"

"Rock it!"

Finally they coordinated Leon's lifting and pushing and Carpathia's alternated gunning the engine and letting up, and the big thing began to sway. When it finally started to move, Leon lost his balance and pitched forward, going completely under. He came up sputtering and trying to wipe his face.

Nicolae pulled the Humvee to slightly higher ground and Leon rushed to get in the passenger side. But when he opened the door, Carpathia was already there.

"I am *not* driving, Leon! How would that look?"

Leon trudged around in front of the car and yanked open the door. Just before climbing in he pulled his sodden robe over his head and left it in the rising river of blood. He clambered aboard in his underwear, assuring Nicolae that he had other clothes in the back.

"Well, put them on immediately!"

The Humvee rocked and bounced as Leon found dry clothes and dressed in the car. Apparently deciding his ornate cap would not work with the new outfit, he tossed it out the window as he slowly pulled away, looking for yet higher ground. The blood had already risen more than four feet.

When the skies cleared and the temperature rose, Mac rubbed his bare arms and emerged from what had been meager cover under sparse trees not far from the Temple Mount. Though not in the uniform of the Unity Army, he must not have looked like a rebel either, as he was virtually ignored. Many of the normal nonfighting citizenry were milling about among the thousands of soldiers, who spent much of their time sitting around. Some platoons were moved here and there, seemingly on the whim of a general or a commander, but all fighting had ceased. The Global Community forces had occupied all of Jerusalem except the Temple Mount, and they had that surrounded. Occasionally a general with a bullhorn tried to persuade the tiny band of rebels inside to surrender and avoid inevitable bloodshed.

Mac was amused that the general assumed the rebels had no access to outside information. But having talked with them, he knew they had radios and even some televisions. They would know what had happened at Petra and Bozrah, and soon they would probably even know the outcome of the battle at Armageddon.

It seemed weird to Mac that soldiers could sit around smoking and playing cards, only occasionally glancing into the sky to see what Jesus was up to. Maybe this was all part of the hardening of hearts, but Mac thought that he, in the same situation, would recognize that his end was near. Theirs was clearly a supernatural foe who had not even been slowed by the most powerful army in history. The war was as good as over.

And yet Nicolae Carpathia, the great deceiver, despite winning not even a skirmish since the appearing of Christ, had somehow convinced his troops that Jerusalem was the key. If they could take the Holy City, he would be returned to his rightful throne, the Son of God would be defeated, and all would again be right with the world.

The only thing that argument had going for it was the current situation in Jerusalem. The idea of the rebels holding anything when they were surrounded and outnumbered a thousand to one was laughable and pathetic. Except, as Mac knew, they were on the right side.

Rayford had assumed he was way past being shocked by now. What could he see that would be more surreal than the last several hours? Yet as Abdullah kept a careful but watchful distance from Carpathia's Humvee, all Rayford could do was stare at the result of the last so-called battle. Of course, there had not been a battle at all. The Unity Army had rattled its sabers, loaded its weapons, and made a lot of noise. And Jesus had killed them all, with mere words.

Of course those words were the words of God, and the effect was overpowering. Mile after mile after mile, Abdullah drove next to a river of blood several miles wide and now some five feet deep. Carpathia's whole-world fighting force of several million troops had been reduced to perhaps a million. That was still huge, of course, and from a human standpoint the rebels could never match it. But the devastation to the Unity Army in a short period should have made plain to Carpathia that his days were numbered.

Rather, to hear him talking earnestly to Leon in the car and to the remaining troops by radio, what had happened served as mere motivation. "Our goal remains," Carpathia said, "and our task is clear. Take the Father's city, wipe out His chosen people, and kill His Son. This has been our design from the beginning. We have drawn Him out, and we will soon have Him where we want Him. Remain loyal, remain true, remain vigilant, and you will be rewarded."

Jesus, meanwhile, had turned to the remnant and addressed them directly as Rayford and Abdullah listened.

"You are of God, little children, and have overcome Antichrist, because He who is in you is greater than he who is in the world. He is of the world. Therefore he speaks as of the world, and the world hears him. You are of God. He who knows God hears Me;

he who is not of God does not hear Me. By this you know the spirit of truth and the spirit of error.

"Beloved, love one another, for love is of God; and everyone who loves is born of God and knows God. He who does not love does not know God, for God is love. In this the love of God was manifested toward you, that God has sent His only begotten Son into the world, that you might live through Him. In this is love, not that you loved God, but that He loved you and sent Me to be the propitiation for your sins.

"Rayford, if God so loved you, you also ought to love one another."

Rayford was always pierced when he heard his name, as he knew Abdullah and all the others had to be. Then Jesus moved from the personal exhortation to clearly explain what had just happened.

"And they gathered them together to the place called in Hebrew, Armageddon.

"Then the seventh angel poured out his bowl into the air, and a loud voice came out of the temple of heaven, from the throne, saying, 'It is done!' And there were noises and thunderings and lightnings. And great hail from heaven fell upon men, each hailstone about the weight of a talent. Men blasphemed God because of the plague of the hail, since that plague was exceedingly great.

"An angel came out of the temple of heaven, crying to Me with a loud voice, 'Thrust in Your sickle and reap, for the time has come for You to reap, for the harvest of the earth is ripe.' So I thrust in My sickle on the earth, and the earth was reaped.

"Then another angel came out of the temple which is in heaven, he also having a sharp sickle. And another angel came out from the altar, who had power over fire, and he cried with a loud cry to him who had the sharp sickle, saying, 'Thrust in your sharp sickle and gather the clusters of the vine of the earth, for her grapes are fully ripe.'

"So the angel thrust his sickle into the earth and gathered the vine of the earth, and threw it into the great winepress of the wrath of God. And the winepress was trampled outside the city, and blood came out of the winepress, up to the horses' bridles, for one thousand six hundred furlongs."

The remnant, full of the glory of God, had been turned and was pointed toward Jerusalem. Chaim believed the Lord would protect them, but strangely, Jesus now moved on ahead with His army. And while the children of Israel seemed to be moving supernaturally fast again, they fell far behind Him and soon lost sight of Him.

Chaim noticed others looking at each other with concern, and he wanted to reassure them. But his place as leader and spokesman had been taken, and he felt no prompting to try to reassert himself. His job was done, and he felt he was just part of the remnant now. They would go where God pointed them and trust the Lord to be their rear guard.

Mac was surprised to discover that the radio waves — and he assumed television as well — were still controlled by the Global Community. That, he knew, would not last long. As he made his way throughout Jerusalem, trying to give Rayford and Abdullah a picture of what they'd find when they arrived, he listened to GC reporters and anchors putting Nicolae Carpathia's spin on everything.

There was no mention, of course, of what could have at least been described as an apparition in the sky — some trick by the enemy to scare everyone. Talk about the proverbial elephant in the room. Mac was certain everyone on earth knew who rode on the clouds. The question was what Jesus was going to do and when He was going to do it.

Jerusalem was replete with makeshift jails and prisons and holding tanks where the captured rebels were starved and tortured. GC personnel reported on these with apparent glee as evidence that victory was at hand. One commentator said that the rebels who thought they were holding the Temple Mount area were themselves in only a larger prison of their own making, for they were helpless to stand against the Unity Army, and there was nowhere they could flee.

It was apparent to Mac that word was beginning to spread throughout the city that the potentate was on his way. The place became a center of activity. Card games ended. Sitting around became a thing of the past. Platoons were coming to attention, areas policed, and the path to the front lines cleared. Every few minutes the news carried a fresh, live quote, right from the commander in chief's own vehicle.

"As we approach what many have referred to as the Eternal City," Carpathia said, "I am pleased to announce that following our victory here, this shall become the new Global Community headquarters. My palace shall be rebuilt on the site of the ruins of the temple, the destruction of which is on our agenda.

"As beautiful as New Babylon was, in

truth it has been my objective all along to one day relocate the seat of government, commerce, and religion to this city, which has meant so much to so many for so long. So, loyal citizens of the New World Order, I trust you will watch with great satisfaction as we complete our takeover of this place, as we root out and destroy the last pocket of resistance, and as we render impotent the One whom the enemy reveres as the reason they have never been able to join our noble cause.

"This One who flits about in the air quoting ancient fairy-tale texts and forcing sycophants to mindlessly run along worshiping Him will soon meet His end. He is no match for the risen lord of this world and for the fighting force in place to face Him. It does not even trouble me to make public our plan, as it has already succeeded. This city and these despicable people have long been His chosen ones, so we have forced Him to show Himself, to declare Himself, to vainly try to defend them or be shown for the fraud and coward that He is. Either He attempts to come to their rescue or they will see Him for who He really is and reject Him as an impostor. Or He will foolishly come against my immovable force and me and prove once and for all who is the better man.

"While I do not expect this to be an extended campaign, as this is the last battle I ever hope to wage, I am bringing in the whole of our resources. Every man and woman under my command and every armament and munition at our disposal shall be employed to make this the most resounding and convincing military victory in history.

"My pledge to you, loyal citizens of the Global Community, is that come the end of this battle, no opponent of my leadership and regime will remain standing, yea, not one will be left alive. The only living beings on planet Earth will be trustworthy citizens, lovers of peace and harmony and tranquility, which I offer with love for all from the depths of my being.

"I am but ten miles west of Jerusalem as we speak, and I will be dismissing my cabinet and generals so they may be about the business of waging this conflict under my command. The Most High Reverend of Carpathianism, Leon Fortunato himself, will serve as my chauffeur for my triumphal entry. Citizens are already lining the roadway to greet me, and I thank you for your support."

Mac hurried into position where he could get a look at the Humvee and the motorcade of military vehicles following it. He stood on a rise on the west side, where he could see the parading army that extended to the horizon. As the procession neared the city, he could hear drums and trumpets, and if he was not mistaken, even from that distance, the royal Humvee looked a mess. Rayford had told him it had been sloshing through the blood in the Valley of Megiddo, but apparently no one had reminded the potentate to get it cleaned.

When it came into view, Mac's suspicions were confirmed. It was ringed with mud and blood to the windows. But sure enough, civilians lined the roadway on either side, cheering, waving, clapping, saluting, and throwing flowers. Carpathia opened the moonroof, stood on the front seat, and appeared in the open air, waving with both hands and blowing kisses.

Enjoy it while it lasts, pal.

"Mac, do you see us?" Rayford radioed over the secure frequency.

"No. Where are you?"

"Third row, behind the Humvee."

"Nobody cares?"

"It's as if they don't even see us."

"What's the plan?"

"As the Humvee reaches Jaffa Road, it

will head for the Jaffa Gate, along with a third of the fighting force. The other two-thirds will split off north and south, surrounding the Old City. Once everyone is in place, Carpathia will lead the charge through the occupied Armenian and Jewish Quarters to the Temple Mount. They plan to batter through the Western Wall and overtake the rebels."

"Plan to."

"Exactly."

Mac finally spotted Rayford and Abdullah's Hummer and was struck by how much it looked like it belonged in the procession. As the cavalcade approached Jaffa Road, Mac began jogging that way, hoping to catch up with his friends when they peeled away from the group.

The cheering crowds grew larger as the cars neared the Old City, and as they slowed, the marching band caught up, its music blaring and drums pounding. Mac was reminded of Memorial Day parades as a child when his father had hoisted him on his shoulders and he had thrilled to the *rat-a-tat-tat* of the snares and the thumping undercurrent of the big bass drums. Back then, of course, he never heard "Hail Carpathia."

The music had stirred the crowd to a fever pitch, and the army that followed was clearly something unlike any of them, loyalists or rebels, had ever seen. There would not be room in the Old City for a fraction of the force. Mac wondered how even Carpathia and the rest of the rolling stock were going to navigate the narrow cobblestone streets.

"I've been wondering the same thing, Mac," Rayford said. "This is some festival, eh?"

"Ridiculous!"

"Frankly, I love it," Rayford said. "The more and the louder the better."

"I don't follow."

"The more pomp and circumstance, the greater the humiliation later."

"Well, that's for sure."

"You find us yet, Mac?"

"I'm headin' your way. When you gonna split off?"

"We're not."

"You're *not?* What? You're gonna go paradin' into the Old City with Carpathia?"

"Why not? See if you can get in."

"Unlikely."

"Try."

* * *

Mac caught up to the parade and had to wonder what all the extra troops were for. The same contingent of soldiers that had been there when he had discovered Buck was more than enough to get the job done from a human standpoint. If they couldn't do it, the rest wouldn't help.

Fortunato steered the wide Humvee through Jaffa Gate, and almost immediately the folly of their plan became clear. There simply wasn't room for the rolling stock to proceed to the Western Wall of the Temple Mount. In his earpiece Mac heard Nicolae trying to enlist engineers to bring in heavy equipment and knock down buildings and walls en route. When told that would take hours, he exploded, swearing and demanding to know who told him his parade through the Old City had been a capital idea.

"Leave the cars where they are!" he announced. "I shall lead the rest of the attack on horseback."

Mac was close enough now to see Carpathia sneak a peek at the sky. Jesus was not there at the moment, and neither was His heavenly army. Mac thought this unnerved Carpathia more than if He'd been there.

Aides immediately attended to Carpathia when he emerged from the Humvee. He straightened his leathers, which seemed no worse for wear since he had not left the vehicle during the debacle at Armageddon. Nicolae also repositioned his garish sword.

But when Fortunato got out, he was wearing plain civilian clothes that made him appear to be on his way to a workday for a local community service club. "Get the reverend a proper uniform and something to clean his face and hair," Carpathia ordered.

Someone ran off, returning presently. "Biggest we have," the man said, handing the folded clothes and a wet towel to Fortunato, who gave him a look that would lift roadkill off asphalt. "Sorry," the man whispered. "Biggest we have."

"You can change in the cathedral," someone else told Leon, and he hurried off with a couple of aides. Meanwhile, more generals and hangers-on and toadies surrounded Carpathia, who asked that they make room for the photographers and TV camera crews.

When Leon returned in the too-short, too-tight Unity Army getup, he looked like Sergeant Garcia trying to fit into Zorro's costume. He had tried to religious-ize the outfit by hanging around his neck a large gold chain with *216* dangling from it.

It was all Mac could do to keep a straight face. He fell into step with Rayford and Abdullah as they approached from their vehicle. They had begun to draw a few stares, though fortunately not from anyone who cared enough to ask questions. All three wore caps pulled low over their foreheads, but without proper uniforms they couldn't pass for Unity Army personnel.

"We'd better split up, eh, Cap?" Mac said.

"I guess. Smitty, you go north. Mac, south. Meet you outside the Eastern Wall at the Golden Gate when this is all over."

Chaim felt the tingle of anticipation as the remnant fell into place at a high point on the western slope overlooking Jerusalem. It still seemed disconcerting not to see Jesus above them, but he knew the Lord knew best. Antichrist had been crowing about luring the Son of God into his trap, when it was clear to Chaim that the opposite had happened. Carpathia had to have read the Bible. He had to know all this was prophesied. He even had to know the predicted outcome. Yet he brazenly came to the very spot he was supposed to, and in spite of the mass execution of his troops in three other confrontations, he still had the gall to believe he would prevail.

This was going to be something to see, and Chaim wanted to say so to the assembled. He had no means to address them all at once, and from looking at those around him, he knew there was nothing they needed to be told. They, like he, looked on with great expectancy.

Ride on, King Jesus!

Fifteen

Rayford was close enough behind Nicolae that he heard him ask a woman general, "What is our equestrian strength?"

She checked via radio and reported, "Excellency, of more than a million soldiers, a little more than a tenth are on horseback."

"Call for as many steeds as we need to get the first wave to the Western Wall, and order Reverend Fortunato and me appropriate mounts."

Within minutes several thousand horses crowded the streets, and Unity Army soldiers were mounting up. A tall, handsome stallion, almost identical to the one Carpathia had ridden out of the city toward Bozrah, was delivered for his use. Cameras clicked and TV crews crowded around as he swung aboard, raising his sword.

He twirled the blade above his head, rousing the troops, who responded with a crescendoing *whoop*, like a football team about to break from the locker room.

Fortunato struggled up onto a smaller black horse and settled himself.

"Follow me to the Western Wall," Carpathia shouted, "and make way for the battering ram and missile launchers! Upon my command, open fire!"

Knowing the Old City by now, Rayford sprinted for side streets, heading toward the Western Wall.

Mac was already at the southern corner of the Old City, a few steps north of Dung Gate. Abdullah contacted him by radio and said he had found a perch near Antonia's Fortress and believed he was safe and undetectable, with a good view of the approaching invaders.

"I am high enough to see the surrounding army forces too, Mac," he said. "They have the entire Old City encircled, several thousand deep. I can see why they are so confident of victory, having cut off all escape routes 360 degrees."

Rayford set up a hundred yards short of the Western Wall and far enough south that he had some underbrush for cover. He thought he saw Mac but couldn't be sure. Almost everyone inside the Old City but the press was part of the attacking force, but the occasional civilian stood atop anything available, cheering and shouting encouragement as Carpathia came into view, valiant and proud on his huge horse, sword pointing to the sky, microphone wrapped around his ear and in front of his mouth so the entire army could hear his commands.

"For the glory of your risen master and lord of the earth!" he shouted, urging his ride to a full gallop, clacking over the cobblestone ground. Fortunato's horse mince-stepped slowly after, which seemed plenty fast enough for Leon.

The band lagged behind the mounted and rolling and marching troops, loudly clanging out a rousing melody. As Carpathia drew within range of the wall, he peeled off to the south with Fortunato trailing him.

"Horsemen, make way for the armaments!" Carpathia bellowed. "Attack! Break through the wall! Take the Temple Mount! Destroy the rebels!"

But when the horsemen whipped their mounts, they did not make way. Rather, the horses bolted as if blind — nickering, whinnying, braying, rearing, bucking, kicking, spinning into each other, running headlong into the wall, throwing riders.

"Make way!" Carpathia screamed. "Make way!"

The riders not thrown leaped from their horses and tried to control them with the reins, but even as they struggled, their own flesh dissolved, their eyes melted, and their tongues disintegrated. As Rayford watched, the soldiers stood briefly as skeletons in now-baggy uniforms, then dropped in heaps of bones as the blinded horses continued to fume and rant and rave.

Seconds later the same plague afflicted the horses, their flesh and eyes and tongues melting away, leaving grotesque skeletons standing, before they too rattled to the pavement.

"Reinforcements!" Carpathia called out. "Charge! Charge! Fire! Fire! Attack!"

But every horse and rider that advanced suffered the same fate. First blindness and madness on the part of the horses, then the bodies of the soldiers melting and dissolving. Then the falling and piling of the bones.

Rayford stood, mouth agape, noticing that neither Carpathia's nor Fortunato's horses had been affected yet. Leon slid off his mount and flopped to the ground, rolling to a kneeling position and burying his face in his hands.

"Get up, Leon! Get up! We are not defeated! We have a million more soldiers and we shall prevail!"

But Leon stayed where he was, whimpering and wailing.

Plainly disgusted, Nicolae urged his horse back to the middle of the wall and looked past the bones of his decimated troops for reinforcements. He lifted his sword and cursed God, but suddenly his attention was drawn directly above.

Rayford followed his gaze to see the temple of God opened in heaven, and the ark of the covenant plain as day. Lightning flashed and thunder roared, and the earth began to shift.

Carpathia's horse reared and high-stepped, and Nicolae fought to control him. Fortunato's horse scampered away without him.

The earth groaned and buckled, and the city of Jerusalem was fractured into three as the great fissures swallowed up Carpathia loyalists and soldiers. Buildings and walls were left intact, except Abdullah reported seeing the cemented-over East Gate — closed off for centuries — blasted open by the movement of the earth.

Rayford slapped his palm over his earpiece and plugged his other ear to hear reports coming in from all over the world. The earthquake was global. Islands disappeared. Mountains were leveled. The entire face of the planet had been made level, save for the city of Jerusalem itself.

And suddenly the Lord Jesus Himself appeared in the clouds again, and the whole world saw Him. He spoke with a loud voice, saying, "Speak comfort to Jerusalem, and cry out to her, that her warfare is ended, that her iniquity is pardoned; for she has received from the Lord's hand double for all her sins.

"Every valley has been exalted and every mountain and hill brought low; the crooked places have been made straight and the rough places smooth. The glory of the Lord has been revealed, and all flesh have seen it together; for I have spoken.

"Behold, the day of the Lord has come, and your spoil has been divided in your midst. For I gathered all the nations to battle against Jerusalem, but the remnant of the people was not cut off from the city. I went forth and fought against those nations, as in the day of battle.

"And the plague with which I struck all

the people who fought against Jerusalem was this: their flesh dissolved while they stood on their feet, their eyes dissolved in their sockets, and their tongues dissolved in their mouths. I sent a great panic over them. Such also was the plague on the horses.

"Behold, I made Jerusalem a cup of drunkenness to all the surrounding peoples, when they laid siege against Judah and Jerusalem. And I made Jerusalem a very heavy stone for all peoples; all who would heave it away were surely cut in pieces, though all nations of the earth were gathered against it.

"I struck every horse with confusion, and its rider with madness; I opened My eyes on the house of Judah and struck every horse of the peoples with blindness.

"I defended the inhabitants of Jerusalem; the one who was feeble among them today is like David, and the house of David shall be like God, like the Angel of the Lord before them. I destroyed all the nations that came against Jerusalem.

"Therefore the curse has devoured the earth, and those who dwell in it are desolate. Therefore the inhabitants of the earth are burned, and few men are left.

"In the midst of the land among the people, it was like the shaking of an olive tree, like the gleaning of grapes when the vintage is done.

"The children of Israel called on My name, and I answered them. I said, 'This is My people'; and each one said, 'The Lord is my God.' "

Though the Lord did not speak audibly to the remnant, Chaim felt as if he and they were being drawn inexorably around the Old City to the east side. As the million-plus slowly made their way past the dead and the dying, a fraction of Antichrist's forces remained alive. They struggled and staggered toward shelter, also apparently drawn to the east.

The Lord sat triumphant on the back of His white horse in the clouds, His army behind Him, gazing upon the one-sided victory over the forces that had come against Jerusalem.

Mac found Rayford and they went looking for Abdullah. They knew he was all right, because they had radio contact. He too was headed east of the city.

"You should have seen Nicolae and Leon," Rayford said.

"I saw them briefly," Mac said, "when Leon fell off his horse."

"Nicolae galloped off a little while ago, heading back the way he had come. Leon was running after him, pleading to let him ride along, but Carpathia ignored him."

"Figures."

The earth still shifted and moved from aftershocks, and Rayford tried to imagine what it must look like from outer space. No more islands. No more mountains. Virtually flat with gently rolling hills. The whole of Israel, except for Jerusalem, was level.

They found Abdullah, who at first looked past them, then smiled and shook his head. "I was looking for two white men, Mac."

Hannah Palemoon caught up with Chaim, who was surrounded by people with questions. She waited until he recognized her, then said, "How long until we are reunited with loved ones who went on to heaven before us?"

"Very soon, I hope," Chaim said. "There are many I wish to see too, but first I want to see Jesus face-to-face."

"What's next?"

"Oh, I think you know. The Lord Himself will set foot on earth again, for only the second time since His ascension. As you know, He came in the clouds for the Rapture, and this time He briefly walked on the ground when He soiled His robe in blood at Bozrah."

"Is the enemy completely gone?" Hannah said.

"Soon," Chaim said. "Very soon."

Illinois, flat as it already was, was hardly affected by the earthquake, though Enoch was certain no one doubted what had happened. The long, low rumbling of the earth continued, and he heard Carpathia loyalists screaming for their lives.

After his people had returned to their homes, Enoch had begun moving his furniture upstairs, looking forward to a life where he could look out the window without caring who might see in. Just before the earthquake one of the few Global Community Peacekeeper patrol cars he'd seen in recent weeks raced down the street. As it came around the curve in front of his place it veered off the road and hit a fire hydrant.

Neighbors ran to the car, collapsing in disbelief when all they found were skeletons and clothes in the front seat. The declared enemies of God were being decimated around the world.

Enoch tried calling his parishioners, reaching many and missing several who called while he was on the phone. No one was hurt, though some of their homes were damaged. Several were badly shaken, telling of seeing government employees disintegrating before their eyes. And all wanted to talk about their new church, where it might be and how soon they might move into it. Many also mentioned their pilgrimage to the Middle East.

"I don't know when it's gonna be," one woman told Enoch, "but I'll be along whenever."

Enoch reminded each that sometime after the earthquake, Jesus would set foot on the Mount of Olives, east of Jerusalem, and the whole world would see Him. "Keep looking up."

"You still in a teachin' mood, Smitty?" Mac said.

"That depends on whether I have studied whatever you are curious about."

"The Mount of Olives, of course."

"Oh yes, I have studied it thoroughly. You can see it from here, naturally. It is only half a mile from the Eastern Wall of the Old City. It is really more of a hill than a mountain, as you can tell. One of Jesus' most famous sermons was preached there. When He made His triumphal entry, He came from the Mount of Olives. And He returned there every night of the last week before the Crucifixion, often praying in the Garden of Gethsemane. The Ascension took place there later too."

"So it makes sense that's where He wants to come now."

"It certainly does to me," Abdullah said.

George Sebastian had never seen anything like it. He told Priscilla he would catch up with her and the kids and the rest of the Tribulation Force traveling with the remnant. He lagged, and rather than following the remnant around the devastated city, he decided to cut directly through it on his way to the Mount of Olives.

As a career military man, Sebastian had seen the spoils of war before, of course, on many fields of battle around the world. He could not recall, however, a quaint, beautiful city so devastated. Most peculiar, it was nearly impossible to determine who had won.

Sebastian had been kept up to speed on the conflict from the beginning and knew from Buck and then Mac how the city had been completely overrun by the Global Community Unity Army. Half the residents had been killed or captured. Many were still imprisoned and had been tortured and starved.

But now as he ambled through the narrow streets, George saw some surviving Unity soldiers leisurely dividing the spoils, while others regrouped for an assault on rebels who would try to escape from the Temple Mount. He also noticed piles of clothes and bones where the Lord had decomposed the bodies of His enemies.

So this was not over. Jerusalem, the jewel City of God, had been violated to the point of ruin. It was a wonder God Himself had not leveled it along with the mountains and islands of the world.

Sebastian scanned the entire area as he walked, heading north to Herod's Gate, where he knew Buck had been killed. He climbed the wall and looked out over the rest of Jerusalem. Perhaps a hundred thousand of Carpathia's troops remained. The rebels still held the Temple Mount, guarding the newly opened East Gate rather than choosing to try to escape through it.

He could see the vast remnant slowly making its way past the South Wall, heading toward the Mount of Olives, and knew he had better catch up or risk leaving his wife with the responsibility of two youngsters by herself. Of course, others would help, but that didn't justify his abandoning her.

Just before Sebastian made his way back

down from the wall, he saw a flurry of activity outside the New Gate in the northwest corner of the Old City. It appeared the press had surrounded Nicolae and Leon and what was left of the potentate's cabinet of advisers and generals. Sebastian shook his head. He knew what was coming, and Carpathia had to as well. Why wasn't he running for his life?

Some men never know when they're beaten, never know when to fold and walk away. Nicolae Carpathia, proving — as if that were necessary — that he was indeed Antichrist, was the epitome of that kind of a man. In a classic case of cosmic denial, his pride still persuaded him he could not lose in the end.

There he stood, pointing, cajoling, scheming, barking orders, talking to the press. Sebastian fired up his radio, and sure enough, his highness was still trying to sell the citizenry on their eventual triumph. "This city shall become my throne," Carpathia said. "The temple will be flattened and the way made for my palace, the most magnificent structure ever erected. We have captured half the enemy here, and we will dispose of the other half in due time.

"The final stage of our conquest is nearly ready to be executed, and we will soon be rid of this nuisance from above."

Rayford, Mac, and Abdullah had also been listening as they watched the crawl of people, mostly the remnant, moving toward the Mount of Olives. Of course, the children of God knew what was supposed to come, and so they kept their distance. No one had any idea of the Lord's timing, but there He remained, hovering over them with His horsemen. And soon He began again to speak words of comfort to His own.

"As you have received Me as your Lord, so walk in Me, rooted and built up in Me and established in the faith, as you have been taught, abounding with thanksgiving. You are complete in Me, the head of all principality and power.

"My Father has said unto Me, 'Your throne, O God, is forever and ever; a scepter of righteousness is the scepter of Your kingdom. You have loved righteousness and hated lawlessness; therefore God, Your God, has anointed You with the oil of gladness more than Your companions.

" 'You laid the foundation of the earth, and the heavens are the work of Your hands. Others will perish, but You remain; and they will all grow old like a garment; like a cloak You will fold them up, and they will be changed. But You are the same, and Your years will not fail.'

"And I, the One about whom these things were said by God Himself, assure you, My children, that I will never leave you nor forsake you. So you may boldly say: 'The Lord is my helper; I will not fear. What can man do to me?' I, your Lord Jesus Christ, am the same yesterday, today, and forever. Therefore, holy brothers and sisters, partakers of the heavenly calling, consider Me the Apostle and High Priest of your confession.

"I was faithful to God who appointed Me, as Moses also was faithful. For I was counted worthy of more glory than Moses, in the same way that God, who built the house, has more honor than the house. For every house is built by someone, but He who built all things is God.

"God has set Me as a High Priest fitting for you — holy, harmless, undefiled, separate from sinners, and higher than the heavens. I do not need daily, as human high priests, to offer up sacrifices, first for My own sins and then for the people's, for this I did once for all when I offered up Myself."

Despite all Jesus' magnanimous comments about Himself, Rayford was struck by how lowly, humble, and compassionate He sounded. He was merely speaking the truth, reminding His children what they enjoyed in Him. The truth of the Word of God, coming from the Living Word, again drove Rayford to his knees, along with his friends and the entire Jewish remnant.

As Rayford knelt, his face in his hands on the ground, Jesus continued to speak directly to his heart.

"God willed to make known the riches of the glory of this mystery, which is Christ in you, Rayford, the hope of glory. I am the hope of Israel, the horn of salvation in the house of God's servant David. Most assuredly, I say to you, before Abraham was, I AM."

Jesus fell silent. From the west Rayford heard the Global Community Unity Army marching band. Their weak rendition of "Hail Carpathia" sounded discordant from a distance, and of course it paled in comparison to the murmured prayers of the million on their knees before the Lord in the sky.

The ground rumbled as what was left of the GC's armaments were rolled into position. It was pathetic and laughable to Rayford that Carpathia had not learned anything from the past several hours. There would be no competing with this force from heaven. No damage would be done to Jesus or to His people with weapons of war.

And yet here Carpathia came, horse at full stride, leathers squeaking in the saddle, sword aloft, the pitiable False Prophet bouncing awkwardly along behind him, holding the reins of his horse for all he was worth. The remnant stood as one, not wanting to miss a thing. Rayford looked fully into the face of his Lord and was again reminded of the biblical description of the man on the white horse with eyes like fire.

The conviction that shone in the eyes of Jesus was of one who had finally had enough. His enemy was right where He wanted him, lured fully into the trap that had been set before the foundation of the world. The fulfillment of age-old prophecies was about to take place, despite the fact that the enemy himself had read them, knew them, and had seen every last one of them come to fruition exactly as it had been laid out.

In all his sick, imitative glory came galloping the quintessence of pride and ego, indwelt by Satan himself. Carpathia swung his sword round and round above his head while Fortunato used one hand to attempt some sort of a weird gesture of worship and the other to keep control of his horse and himself in the saddle.

The band, which led the way, played

louder and louder and, on cue, split right and left to allow the mounted soldiers, then the foot soldiers, then the munitions and armament platoons in rolling vehicles to slowly come into position.

With the remnant just a few hundred yards to the east, the besieged city of Jerusalem a half mile to the west, and the heavenly hosts hovering directly above, Jesus nudged His magnificent white charger and descended to the top of the Mount of Olives.

As He dismounted, Carpathia shrieked out his final command, "Attack!" The hundred thousand troops followed orders, horsemen at full gallop firing, foot soldiers running and firing, rolling stock rolling and firing.

And Jesus said, in that voice like a trumpet and the sound of rushing waters, "I AM WHO I AM."

At that instant the Mount of Olives split in two from east to west, the place Jesus stood moving to the north and the place where the Unity Army stood moving to the south, leaving a large valley.

All the firing and the running and the galloping and the rolling stopped. The soldiers screamed and fell, their bodies bursting open from head to toe at every word that proceeded out of the mouth of the Lord as He spoke to the captives within Jerusalem. "You shall flee through My mountain valley, for the mountain valley reaches to Azal. Yes, you shall flee as you fled from the earthquake in the days of Uzziah king of Judah. The Lord your God has come, and all the saints with Me."

With shouts and singing, it was as if Jerusalem burst forth; the captives, who had been imprisoned in Jerusalem, came running toward the great rift between the two sides of the Mount of Olives. And as the earth continued to rumble and shift, Rayford watched in awe as the whole city of Jerusalem rose above the ground some three hundred feet and now stood as an exalted jewel above all the surrounding land that had been flattened by the global earthquake.

Mac struggled to his feet and grabbed Rayford. "You see 'em?" he said, pointing. "See Nicolae and Leon lighting out for safety? And look at that big glob of bobbing light bouncin' along ahead of 'em! 'Member what I told you about Lucifer showing up at Solomon's Stables? That's got to be him, and he's deserted ol' Nick again!"

Mac and Abdullah and Rayford stood,

arms around each other's shoulders, taking in the spectacular scene. Rebels from the Temple Mount and the captives fled through the new valley, chased by the last feeble vestiges of the Unity Army. But when Jesus spoke, the pursuers died at His words.

"Living waters shall flow from Jerusalem," He said, "half of them toward the eastern sea and half of them toward the western sea; in both summer and winter it shall occur. And I the Lord shall be King over all the earth. Today the Lord is one and His name one.

"All the land has been turned into a plain from Geba to Rimmon south of Jerusalem. Jerusalem has been raised up and inhabited in her place from Benjamin's Gate to the place of the First Gate and the Corner Gate, and from the Tower of Hananeel to the king's winepresses. You, the people, shall dwell in it; and no longer shall there be utter destruction, but Jerusalem shall be safely inhabited."

With that, Jesus mounted His horse and began His final triumphal entry toward Jerusalem. During His first visit to earth He had ridden into the city on a lowly donkey, welcomed by some but rejected by most. Now He rode high on the majestic white steed, and with every word that came from

His mouth, the rest of the enemies of God — except for Satan, the Antichrist, and the False Prophet — were utterly destroyed where they stood.

"This is the day of vengeance, that all things which were written have been fulfilled. The loftiness of man shall be bowed down, and the haughtiness of men shall be brought low; the Lord alone will be exalted today."

Loud voices from heaven said, "The kingdoms of this world have become the kingdoms of our Lord and of His Christ, and He shall reign forever and ever!

"We give You thanks, O Lord God Almighty, the One who is and who was and who is to come, because You have taken Your great power and reigned. The nations were angry, and Your wrath has come, and the time of the dead, that they should be judged, and that You should reward Your servants the prophets and the saints, and those who fear Your name, small and great, and should destroy those who destroy the earth."

The remnant trailed Jesus, raising their hands, singing *hosanna*, and praising Him. They fell silent when He spoke again.

"It is a righteous thing with God to repay with tribulation those who trouble you, and to give you who are troubled rest. I have taken vengeance on those who do not know God, and on those who do not obey My gospel. These shall be punished with everlasting destruction from the presence of the Lord and from the glory of His power. I have come to be glorified in My saints and to be admired among all those who believe."

Sixteen

Kneeling in his front yard in suburban Chicago, Enoch wept at the glorious triumphant words of Christ. He also wept because of his deep longing to be in Jerusalem. He had studied these passages for years and knew what was happening. He couldn't wait to get there, to reunite with his friends from the Tribulation Force, and to hear every detail of the great day of God the Almighty.

More than anything, however, he wanted to see Jesus.

With every moment it became more and more difficult for Rayford to take in the magnitude of the supernatural events. Sensory overload was a gross understatement. He never once had to pinch himself to determine whether this was a dream. It was all so real, so massive, that even what he might have considered smaller miracles took their place alongside the global and local earthquakes in importance. Like the fact that he still felt no fatigue, despite no rest — let alone sleep — in he didn't know how long.

But when he and Mac and Abdullah parked the Hummer outside the Old City and followed the vast procession in the newly burst-open East Gate, a new phenomenon awaited him. It was one thing to follow his Lord, the King of kings, on His ultimate triumphal entry into the City of David, but to see what he saw there compared with what he expected to find . . .

Jerusalem, particularly the Old City, should have been filled with the gore of the dead. Hundreds of thousands had been slain here, the majority in most grotesque ways. There should have been stench, blood, and flesh, not to mention the skeletal remains of Unity Army soldiers and horses.

But the earthquake that had rent in two the Mount of Olives and elevated the Eternal City some three hundred feet had accomplished a macabre cleanup operation as well. Jesus led the happy throng in and around the inside borders of the Old City, stretching the parade of singing, dancing, chanting, embracing, praising, worshiping, celebrating people for several miles. Strangely, the walls had been leveled, all of them. No more battle scars, no more jagged edges from bombs and battering rams, no more uneven heights. Where the walls had stood were gently rolling mounds of fine, crushed stone.

Even the Wailing Wall had disappeared, and Rayford had the full-hearted feeling that Jesus had replaced it with Himself. Sure enough, as the head of the procession came within sight of the Western Wall, Jesus began to speak. And while in the saddle He was only slightly higher than the people in line and was facing away from them, Rayford knew all could hear Him as clearly as he himself could, about a third of the way back in the throng.

"There is one God and one Mediator between God and men, I, the Man Christ Jesus. I gave Myself a ransom for all."

Where was the residue of war? Rayford could only guess. It was as if the city had been shaken and tilted this way and that. And while the buildings and landmarks remained, the rubble of the walls had apparently scrubbed the streets and pushed the gruesome evidence — all of it — into crevasses now covered over for the rest of eternity. The City of God was pristine anew, and the people seemed astonished by it.

When the Lord had ridden His horse far enough into the city to allow all those following to also enter in, He circled so that the entire host was in a great circle, thousands deep. Behind everyone, almost as an afterthought, were the hosts of heaven, also still on horseback.

The remnant ignored them, as if temporarily unaware of them. Rayford saw them clearly and knew that everyone else could too. In the back of his mind was the prospect — soon, he hoped — of reunions with loved ones. But having Jesus in their midst made everyone think only of Him. Everything else, pleasant or not, faded to insignificance.

When everyone had finally stopped walking and shuffling and maneuvering into place, Jesus dismounted and stretched out His arms. "O Jerusalem, Jerusalem," He cried, "the one who kills the prophets and stones those who are sent to her! How often I wanted to gather your children together, as a hen gathers her chicks under her wings, but you were not willing! See! Your house was left to you desolate; for I said to you, you shall see Me no more till you said, 'Blessed is He who comes in the name of the Lord!' "

Jesus looked to the remnant, and Rayford knew intuitively that each one had the same feeling he did, that He was looking directly into their eyes alone. Rayford could not contain himself. He took a huge breath and shouted for all he was worth, "Blessed is He who comes in the name of the Lord!" And every soul there had shouted the same thing, bringing the most beatific smile to the face of Jesus.

Ming Toy Woo, standing hand in hand with her new husband, Ree, drank this all in with a lump in her throat, her heart full to bursting. She heard every word in her native tongue and had to remind herself that Jesus was doing this for each person in his or her own language. Though she and Ree were at least a hundred deep in the crowd, and everyone was standing, she had a clear and perfect view of Jesus without having to stand on tiptoe or lean between bodies.

Suddenly standing behind Jesus were five heavenly beings, three of whom she recognized: Christopher, the angel with the everlasting gospel; Caleb; and Nahum. These were the three angels of mercy who had delivered her from certain death when she was working undercover for the Global Community. They were also the ones who told her she would not die before the Glorious Appearing of Christ.

The other two angels were quickly identified when Jesus handed the reins of His horse to one, saying simply, "Gabriel." The other set a stone bench in place, and as Jesus sat He said, "Thank you, Michael."

Then the Son of God, Maker of heaven and earth, Savior of mankind, looked directly into Ming's eyes and said in Chinese, "Come to Me, My child."

Ming stared as if struck with paralysis. Finally able to move, she touched her chest and asked, "Me?"

Jesus seemed to look into her soul, concentrating only on her. "Yes, dear one. Come to Me, Ming."

She wanted to run, to push others aside, to leap into His arms. But it was all she could do to put one foot in front of the other. She let go of Ree's hand and slowly began to move, realizing that the entire band, many more than a million now, was moving toward Jesus as one.

It had been plain as day and no mistake. Jesus had looked right at Rayford, deep in the crowd, and singled him out. He had called him by name and told him, "Come to Me, My child."

Rayford tore his eyes away and looked to his right and his left. Both Abdullah and Mac looked shocked, also staring at Jesus and questioning, by gesture or word — Abdullah in Arabic — whether He was talking to them.

But He was not, Rayford knew. *He is talking to me.* Rayford pointed at himself with both hands and raised his brows. And Jesus nodded. He began to move toward his Savior. How could this be? How could Jesus give individual audiences before a crowd this size? How much time could He give each person? This could take months! And how was it possible that Rayford was selected first?

As he moved stiff-legged toward Jesus, Rayford's mind reeled. What were the odds? How could he quantify the privilege of locking eyes with the eternal God of the universe? He began to hurry, and Jesus said, "Come unto Me, Rayford, and I will give you rest."

Though his eyes were on Jesus and his body moved forward, Rayford suddenly became aware of everything. He was coming out of a crowd of well over a million. Five angels stood sentry behind the Master. Rayford's friends and family would see him. What had he done to deserve this privilege?

Rest — yes, for the first time he felt that need. The fatigue of the last several hours washed over him and he felt as if he could sleep if only given the opportunity.

But as he came within steps of Jesus and saw His welcoming smile, he was struck that the Lord seemed as thrilled to see him as he was to see the Lord. And he was overcome with the shame of his sin. Unworthy. So unworthy. He slowed almost to a stop, fearing he would collapse in disgrace and humiliation.

"No, no," Jesus said, still smiling, and now leaning forward and reaching for him with scarred hands. When Rayford saw that, he nearly dissolved. He forced himself to keep moving, though he had lost control of his own coordination and feared he would stumble and fall into Jesus' lap.

He dropped to his knees at Jesus' feet, sobbing, reminded of every sin and shortcoming of his entire life. Loving hands gathered him in, and he was drawn to Jesus' bosom. "Rayford, Rayford, how I have looked forward to and longed for this day."

Rayford could not speak.

"I knew your name before the foundation of the world. I have prepared a place for you, and if it were not so, I would have told you."

"But, Lord, I — I —"

Jesus took Rayford by the shoulders and gently pushed him back and cupped his face in His hands. He stared into his eyes from inches away, and Rayford could barely hold His piercing gaze. "I was there when you were born. I was there when you thought your mother had abandoned you. I was there when you concluded that I made no sense."

"I am so sorry. I —"

"I was there when you almost married the wrong woman. I was there when your children were born. I was there when your wife chose Me and you did not."

"I —"

"I was there when you nearly broke your vows. When you nearly died, before you knew Me. I was there when you were left behind. And I was waiting when finally you came to Me."

"Oh, Lord, thank You. I'm so —"

"I have loved you with an everlasting love. I am the lover of your soul. You were meant to be with Me for eternity, and now you shall be."

Rayford had so many questions, so many things he wanted to say. But he could not. Looking into Jesus' face transported him to his childhood and he felt as if he could stay kneeling there, childlike, letting his Savior love and comfort him forever.

Jesus put one hand on Rayford's shoulder and the other atop his head. "I pray to My Father, from whom the whole family in heaven and earth is named, that He would grant you, according to the riches of His glory, to be strengthened with might through His Spirit in the inner man, that I may dwell in your heart through faith; that you, being rooted and grounded in love, may be able to comprehend with all the saints what is the width and length and depth and height — to know My love which passes knowledge; that you may be filled with all the fullness of God.

"Now to Him who is able to do exceedingly abundantly above all that you ask or think, according to the power that works in you, to Him be glory in the church to all generations, forever and ever. Amen."

As Rayford seemed to walk on air back to his place among the throng, something deep within him understood that as personal as that had been, Jesus was bestowing the same love and attention on everyone present. He suddenly became aware that Mac and Abdullah were also returning to the crowd, tears streaming, body language evidencing that they had also been with the Master. The three stood again with arms around each other's shoulders, unashamedly worshiping.

As Rayford looked around, he could see from every face that each person had personally encountered Jesus.

The Savior had come to Enoch in his sleep, and yet the encounter was so real and deep that the young man didn't question it for a second. When it was over he found himself on his knees on the floor, feeling as if Jesus had been right there in the room. He had been reminded of significant events in his life, of his journey first away from and then toward true faith. Enoch was able to see anew the hand of God throughout his entire life, and to know that Jesus had known him by name before the foundation of the world. . . .

His phone was chirping, and as Enoch took the first call it began to signal that more and more calls were coming in. An hour later he had heard from almost everyone in his congregation. "I still want to go over there," was a common theme, "but if Jesus is going to come here like that, maybe I don't need to."

Jesus stood and stretched His arms wide, and Rayford was struck that the experience of watching and hearing Him was more personal than ever, despite the numbers of those all doing the same.

"I beseech you," He said, "to walk worthy of the calling with which you were called, with all lowliness and gentleness, with long-suffering, bearing with one another in love, endeavoring to keep the unity of the Spirit in the bond of peace.

"Never again put your trust in men, in whom there is no help. Man's spirit departs, he returns to the earth; in that very day his plans perish. Happy are you who have the God of Jacob for your help, whose hope is in the Lord your God, who made heaven and earth, the sea, and all that is in them; who keeps truth forever, who executes justice for the oppressed, who gives food to the hungry. The Lord gives freedom to the prisoners.

"The Lord opens the eyes of the blind; the Lord raises those who are bowed down; the Lord loves the righteous. The Lord watches over the strangers; He relieves the fatherless and widow; but the way of the wicked He turns upside down.

"The Lord shall reign forever — your God, O Zion, to all generations. Praise the Lord!"

And Rayford did. They all did.

For the first time since His appearing, Rayford saw Jesus speaking and yet did not hear Him. He was conferring with the angelic beings behind Him, and naturally, this attracted the attention of the entire gathering with as much curiosity as when they could hear Him.

The one He had called Gabriel stepped forward. "Remnant of Israel!" he began, with a voice clear as crystal and able to be heard by all. "And Tribulation saints! In truth I perceive that God shows no partiality.

"But in every nation whoever fears Him and works righteousness is accepted by Him.

"The word which God sent to the children of Israel, preaching peace through Jesus Christ — He is Lord of all — that word you know, which was proclaimed throughout all Judea, and began from Galilee after the baptism which John preached: how God anointed Jesus of Nazareth with the Holy Spirit and with power, who went about doing good and healing all who were oppressed by the devil, for God was with Him.

"And we are witnesses of all things which He did both in the land of the Jews and in Jerusalem, whom they killed by hanging on a tree.

"Him God raised up on the third day, and showed Him openly, not to all the people, but to witnesses chosen before by God, even to those who ate and drank with Him after He arose from the dead.

"And He commanded some to preach to the people, and to testify that it is He who was ordained by God to be Judge of the living and the dead.

"To Him all the prophets witness that, through His name, whoever believes in Him will receive remission of sins. Amen."

The gathered repeated the amen in unison. And Jesus once again addressed them:

"In this manner, therefore, pray: Our Father in heaven, hallowed be Your name.

"Thank You that Your kingdom has come. Your will has been done on earth as it is in heaven.

"Give us this day our daily bread. And forgive us our debts, as we forgive our debtors. And do not lead us into temptation, but deliver us from the evil one. For Yours is the kingdom and the power and the glory forever. Amen."

After praying with Him in unison, they opened their eyes and Rayford noticed that only four angels now stood behind Jesus. Michael was gone.

And Jesus said, "I am not alone, because the Father is with Me. In Me you have peace. In the world you had tribulation; but be of good cheer, I have overcome the world."

Jesus lifted up His eyes to heaven, and said: "Father, You glorified Me that I also may glorify You, as You have given Me authority over all flesh, that I should give eternal life to as many as You gave Me.

"And this is eternal life, that they may know You, the only true God, and Me whom You have sent.

"I glorified You on the earth. I finished the work which You have given Me to do.

"And now, O Father, glorify Me together with Yourself, with the glory which I had with You before the world was.

"I do not pray for the world but for those whom You have given Me, for they are Yours. And all Mine are Yours, and Yours are Mine, and I am glorified in them. Those whom You gave Me I have kept; and none of them is lost except the son of perdition, that the Scripture might be fulfilled.

"I do not pray that You should take them out of the world, but that You should keep them from the evil one. Sanctify them by Your truth. Your word is truth.

"O righteous Father! The world has not

known You, but I have known You; and these have known that You sent Me. And I have declared to them Your name, and will declare it, that the love with which You loved Me may be in them, and I in them."

Again Gabriel stepped forward. "The Lord is faithful, who will establish you and guard you from the evil one."

With the mention of the evil one, Mac saw commotion in the crowd far behind Jesus and the angelic beings. People were moving aside and murmuring, making way for the archangel Michael. With him were Nicolae Carpathia, in his now disheveled leathers, sans sword; a worn and exhausted looking Leon Fortunato in one of his lesser, simpler robes and no head adornment; and the three ghastly robotic Carpathia look-alikes Mac and the others had seen over the hidden camera when Carpathia and Fortunato had introduced them to the ten kings of the world. These were Ashtaroth, Baal, and Cankerworm, the three froglike demonic creatures who had been sent out to deceive the nations, persuading them to gather together in Megiddo to fight the Son of God.

They were hideous, chalky white beings that had taken on human form and wore identical black suits. They looked defeated, bent, as if crippled by their own evil. They stuck together but separated themselves from Carpathia and Fortunato, and Nicolae and Leon seemed not to want to have anything to do with each other either.

Michael led the five in front of Jesus, and Mac was struck by His countenance. He detected righteous anger, of course, but also what appeared to be disappointment, even sadness. There was no gloating.

The pathetic trio locked arms and knelt before Jesus, whimpering in annoyingly screechy tones. Carpathia turned his back on Jesus and faced the remnant, hands on his hips, defiant and bored. Leon wrung his hands and occasionally fingered his gaudy gold 216 necklace. He half faced Jesus, looking guilty and full of dread, peeking at Carpathia every now and then as if for direction.

Gabriel stepped between Jesus and the three and bent at the waist to get in their faces, and in a loud voice said, "As a fulfillment of age-old scriptural prophecy, you kneel this day before Jesus the Christ, the Son of the living God, who, being in the form of God, did not consider it robbery to be equal with God, but made Himself of no reputation, taking the form of a bondservant, and coming in the likeness of men.

"And being found in appearance as a man, He humbled Himself and became obedient to the point of death, even the death of the cross."

"Yes!" the beings squealed, hissing. "Yes! We know! We know!" And they bowed lower, prostrating their deformed bodies.

Gabriel continued: "Therefore God also has highly exalted Him and given Him the name which is above every name, that at the name of Jesus every knee should bow, of those in heaven, and of those on earth, and of those under the earth — like you — and that *every* tongue, even yours, should confess that Jesus Christ is Lord, to the glory of God the Father."

"Jesus Christ is Lord!" they rasped, and Gabriel stepped back behind Jesus. "Jesus Christ is Lord! It is true! True! We acknowledge it! We acknowledge Him!"

Jesus leaned forward and rested His elbows on His knees. The three kept their faces to the ground, not looking at Him. " 'As I live,' says the Lord God, 'I have no pleasure in the death of the wicked, but that the wicked turn from his way and live.' "

"We repent! We will turn! We will turn! We worship You, O Jesus, Son of God. You are Lord!"

"But for you it is too late," Jesus said, and Mac was hit anew by the sorrow in His tone. "You were once angelic beings, in heaven with God. Yet you were cast down because of your own prideful decisions. Rather than resist the evil one, you chose to serve him."

"We were wrong! Wrong! We acknowledge You as Lord!"

"Like My Father, with whom I am one, I have no pleasure in the death of the wicked, but that is justice, and that is your sentence."

And as the three shrieked, their reptilian bodies burst from their clothes and exploded, leaving a mess of blood and scales and skin that soon burst into flames and was carried away by the wind.

Leon flopped to the ground with such force that his palms smacked loudly and his forehead bounced with a crack. He ripped off his necklace and tossed it away. As Jesus sat staring intently at him, Leon rose and tore off his robe, casting it aside and kicking off his shoes. Then he lay face-first on the ground, clad only in plain pants and shirt and socks, his great belly pressing the pavement.

"Oh, my Lord and my God!" he wailed, sobs gushing from him. "I have been so blind, so wrong, so wicked!"

"Do you know who I am?" Jesus said. "Who I truly am?"

"Yes! Yes! I have always known, Lord! Thou art the Christ, the Son of the living God!"

Jesus stood. "You would blaspheme by quoting my servant Simon, whom I blessed, for flesh and blood had not revealed it unto him, but My Father who is in heaven?"

"No, Lord! Your Father revealed it to me too!"

"I tell you the truth, woe to you for not making that discovery while there was yet time. Rather, you rejected Me and My Father's plan for the world. You pitted your will against Mine and became the False Prophet, committing the greatest sin known under heaven: rejecting Me as the only Way to God the Father and spending seven years deceiving the world."

"Jesus is Lord! Jesus is Lord! Don't kill me! I beg you! Please!"

"Death is too good for you. How many souls are separated from Me forever because of you and the words that came from your mouth?"

"I'm sorry! Forgive me! I renounce all the works of Satan and Antichrist! I pledge my allegiance to You!"

"You are sentenced to eternity in the lake of fire."

"Oh, God, no!"

Gabriel said, "Silence!"

Leon rolled and then crawled several feet away, where he lay in a fetal heap, sobbing.

Jesus sat again and Nicolae Carpathia, still facing the assembled crowd, shrugged and thrust his hands deep into his pockets. His eyebrows were raised, a smirk planted, and Mac had to wonder how this would play out. Even Carpathia was to bow and confess that Jesus was Lord, but he exuded no fear and certainly no humility.

Michael advanced to one side of him, Gabriel the other. Michael grabbed an elbow and spun him around as Gabriel shouted, "Kneel before your Lord!"

Carpathia wrenched away from Michael and again stood arms akimbo. Jesus said, "Lucifer, leave this man!"

And with that, Carpathia seemed to shrink. He looked again the way Mac had seen him below the Temple Mount in Solomon's Stables. His leathers were now too roomy for him and hung on him like limp robes. His hands and fingers became bony. His neck seemed to swim inside a collar now much too large.

Nicolae's hair was sparse and nearly colorless, and dark veins appeared on his exposed skin. He was pale and pasty, as if his skin could be easily rubbed away. Again Mac had the feeling that this was what the body of Carpathia would have looked like, had it been moldering in the grave since his assassination three and a half years before.

Nicolae shivered and quivered despite the heat, and he slowly, clearly painfully, reached up and spread his cape around both shoulders, covering himself and seeming to hide within it as if it were a cocoon.

"Kneel!" Gabriel shouted, and he and Michael moved back behind Jesus.

Nicolae nodded weakly and deliberately lowered himself, like an old man, to one knee. It was as if the pavement was too hard for him and his other knee quickly came down, his hands splaying to the sides to keep himself from pitching to his face. There he knelt, on all fours, weak and pathetic and frail, leather cape hanging limply off bony shoulders.

Mac had to contrast the righteousness of Christ with his own humanity. Had he been in Jesus' place now, he would have been unable to resist rejoicing in the triumph. Mac would have said, "Not such a big man now, are you? Where's the sword? Where's the army? Where's the cabinet, the sub-potentates? Now you're only the supreme *im*potentate, aren't you?"

But this was not about winning. This was about justice.

Jesus said, "You became a willing tool of the devil himself."

Nicolae did not protest, did not beg. He merely lowered his head even more and nodded.

"You were a rebel against the things of God and His kingdom. You caused more suffering than anyone in the history of the world. God bestowed upon you gifts of intelligence, beauty, wisdom, and personality, and you had the opportunity to make the most of these in the face of the most pivotal events in the annals of creation.

"Yet you used every gift for personal gain. You led millions to worship you and your father, Satan. You were the cunning destroyer of My followers and accomplished more to damn the souls of men and women than anyone else in your time.

"Ultimately your plans and your regime have failed. And now, who do you say that I am?"

The pause was interminable, the silence deadly. Finally, in a humble, weak voice, Nicolae croaked, "You *are* the Christ, the Son of the living God, who died for the sins of the world and rose again the third day as the Scriptures predicted."

Jesus reached and gestured as He spoke, and Mac had the impression He wished that Nicolae would look at Him. But he did not. "And what does that say about you and what you made of your life?"

Carpathia sank even lower than Mac thought possible. "I confess," he whispered, "that my life was a waste. Worthless. A mistake. I rebelled against the God of the universe, whom I now know loved me."

Jesus shook His head and Mac saw a great sadness in His face. "You are responsible for the fate of billions. You and your False Prophet, with whom you shed the blood of the innocents — My followers, the prophets, and My servants who believed in Me — shall be cast alive into the lake of fire."

The archangels Michael and Gabriel stepped forward, Michael to pull the False Prophet from the ground and Antichrist to a standing position. He stood before Jesus as if awaiting instructions while the wasted Nicolae Carpathia was hunched and elderly looking, hanging his head. Leon Fortunato looked a mess, hair askew, face flushed and tear-stained, hands clasped tightly in front of him.

Gabriel pronounced to the crowd, "And I

saw the Beast, the kings of the earth, and their armies, gathered together to make war against Him who sat on the horse and against His army.

"Then the Beast was captured, and with him the False Prophet who worked signs in his presence, by which he deceived those who received the mark of the beast and those who worshiped his image.

"These two were cast alive into the lake of fire burning with brimstone."

Gabriel moved out of the way, and on the spot where he had stood, a hole three feet in diameter opened in the ground and a putrid, sulfuric odor burst forth, making Mac and everyone in the city hold their noses. This was followed by a whistling blue flame that erupted from the hole and rose twenty feet, which Mac could only compare to a monstrous acetylene torch. This added the smell of ether to the mix, and Mac found the front lines of the crowd backing away.

Even as far as he was from the action, Mac felt the tremendous heat emitted by the raging pillar of fire. Jesus and the five angelic beings were apparently immune to the smell and the heat, but both Carpathia and Fortunato tried to back off. Michael held tight to each, still looking to Jesus.

The Lord nodded sadly, and without hesitation, Michael briskly walked the two to the edge of the hole. Fortunato caterwauled like a baby and fought to escape, but with one mighty arm Michael pushed him into the hole. His keening intensified and then faded as he fell. Carpathia did not struggle. He merely covered his face with his forearms as he was dropped in, and then his bawling echoed throughout Jerusalem until he had fallen far enough away. The hole closed as quickly as it had opened, and the Beast and the False Prophet were no more.

Seventeen

Rayford was reeling, and he could only imagine what the rest of the throng must have thought. He knew these things were supposed to happen, and he also knew what was next, but he had never imagined being an eyewitness to all of it. He believed George and Priscilla Sebastian had their ways of shielding the eyes of the children from the gruesome sights, but he also counted on the supernatural power of Jesus Himself to protect Kenny from such images.

How he wanted to see Irene and Raymie and Chloe and Buck, and yes, Amanda. Somehow he understood that the awkwardness of two wives meeting each other in the natural world would not be an issue in the new world. Their full focus and attention would be on Christ and what He had accomplished in all of their lives.

But that would have to come in due time. Gabriel, the pronouncing archangel, appeared ready to speak again. And as soon as he began, Rayford had the feeling that this was the plan of the Lord, to settle the minds of His people after what they had just seen.

"Jesus is the true Light," Gabriel began, "who gives light to every man coming into the world.

"He was in the world, and the world was made through Him, and the world did not know Him.

"He came to His own, and His own did not receive Him.

"But as many as received Him, to them He gave the right to become children of God, to those who believe in His name: who were born, not of blood, nor of the will of the flesh, nor of the will of man, but of God.

"And the Word became flesh and dwelt among you, and you beheld His glory, the glory as of the only begotten of the Father, full of grace and truth. Amen."

"Amen!" the people shouted, and many seemed comforted.

No food, no rest, and now nowhere to sit but on the pavement — so long as one didn't care if he missed some of the action. And of course Rayford did care. Yet once again he felt no hunger, not even the fatigue that had overcome him on his way to see Jesus. And standing was fine.

Again Jesus conferred with the heavenly beings, and Michael disappeared. Would the big event happen this soon, this close to the first judgments? Rayford couldn't imagine, but it was certainly something he didn't want to miss.

Gabriel spoke once more: "But now in Christ Jesus you who once were far off have been brought near by the blood of Christ.

"For He Himself is your peace, and He came and preached peace to you who were afar off and to those who were near. For through Him those both near and far have access by one Spirit to the Father.

"Now, therefore, you are no longer strangers and foreigners, but fellow citizens with the saints and members of the household of God, having been built on the foundation of the apostles and prophets, Jesus Christ Himself being the chief cornerstone, in whom the whole building, being fitted together, grows into a holy temple in the Lord, in whom you also are being built together for a dwelling place of God in the Spirit.

"You, then, who were raised with Christ, sought those things which were above, where Christ was, sitting at the right hand of God.

"You set your mind on things above, not on things on the earth. For you died, and your life was hidden with Christ in God. So when Christ who was your life appeared, then you also appeared with Him in glory.

"And now, dear ones, be sober, be vigilant; because your adversary the devil still walks about like a roaring lion, seeking whom he may devour. You have resisted him, steadfast in the faith, knowing that the same sufferings were experienced by your brotherhood in the world. But now the God of all grace, who called us to His eternal glory by Christ Jesus, after you suffered a while, perfected, established, strengthened, and settled you. To Him be the glory and the dominion forever and ever. Amen."

"Amen!" the crowd shouted, and as they broke into spontaneous worship and singing, Gabriel concluded: "Then I saw an angel coming down from heaven, having the key to the bottomless pit and a great chain in his hand."

The crowd began to cheer.

"He laid hold of the dragon, that serpent of old, who is the Devil and Satan, and bound him for a thousand years."

Hands raised, they were screaming now.

"And he cast him into the bottomless pit, and shut him up, and set a seal on him, so that he should deceive the nations no more till the thousand years were finished."

Rayford sensed apprehension on the part of the people, because anyone who was not up to speed on what was next had begun to figure it out. And when the mighty warrior archangel Michael suddenly reappeared with a gargantuan lion — easily three times larger than any natural king of beasts — the crowd let out a collective gasp and shriek and embraced each other in fear.

But Gabriel quieted them with this assurance: "You are of God, little children. Fear not, for He who is in you is greater than he who is in the world."

The roar of the prodigious carnivore hurt Rayford's ears and echoed off the surrounding buildings. The lion swiped at Michael and snarled, stamping and turning on its ridiculously muscled haunches. But he held it firm. As the lion set itself for another attempt to break free and devour its captor, Michael tightened his grip and twisted the tree-trunk neck further.

Suddenly the lion transformed itself into a titanic, hissing serpent, coiling itself around the angel's arms and legs and squeezing, its tongue darting between shows of its elongated fangs. Michael quickly wrestled it to the ground and tightly clamped its mouth shut. Whereupon the creature transformed itself yet again.

Now it grew and bulged and covered itself with slimy scales, sprouted four thick legs with horny toes, a lashing tail, a long neck, broad head and face, pointed ears, horns, and a fire-breathing mouth full of canines. This was the greatest test for Michael, who seemed to produce from thin air a heavy linked chain with which he was able to hog-tie the monster.

It rolled onto its back, snorting flames, hissing and drooling, struggling against the restraints. Its tail swept again and again at the angel, its great head shaking back and forth. Michael finally succeeded in lassoing the neck with the remains of the chain and with a powerful yank pulled the head toward the torso, rendering the dragon virtually immobile.

It lay there, snorting and writhing, and anyone watching knew what it would do if it could somehow free itself. Finally it appeared to relax, but that only preceded its final incarnation. The dragon gave way to what appeared to be one more angel, brighter than the archangels and the three angels of mercy, including Christopher, the angel with the everlasting gospel. Yet its light paled to insignificance next to that of Christ, whose glory lit the whole world.

Now the being stood docile, the chain having slid into a tall coil on the ground. It looked menacingly at Michael, who did not retreat. Gabriel spoke with a loud voice, "Lucifer, dragon, serpent, devil, Satan, you will now face the One you have opposed from time immemorial."

"Oh no!" the being rasped. "The last time you contended with me, Michael, it was over the body of Moses, and you dared not even bring against me a reviling accusation, but said, 'The Lord rebuke you!' I do not answer to you!"

"No," Jesus said quietly, though Rayford heard Him distinctly. And with the authority of the ages He said, "But you *do* answer to Me. Kneel at My feet."

"I will do no such thing!"

"Kneel."

And he did, shoulders hunched in rebellion and anger.

"I have fought against you from shortly after your creation," Jesus said.

"My *creation!* I was no more created than You! And who are You to have *anything* against *me?!*"

"You shall be silent."

The angel of light appeared to Rayford to try to stand, but he could not. He also appeared to try to speak, straining, shaking his head.

Jesus continued: "For all your lies about having evolved, you are a created being."

The creature violently shook its head.

"Only God has the power to create, and you were Our creation. You were in Eden, the garden of God, before it was a paradise for Adam and Eve. You were there as an exalted servant when Eden was a beautiful rock garden.

"You were the seal of perfection, full of wisdom and perfect in beauty. Every precious stone was your covering: the sardius, topaz, and diamond, beryl, onyx, and jasper, sapphire, turquoise, and emerald with gold. The workmanship of your timbrels and pipes was prepared for you on the day you were created.

"You were the anointed cherub who covers; God established you; you were on His holy mountain; you walked back and forth in the midst of fiery stones. You were perfect in your ways from the day you were created, till iniquity was found in you.

"But you became filled with violence within, and you sinned; therefore We cast you as a profane thing out of the mountain of God; and We destroyed you, O covering cherub, from the midst of the fiery stones. Your heart was lifted up because of your beauty; you corrupted your wisdom for the sake of your splendor; We cast you to the ground, laid you before kings, that they might gaze at you.

"You defiled your sanctuaries by the multitude of your iniquities, by the iniquity of your trading; therefore God brought fire from your midst; it devoured you, and He turned you to ashes upon the earth in the sight of all who saw you.

"All who knew you among the peoples are astonished at you; you have become a horror, and shall be no more forever."

The kneeling angel of fading light seemed to writhe in pain, eager to retaliate.

Jesus said, "You have opposed My Father and Me from before the creation of man. A third of the angels in heaven and most of the population of the earth followed your model of rebellion and pride. This will earn for them and for you separation from Almighty God in the everlasting fire prepared for you and your angels.

"You deceived Eve into sinning. During the next millennia you attempted to pollute the bloodline of Adam, putting it into Cain's heart to murder Abel and thus eliminating Adam's first two sons. You encouraged the cohabitation of fallen angels with human women to produce Nephilim, fallen ones. Because of you, within sixteen hundred years, only eight humans were found faithful and worthy of preserving from the Flood.

"It was you who attempted to establish a universal, idolatrous religion in Babel, then the largest city in the world, to keep mankind from worshiping the one true God.

"It was you who tried to destroy the Hebrew race, filling Pharaoh's mind with the idea to kill the male babies at the time of Moses' birth.

"I lay at your feet all the suffering of mankind. The earth was created as a utopia, and yet you brought into it sin, which resulted in poverty, disease, more than fifteen thousand wars, and the senseless killing of millions. You and your sin of pride spawned the rebellion of mankind against God, hatred, murder, and the damning of billions of souls from the time of Adam.

"You tried to attack Me upon My earthly birth by filling Herod's mind with the idea of killing all the male babies in Bethlehem. You tempted Me in the wilderness and tried to destroy My church through persecution and false teaching. You brought the storm to the Sea of Galilee while I slept. It was you who entered Judas Iscariot, you who filled the heart of Ananias with deceit. It was you, as the god of this evil world, who blinded the minds of those who do not believe.

"You were at work in the hearts of those who refused to obey God. It was you who prevented My servants from ministering, you who sowed discord in the churches, you who attacked the weak, the suffering, the lonely."

By now Satan had toppled onto his side, gasping and snorting, struggling to get back to his feet, to fight back, to speak.

"It is contrary to the will of God not only that humans sin, but also for them to reject Me. It is the will of My Father who is in heaven that not one of these little ones should perish. He is not slack concerning His promise, but is longsuffering, not willing that any should perish but that all should come to repentance.

"During the last seven years," Jesus said, "you have deceived millions with false teachers, false messiahs, a false prophet, and an antichrist. You gave him his power, his throne, and great authority. And all the world marveled and followed him.

"They worshiped you who gave authority to the Beast; and they worshiped the Beast, saying, 'Who is like the Beast? Who is able to make war with him?' And you gave him a mouth speaking great things and blasphemies, and he was given authority to continue for forty-two months.

"He opened his mouth in blasphemy

against God, to blaspheme His name, His tabernacle, and those who dwell in heaven. You granted to him to make war with the saints and to overcome them. And you gave him authority over every tribe, tongue, and nation.

"All who dwelt on the earth worshiped him, whose names have not been written in the Book of Life of the Lamb slain from the foundation of the world. He performed great signs, so that he even made fire come down from heaven on the earth in the sight of men.

"And you deceived those who dwell on the earth by those signs.

"You have a hatred for Me, a hatred for My people. You made war with those who kept the commandments of God. When anyone heard the word of the kingdom and did not understand it, you came and snatched away what was sown in his heart.

"You were the reason My servant had to remind My people that they did not wrestle against flesh and blood, but against principalities, against powers, against the rulers of the darkness of that age, against spiritual hosts of wickedness in the heavenly places. You were why they had to be instructed to take up the whole armor of God, that they would be able to withstand in the evil day, and having done all, to stand.

"I pledged ages ago that I would build My

church, and that the gates of Hades would not prevail against it. Your time has come. I have sent out My angels and they have gathered out of My kingdom all things that offend, and those who practice lawlessness, and I will cast them into the furnace of fire. There will be wailing and gnashing of teeth.

"Then the righteous will shine forth as the sun in the kingdom of their Father."

Michael grabbed Satan and pulled him back up to his knees, where he continued to thrash as if he were about to burst.

"It is you who have brought this on yourself," Jesus said. "For you have said in your heart: 'I will ascend into heaven, I will exalt my throne above the stars of God; I will also sit on the mount of the congregation on the farthest sides of the north; I will ascend above the heights of the clouds, I will be like the Most High.'

"Yet you shall be brought down to Sheol, to the lowest depths of the pit. Those who see you will gaze at you, and consider you, saying: 'Is this the man who made the earth tremble, who shook kingdoms, who made the world as a wilderness and destroyed its cities, who did not open the house of his prisoners?' "

Like everyone else, Abdullah was fascinated by this trial and judgment of Satan himself. In all his study of Scripture and prophecy, he never expected to witness it firsthand. He wished he could ask questions, like why the Antichrist and False Prophet were cast forever into the lake of fire, while Satan himself was set to be bound for a thousand years, only to be released again for a time at the end of the Millennium.

But Abdullah had found that most of his questions were eventually answered without anyone's asking them.

He couldn't get over the beauty of Jerusalem, given what had gone on in the previous several days. It looked pristine, scrubbed clean, and even the foliage seemed in full bloom and fragrant. What an impact on the world the presence of Jesus made!

Most of the remnant was made up of people from greater Jerusalem, far beyond the former walls of the Old City. The enemy had been driven out and killed, and so all the dwelling places in the Holy City were available again. People would be going back to their homes. Abdullah didn't know what that meant for him and other Gentile members of the Tribulation Force. They could always go back to Petra, of course. There was plenty of room there.

But for himself, he wanted to be where Jesus was, and he knew that prophecy said He would rule from the throne of David. That meant that when all this public stuff was over, people would still have access to Him, but of course a million-plus would not fit inside the temple. Maybe He would have supernatural audiences with them all at the same time once again. Otherwise, that would be His headquarters for ruling the nations of the world "with an iron rod."

Would Abdullah live with his wife? He couldn't wait to reunite with her, but he did not know all the ramifications of life now. She would exist in her glorified body, while he would bring to the millennial kingdom his mortal frame. There was so much to learn, so much to know.

Chang and Naomi, though they stood watching hand in hand, had barely spoken for hours. The day, in fact the whole time since the Glorious Appearing, had flown by. When Jesus had held Chang, and then cupped his face in His hands and spoken to him in Chinese, Chang had realized that everything he had been through was worth it. He would have given anything for that encounter with his Savior.

Jesus had told him that He was there

when Chang was born, when he was raised in a godless home and an aberrant religion. He was there when Chang was sent many miles away to school because of his intellect, and it was He Chang prayed to for strength and comfort and companionship, even though at that time he had never heard of Jesus.

"I was there, Chang," Jesus had told him, "when you came to believe deep in your heart that no god existed, certainly not One you associated with capitalists of the West. I was there when you rebelled against your parents and tried to teach them a lesson for sending you away. I was there when you abused your body and your mind with substances not intended for your nourishment.

"I was there when your mind was deceived by philosophy and vain deceit. I was there when you were discovered by the government of this world and pressed into service for the evil one.

"I rejoiced with the angels when you learned of Me and turned to Me and were used for My glory in the lair of Antichrist.

"And I was there when the mark of the beast was forced upon you and you feared you had lost your salvation. I have loved you from eternity past with an everlasting love, and I have looked forward to this day."

Chang was still glowing from that experience, even though he had finally figured out that everyone there had enjoyed their own personal encounter with Jesus. That it was not unique to him made it no less special. The message his Savior imparted was definitely for him alone, and the fearful, ugly things that had happened over the last few hours did nothing to temper the thrill of it.

It was time, Rayford realized. Jesus had finished His charges, and nothing was left but to carry out the sentence. Satan rocked on his knees, forcing gasping breaths through clenched teeth.

Gabriel leaned over the angel of light and shouted, "Acknowledge Jesus as Lord!"

Satan had been struck dumb, and as much as it appeared he was trying to speak, no words came out. But it was clear he had no interest in acceding to the order. He vigorously shook his head and clenched his fists before Jesus.

Jesus looked briefly to His left, and Rayford guessed thirty yards in that direction, farther from the angels and from the crowd, a great gaping hole appeared in the ground. Black smoke belched from deep within and nearly blotted out the sky. Again, no shadows were produced, because the light of day no longer came from the sun, but rather from the Lord Himself.

He nodded to Michael, who scooped up the long, heavy chain and draped it over his sinewy forearm. As he approached the condemned, Satan sprang to his feet and began to fight. Again he morphed, first into the dragon, then the snake, and finally the lion. The conflict covered the distance between the remnant and Jesus and the other angels. Every time Michael and Satan tumbled near the crowd, people backed into each other.

Rayford had no misgivings about the outcome of the tussle. Jesus seemed to look on with abject sadness and no concern. Gabriel, who had always served as a herald and not a warrior, looked every bit as capable as Michael and could have stepped in at any time. The three angels of mercy, including the preacher of the everlasting gospel, were close by as well.

Finally, in his form as the lion, Satan was strangely without a roar. Jesus had silenced him, and the curse carried over regardless of his disguise. Michael finally worked the chain about him and drew it tight, forcing the animal into a bound mass.

As he lifted the captive toward the smoking abyss, Satan altered himself yet again, back to the angel of light. With that he slipped out of the chain and made one last feeble attempt to escape. Michael swung the chain and let it slide through his hands until the extended portion was at least twenty feet long. This he flung at the devil, catching him at the midsection and causing the chain to wrap itself around him.

Michael rushed him, tackled him to the ground, completed the chain-wrapping operation, and jumped to his feet, carrying the bound devil. Just before he reached the smoldering, smoke-belching chasm, Michael left his feet and flew — Satan under his arm — about ten feet into the air and then headfirst down into the abyss.

This Jesus did not watch, though the other angelic beings did. The crowd roared and cheered and applauded, but they quieted quickly when Jesus stood and gestured with a hand.

"And now," He said, "to My Father God, the King eternal, immortal, invisible, to Him who alone is wise, be honor and glory forever. Beloved, sin reigned in death, but even so grace reigns through righteousness to eternal life. Even the demons recognized Me as the Holy One of God. I stand before you this day as the King of Israel, He who comes in the name of the Lord."

He gazed above, and from beyond the

clouds came a chorus from those Rayford could only assume were gathered around the throne of God. They sang the song of Moses, the servant of God, and the song of the Lamb, saying: "Great and marvelous are Your works, Lord God Almighty! Just and true are Your ways, O King of the saints! And He will reign over the house of Jacob forever, and of His kingdom there will be no end."

Still the smoke poured from the bottomless pit, and Rayford wondered if others, like he, had begun to worry about Michael. But presently he reemerged with a key in his hand. Satan and the chain were no longer to be seen.

Michael rejoined the others behind Jesus, who turned and mounted His horse. He slowly led the white stallion away from the open square and through the crowd toward the Temple Mount, where He would take His rightful place on the throne of King David.

And finally, Rayford felt a twinge of hunger and a new wave of fatigue. Without instruction or a word about it, the remnant seemed to be slowly scattering to return to their homes. Rayford would have to reconnect with his friends and see who might have room for him.

Eighteen

Rayford could not think of a word to describe how he felt, other than *euphoric*. He knew there would be times when Jesus would not be visible, like now. It only made sense. But he had feared he would have such a longing for Him that he might be depressed, out of sorts, when Jesus was otherwise occupied. Rayford was thrilled to realize this was not the case.

His heart was still with Jesus, of course. He thought about Him constantly. And he wanted to see Him, sure. But because Rayford was so preoccupied with Him, eager to love and serve Him forever, he found himself free from his normal temptations. He had to wonder if this was temporary. Was he free from lust, from pride, from greed only because this was like being in church, in the presence of your pastor? Or did the binding of Satan and the death of his demons have something to do with it? Rather than being tempted by the world, the flesh, and the devil, he had to worry about only two of the three. And the world was new and ruled by Jesus.

Would the novelty of having Jesus physically present eventually wear off? *I mean, a thousand years, and then eternity . . .*

The way Jesus had talked to him, connected with him, made Rayford feel as if He were still right there, even though he couldn't see Him. When he prayed, it was as if Jesus conversed with him immediately. Rayford had so many questions, so many things he would have to ask Chaim.

First, of course, was whether Chaim had any idea where Rayford might find lodging. He was amused to discover, upon reuniting with the rest of the Tribulation Force personnel who had been at Petra, that this had already been thoroughly thought through, discussed, and even decided.

Rayford and Mac and Abdullah had stayed in the public square, searching the crowd for anyone they recognized. "We had better separate," Abdullah suggested. "If any of us finds someone, he can call the others and arrange a meeting place."

Abdullah headed west, Mac east. Rayford

stayed in the center, searching faces for the familiar. What a sight! Everywhere he looked, people looked like friends, though they were mostly strangers. He recognized some from having seen them in Petra, but when he asked if they had seen his friends and acquaintances, none had. And yet all wanted to talk. Mostly about Jesus. But about the earthquake too, and the splitting of the Mount of Olives. The slaying of the enemy. The sentencing of Carpathia, Fortunato, and Satan.

Others mentioned the weather — hot, clear, refreshing, as if they were breathing new air. A woman pointed out the trees and bushes and how suddenly full and healthy they looked. "They did not look this way twenty-four hours ago," she said.

Something hit Rayford. He asked where she was from. "Russia," she said.

"And what language are you speaking?"

"Russian, of course. I know only a little English. And you?"

"English. It's all I know."

Rayford kept moving, looking, asking. Here and there groups were praying, singing, some just lifting their hands toward heaven and smiling. Finally he got a call from Mac.

"Seems strange that these contraptions

are still workin', doesn't it?" Mac said. "You'd think maybe we could just talk to each other without machines now."

Rayford laughed. "Why?"

"Why not? Anyhoo, you know Christ Church, a tick southeast of David's Tower?"

"Sure."

"That's where we all are."

"Smitty too?"

"Everybody."

The names of all the landmarks had been changed when Carpathia came to power, but the believers knew what was what. Outside Christ Church, at the southeast corner of the building, Rayford found his circle of friends from Petra. All but Otto.

Besides Abdullah and Mac, Chaim was there with Chang and Naomi and her father, Eleazar. Hannah and Leah were there. When Rayford saw Razor chatting with the Woos, he knew Sebastian and Priscilla and Beth Ann had to be close by, and that meant Kenny couldn't be far off. And here he came.

The boy leaped into Rayford's arms. "Grandpa! I saw Jesus! And He talked to me!"

"Isn't that the best?"

"Yeah! Gonna see Mommy and Daddy too."

Rayford looked at Priss. She mouthed, "Soon."

"Yeah, pretty soon," Rayford said.

As he held Kenny, Rayford was brought up to speed on what had been decided. "Otto has somehow secured an abandoned hotel for his people," Chaim said.

"Already?"

"Oh, Rayford, people are eager to accommodate each other. And as you can imagine, a little over a million people will rattle around in this country. Nearly three quarters of a million used to live in greater Jerusalem alone. There are thousands of deserted residences, but most people seem to be returning to their own homes and inviting in those from other places. Eleazar and Naomi have agreed to take the single women and the married couples, and I have plenty of room for the single men."

"Kenny," Rayford said, "you want to stay with Grandpa at Uncle Chaim's? Or with Beth Ann and Aunt Priscilla?"

"Where's Mommy gonna be?"

"Probably with us," Priss said, and Kenny wriggled down.

"Okay, Grandpa?"

"Okay, Kenny. I'll see you a lot."

"I'll get the car," Abdullah said, and he jogged off.

With Rayford crammed all the way in the back, facing the back window with his knees pulled to his chest, they somehow managed to fit Chaim, Chang, Lionel, Mac, and Razor into the Hummer, with Abdullah behind the wheel.

On the way to Chaim's house, Chang spent the whole time on the phone with Naomi. Razor teased him that he had just been with her for days, but Rayford noticed that they weren't talking about each other anyway. Like everyone else in the car, they were talking about Jesus.

"I have so many questions, Chaim," Rayford called out from the back.

"Probably not as many as I do," Chaim said, "but for those who are interested, we will open the Scriptures and try to make sense of all this."

"Are you all seeing what I'm seeing?" Rayford said, studying the landscape and the people and the animals as Abdullah steered through the happy crowds. All the animals were docile. Sheep, dogs, wolves, critters of all types roamed everywhere. Shops had already reopened and butchers were working in the open air. Trucks delivered fresh fruits and vegetables from nearby groves. "Who'd have had time to pick these, and where are butchers getting their meat?"

"That butcher is a friend of mine," Chaim said. "Let me find out."

Abdullah pulled over and everyone got out, Razor heading for a produce stand. Rayford followed Chaim.

"Ezer!" Chaim shouted, embracing the tall, thin man who wielded a cleaver and wore a blood-spattered apron. "I did not know you were a believer!"

"I wasn't," Ezer said. "I resisted and resisted, blind, so blind. But during the fighting to hold Jerusalem I heard a rabbi in the Old City talk of Messiah. And I was spared."

"Back to butchering already! How does this happen?"

"I was driven underground by the GC because I refused to take the mark. I lost this shop and my home. After what we just witnessed in the Old City, I wanted to see what was left. My home is intact. And my shop stood empty. You will not believe it, Chaim, but fattened animals, ready for slaughter and butchering, milled about the place as if volunteering! Cows, sheep! Imagine! I found my tools and got to work immediately. What do you need?"

"A lot of beef and lamb. I have six houseguests, all hungry grown men."

"Take all you need. It's on me."

"Oh no, I couldn't!"

"You don't have money anyway, do you? And I wouldn't want Nicks."

"No, but start a bill for me, and when we discover what shape the economy takes, I will settle up."

"You opposed Carpathia, Chaim. That is all the pay I need."

"No, I insist. How will you live?"

"I told you! The goods cost me nothing, and look!" He pointed behind the shop and Chaim and Rayford stepped to where they could see. From miles around, the sheep and the cows kept coming. Men were already building pens. "My new employees," Ezer said. "I pay them in meat. I have more than I need, and apparently God is providing. Please, do me the honor of taking all you need. They are the freshest, fattest, finest cuts I have ever produced."

Chaim finally relented, and Ezer was resolute in enlisting all the houseguests to take several pounds each. "To hold in your lap on the trip home. Please, please. You are doing me a favor. I have too much and nowhere to store it."

As they returned to the car, Rayford heard Ezer shouting to the crowds in the streets, "Free meat from the hand of God! Come, please, and take all you need!"

Razor returned from the produce stand, laden with sacks of fruit and vegetables. "The woman would take nothing for these!" he said. "She claims they are falling off the trees, not just in the orchards but right here in the city."

"Hold on," Chang said into the phone, then covered it as Abdullah pulled away and headed for Chaim's. "Naomi says it is a widespread miracle. They too have stopped to stock up on fresh meat and produce. She said they gathered oranges and grapefruit from beneath trees and saw the branches ripen again before their eyes."

That evening — Rayford could tell it was evening only by his watch; the brightness of the day never changed — the men settled into Chaim's spacious home, room assignments seeming to take care of themselves. It turned out that Razor and Abdullah considered themselves cooks and proved it by grilling the meat and preparing heaping bowls of sliced fruit and steaming vegetables.

Rayford had always been impressed with how the Trib Force and Co-op believers worked together, but he had never seen anything like this. In fact, he wondered if a thousand years with zero strife or conflict would get boring. Despite the generally good attitudes of the people under his charge over the last seven years, part of the challenge of his job had been refereeing battles of ego and turf. Now he just watched as people got along and worked together. Admittedly, it was the first day in their new home. They had just witnessed miraculous fulfillments of prophecy and had been in the physical presence of Jesus. And they had been provided the most comfortable lodging they'd had in years, not to mention they were about to eat free food — and a feast at that.

Mac found chairs and tables and enlisted Chang and Lionel in the setup process, while Chaim asked Rayford to help him assess the home he had not seen for three and a half years. All the old man could do was shake his head at the memories. There was no evidence of damage to the place by the GC. He found no residue from three separate earthquakes, including the most recent global upheaval and the raising of the entire city some three hundred feet at the cleaving of the Mount of Olives.

As Rayford followed him about the place, Chaim said, "I am tired of my own disbelief. I must simply once and for all accept that God is the author of all this. He can do anything, and He has done everything. I had heard that the GC took over this house as a command center almost three years ago. Can you imagine, Captain Steele, what it should look like after dozens of different men have lived and worked in it? I expected the stench of tobacco, garbage, a mess. Yet look."

Rayford *was* looking. It was as if a cleaning crew had swept through the entire place. Floors, walls, ceilings were clean. Furniture was in place. Rayford wouldn't have been more surprised if there had been slipcovers draped on each piece. But there didn't need to be. He couldn't find a speck of dust anywhere.

"Well, the refrigerator and freezer and pantry are empty," Chaim said. "And yet look what the Lord provided on our way here."

"Guess He thought you could stock the shelves yourself."

"I do not know. I could get used to all this."

When it was time to sit and eat, Chaim stood at the head of the table. "Let us pray," he said.

And Rayford had the strangest experience. As he prayed along with Chaim, thanking God for the privilege of witnessing what they had seen that day, for the food He had provided, and for the move-in-ready home He had preserved, it was as if Jesus answered audibly and immediately and personally.

"You're welcome, Rayford," He said. "It is My delight to shower you with love in tangible ways." And before Rayford could pray for Kenny, the Lord said, "I know of your concern. He will be reunited with his parents, as will you, very soon."

It was as if Jesus were sitting right next to Rayford, His arm around him, speaking directly to him. It broke Rayford anew and he couldn't stanch the tears. He folded his hands on the plate before him and rested his face on them, worshiping God.

And Jesus said, "I will reign over the house of Jacob forever, and of My kingdom there will be no end. As the Father knows Me, even so I know the Father; and I laid down My life for the sheep. I am the Lamb who will lead you to living fountains of waters, and God will wipe away every tear from your eyes."

Rayford rested there, listening and worshiping, knowing that the tears Jesus mentioned were those of sadness, and his were anything but. He couldn't imagine ever being sad again.

He heard the rest of the men murmuring

their praise and knew they had had the same experience he had. While Rayford could smell the delicious food in heaping serving bowls inches from his plate, his hunger could wait. He never wanted this moment of worship to end.

After several minutes, Chaim picked up his prayer again. "And now, O Lord, our Redeemer and Friend, we thank You for this bounty. I confess, Father, that as grateful as I was for the manna, and as satisfying as it was . . ." He didn't have to finish. Rayford sat up and covered his mouth, but he couldn't stifle the laugh. And in his soul he believed with all his heart that he heard Jesus chuckle too. Yes, manna was one thing. This was something else entirely.

Chaim sat down and the men opened their eyes, looking at each other. "Jesus spoke to me again in Chinese," Chang said.

"Spanish," Razor said.

"Hebrew," Chaim said.

"English," Rayford said.

"Sout' side o' Chicago," Lionel said, and they laughed.

"He worked a little west Texan in there too, I believe," Mac said. "That's the language of heaven, ya know."

Rayford cleared his throat. Still no one had reached for the food. "Ah, was it just me, or did any of you hear Jesus laugh at Chaim's manna crack?"

They all smiled and nodded. Chaim said, "No question the Lord has a sense of humor. Gentlemen, can you believe the food is still steaming as if we hadn't left it out here for several minutes?"

"The fruit looks crisp and fresh too," Razor said. "And no flies."

And so they ate. Rayford assumed that for the others it was as it was for him — the tastiest meal he had ever enjoyed. "The real miracle," he said later, "will be eating like this all the time without gaining weight."

During cleanup, Rayford and Chaim spoke with Eleazar by phone. It was great for Rayford to hear that they had enjoyed the same type of time with the Lord and a wonderful meal as the men had. Chaim reminded Eleazar of what they planned to cover that evening from the Scriptures, and they compared notes on difficult passages. "If we are left with confusing questions," Eleazar boomed, "we shall simply ask Jesus, next time we see Him."

Later that evening, the men gathered in Chaim's great room, and he opened his Bible and spread his notes and a couple of commentaries before him. "Books by men seem superfluous now," he said. "Whenever we pray I feel as if Messiah is here with me, answering questions even before I ask. Let us begin with a time of worship and prayer."

As one the men slipped from their chairs and knelt on the floor, each praying in his native tongue.

Mac was about to tell the Lord that there were people — particularly from the previous seven years — that he was eager to see. Each had meant something special to him, had made a significant impact on his life. But before he could articulate it, Jesus spoke to him by name. "I know, Cleburn. And you shall see them soon. I long for that reunion as much as you do and will rejoice with you when you see them."

As Rayford received answers to prayers he had not yet even uttered, he prostrated himself on the floor and could see the others doing likewise. He decided that what Jesus was trying to tell him was the same as he had heard from Bruce Barnes years before, and the same as he had heard from Tsion and Chaim: Prayer was as much, or more, about listening as it was about talking. Rayford had never accomplished that balance. It seemed he was always beseeching, asking, requesting. Yes, he thanked God for things and often worshiped Him in prayer, but he was starting to get the picture now. It was time to simply be quiet and listen. And even if God said nothing, Rayford was to rest in the peace of His presence.

Rayford lay there on his stomach and basked in the warmth of God's love. And Jesus said, "God is your refuge and strength, a very present help in trouble. Therefore do not fear, even though the earth be removed, and though the mountains be carried into the midst of the sea; though its waters roar and be troubled, though the mountains shake with its swelling.

"There is a river whose streams shall make glad the city of God, the holy place of the tabernacle of the Most High. God is in the midst of her, she shall not be moved; God shall help her, just at the break of dawn.

"The nations raged, the kingdoms were moved; He uttered His voice, the earth melted. The Lord of hosts is with you; the God of Jacob is your refuge.

"Come, behold the works of the Lord, who has made desolations in the earth. He made wars cease to the end of the earth; He broke the bow and cut the spear in two; He burned the chariot in the fire.

"Be still, and know that I am God; I will

be exalted among the nations, I will be exalted in the earth!

"The Lord of hosts is with you; the God of Jacob is your refuge."

Suddenly Chaim rose back to his knees and said, "Oh, clap your hands, all you peoples! Shout to God with the voice of triumph! For the Lord Most High is awesome; He is a great King over all the earth. He has subdued the peoples under us, and the nations under our feet. . . . God reigns over the nations; God sits on His holy throne."

Rayford lay communing with God, only vaguely aware of the others. Finally, when it felt as if he actually needed a break from the loving hand of Jesus, he moved back to his chair. Strange how everyone seemed to have the same experiences at the same time and for the same duration.

"Before you start, Chaim, I have a question, maybe more of a confession. This newly close presence of God, through Jesus, is so fresh, so special, that at times I can't seem to get enough of Him. But at other times, like just now, it was almost as if I was so filled to overflowing that if I stayed there, I could take no more."

Others nodded, which Rayford found comforting. Chaim said, "That reminds me of a story I once read of a great evangelist from the nineteenth century, Dwight L. Moody. He wrote of having an experience with the Lord where His presence and fullness were so overwhelming that Moody had to ask God to 'stay His hand.' "

"Exactly," Rayford said.

"I have felt that too," Chaim said. "Perhaps in the presence of Jesus we will build the spiritual muscle necessary to endure such blessings."

Chaim seemed to look at each man individually, as if to ask if there was anything else before he got started. Then he explained that he and the elders had spent the last month vigorously searching the Scriptures for clues to what to expect after the Glorious Appearing.

"Like cramming for a test," Razor suggested.

"I am not familiar with that term," Chaim said, "but it seems self-explanatory and I would have to agree. Not that we are going to be tested. In fact, there was much discussion among the elders at first over how necessary this was. Some held that Jesus would be our teacher and would explain everything along the way.

"Well, maybe He expects us to know this material, hmm? Today we witnessed His victory ascent to Mount Olivet, also known as the Mount of Olives. We saw it split in two. He conquered the invading armies, slaying them with the Word of God. We were with Him for His triumphal entry into Jerusalem, and we saw Him capture and judge demons, the False Prophet, Antichrist, and even Satan himself. And yet never once did He stop and say, 'Beloved, you'll find this on page so-and-so of your text, and it *will* be on the final.'

"These things happened as they were prophesied, and no explanation is forthcoming. That is much the same way Jesus taught and preached the first time He was on earth. Only occasionally did He follow a parable with an explanation. And when He did, it was only enough for those 'who have ears to hear.'

"I suppose there were many in the crowd today who had little idea what was going on. They probably could have figured out who was who and what was what, and in the end they knew that Jesus had won again, conquering more foes. But they are probably wondering where He has gone, what He is doing. Well, gentlemen, the answers are in the Book, and if you are interested, we shall plumb the riches herein and see what we can learn."

Each enthusiastically expressed his interest, and Chaim began.

"I fear that many — and I confess this was true of me and most of the elders — believed that the Glorious Appearing ushered in the millennial kingdom, which, as you know, means the thousand-year reign of Christ on earth. Anyone here in that camp?"

Several nodded, Rayford included. He glanced at Abdullah, who was smiling. It was not the smile of the condescendingly superior, but of one who had apparently done his homework and knew what was coming. Rayford was most impressed that, despite this, Abdullah did not call out, "Not me! I know!"

Rayford raised his hand. "Chaim, I'll bet Smitty knows what you're talking about. He's become quite the student."

"Is that true, Mr. Smith?" Chaim said.

"I am not well versed in it," Abdullah said, "but my studies, mostly with Dr. Ben-Judah, reveal that there is actually a gap between the Glorious Appearing and the Millennium, much as there was between the Rapture and the Tribulation."

"There was?" Razor said.

"Oh yes," Abdullah said. "You'll recall that the seven years did not begin with the disappearances of the believers, but rather with the signing of the covenant between

Antichrist and Israel. That came a couple of weeks later, but it could have come a couple of years later, and the signing, not the Rapture, would have been the start of the Tribulation."

"Excellent!" Chaim said. "That is indeed where I was going and what we will discuss this evening. From the Glorious Appearing to the actual beginning of the millennial kingdom, there is a seventy-five-day interval. If it took God just six days to create the heavens and the earth and man himself, imagine how much work Jesus must have if He has been allotted seventy-five days in which to do it."

"Where do you get that out of the Bible?" Rayford said. "I mean, I'm no great student or anything, but I've tried to read a lot."

"Good question. The answer is found partly in Daniel 12:11–12. Listen to the first of those verses: 'And from the time that the daily sacrifice is taken away, and the abomination of desolation is set up, there shall be one thousand two hundred and ninety days.' Rayford, you remember when Antichrist defiled the temple?"

"*Do* I."

"That was the abomination of desolation. And that was one thousand two hundred and *sixty* days before the Glorious Appearing. So we are already talking about thirty more days. And the next verse says, 'Blessed is he who waits, and comes to the one thousand three hundred and thirty-five days.' That's another forty-five days, giving us a total of seventy-five more days."

"What does the first thirty days refer to?" Rayford said.

"Well, the verse is talking about the temple sacrifice and the abomination, so I think it is fair to assume the first interval relates to the temple. I cannot imagine Jesus wanting to take the throne of David in a temple that has been defiled by Antichrist — at least not before He cleanses it. We know from Ezekiel 40–48 that the Lord will establish a temple during the Millennium, so I conclude that the first thirty days of the interval will be devoted to setting up the temple and preparing it for use.

"The other forty-five days are more open to speculation, but notice that verse 12 says that those who make it through that time will be blessed. If that is a personal, individual blessing, it indicates that the person is qualified to enter into the millennial kingdom. Matthew 25:34 says, 'Then the King will say to those on His right hand, "Come, you *blessed* of My Father, inherit the kingdom prepared for you from the foundation of the world." '

"That makes it sound to me as if the seventy-five-day interval is a time for preparation for the kingdom. So much of the globe has been destroyed during the judgments of the Tribulation, I suppose it should not surprise us that the Lord will take some time to renovate His creation for the Millennium. The beautification of Jerusalem was done in an instant with the elevating of the city from the splitting of the Mount of Olives, but imagine the work that needs to be done around the world. The mountains have been leveled, filling much of the seas. Islands have vanished. Surely God wants to put the earth back into its Edenic state for the enjoyment of those who will share it with Jesus for the next thousand years."

Nineteen

Leah Rose had come a long way from nursing supervisor at Arthur Young Memorial Hospital in Palatine, Illinois. How was she to know what would become of her when she first encountered Rayford Steele and the fledgling Tribulation Force nearly seven years before? She and Rayford had spotted each other's seal of the believer, visible only to others of like faith. Otherwise, she might not have given him the time of day.

To think that since then she had been all over the world with the Force in a variety of roles, mostly medical but not exclusively. She had made new friends, seen them become loved ones, and then seen them die. There had been times when she wouldn't have given two cents for her chances to make it to the Glorious Appearing. At least not until she was assigned duty at Petra, where in three and a half years, no one had died.

Privileged, that's what she called herself. Certainly nothing she had ever done had earned her the benefits she had enjoyed. It had not been an easy life. Hardly. No one who had lived through the Tribulation had it easy. That she had to live through it at all was her own fault — for having heard the message and ignored it for so long. She had not considered herself a rejecter. Leah had seen herself as an intellectual, a thinker, a ponderer.

Evangelists and evangelistic-minded friends had told her and told her that a nondecision was a "no" decision. She had argued. She wasn't saying no, she said; she was still thinking. Well, one of her well-meaning friends had said, don't think yourself into hell. Or into being left behind.

That had been a laugh. While Leah had seriously considered the claims of Christ on her life, that He had died for her sins — of which she acknowledged there were many — the idea of His showing up in the clouds someday, in an instant so quick you could blink and miss it, well . . . come on now.

And then she had been left behind. Leah

took care of that issue immediately. Then, while she floundered spiritually, looking for more, looking for truth, looking for answers, she believed God sent Rayford and the Trib Force into her life.

They were all in the same boat, of course, latecomers to the kingdom. But among them were men of the Bible, lifelong students like Tsion Ben-Judah, from whom she believed she had learned more than she had in nursing school.

And now here she was in Jerusalem, in the home of an elder. With friends who had become dear and who had experienced with her, firsthand, the fulfillment of prophecy in the presence of Jesus Himself. Leah had seen it with her own eyes, talked to Him, and met with Him personally. When He embraced her and called her by name and told her how much He loved her, she could not speak. And yet He heard her heart. He had been with her, known her since the foundation of the world, He said. Was with her all her life, at the high and low points, the turning points, loving her, waiting for her, longing to meet her.

Leah was so full of Jesus she hardly knew if she could stand it. And while others cowered and hid their faces and grimaced at the awful reality of Satan and his lackeys getting theirs, she would not turn away. This, she knew, was justice, and she wanted to see it.

Leah had been a victim of Satan, and of course she had suffered under the rule of Nicolae Carpathia. To be made an international fugitive simply because she loved the one true God and His Son was an unspeakable, unforgivable offense. Antichrist, indwelt by Satan, had exalted himself over God, and Leah's lifelong sense of right and wrong — cultivated even before she became a believer — told her he would have to pay. And when the time came, gruesome and graphic as it was, to her it was fitting.

Leah had seen the physical ravages of sin, what war could do to the human body. When she tried to repair dying comrades she couldn't help but lay the blame at the feet of Antichrist and his False Prophet. She didn't avert her eyes from that carnage, and so she didn't when Satan's demons were put to death by the words of Jesus. And when Nicolae and Leon were sent to eternal torment. And especially when Satan himself was locked away for a thousand years.

Leah still didn't understand that one. It was something she could ask Eleazar when he led the group in Bible study that night. Word was that the elders were all teaching the same stuff, wherever they wound up and with whom. She considered it another privilege to have landed in the lovely Tiberius home.

Naomi's late mother's touches remained, even after all this time. The place had been taken over by the GC, just like any home of some worth. The result of that could have been disappointing, yet when the ten of them settled in, unloading their haul of fresh meat and produce in the generous kitchen, no one was more surprised than Eleazar at the state of the place. It looked as if someone had been hired to make it perfect for their stay.

They had found their quarters — just enough space for everyone — and had worked together watching the children, setting the tables, preparing the food. They had prayed and feasted, cleaned up, and prayed some more. Jesus had spoken to them in three different languages simultaneously. Leah then helped Priss Sebastian get the kids to bed, and now it was time to study.

She found the teaching on the next seventy-five days fascinating, having never heard of it before. What Leah appreciated most about Eleazar was his own bright, inquisitive mind and how he didn't pretend to know things he didn't. "Some things," he said in his jolly basso profundo, "are apparently unknowable, at least for now. Other truths are fascinating to ferret out of the Scriptures."

Leah asked her question about why Antichrist and the False Prophet were sentenced for eternity while Satan would be released at the end of the Millennium.

"The binding of Satan," Eleazar said, "restricts him from what he does best, of course. Revelation 20:3 indicates that God's goal in this binding is 'so that he should deceive the nations no more till the thousand years were finished.' "

"Yes," Leah said, "but it goes on to say, 'But after these things he must be released for a little while.' Why must he?"

"I once asked the same question of Dr. Ben-Judah, and I recently asked Dr. Rosenzweig," Eleazar said. "Neither was entirely sure, and neither am I, but they suggested some remarkable things I had been unaware of, and I'll bet you have been too."

"That wouldn't surprise me," Leah said.

"Here's the way I understand it, based on what I have been taught. Look at it this way: If God did not allow Satan one more chance to deceive the nations, all the people who are born and live during the millennial kingdom would be exempt from the decision to follow God or follow Satan. By releasing him one more time, all people are given equal standing before God."

"Interesting."

"But where it gets dicey is that those who reject Christ during the Millennium will all be young people, relatively. You will see when we dig into the Scriptures that anyone born during the Millennium who does not trust in Christ by the time he or she is a hundred years old will be accursed and die."

"I thought you said young people."

"Relatively. You see, those who do trust in Christ will live to the end of the Millennium."

"So someone born today, who becomes a believer, will live to be a thousand."

"Exactly."

"But the unbelievers, whenever they are born during this period, will die at a hundred?"

"Now you've got it."

"I don't know what I have," Leah said. "But it *is* interesting. If I'm figuring it right, what Satan will have to do at the end of the Millennium is try to organize all the people who were born at the nine-hundred-year mark or after — who haven't become believers — and get them to make one last-

442

gasp effort to fight Jesus."

"There you go."

"Wow. And there's Scripture for this."

"There is. Let's read it together from Isaiah 65:17–25: 'For behold, I create new heavens and a new earth; and the former shall not be remembered or come to mind.

" 'But be glad and rejoice forever in what I create; for behold, I create Jerusalem as a rejoicing, and her people a joy.

" 'I will rejoice in Jerusalem, and joy in My people; the voice of weeping shall no longer be heard in her, nor the voice of crying.

" 'No more shall an infant from there live but a few days, nor an old man who has not fulfilled his days; for the child shall die one hundred years old, but the sinner being one hundred years old shall be accursed.'

"Let me just interject an explanation here," Eleazar said. "This is saying that a person who dies at a hundred will be considered a child, because everyone else is living until the end of the Millennium. And that the 'child' who does die at a hundred will die because he is a sinner. Now, let's read on:

" 'They shall build houses and inhabit them; they shall plant vineyards and eat their fruit.

" 'They shall not build and another in-habit; they shall not plant and another eat; for as the days of a tree, so shall be the days of My people, and My elect shall long enjoy the work of their hands.'

"Again," Eleazar interrupted, "here's what I believe is being said here. We will not be serving landlords and despots. What we build we will enjoy ourselves. And what we plant and harvest will be for us, not a boss or an occupying government. Reading on:

" 'They shall not labor in vain, nor bring forth children for trouble; for they shall be the descendants of the blessed of the Lord, and their offspring with them.

" 'It shall come to pass that before they call, I will answer; and while they are still speaking, I will hear.' "

"I've already experienced that!" Leah said. "Haven't you all?"

"Yes!" several others said. "Jesus often an-swers a prayer before I have prayed it."

"Continuing," Eleazar said. " 'The wolf and the lamb shall feed together' — we saw that in the street today — 'the lion shall eat straw like the ox, and dust shall be the ser-pent's food. They shall not hurt nor destroy in all My holy mountain,' says the Lord. "

Rayford's brain was spinning. This was

new to him, and he assumed it was to the people at Eleazar Tiberius's home as well. He couldn't wait to discuss it with some of them.

Chang raised his hand. "Chaim," he said, "where are all the people who died before the Rapture? The people from the Old Testament, the believers before Jesus came, and the ones who died during the Tribulation? Were they all in the army that appeared with Jesus in the clouds?"

Chaim sat back and smiled. "You have raised an interesting issue," he said. "Do we want to get into this tonight, or are you all ready to pull the shades and see if we can pretend it is dark enough to sleep?"

Rayford was tired, but he was no more interested in going to bed than any of the rest of the men were. And they said so.

"Fair enough," Chaim said. "It all begins with the Bible's teaching about resurrection day. I had always thought there was only one and that it coincided with the Rapture."

"Me too."

"Apparently, this is not the case, for the resurrection that took place at the Rapture was of what the Bible refers to as 'the dead in Christ' and did not include the saints from the Old Testament. When they died, Christ had not yet come to earth, so even though they were justified by faith, they technically cannot be referred to as 'the dead in Christ.' The resurrections in Scripture fall into two categories: the first resurrection, or the resurrection of life; and the second resurrection, the resurrection of judgment. John 5:28–29 quotes Jesus saying, 'Do not marvel at this; for the hour is coming in which all who are in the graves will hear His voice and come forth — those who have done good, to the resurrection of life, and those who have done evil, to the resurrection of condemnation.'

"The first resurrection includes the redeemed of all the ages, but the timing of the resurrection of these people varies, based on whether they are an Old Testament saint, a Christian who lived before or at the time of the Rapture, or a Christian martyred during the Tribulation. All of them will take part in the resurrection of life. The resurrection of judgment will include the unredeemed of all the ages, and this will happen at the end of the Millennium during what the Bible calls the Great White Throne Judgment. The unredeemed will be cast into the lake of fire."

"So let me get this straight," Rayford said. "Christians who died before the Rapture were resurrected at the time of the Rapture."

"Right."

"Old Testament saints will be resurrected when?"

"Soon. During this interval between the Glorious Appearing and the Millennium."

"And Tribulation martyrs?"

"At the same time. Old Testament saints and Tribulation martyrs will live and reign with Christ in the millennial kingdom."

"What about people who become believers during the Millennium?"

"They will be resurrected at the end of the Millennium."

"Even though they're alive."

"Correct."

"And the unredeemed won't be resurrected until after the Millennium either, for the Great White Throne Judgment."

Chaim smiled. "Now you know as much as I do."

"So," Rayford said, "my wife and son, who were raptured, were in that army of heaven behind Jesus."

"Yes."

"But my daughter and son-in-law, who were martyred during the Tribulation, will soon be resurrected."

"Precisely."

"So, we'll get to see our friends and loved ones soon."

Enoch Dumas and his people from the tiny The Place congregation, formerly of inner-city Chicago, began discovering a few tiny pockets of fellow believers here and there. Employees of Antichrist or his government, even in America, had died at the words that came from the mouth of the Lord, but apparently it was God's intent that the Millennium start with a clean slate. *All* unbelievers would soon die.

The group reunited, and immediately everyone had the same idea. They should head back into Chicago to reminisce at their old meeting place, see what the former Tribulation Force safe house — where they had been guests before it was compromised — looked like now. Most of all, they needed to see what living accommodations were available in the city. Were the hotels and flophouses and fleabag apartments still around? And what about the high-rent district not so many blocks from where they had plied their trades before they became believers? If everyone else was going to die, what would keep them from living in the fancy hotels downtown?

Chicago had been considered radioactively contaminated for years, and even members of The Place had believed it, feeling forced to live inside, underground. When Chloe Steele Williams had discovered them and convinced them that the nuclear readings in Chicago were phonies planted by a Trib Force mole at the GC palace in New Babylon, they finally ventured out.

Once the GC discovered the scheme, the Trib Force and The Place members had to relocate — and fast. Since then GC operatives had determined Chicago was safe again, and the city had begun to rebuild. But if what was true in Palos Hills and the surrounding suburbs was also true in the city, Enoch and his people would virtually have the place to themselves.

Enoch expected to see the grisly effects of the worldwide slaughter of Christ's enemies, much as he had seen in his neighborhood when the GC car had hit the hydrant. Would there be bodies lining the streets, blood and flesh everywhere? Piles of bones? There were not. The global earthquake had apparently been a work of cleanup. Many skyscrapers had toppled, including the Strong Building, where the Trib Force safe house had been. But even these piles of rubble had been so shaken that they merely buried the ugliness of the bloodbath among Carpathia's employees.

Enoch had to talk with God about what to do. If only believers would be left in the United States, with scriptural prophecy seeming to ignore America, it was going to be one sparsely populated country. The various groups of believers might find each other, but what were they to do? Would there be enough of them to start rebuilding the country as, finally for real, a Christian nation? Was this why God was going to purge it of the unredeemed and had already leveled it, making the entire planet as flat as the state of Illinois? None of the believers had worked in public for years. Anyone responsible for any public service or utility would soon be dead. Maybe this was God's way of drawing all His people to be with Jesus in Israel.

As Enoch slowly drove through Chicago, Jesus spoke to him. "Fear not, Enoch, for you have rightly deduced that you and your flock are to be with Me."

"But, Lord, we —"

"I will transport you. You need not trouble yourselves."

"When? What will we do about clothes and — ?"

"Now, Enoch, if God clothes the grass of the field, which today is, and tomorrow is thrown into the oven, will He not much more clothe you, O you of little faith?

"Therefore do not worry, for your heavenly Father knows that you need all these things. Do not worry about tomorrow."

Enoch would never forget the looks on the faces of his people when he reunited them and told them, "We're going to Israel. Don't ask how. God will make a way."

"When?"

"That you *can* ask. I believe we're going tomorrow."

Leah was finally tired and longed for sleep, but she wanted to know about the coming judgments. Apparently there were several, and everyone else seemed curious too.

"I remain up to teaching if you remain up to learning," Eleazar said. "I do not yet know how we will sleep with so much light anyway."

"Today was clearly Judgment Day for Satan and his puppets," Leah said. "But there must be more than one Judgment Day."

"There is," Eleazar said. "Actually there are several times of judgment, each with a specific purpose. Drs. Ben-Judah and Rosenzweig and the elders have come to believe that there are different judgments for the sins and works of believers, Old Testament saints, Tribulation saints, Jews still alive at the end of the Tribulation, Gentiles still alive at the end of the Tribulation, Satan and the fallen angels — which we saw today — and all the unredeemed people of all time.

"Christ's death on the cross was where God placed upon Jesus the sin of all who would become believers. Christ paid for our sins and thus we will face only the judgment seat of Christ and not any of the other judgments. Jesus Himself said in John 5:24, 'Most assuredly, I say to you, he who hears My word and believes in Him who sent Me has everlasting life, and shall not come into judgment, but has passed from death into life.'

"Romans 8:1–4 says, 'There is therefore now no condemnation to those who are in Christ Jesus, who do not walk according to the flesh, but according to the Spirit. For the law of the Spirit of life in Christ Jesus has made me free from the law of sin and death. For what the law could not do in that it was weak through the flesh, God did by sending His own Son in the likeness of sinful flesh, on account of sin: He condemned sin in the flesh, that the righteous requirement of the law might be fulfilled in us who do not walk according to the flesh but according to the Spirit.' "

"Then why," Leah said, "do we face the judgment seat of Christ, and what is that?"

"We believe the judgment seat of Christ is distinct from the judgment of unbelievers. Paul told the Corinthian believers, 'We make it our aim . . . to be well pleasing to Him. For we must all appear before the judgment seat of Christ, that each one may receive the things done in the body, according to what he has done, whether good or bad.' "

"But if Jesus took our punishment and paid for our sins," Naomi said, "on what basis will we be judged?"

Eleazar smiled at his daughter. "So young, yet so bright."

"Daddy," she said, blushing, "stop."

"I am sorry. Your question is a good one." He flipped through his Bible. "Listen to what the apostle Paul told the Corinthians: 'For no other foundation can anyone lay than that which is laid, which is Jesus Christ. Now if anyone builds on this foundation with gold, silver, precious stones, wood, hay, straw, each one's work will become clear; for the day will declare it, because it will be revealed by fire; and the fire will test each one's work, of what sort it is.

" 'If anyone's work which he has built on it endures, he will receive a reward. If anyone's work is burned, he will suffer loss; but he himself will be saved, yet so as through fire.

" 'Do you not know that you are the temple of God and that the Spirit of God dwells in you? If anyone defiles the temple of God, God will destroy him. For the temple of God is holy, which temple you are.'

"He also said, 'Do you not know that those who run in a race all run, but one receives the prize? Run in such a way that you may obtain it. And everyone who competes for the prize is temperate in all things. Now they do it to obtain a perishable crown, but we for an imperishable crown. Therefore I run thus: not with uncertainty. Thus I fight: not as one who beats the air. But I discipline my body and bring it into subjection, lest, when I have preached to others, I myself should become disqualified.'

"Actually, Naomi, 'the judgment seat of Christ' has already taken place. It happened in heaven so that the church that was raptured with Jesus could be adorned as His bride when it descended with Him at the Glorious Appearing. Revelation 19:7–8 says, 'Let us be glad and rejoice and give

Him glory, for the marriage of the Lamb has come, and His wife has made herself ready. And to her it was granted to be arrayed in fine linen, clean and bright, for the fine linen is the righteous acts of the saints.' Those of us who remain alive will be judged by Christ soon, before the Millennium actually begins.

"As for us Jews, the Tribulation itself was the time when God made Israel 'pass under the rod,' according to Ezekiel 20. God says, 'I will bring you into the bond of the covenant; I will purge the rebels from among you, and those who transgress against Me; I will bring them out of the country where they dwell, but they shall not enter the land of Israel. Then you will know that I am the Lord.

" 'As for you, O house of Israel, . . . go, serve every one of you his idols — and hereafter — if you will not obey Me; but profane My holy name no more with your gifts and your idols. For on My holy mountain, on the mountain height of Israel, . . . there all the house of Israel, all of them in the land, shall serve Me. . . . Then you shall know that I am the Lord, when I bring you into the land of Israel, into the country for which I raised My hand in an oath to give to your fathers.'

"Zechariah 13 says that two-thirds of Israel would die, so that of those left, 'all Israel will be saved.' According to Romans 11:26–27, 'The Deliverer will come out of Zion, and He will turn away ungodliness from Jacob; for this is My covenant with them, when I take away their sins.'

"We elders have estimated that there are between five and ten million of us Jews who will enter the Millennium. But the Tribulation was also a time of judgment of unbelieving Gentiles. That should have been obvious from the twenty-one judgments that came from heaven during the past seven years."

George Sebastian raised a hand. "Elder Tiberius, Tsion and Chaim taught us there would also be a judgment of nations, but either I missed it or we didn't get into it. What's that about?"

"That is yet to come, and likely soon. The Scriptures seem to indicate that the valley created by the splitting of the Mount of Olives is called the Valley of Jehoshaphat, which means 'Jehovah judges.' The forming of that valley buried the rubbish of nearly four thousand years of civilization and runs from the Mount of Olives right through Jerusalem. In that newly purified area it appears the Lord will conduct three judgments: He will restore the Jewish nation; He will judge the sheep; and He will judge the goats."

"I remember studying the sheep-and-goats judgment," Hannah Palemoon said. "But I forget who they are."

"Some call this a Semitic judgment," Eleazar said. "Jesus will judge you Gentiles on how you have treated His chosen people. Those who honored the Jews are the sheep, and those who did not are the goats.

"When Jesus slayed all His enemies by the sword that came out of His mouth — the very Word of God — Antichrist's armies were put to death in preparation for the millennial kingdom. Soon all remaining unbelievers — yes, including those who did not take the mark of the beast and yet who never decided for Christ either — will also face death."

"Just people here in Israel?" Ming Woo said. "Or from all over the world?"

"Oh, from the entire world, I'm sure."

"And they will be judged here? Or in their own countries somehow?"

"Good question. I don't know. The Bible seems to indicate that this all takes place in the Valley of Jehoshaphat."

"So it might be awhile before everyone can get here. And what if they choose not to come?"

Eleazar chuckled. "Did you see anyone at the judgment today who appeared to have a choice?"

"So what you're saying," Ree Woo said, "is that only believers populate the Millennium?"

"It appears that way, yes. At least at the beginning. People born during the Millennium will have to make their choice, of course."

Priscilla Sebastian said, "Then the Great White Throne Judgment, at the end of the Millennium, is the final one?"

"Yes."

"But it doesn't sound like there will be much to judge. People either received Christ as their Savior, or they didn't."

"Right, but we believe that God, being wise and fair and wanting to demonstrate how far men and women fall short of His standard, will judge them based on their own works. Obviously, all will fail to measure up. This will show that the punishment is deserved, and as I have said, they will be sent to the lake of fire for eternity."

"But what about the goats in the coming judgment? Where do they go? And will they also be judged again at the great white throne a thousand years from now?"

"Yes. For now they will be sent to hades,

apparently a compartment of hell, where they will suffer until that final judgment, and then they will be cast into the lake of fire."

"Sad."

"Yes, it is. Very. And yet I believe all these judgments will demonstrate to the whole world God's justice and righteousness and will finally silence all who have scoffed."

Just before turning in, Rayford called George Sebastian to check on Kenny, hoping the phone wouldn't wake the children.

"He's out cold," Sebastian reported. "Priss is a little surprised, because all he can talk about is Jesus and seeing Mommy and Daddy tomorrow."

"We covered everything from the millennial kingdom to the resurrections and judgments tonight. You?"

"The same. Fascinating stuff."

"Tired, Sebastian?"

"Exhausted. It's about time. I had begun to wonder if I would ever be hungry or thirsty or tired again."

"And were you hungry?"

Sebastian laughed. "After the dinner we had tonight, I'm still wondering if I ever will be again."

"I hear you. I can still taste the lamb."

"I can still taste everything."

Rayford closed the shades and lay on his back, pulling a single blanket over himself. The light streaming through the cracks around the shade was so bright he had to cover his eyes with the crook of his elbow. He began thanking God for the events he had witnessed, beginning with his own healing, but before he could even mention them, Jesus said, "I know, Rayford. I know. I am right here, and I will always be right here. I will never leave you nor forsake you.

"My blood is precious, as of a lamb without blemish and without spot. I am the light of the world. He who follows Me shall not walk in darkness, but have the light of life."

"Thank You, Lord."

And believing Jesus was there, Rayford drifted off into the sleep of the redeemed.

Twenty

Leah could tell it was morning only because of the dew on the roses and the coolness of the air. It was as bright as it had been at midnight, the last time she checked her watch before falling asleep. She had awakened with the knowledge that she was to go to the new Valley of Jehoshaphat. There was no question in her mind. As she showered and dressed, she knew she was not to eat, not to do anything else. Just go.

Leah had not been aware of Jesus speaking to her again in the night or in the morning, but this inner conviction about what she was to do was so strong and persuasive that He might as well have shown up in person and told her.

She hurried to the front of the house where Eleazar and Naomi were greeting their guests as they emerged from various sleeping quarters. Not a word was said about breakfast or plans for the day. Leah thought about mentioning her urge and asking how she might get there, but she could tell from the looks on the faces of George and Priscilla Sebastian, Hannah Palemoon, and Ree and Ming Woo that they too were on a mission that needed no words. Even the children, Beth Ann and Kenny, seemed eager to get moving.

When everyone was there, Kenny said, "Can we go now?"

Eleazar roared, his bulging eyes twinkling. "And where would you like to go, little one?"

Kenny shrugged. "To see Jesus."

Leah was struck that he didn't mention his mother or dad. For some reason, he too was being drawn to Jesus so forcefully that nothing else seemed to matter.

They all crowded into a vehicle driven by Eleazar, and Leah found herself next to the Woos. "Where're we going, Ming?" she said.

Ming said, "I don't know where anyone else is going. I just hope Elder Tiberius stops within walking distance of the new valley."

Walking distance didn't begin to describe it. Eleazar drove directly to the valley. As they got out, Leah was staggered to see millions and millions of people. They were white and black and red and yellow, and they were all headed the same direction. Leah sensed Jesus was at the end of this rainbow of humanity, and she knew where to find Him as soon as she turned her eyes to the sky. He was not there, but not only was His heavenly army host hovering on horseback, but also tens of thousands of angels flanked them on the sides and behind.

Leah stopped walking, already separated from her friends. She simply had to stare. The sky seemed nearly filled with heavenly beings, forcing her to shield her eyes. But that did no good. The light of the glory of Christ was all about her, and even behind her hands it glared into her eyes. It felt as if she were staggering toward the object of everyone's attention.

Leah had been to professional sporting events where the crowds were so huge going in and out of a stadium that one could not see the end of the people. This was a million times bigger. As she began to walk again, snatches of conversations grabbed her interest.

"I was in my home, minding my own business."

"Where?"

"Johannesburg."

"When was this?"

"Not ten minutes ago!"

"I was asleep in Michigan!"

Leah followed the gently rolling terrain until it opened on an area just enough below Jerusalem that she could look up and see the Eternal City. She also had a view of Golgotha, the site of Calvary, which took away her breath. Again, Leah had to stop and stare.

"Leah," Jesus said.

"Yes, Lord."

"When you see My throne, join those on My right, your left."

"Yes, Lord."

She turned and continued to follow the crowd, realizing that everyone must have been given personal directions. The masses were breaking to the right and to the left and heading for separate destinations.

Rayford tried to stay with Chaim. The men had left the Rosenzweig home without breakfast and without a word, as if they all somehow knew where they must go. Rayford decided that whatever was to come, he wanted to be close enough to Chaim to ask questions. The others must have had the same idea, as they all stuck together despite the crowds.

When Jesus told Rayford where he should go, he moved to his left without question, and as waves of people moved both directions, suddenly the view before Rayford became clear. Directly below and centered under the vast heavenly hosts, saints, and angels, a great raised platform stood, bearing a throne on which Jesus sat. Behind Him were the three angels of mercy. On either side of Him stood the archangels Michael and Gabriel.

Rayford knew instinctively that every living person on earth was gathered in that valley. "I'm guessing several million, Chaim, but it's really not many compared to how the earth was once populated."

"Very few," Chaim said, keeping up with Rayford. "Half a billion or more were raptured seven years ago. Half the remaining population was killed during the seal and trumpet judgments during the next three and a half years. Many more were lost during the vial judgments, and millions of believers were martyred. What you are looking at is probably only one-fourth of those who were left after the Rapture. And most of these will die today."

Indeed, Rayford realized, those assembling on Jesus' right were scant compared to those on His left.

Enoch was sitting behind the wheel of his car in his Palos Hills, Illinois, driveway, praying. When he finished and opened his eyes, he was sitting in the sand in Israel with millions of people moving past him. Enoch stood and saw the heavenly hosts, the City of God, and the Place of the Skull. And Jesus told him where he should go.

"And, Lord, my flock. Are they — ?"

"Of course they are, beloved. I will direct them to you."

It took most of the morning for the masses to find their places and settle. To Rayford it appeared that those to Jesus' left were puzzled at best, frightened at worst.

Gabriel stepped to the front of the platform and stretched out his arms for silence. "Worship the King of kings and Lord of lords!" he shouted, and as one the millions on both sides of the throne fell to their knees. In a cacophony of languages and dialects they cried out, "Jesus Christ is Lord!"

Those on the left of Jesus began rising to their feet, while all around Rayford, everyone remained kneeling. "Clearly two different groups of people here, eh, Chaim?"

"Actually three," the old man said. "Those are the 'goats' over there, the followers of Antichrist who somehow survived to this point. You are among the 'sheep' on this side, but I represent the third group. I am part of Jesus' 'brethren,' the chosen people of God whom the sheep befriended. We are the Jews who will go into the Millennium as believers, because of people like you."

Hannah Palemoon knelt in the sand, worshiping her Savior. Those millions in the crowd to Jesus' left had acknowledged Him, but she sensed no worship was involved.

Since the moment she had awakened, she had wanted — needed — to be here. To have Jesus speak to her in her native tongue was more than she ever could have dreamed or asked for.

Now people around Hannah began to rise, and she looked to the platform to see why. Gabriel was gesturing that they should stand. When everyone was in place and quiet, Gabriel spoke in a loud voice, saying:

"John the revelator wrote: 'I saw an altar, and underneath it all the souls of those who had been martyred for preaching the Word of God and for being faithful in their witnessing.

" 'They called loudly to the Lord and said, "O Sovereign Lord, holy and true, how long will it be before You judge the people of the earth for what they've done to us? When will You avenge our blood against those living on the earth?"

" 'White robes were given to each of them, and they were told to rest a little longer until their other brothers, fellow servants of Jesus, had been martyred on the earth and joined them.'

"People of the earth, hearken your ears to me! The time has been accomplished to avenge the blood of the martyrs against those living on the earth! For the Son of Man has come in the glory of His Father with His angels, and He will now reward each according to his works! As it is written, 'At that time, when I restore the prosperity of Judah and Jerusalem,' says the Lord, 'I will gather the world into the Valley Where Jehovah Judges and punish them there for harming My people, for scattering My inheritance among the nations and dividing up My land.

" 'They divided up My people as their slaves; they traded a young lad for a prostitute, and a little girl for wine enough to get drunk.' "

Hannah was startled when the larger mass, the group to Jesus' left, immediately fell to their knees again and began shouting and wailing, "Jesus Christ is Lord! Jesus Christ is Lord!"

She wondered if she should be doing the same, but Jesus said, "Hannah, I know your heart."

"Thank You, Lord," Rayford said. "I know You do."

"Cleburn," Jesus said to Mac, "come, you blessed of My Father, inherit the kingdom prepared for you from the foundation of the world: for I was hungry and you gave Me food; I was thirsty and you gave Me drink; I was a stranger and you took Me in; I was naked and you clothed Me; I was sick and you visited Me; I was in prison and you came to Me."

Priscilla Sebastian responded, "Lord, when did I see You hungry and feed You, or thirsty and give You drink?"

Enoch said, "When did I see You a stranger and take You in, or naked and clothe You?"

Razor said, "When did I see You sick, or in prison, and come to You?"

And Jesus said in Spanish, "Assuredly, I

say to you, Razor, inasmuch as you did it to one of the least of these My brethren, you did it to Me."

"Thank You, Jesus," Razor said, bowing his head. But he was distracted by a commotion from those to the left of the throne. He looked up in time to see Jesus stand and walk to the edge of the platform.

With anger and yet sadness, He said, "Depart from Me, you cursed, into the everlasting fire prepared for the devil and his angels: for I was hungry and you gave Me no food; I was thirsty and you gave Me no drink; I was a stranger and you did not take Me in, naked and you did not clothe Me, sick and in prison and you did not visit Me."

The millions began shouting and pleading, "Lord, when did we see You hungry or thirsty or a stranger or naked or sick or in prison, and did not minister to You?"

Jesus said, "Assuredly, I say to you, inasmuch as you did not do it to one of the least of these, you did not do it to Me. You will go away into everlasting punishment, but the righteous into eternal life."

"No! No! No!"

But despite their numbers and the dissonance of their desperate bawling, Jesus could be heard above them. "As the Father raises the dead and gives life to them, even so the Son gives life to whom He will. For the Father judges no one, but has committed all judgment to the Son, that all should honor the Son just as they honor the Father. He who does not honor the Son does not honor the Father who sent Him."

"We honor You! We do! You are Lord!"

"Most assuredly, I say to you, he who hears My word and believes in Him who sent Me has everlasting life, and shall not come into judgment, but has passed from death into life.

"But My Father has given Me authority to execute judgment also, because I am the Son of Man. I can of Myself do nothing. As I hear, I judge; and My judgment is righteous, because I do not seek My own will but the will of the Father who sent Me."

"Jesus is Lord!" the condemned shouted. "Jesus is Lord!"

Gabriel stepped forward as Jesus returned to the throne. "Silence!" Gabriel commanded. "Your time has come!"

Rayford watched, horrified despite knowing this was coming, as the "goats" to Jesus' left beat their breasts and fell wailing to the desert floor, gnashing their teeth and pulling their hair. Jesus merely raised one hand a few inches and a yawning chasm opened in the earth, stretching far and wide enough to swallow all of them. They tumbled in, howling and screeching, but their wailing was soon quashed and all was silent when the earth closed itself again.

Everyone on the platform was back in their place, and from the throne Jesus said, "Surely, as I have thought, so it shall come to pass, and as I have purposed, so it shall stand."

"Astounding," Chaim said.

"Hmm?" Rayford said.

"I know that verse," Chaim said, "but think about it. What He merely thinks comes to pass, and whatever He purposes will stand."

Rayford was spent, as he assumed all the "sheep" and "brethren" were. Despite every horror he had witnessed during the Tribulation and the Glorious Appearing, the death and eternal punishment of millions all at once overwhelmed everything else.

"I know, Rayford," Jesus said. "Now rest your mind. My peace I give to you; not as the world gives do I give to you. Let not your heart be troubled, neither let it be afraid. Listen now as My servant comforts you."

Gabriel came forward again. He said, "God's Son, Jesus Christ our Lord, was born of the seed of David according to the flesh, and declared to be the Son of God with power according to the Spirit of holiness, by the resurrection from the dead.

"Through Him you have received grace. You also are the called of Jesus Christ; grace to you and peace from God our Father and the Lord Jesus Christ. In His gospel the righteousness of God is revealed from faith to faith; as it is written, 'The just shall live by faith.'

"The wrath of God has been revealed from heaven against all ungodliness and unrighteousness of men, who suppressed the truth in unrighteousness, because what may be known of God was manifest in them, for God had shown it to them.

"For since the creation of the world His invisible attributes were clearly seen, being understood by the things that were made, even His eternal power and Godhead, so that they are without excuse, because, although they knew God, they did not glorify Him as God, nor were thankful, but became futile in their thoughts, and their foolish hearts were darkened. Professing to be wise, they became fools, and changed the glory of the incorruptible God into an image made like corruptible man — and birds and four-footed animals and creeping things.

"Therefore God also gave them up to uncleanness, in the lusts of their hearts, to dishonor their bodies among themselves, who exchanged the truth of God for the lie, and worshiped and served the creature rather than the Creator, who is blessed forever. Amen."

"Amen!" the assembled shouted.

"These who have been cast into outer darkness and await the Great White Throne Judgment a thousand years hence were indeed without excuse. God sent His Holy Spirit as on the Day of Pentecost, plus the two preachers from heaven who proclaimed His gospel for three and a half years, plus 144,000 thousand witnesses from the twelve tribes. Endless warnings and acts of mercy were extended to these who continued to be lovers of themselves rather than of God."

It hit Rayford that all who were left were believers, worshipers of Christ, and that he was among those who would populate the Millennium.

Gabriel gestured that everyone should sit. When all were situated, he smiled broadly and pronounced loudly, "Blessed and holy is he who has part in the first resurrection. Over such the second death has no power, but they shall be priests of God and of

Christ, and shall reign with Him a thousand years.

"The Mighty One, God the Lord, has spoken and called the earth from the rising of the sun to its going down. Out of Zion, the perfection of beauty, God will shine forth. Our God has come, and shall not keep silent; He shall call to the heavens from above, and to the earth, that He may judge His people!"

With that Jesus stood and Gabriel moved to stand behind the throne with the other angels. And Jesus said, "Gather My saints together to Me, those who have made a covenant with Me by sacrifice! Come forth!"

From everywhere, from the earth and beyond the clouds, came the souls of those who had died in faith, whom Chaim and Tsion had often referred to as "the believing dead," and whom Rayford knew now also included Tsion himself — along with many more of Rayford's friends and loved ones.

All these were gathered around the throne between Jesus and the assembled tribulation saints. They were arrayed in white robes, gleaming and pristine. Rayford looked for Chloe and Buck, for Tsion and Albie, Bruce Barnes, Amanda, Hattie, Ken, Steve, and the rest, but there were too many.

Jesus began by honoring the saints of the

Old Testament, those Rayford had only heard and read about. Rather than handling this the way He had the individual audiences with the tribulation saints — supernaturally doing them all in what seemed to be an instant — Jesus this time gave the spectators His strength and patience. The ceremony must have gone for days, Rayford eventually decided, but he felt neither hunger nor thirst, no fatigue, not even an ache or a cramp from sitting in the sand that long. He loved every minute, knowing that when Jesus finished with the Old Testament saints, he would get to the tribulation martyrs. Waiting for his friends and loved ones to be recognized would be akin to waiting for Chloe's name to be called when she graduated from high school, but the reunion afterward would make it all worthwhile.

Abdullah drank it all in. He glanced at his watch every few hours and realized how long it had taken to cover most of the Old Testament saints. Many he had never heard of — either he had not studied enough or these were some whose exploits had not been recorded. And yet God knew. He knew their hearts, knew of their sacrifice, knew of their faith. And one by one Jesus honored them as He embraced them and they knelt at His feet, and He said, "Well done, good and faithful servant."

Enoch Dumas reveled in the privilege. He was most fascinated by the names he had read about and studied. He perked up when Jesus said of Abel, the son of Adam, "By faith you offered to God a more excellent sacrifice than Cain, through which you obtained witness that you were righteous, God testifying of your gifts; and through that, though dead for generations, your life still spoke."

Enoch was intrigued to finally get a look at these famous men and women. As they came to Him one by one, Jesus said, "Without faith it is impossible to please God, for he who comes to My Father must believe that He is, and that He is a rewarder of those who diligently seek Him."

There was Noah, humbly kneeling, receiving his reward. Jesus said, "By faith, being divinely warned of things not yet seen, you moved with godly fear, prepared an ark for the saving of your household, by which you condemned the world and became heir of the righteousness which is according to faith."

Hours later it seemed everyone roused when it was Abraham's turn. Jesus said, "By faith you obeyed when you were called to go out to the place you would receive as an inheritance. And you went out, not knowing where you were going. By faith you dwelt in the land of promise as in a foreign country, dwelling in tents with Isaac and Jacob, the heirs with you of the same promise; for you waited for the city which had foundations, whose builder and maker was God."

Sarah was right behind him, and Jesus said to her, "By faith you yourself also received strength to conceive seed, and you bore a child when you were past the age, because you judged Him faithful who had promised. Therefore from one man, your husband, and him as good as dead, were born as many as the stars of the sky in multitude — innumerable as the sand which is by the seashore."

Jesus addressed the spectators. "These all died in faith, not having received the promises, but having seen them afar off were assured of them, embraced them and confessed that they were strangers and pilgrims on the earth. For those who say such things declare plainly that they seek a homeland. And truly if they had called to mind that country from which they had come out, they would have had opportunity to return. But now they desire a better, that is, a heavenly country. Therefore I am not ashamed to be called their God, for I have prepared a city for them.

"By faith Abraham, when he was tested, offered up Isaac, and he who had received the promises offered up his only begotten son, of whom it was said, 'In Isaac your seed shall be called,' concluding that God was able to raise him up, even from the dead."

Later Jacob approached the throne, and Jesus said, "By faith, when you were dying, you blessed each of the sons of Joseph, and worshiped, leaning on the top of your staff."

And behind him, Joseph. Jesus told him, "By faith you, when you were dying, made mention of the departure of the children of Israel, and gave instructions concerning your bones."

All around Enoch Dumas, Jews began to stand. Soon everyone was on their feet. Moses himself was kneeling at the feet of Jesus with a man and a woman, and the Lord embraced them and said, "Well done, good and faithful servants. By faith, when your son was born, you hid him three months, because you saw he was a beautiful child; and you were not afraid of the king's command.

"And you, Moses, when you became of age, by faith refused to be called the son of

Pharaoh's daughter, choosing rather to suffer affliction with the people of God than to enjoy the passing pleasures of sin, esteeming My reproach greater riches than the treasures in Egypt; for you looked to the reward. By faith you forsook Egypt, not fearing the wrath of the king; for you endured as seeing Him who is invisible.

"By faith you kept the Passover and the sprinkling of blood, lest he who destroyed the firstborn should touch them.

"By faith you led My children through the Red Sea as by dry land, whereas the Egyptians, attempting to do so, were drowned."

A woman knelt before Jesus. He said, "By faith, Rahab, you did not perish with those who did not believe, because you received My spies with peace."

By the time Leah had seen all the heroes of the Old Testament, including Gideon and Barak and Samson and Jephthah, also David and Samuel and the prophets, she felt as if she were already in heaven. Jesus stood and said, "These through faith subdued kingdoms, worked righteousness, obtained promises, stopped the mouths of lions, quenched the violence of fire, escaped the edge of the sword, out of weakness were made strong, became valiant in battle, turned to flight the armies of the aliens.

"Women received their dead raised to life again. And others were tortured, not accepting deliverance, that they might obtain a better resurrection.

"Still others had trial of mockings and scourgings, yes, and of chains and imprisonment. They were stoned, they were sawn in two, were tempted, were slain with the sword. They wandered about in sheepskins and goatskins, being destitute, afflicted, tormented — of whom the world was not worthy. They wandered in deserts and mountains, in dens and caves of the earth.

"And all these obtained a good testimony through faith."

Twenty-one

Rayford Steele's mind was on a woman he had not touched in more than seven years. What would Irene look like in her glorified body? What would they say to each other? Had she been aware of him all this time, watching, knowing what he was doing? Did she know he had become a believer?

"Do you realize how long we've been here?" he said.

Chaim looked at his watch. "Days, and yet it seems less than an hour. You know it is unlikely Jesus will handle the tribulation saints and martyrs the way He did the Old Testament saints."

"Why?"

"Think about it. It would take years."

"How many are there?" Rayford said.

"More than two hundred million martyrs alone."

"How can you be so sure?"

"I read the Book. Revelation says the martyrs under the throne who had come out of the Tribulation constitute a multitude no man can number."

"Then how can you say — ?"

"Stay with me. Earlier it refers to the demonic horsemen — remember them?"

"Don't ask."

"It refers to two hundred million of them, obviously a multitude that *can* be numbered. So, if there are so many martyrs that they cannot be numbered, how many must there be?"

Mac tried to imagine how he would have felt, before the Glorious Appearing, had he sat in the desert this long without food, water, or sleep. *These old bones would be dried up and blowin' away.*

He recalled that as a child he'd worried about the afterlife. His friends, most of them, were church kids, and they talked about dying and going to heaven as if it was simply expected. "Yeah," he had said, "but what'll we *do* there?" His idea of heaven was ghosts in white robes with halos sitting on clouds and playing harps.

His friends could only shrug and say, "Better there than in hell."

He hadn't been so sure. His uncles always kidded about wanting to go to hell, "because that's where all our friends will be."

Needless to say, Mac was grateful to have avoided hell. And if heaven was as fascinating as this interval before the Millennium, it was going to be more than okay.

"It might be a little late to be asking this, Chaim," Rayford said, "but what kind of a relationship will I have with Irene now? And Amanda. I know that's the kind of question Jesus was asked when the Pharisees were trying to trip Him up, but I sincerely need to know."

"All I can tell you is what Jesus said. 'In the resurrection they neither marry nor are given in marriage, but are like angels of God in heaven. For when they rise from the dead, they neither marry nor are given in marriage. But those who are counted worthy to attain that age' — meaning this time period right now — 'and the resurrection from the dead, neither marry nor are given in marriage.' I cannot make it any plainer than that."

"So only the people who reach the Millennium alive will marry and have children."

"Apparently."

Rayford also looked forward to meeting his heroes from the Old Testament. "We *do* get to interact with those guys, don't we?"

"Absolutely," Chaim said. "In Matthew 8:11 Jesus says, 'Many will come from east and west, and sit down with Abraham, Isaac, and Jacob in the kingdom of heaven.'"

But for now the Old Testament saints were not mingling. They too had become spectators, because the multitude that no man could number was lined up at the throne, awaiting their rewards.

"Those who were killed for the testimony of Jesus," Chaim said, "which pretty much covers any believer who died during the Tribulation, will be honored. But those who were actually martyred will be given a special crown."

Gabriel stepped forward one more time and announced, "John the revelator wrote, 'And I saw the souls of those who had been beheaded for their testimony about Jesus, for proclaiming the Word of God, and who had not worshiped the Creature or his statue, nor accepted his mark on their foreheads or their hands. They had come to life again and now they reigned with Christ for a thousand years.'"

Chaim's assessment proved accurate.

Somehow the Lord arranged it so that only those who knew each tribulation saint witnessed them getting their reward. So, rather than Rayford's having to wait through the ceremonies for a million or two strangers to see a friend or loved one, as soon as the festivities began, Bruce Barnes approached the throne.

"Bruce!" Rayford called out, unable to restrain himself, and he stood and applauded. All around him others were doing the same, but they were calling out other names. "Aunt Marge!" "Dad!" "Grandma!"

From that distance, Rayford could tell only that Bruce looked like himself. Of course he had never seen him in a white robe, and he didn't know what a glorified body would be like, but Rayford couldn't wait to see him face-to-face.

Soon he saw Loretta, Bruce's secretary, who had died in the first global earthquake.

And then came Amanda, Rayford's second wife.

He saw Dr. Floyd Charles, who had worked with the Tribulation Force. And David Hassid, the first mole in the Global Community Palace, who had been shot and killed at Petra, just before the remnant began to move in.

T Delanty was there, and sweet Lukas

Miklos and his wife, who received a martyr's crown for enduring the guillotine. Soon came Ken Ritz, who had taken a bullet to the head from the GC in an escape attempt.

What memories! How good it would be to reminisce. Jesus honored Ken by mentioning how he had "used your God-given mind and abilities to often thwart the works of the enemy and encourage your brothers and sisters in Christ."

Melancholy washed over Rayford when he recognized Hattie Durham embracing Jesus. How he had misused her and nearly given up on her, but what a brave saint she had become in the end. When she knelt, Michael the archangel handed Jesus a crystalline tiara, which He placed on her head. "My daughter," He said, "you were martyred for your testimony of Me in the face of the Antichrist and the False Prophet, and so you will bear this crown for eternity. Well done, good and faithful servant."

There was Annie Christopher, who had worked underground at the GC palace. Steve Plank, Buck Williams's former boss, who was thought dead in the wrath of the Lamb earthquake, only to resurface undercover as a GC operative under the name Pinkerton Stephens.

"You suffered the blade for My sake,"

Jesus said, "and maintained your testimony to the end. Wear this crown for eternity."

Albie appeared, Rayford's old friend and faithful compatriot.

And finally, there was Chloe, and right behind her Buck and Tsion. Rayford kept shouting and clapping as his daughter, son-in-law, and spiritual adviser received their *well-done*, their embrace, and their martyr's crown. The entire heavenly host applauded each martyr, but Caleb, one of the angels of mercy, came out from behind the throne to embrace Chloe. Rayford would have to ask her about that.

Of her, Jesus said, "You too suffered the guillotine for My name's sake, speaking boldly for Me to the end. Wear this for eternity."

Of Buck he said, "You and your wife gave up a son for My sake, but he shall be returned to you, and you shall be recompensed a hundredfold. You will enjoy the love of the children of others during the millennial kingdom."

Jesus took extra time with Tsion Ben-Judah, praising him for "your bold world-wide proclamation of Me as the Messiah your people had for so long sought, the loss of your family — which shall be restored to you — your faithful preaching of My gospel

488

to millions around the world, and your defense of Jerusalem until the moment of your death. Untold millions joined Me in the kingdom because of your witness to the end."

Rayford enjoyed Jesus' welcome to dozens of others whose names he had forgotten, underground believers in various countries who had worked through the Co-op, hosted Trib Force people, and sacrificed their lives in defense of the gospel.

Only by the miraculous work of God through Jesus, the honoring of more than two hundred million tribulation martyrs and saints was suddenly over. Jesus stood at the front edge of the vast platform and spread His arms as if to encompass the mighty throng of souls, most with glorified bodies, the rest mere mortals who had survived the Tribulation.

"I will declare the decree," He said. "The Lord has said to Me, 'You are My Son, today I have begotten You. Ask of Me, and I will give You the nations for Your inheritance, and the ends of the earth for Your possession. You shall break them with a rod of iron; You shall dash them to pieces like a potter's vessel.'

"Now therefore, I say be wise, O kings; be instructed, you judges of the earth. Serve the Lord with fear, and rejoice with trembling. Kiss the Son, lest He be angry, and you perish in the way, when His wrath is kindled but a little. Blessed are all those who put their trust in Him.

"I welcome you, one and all, to the kingdom I have prepared for you. Rayford, welcome."

"Thank You, Lord."

How anyone found anyone else in the endless mass of souls was a miracle in itself. Rayford saw Chaim making a beeline to Tsion, who was already in the embrace of his wife and two children. Albie and Mac were laughing and shouting and hugging.

There were Buck and Chloe running to Kenny as he ran to them.

And seemingly out of nowhere, at Rayford's elbow stood Irene. One thing he could say for the glorified body: She looked herself, and as if she had not aged. No way she could say the same for him.

"Hi, Rafe," she said, smiling.

"Irene," he said, holding her. "You're permitted one cosmic I-told-you-so."

"Oh, Rayford," she said, stepping back as if to get a good look at him. "I've just been so grateful that you found Jesus and so thrilled at how many souls are here because of what you and Chloe and the others did."

She looked behind him. "Raymie," she said, "come here."

Rayford turned and there was his son. He scooped him up in a tight embrace. "Even you knew the truth that I didn't," he said.

"I can't tell you how great it is to see you here, Dad."

Rayford pointed to Buck and Chloe and Kenny. "You know who that is?"

"Of course," Irene said. "That's my grandson — your nephew, Raymie."

They approached shyly, but it was Buck who broke the ice as Chloe gathered in her parents. "So nice to meet you, finally," he said, shaking his mother-in-law's hand. "I've heard so much about you."

Kenny seemed fascinated to have a real uncle, and one so young.

As they laughed and hugged and praised God for each other and for their salvation, Amanda White Steele approached. "Rayford," she said. "Irene."

"Amanda!" Irene said, pulling her close. "Would you believe I prayed for you even after I was raptured?"

"It worked."

"I know it did. And you and Rafe were happy for a time."

"I was so afraid this would be awkward," Rayford said.

"Not at all," Irene said. "I didn't begrudge you a good wife and companionship. I was so thrilled that you both had come to Jesus. You're going to find that He is all that matters now."

"And I," Amanda said, "am just so happy you made it through the Tribulation, Rayford." She turned back to Irene and took her arm. "You know, your witness and character were the reasons I came to the Lord."

"I knew that was your testimony," Irene said. "But I hadn't recalled making any impression on you."

"I don't think you tried. You just did."

Rayford had the feeling that his family would be close, affectionate friends throughout the Millennium. He didn't understand it all yet, in fact hardly any of it. But he had to agree with Irene: Jesus was all that mattered anymore. There would be no jealousy, envy, or sin. Their greatest joy would be in serving and worshiping their Lord, who had brought them to Himself.

As Buck and Chloe continued to interact with Irene and Amanda, Rayford borrowed Raymie. "There are so many people I want to see, Son. You must meet them all. And we've only got a thousand years."

Epilogue

But after these things [Satan] must be released for a little while.

Revelation 20:3

About the Authors

Jerry B. Jenkins (www.jerryjenkins.com) is the writer of the Left Behind series. He owns the Jerry B. Jenkins Christian Writers Guild (www.ChristianWritersGuild.com), an organization dedicated to mentoring aspiring authors. Former vice president for publishing for the Moody Bible Institute of Chicago, he also served many years as editor of *Moody* magazine and is now Moody's writer-at-large.

His writing has appeared in publications as varied as *Reader's Digest, Parade, Guideposts,* in-flight magazines, and dozens of other periodicals. Jenkins's biographies include books with Billy Graham, Hank Aaron, Bill Gaither, Luis Palau, Walter Pyton, Orel Hershiser, and Nolan Ryan, among many others. His books appear regularly on the *New York Times, USA Today,*

Wall Street Journal, and *Publishers Weekly* best-seller lists.

Jerry and his wife, Dianna, live in Colorado and have three grown sons.

Dr. Tim LaHaye (www.timlahaye.com), who conceived the idea of fictionalizing an account of the Rapture and Tribulation, is a noted author, minster, and nationally recognized speaker on Bible prophecy. He is the founder of both Tim LaHaye Ministries and the Pre-Trib Research Center.

He also recently cofounded the Tim LaHaye School of Prophecy at Liberty University. Presently Dr. LaHaye speaks at many of the major Bible prophecy conferences in the U.S. and Canada, where his current prophecy books are very popular.

Dr. LaHaye holds a doctor of ministry degree from Western Theological Seminary and a doctor of literature degree from Liberty University. For twenty-five years he pastored one of the nation's outstanding churches in San Diego, which grew to three locations. It was during that time that he founded two accredited Christian high schools, a Christian school system of ten schools, and Christian Heritage College.

Dr. LaHaye has written over forty books that have been published in more than thirty languages. He has written books on a wide variety of subjects, such as family life, temperaments, and Bible prophecy. His current fiction works, the Left Behind series, written with Jerry B. Jenkins, continue to appear on the best-seller lists of the Christian Booksellers Associations, *Publishers Weekly*, *Wall Street Journal*, *USA Today*, and the *New York Times*.

He is the father of four grown children and grandfather of nine. Snow skiing, waterskiing, motorcycling, golfing, vacationing with family, and jogging are among his leisure activities.